RESISTING THE *Running Back*

LISA SUZANNE

RESISTING THE RUNNING BACK
THE NASH BROTHERS BOOK 5
© 2025 LISA SUZANNE

Published in the United States of America by Books by LS, LLC.

ISBN: 978-1-963772-19-7

Cover Design by Qamber Designs.

Dedication

To the three people who make me smile every day.

Chapter 1: Sophie Summers

This Is Because of Your Books

"It just feels like all we do lately is argue. We've been growing apart for some time now, and I think it would be for the best for us to end things." I let out the breath I definitely know I was holding as I finally say the words I've been practicing for weeks.

"We do *not* argue all the time," Tyler protests.

I think about pointing out the fact that, well, it's *another* argument, but I stop myself. I just want to get this over with.

"It's not like this is coming out of nowhere," I say quietly, calling on those teacher instincts deep inside to remain calm in any situation. "I know it might take some time to figure out how we move on from here, but I'd like to talk about how to split things up and which one of us should move."

"Move?" he repeats, his volume higher than it needs to be since I'm sitting two feet away from him. He sits back and folds his arms across his chest, and he shakes his head. "No. Nobody's moving."

He clearly doesn't want this, though I think it has more to do with the way he tends to hold onto things than with the actual state of our relationship.

I haven't been happy for a while, but I stayed anyway because I thought we could fix things. As it turns out, he doesn't want to put in the work.

I can't be with someone who doesn't put in the work.

"This is because of your books, isn't it?" he asks.

I clench my jaw together at his words, and my back teeth grind as I try my hardest to keep my composure…but he just hit me where he knew it would hurt the most.

He just doesn't get it, and *that* is why I'm ending things.

Maybe if he supported my hobby-turned-side hustle, we wouldn't be in this exact predicament.

But he's never supported my writing. Instead, he makes fun of it. He calls it porn. He treats it like it's trash.

It's none of those things. It may not win the next Nobel Prize, but I have an email from Rozlyn telling me how my words distracted her from her mother's long battle with a disease, another from Kathy telling me how my words helped get her through a dark time in her life, and one from William telling me that he and his wife reconnected because of my books.

I know my words matter even if it's just to those three people, but all Tyler ever does is belittle it. He calls it my hobby. He doesn't believe in it—or in me.

And that is why I'm done with him.

I make enough between my job teaching high school language arts and my royalties from my books that I can walk out of this apartment and find my own place to rent. It'll be tight, but it'll be better than living another minute with someone who tries to use my books against me as I'm breaking up with him.

"Why would it be because of my books?" I ask through that clenched jaw.

"Because you create this perfect man that doesn't exist, and you expect me to act like that." He purses his lips and shakes his head as if it's some sort of crime.

"You know what, Tyler? The truth is that the men I create are visions of what I want in a man. What I want in a *relationship*. No…not what I want," I amend, shaking my head. "What I *deserve*. And you…you aren't it."

He rolls his eyes, which only serves to further prove my statement, and I let out a heavy sigh. Before he can start in on me again, I say, "I'll stay in the guest room tonight, and I'll start looking at places tomorrow."

"Suit yourself." He grabs the remote and turns on the television, and even though every instinct is telling me to stomp off, I also don't want him to see that he's affecting me.

I calmly walk out of the room, head to the bedroom, change into my pajamas, and then settle into the guest room.

I play games on my phone to try to calm my mind, and I'm on track for a new high score when my phone starts to ring.

I glance at the clock. It's nearly nine o'clock, and it's my department chair calling—probably to ask me to sub for someone's zero hour class bright and early tomorrow morning. She knows I'm almost always an automatic yes since I haven't learned the skill of telling my boss no, so I answer.

"Hello?"

"Hi, Sophie. It's Elizabeth Watson."

"Hey, Elizabeth. Do you need me to cover for someone tomorrow?"

"No, I'm calling to talk to you about the post you made to your message board a half hour ago. I, uh…" She stutters and trails off. "I'm going to have to place you on administrative leave while the district investigates this."

"My message board?" I glance around the guest room and realize I left my laptop on the kitchen table. "I didn't post to my message board a half hour ago."

My heart leaps up into my chest as I realize *I* didn't post…but I did have my message board open because I was responding to students before Tyler got home. I abandoned my laptop to break up with him.

Oh no. Oh, God, no.

What did he do?

"There's a post here from you, Sophie. As I said, you'll be on leave until further notice."

"What does it say?" I beg.

She clears her throat. "Surprise! I've been publishing books under a pen name for years. Buy my new erotic romance, *Second Chances* by Summer Love, available now."

"What?" I screech. "Elizabeth, be serious. Why would I post that to my message board?"

"I don't know, Sophie. That's what the district plans to investigate. I will be in touch when I know anything more." She cuts the call, and I stare at the phone as my hands shake.

Anger plows into me, and I'm done remaining calm.

I leap out of bed and throw the door to the guest room open. It hits the wall behind it with a thud, and I storm through the apartment back to where the asshole was sitting not a half hour ago.

He's not on the couch. He's not in the kitchen, and my laptop is sitting right where I left it. He's not in the bedroom or the bathroom, either, and I storm toward the slider to check for his car in the space outside.

It's gone.

He did what he did, and then he left like the fucking coward he is.

I'm positively quaking with fury. I can't believe he did this to me.

Fear plows into me. I'm going to lose my job. I'm going to lose my friends. I'm going to lose the respect of this entire community. I'm going to lose the niche I carved out for myself.

And I'm not going to be able to find another job—at least not one teaching high school students after this scandal.

It won't matter that I'm not the one who posted it. It's under my name, and they'll do their investigation, and I will look guilty as sin because I do, in fact, publish romance novels, though I would never categorize them as *erotic*.

Shows what that stupid asshole knows.

The anger turns into grief as I start to cry.

I pick up my phone and dial the one person who is always there for me. He'll know just the right thing to say to help me figure out where the hell I go from here.

Chapter 2: Miller Banks

I rub my hands together nervously, and that's when I realize…I shouldn't be nervous.

It's that damn twintuition at work again.

This is my twin brother Tanner's deal, not mine. He's about to propose to his girl tonight on our thirtieth birthday.

Maybe I'm nervous about turning thirty. The whiskey hasn't really helped calm that nerve. There's something in my chest that feels off, but I'm chalking it up to Tanner.

I pull him aside. "When are you going to do it?" I ask.

He shrugs. "I think I'm ready."

I'm about to congratulate him when the buzz of my watch tells me someone's calling. I glance at it and see it's Sophie. I flash my phone at my brother before I answer. "Soph?"

"Miller?"

I can hardly hear her since the music is blaring at this club, so I hold a hand over my ear.

"Where are you?" she asks, her voice loud and clear…and hoarse, as if she's been crying.

"I'm in Vegas."

She lets out a small sob. "Okay. I'll, uh—" She interrupts herself with another sob.

"Who did this to you?" I demand.

"I broke up with Tyler, and—"

"I'll be right there," I say, cutting her off and ending the call.

This is an important night for Tanner, of course. It's my thirtieth birthday, too.

And there's no one I'd rather spend my thirtieth birthday with than the girl I've loved since I was fourteen.

Sophie Summers.

"I need to go," I say to Tanner.

"Where?" he asks.

"Phoenix."

"Is everything okay?" he asks.

I shrug, and I glance around the room because we didn't get far enough into the conversation for me to know what's going on. All I know is that she called, so I will drop everything to be there for her.

"I don't know. Happy birthday, bro." I slap his shoulder, and then I lean in so Cassie doesn't hear me. "Good luck tonight. We'll celebrate when we're back in San Diego," I promise, and then I head out.

My phone starts to ring again, and I see it's her calling again.

"Soph?" I answer.

"Oh my God, it's your birthday. I'm so sorry. Happy birthday," she says. She sniffles.

"Don't be sorry."

"Don't come all the way here, Miller. I didn't mean to interrupt your night out celebrating."

"It's fine. I'm already en route to my hotel to grab my suitcase, and then I'll hop on the first flight. It'll be a quick trip from Vegas, and it's been too long since I've seen you anyway."

"It has," she agrees.

Not seeing her was both one of the drawbacks and benefits of moving to San Diego.

She's been with that douchebag for two years now, and seeing her with anyone is tough, but seeing her with someone who never deserved her was excruciating.

"It's not just any birthday, you know," I say casually.

"Your thirtieth," she says flatly—probably because it means that one month from tomorrow is *her* thirtieth birthday, and I'm not sure either one of us was really ready to face that number just yet.

I wonder if she remembers the promise we made over fifteen years ago. She probably didn't mean it. I did.

"Do you want to talk about what happened with Tyler?" I ask as I walk back to the Bellagio rather than asking if she remembers.

"We've just been growing apart for a while now, so I ended things."

"And?" I ask. Sophie is a badass. She's not the type to sit around crying, which tells me that he did something.

Something bad.

"And, uh…it's a long story."

"But you called me," I point out.

"Yeah. Are you really coming to Phoenix?"

"I'm walking into my hotel to grab my suitcase right now," I say.

"I'm so sorry for ruining your trip. For ruining your birthday."

"You're not," I say softly. If anything, getting to see her is the only gift I could ask for this year. You know…aside from learning she ended things with that asshole.

"Let me know when you land. I'll pick you up."

"Don't you have work tomorrow?" I ask since that's the reason she's not in Vegas celebrating with me tonight.

Apparently that was the wrong question. She bursts into tears, and I realize I need to get a move on.

I rush through the hotel to the elevator. "Fuck, Soph. What did I say? I'm sorry. Let me book a flight, and I'll call you right back."

She sobs out some reply, and what the hell am I walking into?

I don't have any idea.

I pull up flights on the elevator. I book the first one I find. It leaves in a half hour, so I bust my ass packing my shit and rushing out to the valet, where I offer a decent sum of money to get me to the airport quickly. They offer me the hotel limo, and I get to the gate as they make the final call for boarding.

I realize in all the rushing that I didn't call her back, but I slip into airplane mode, pay for the WiFi, and shoot her a text as the plane pulls back from the gate.

Me: *I'm on a plane. Landing at 11:45.*
Sophie: *I'll be at the usual doors.*
Me: *Just be safe. No driving and crying.*
Sophie: *No promises.*

I text her again when the plane touches down, and once the doors open, I run through the airport with the suitcase I carried on to get to her.

She's waiting there where she said she'd be. Dependable as always.

She rushes around the car and practically attacks me with a hug, and I drop my suitcase and hold her tightly to me.

I lean down and draw in a deep breath, the warm scent of her shampoo wrapping around me and climbing into my chest the way it always does. It's a clean scent, fresh and a little fruity, like a summer garden. It's the same way she has smelled since the day I met her, and any time I catch a whiff of it, I'm immediately transported to this spot right here—no, not the airport, but a place with her in my arms.

She just…fits. She's maybe eight inches shorter than me, and her body just seems to nestle right into mine as she leans her head against my chest, and I hold her in my arms where she belongs.

She draws in a deep breath, and I have the strongest urge to lean down and kiss her.

It's the same urge I've fought for half my life now.

I met her when I was fourteen—our freshman year of high school. We were in the same English class, and we would laugh together every single day. Our friendship grew from there.

But that's all it ever grew into.

Friendship.

I don't know if I was friend-zoned or what, but I never made the move even though I always wanted to, and eventually it became what it is now. I'm too afraid to make a move because I'll lose the best friend I've ever had aside from my brother.

We've always been there for each other through breakups, makeups, and hookups. Sometimes—oftentimes—she shares more details than I'd prefer to know, but I've learned to live with my lot in life.

I'd rather be her friend than not have her in my life at all.

She sniffles against me, and eventually she sighs again and backs up out of my arms. "Welcome home," she says.

I give her a half smile. "Thanks. You doing okay?"

She shakes her head, and then she slips into the passenger seat of her own car without asking me to drive. It's a given that I'll drive. I always do when we're together, and it spans back to high school when we'd go to parties and I would opt out of drinking the night before a game, so I'd end up driving her home in her own car, and then I'd walk the few blocks to my house from there.

Her head is leaned back on the seat and her eyes are closed when I take the driver's seat after depositing my suitcase in her trunk, and I have to adjust the seat to give myself a bit more legroom.

"Okay, Summers. Spill it. Why am I here?" I fire up the engine, and I'm about to ease into traffic when her reply comes.

"I'm pretty sure I'm going to lose my job because of Tyler."

I slam on the brakes and stare over at her. "What? How?"

She licks her lips and chews on the bottom one for just a beat as I resist the urge to reach over and pull her lip out from the clutches of her teeth. "He snuck onto my computer and posted about my books under my account on my student message board."

My jaw drops. "What?"

She presses her lips together. "He always hated that I wrote. He's not like you."

She says that last part quietly.

I couldn't be prouder of her for reaching for her dreams. She's been quietly publishing books under a pen name for the last four years, and I'll admit that I've bought every single one of them.

All eleven of them.

And I've read them.

All of them.

And when I'm finding myself in a moment of missing her, which is fairly often, I like to reread them just to listen to her beautiful voice through her words.

I've never told her that.

She writes about strong, badass women much like herself falling in love with billionaires, and her stories are the kind that are hard to put down because I want to know what happens next.

I love the way her mind works, and to hear that she was with someone who didn't fully appreciate it is nothing short of totally infuriating.

"I'm so sorry, Soph. That was a dick move. What can you do to fix it?" I ask.

She lifts a shoulder. "Doesn't matter. Damage is done. You can go," she says, looking at the empty road beside me.

She only adds more detail once I start driving. "Only you and Tyler knew my pen name. I didn't tell anyone else because I was afraid of my students finding out. I love my job, and I love teaching, and my department chair called me to tell me I'm on administrative leave until further notice." She swipes at her cheek. "They'll investigate, find out that my pen name is indeed Summer Love, and that'll be the end of it. It was my own fault for leaving my laptop where he could access it."

"You had no idea he would stoop that low," I say.

She shakes her head. "No, I didn't." She reaches over and touches my arm. "I'm glad you're here."

I set my hand on top of hers for a second as I glance over at her. "Me, too."

I just have no idea where we go from here.

Chapter 3: Miller Banks

Only One Bed

"I don't want to go to the apartment," she blurts. "Can we just…I don't know. Go to a hotel? Would that be weird?"

"It wouldn't be weird at all. Whatever you need."

I know the area well since I lived around here my entire life up until a little under a year ago, so I pull off the highway and head toward one of the nicer hotels in town.

"Is this okay?" I ask when I stop in front of the hotel entry.

She nods. "I didn't bring anything with me."

"Do you want to go grab anything?"

She shakes her head. "We'll go tomorrow when he's at work."

We head inside to the front desk, and the clerk working there immediately recognizes me. I did attend the university in this town, and I did play for the local pro football team for a number of years, so I guess I'm somewhat well known around these parts.

"Miller Banks," the clerk says. "Wow, what an honor to meet you."

"And you," I say politely.

"Can I get a photo with you?" He pushes his phone across the counter toward Sophie.

I chuckle. "Do you mind?" I ask her.

She's used to this. She snaps our picture, and then the clerk asks what he can do to help us.

"I'm looking for a room tonight. A suite if you have one, preferably with two beds." I clear my throat awkwardly. I don't *want* two beds, but Sophie certainly does.

He taps around on his computer. "We're sold out, but let me see what I can do."

"Sold out?" I repeat.

"It's the Duel in the Desert tonight," he explains, which means the University of Arizona is up here from Tucson playing the Arizona State University men's basketball team.

"Shit," Sophie mutters.

We exchange a glance.

"Looks like we have one room available, but it's just a regular king room. Will that work?" he asks.

Only one bed.

I look over to Sophie. "Your call."

She presses her lips together as she nods. "We'll take it." She looks at me. "It's fine."

"I can sleep on the floor," I offer.

"Don't be ridiculous." She looks at the clerk. "We've been best friends since high school, and I broke up with my boyfriend tonight." It's cute that she's justifying this to a complete stranger.

He raises his brows, and I can hear his sarcastic, *okay, sure.* He doesn't voice it even though his face doesn't hide it.

We move the car from the entry to a parking space, grab my suitcase, and head up to our room. It's small, and there's not even a couch that I could try to get comfortable on.

She collapses on the right side of the bed, and I collapse next to her on the left a minute later.

"You doing okay?" I ask.

"I just…I don't know. It's like I'm waiting for the phone to ring to confirm I'm fired, and I don't know what to do. I'll tell you one thing, though. I don't feel bad about dumping Tyler anymore."

I laugh as we both stare up at the ceiling. "I always knew you deserved better, Soph."

"I love you, Millby." Millby, or Mill-B, short for Miller Banks, is the nickname she gave me when we were freshmen in high school, and hearing it brings me back to that time in our lives.

Everything seemed so much simpler back then.

Back then, it was just a crush on a cute girl. It wasn't deep feelings of love for my best friend. It wasn't the risk of losing someone I've been close to for more than half my life.

It's too far out of left field to even consider it at this point.

But that doesn't mean I don't think of her every minute of every day. It doesn't mean I don't pine for what could have been if I could've gotten up the nerve to ask her out when I was fourteen.

I didn't. Bryce McDaniels did before me. They dated for two years, and it was too late by that point. I was firmly stuck in the friend zone, where I've spent the last sixteen years.

"I love you, too, Summers." More than I can even admit to her.

She yawns, and I realize how late it got. It's been an emotional day for her, and a strange one for me, too.

"Bet you didn't think you'd end up in Arizona for your thirtieth," she says.

I chuckle. She's not wrong about that—not when the day started out in Vegas, anyway.

But sharing a bed with her? Not the worst birthday present I can think of.

We get ready for bed. She uses my soap to remove her makeup, and she finger brushes her teeth with my toothpaste. And then we get in bed.

"Goodnight," she says quietly.

"Night." I flip off the light, and we lie in darkness for a few minutes.

I think she might be asleep, but I ask the question anyway. "Do you remember the promise?"

"Hm?" she murmurs.

"That if we're both thirty and neither one of us is married, we marry each other." I whisper the words.

"Mm-hm."

"I'm game." I realize there's another month to go before we have to worry about that, but I'd marry her in a heartbeat if I could.

She doesn't say anything, and I hear even breathing after that.

I'm not sure I'll have the nerve to bring it up again, but at least we're sharing a bed tonight. It's a step in the right direction.

And I sleep better than I have in months. Years, even.

When morning dawns, I'm thirty and single, she's twenty-nine and single, and I have an erection the size of Texas.

My arms are around her.

She's snuggled into my chest.

I could stay like this forever, but I also don't want her to wake up and find herself in my arms. That's not what this is supposed to be…as much as I want to let her help with the Texas-sized erection.

It's just not in the cards for us. Instead, I sneak out of bed to take care of the problem in the shower.

The relief of a release helps, but the ache is back the second I step out of the bathroom and see her sitting in the bed we slept in together. She's rubbing the sleep from her eyes as she talks on the phone.

"I understand. Thank you for the call." She hangs up, lowers the phone from her ear, and stares blankly at the phone.

"Everything okay?"

She glances up at me, her brown eyes misty as she shakes her head. "That was my department chair. They're just starting their investigation, but she's not very optimistic things will work in my favor. I mean, people have kept their jobs in worse situations, but this was advertising a personal side hustle to kids."

I sit next to her. "I'm so sorry. What do you want to do?"

She sighs and averts her gaze to the window. I can't help but study her in the natural light coming in the window. She's gorgeous even with no makeup, her face fresh and bright despite the desperate situation she currently finds herself in. She sighs and glances back at me. "I don't know. Get breakfast?"

I nod, and we head down to the restaurant in the hotel.

Chapter 4: Sophie Summers

New Job Isn't on the Menu

I stare at the menu as I try to figure out what I want to order. Since "New Job" doesn't appear to be on the menu, I settle for two eggs, bacon, and toast. We both opt for a cup of coffee along with a glass of orange juice, too, and Miller asks the waitress if they have Cholula.

I giggle. "You still put hot sauce on everything?"

He nods. "On everything. Not Tabasco. It has to be Cholula."

I narrow my eyes at him. "New life goal unlocked. Get Miller Banks hooked on a new hot sauce."

"Pfft," he scoffs. "Like that'll ever happen."

We settle into easy conversation as our coffee is delivered to our table, and I'm debating whether to bring up the promise we made at the beginning of our sophomore year of high school or not. For some reason, I woke up thinking about that promise, but I feel like it was just something fifteen-year-olds say, not something they really intend to act upon.

"Does Tanner still not drink coffee?" I ask instead of the real question on my mind.

It's funny how Miller and I have always been so close, and while Tanner and I were always friendly, we never made that same connection.

There's a pretty good difference between the brothers. I love both of them dearly, but Tanner was always a little more on the wild side than his brother. He was the one who went crazy at parties, doing the things he shouldn't, while Miller was the more responsible one who drove us home.

I would see Tanner making out with different girls in the corner at every party, breaking hearts all over Phoenix, while Miller was always a little more dependable and responsible.

"Yeah," he says. "He's on a pretty strict diet, and I should be too, but it's the offseason." He gives me a wide smile, and it's that smile that always causes my chest to flutter just a little bit.

Has he always been this cute?

I've never looked at Miller as anything more than a friend because it felt like he never was looking at me that way. Plus, our timing just never seemed to work out. I wanted to ask him to homecoming, but I was too nervous. Then Bryce asked me, and the rest was history. Somehow, we slipped into an easy friendship that neither of us ever wanted to ruin with anything more than that, and now I genuinely can't imagine my life without Miller as my best friend.

"What are you thinking?" he asks.

I lift a shoulder. "To be perfectly honest, I have no idea. I'm about to lose my job based on what my department chair told me and…" I trail off.

"And what?"

"I don't know where I go from here. If I'm getting fired because I told minors to buy an erotic romance novel with explicit sex scenes and admitted my name in a single post…how do you come back from that?"

I won't get a job anywhere because this will be on my record. An English teacher telling students to read a book with sex in it? I never would've thought to say anything about it to my students at all. They don't even know I've published books. Or, they didn't, anyway. And neither do my parents. I love my family dearly, but they are much more conservative than I turned out to be.

Besides, it's kind of embarrassing to admit to your mom and dad that you write explicit sex, no matter how proud you are of the product you produce. We never talk about sex in my family, and it's always felt like a taboo subject. Maybe that's why I write about it instead.

But now they'll know. Everyone in the conservative community in which I grew up will know. I teach at the high school I graduated from, and my colleagues are my former teachers. Nobody around here will understand, and anytime I even have a conversation with a colleague about what I like to read in my spare time, I get the same sort of reactions I got from Tyler.

Miller's eyes light up before I answer his question. He's the only person I've really confessed any of this to. He's the only one who knows my pen name. Tyler never supported my writing, but Miller always has. I think he's even bought a couple of my books.

"I can tell you're thinking something, so just come on out with it," I say, pursing my lips and raising a brow as I fold my arms across my chest.

He shrugs innocently, but then he says, "What if this is the push you needed to do this dream of yours full-time?"

I sink back into the booth. On one hand, it's not like I haven't wanted to make writing my full-time job for years. On the other hand, it always just felt way too far out of reach. Turning hobbies into careers doesn't always pan out. The last thing I want is to develop negative feelings toward one of the things I love doing most in the world because it becomes my sole way of earning money to support myself.

But on the other hand, maybe he's right. Maybe this is exactly what I need to push me out of my comfort zone and take the risk by doing the damn thing.

I chew on the inside of my cheek as I think it over. "Where will I live? My royalties have been nice bonus money in addition to my teaching salary, but I don't think it's enough to pay rent."

"Look, Sophie. I've read your books. You have what it takes to be successful. Your words are as incredible as you are, and you deserve the chance to make this happen." His blue eyes are warm and sincere across the table.

My jaw slackens as his words register. "You've read my books?"

"Every single one of them."

I gasp. A long silence fills the space between us, and then I ask, "Which is your favorite?"

He chuckles. "*Second Chances* was pretty good, but I think *Married to the Enemy* was my favorite. That tension when they got married but you knew they both wanted it to be real was next level." He's talking about my fourth book, still one of my best sellers to this day. "I mean it. I know anybody can publish a book these days, but not everybody has the talent you have. I believe in you, and I want to see what you can do with giving this a shot full-time."

"The problem is that it takes more than just writing a book to get people to buy it. There's a marketing side of it, and having been in the classroom full-time since I started publishing, it's difficult to find enough hours to get everything done." I don't even know where to start, if I'm being honest.

"So hire an assistant," he suggests.

"With what money?" I ask.

His eyes light up some more, and to be honest, I'm a little fearful of what he's thinking.

"Come live with me. Come to San Diego. Quit your job before they force you into an investigation you don't want. Blow this town and use this as your moment to give your dream a try."

"I can't do that, Miller," I protest. "I won't have an income."

"I have plenty for both of us," he says, and his voice is low and incredibly convincing. He's not bragging about the amount of money he has but rather seems to be telling me he has enough to support the two of us, as if he wants to share it with me. "Stay with me and let me invest in my favorite author."

My chest tightens and my heart squeezes as this overwhelming feeling of gratitude washes over me. "I can't do that," I protest.

For a split second, I wonder why exactly I'm protesting. What do I have to lose by giving this a try? I don't want to mooch off my best friend, but he's offering my dreams on a platter, and that is a difficult deal to resist. I'm not sure it makes any sense at all to say no.

"I want this for you, Sophie. Let me do this for you. I will lend you what you need to get it off the ground."

I think quickly. I was splitting rent with Tyler for the last year and a half, so I saved a bit between my teaching job and my royalties. I have probably six months or so worth of expenses saved, so I can get by for now.

Maybe this isn't such a bad idea. Maybe getting out of this town for a little while is exactly what I need.

Before I get a chance to answer, the waitress comes by with our food. Neither of us picks up our forks to start eating despite the rumbling in my stomach. I feel hopeful and excited and a little less sad for the first time since I told Tyler I was done last night.

And I also see the hope and excitement in Miller's eyes.

He's in a new city, though he's been there for nearly a year at this point. But I know how important it is to him to be surrounded by people he trusts. He's had a rough year and a half between finding out the man who raised him isn't his biological father and then losing his biological father before he had the chance to really get to know him. He found out his parents had been lying to him his entire life. And then he left the team he'd been playing for his entire career and moved to a completely new city. Only his twin brother has been with him through it all.

So part of this feels like a new beginning for both of us. To live with my best friend for a bit after a bad breakup doesn't really sound so bad.

I pick up my phone before I give him an answer, and I dial Elizabeth.

"Sophie?" she answers. "I haven't heard anything yet."

"I know. I'm calling because I want to resign." I blurt the words and realize my hands are shaking. "The investigation is only going to waste everyone's time, and it's going to come out that I am, in fact, publishing romance books under a pen name. So let's save everyone the time and just call it what it is."

"Oh, Sophie. I don't want to lose you as a teacher in our department. Are you sure about this?"

I'm not. This feels like a split-second decision over breakfast with my best friend, but as my eyes edge over to his, I suddenly feel certain that this is the right choice for me. Something about the way he's looking at me is convincing enough to push me to take this risk.

I draw in a deep breath, and I nod. "I'm sure."

She's quiet for a few seconds, and then she sighs. "Okay, then. Email me your official letter of resignation as soon as you can."

"Thank you for everything." We hang up, and I look at Miller again. "Let's do this damn thing."

"Yeah?" he asks, his eyes still all lit up and bright blue as they crinkle at the corners with excitement.

"Yeah," I confirm. And then we toast with our orange juice glasses and celebrate with our breakfasts.

Chapter 5: Miller Banks

Mr. Wiggles

The strangest feelings pulse through me as I look at her face across the table from me.

She's smiling despite breaking up with her long-term boyfriend last night and subsequently getting fired because of the douchebag move on his part.

And I am the one who put the smile on her face. This may be a crazy plan, but it feels right. This is her chance to take a leap, and if I can support the person I believe in most in the entire world, then it's my responsibility to help her take that leap.

"When I first moved to San Diego, Tanner and I got a place together. He moved out, but I stayed, and it's way too big for just me. So just come live with me a while. It'll be your chance to get away and build your business," I say.

She looks at me a little doubtfully. "Are you sure?"

I chuckle. "Absolutely."

"I just don't want you to feel like you can't keep living your life just because I'm there," she says.

My brows dip together. "What do you mean by that?"

"You know, if you're seeing anybody or want to bring someone back…" She trails off, and somehow the permission to keep living my life feels like a knife right through my heart.

There's no one else.

It's her. It's always been her.

I've tried. Believe me, I've tried. I've experimented with the competition, but she's the reigning champ.

But her words are yet another reminder that she doesn't feel the same way I do, and she never has.

It's probably a little on the masochistic side to even suggest living together since I'll be subjecting myself to the daily agony of living with a person that doesn't feel the way I do, but it also feels like having her so close is good for my soul.

Maybe she doesn't love me the way I love her, but regardless, she is still my best friend. We share a history and inside jokes and a lot in common. Even if I have to be subjected to her moving on from her previous relationship, I still have the friendship that means so much to me. And that's better than nothing.

We finish breakfast, and I grab the bill. She gives me a warning, to which I reply, "Get used to it."

She lets out a soft sigh that feels a bit like she's relenting.

"Where to?" I ask once we're out in the parking lot by her car.

"San Diego?" she suggests, and I laugh.

"Do you need to go back to your place to pack your stuff first?"

"Yeah, I probably should. Tyler will be at work by now so I can get in, get what I need, and get out."

"And you've got me here to help if you want to mess any of his shit up," I say.

She rewards me with a laugh, and we head over to her place.

"Do we need anything for your place?" she asks on the way over.

"Like what?" I ask.

She lifts a shoulder. "I don't know, like dishes or pots and pans or…" She trails off.

I shake my head. "As of yesterday, I am thirty years old, you know. I sort of know how to cook for myself and actually own a set of pots and pans. I mean, I eat off paper plates, but…"

She looks at my profile as I drive and studies me as she tries to figure out whether I'm teasing her, and when she determines that I am, she says, "Okay, fine. So we don't need dishes."

I reach over and squeeze her forearm. "You can bring whatever will make it feel like home to you because it'll be your home, too."

She pats my hand on her arm. "I'll just take what I need and take stock of what you got when we get there."

"Anywhere else you want to go before we head out of town?"

She scrunches up her nose in this cute way she has, and I already know what's coming.

"I should probably stop by the school to grab my things and my parents' house to let them know what's going on," she says.

"Are you going to tell them about your books?"

Her brows furrow tightly together as they create a shadow over her lids, and her lips turn down. "That's a solid hell to the no, Banks."

I have no idea what, exactly, she plans to tell them, but something tells me it'll be good.

Once we get to her place, or her *former* place, she heads to the bedroom and grabs the suitcase, which she starts to fill with the clothes stored in the dresser. She directs me to the closet to grab her clothes on hangers, and I fill the backseat of her car pretty quickly. The trunk holds her suitcase and a couple of boxes, mostly filled with perfume and makeup, along with a few blankets and stuffed animals that span all the way back to the time before I even met her.

I pick up her unicorn. "You still have Mr. Wiggles?"

She takes it from my hands. "I can't believe you remember her name."

"Who could forget a unicorn named Mr. Wiggles that's female?"

She giggles. "Good point. I used to make up the craziest adventures for Mr. Wiggles and me."

"Tell me about them," I say.

"Oh, we'd go find rainbows and ride them all the way to the end. We'd land in the pot of gold, but it was such a big pot that the whole entire city fit inside, and it was all made of gold. We'd go into the local pubs with the local unicorns and their owners, and we would eat glitter and drink clouds and go on magical adventures." She has a dreamy look in her eyes.

"So you're telling me you had a vivid imagination even as a child," I say.

"Absolutely," she says, setting Mr. Wiggles into a box and picking up a penguin, her favorite animal, who I believe is named Penelope. "I've been making up stories my whole life. They just happen to be a little sexier now."

"A little?" I ask, and she ducks her head a little as her cheeks turn pink. I walk over and give her a quick hug even though I want to hold her in my arms. "Don't you dare be embarrassed about that. Your words are powerful and wonderful and sexy as fuck."

Her brown eyes are so sweet and innocent as they meet my blue ones.

They look a little misty as she lets out a soft sigh. "Thank you," she says. "I've gotten the email here and there from readers telling me how much my words mean to them, but nobody in my life has ever made me feel like what I do is important until you did just now."

"Well, get used to it," I say, repeating the words I said earlier when I paid the bill at the restaurant.

She deserves the world, and I want to be the one to give it to her.

Chapter 6: Miller Banks

It's been years since I pulled into the driveway of Mr. and Mrs. Summers' house.

This is the same house where she grew up, the same house where I picked her up before school, the same house where she helped me write my essays, and I helped her pass algebra.

We were never together then, and we're not together now—but one thing remains true. I wish we were.

She draws in a deep breath as I cut the engine.

"You okay?" I ask.

She leans her head back on the headrest, then slides it to the side to look at me. "No."

I reach over and squeeze her thigh. "You don't have to be. It's why I'm here."

Her eyes soften at my words, and she presses her lips together and nods her head. "Let's do this. And just…whatever she asks, whatever I say, just play along, okay?"

"Of course," I say.

She opens the door, and we both get out and meet at the front of the car. She slides her hand into mine for fortitude as we approach the door together, and she rings the bell.

When I go to my parents' house, I just walk in. It's the difference between our families, and it makes me think for just a split second that I should stop by to see my mother while I'm in town.

But this trip isn't about me. It's about Sophie.

The door opens, and Mrs. Summers looks surprised to see the two of us standing on her front porch holding hands. Her brows dip together as her eyes flick to our joined hands before she looks up at the two of us.

"What are you doing here, honey?" she asks her daughter. "Shouldn't you be at school?"

She hasn't even invited us in yet.

Sophie clears her throat. "Could we, uh…come in and talk to you?"

"Of course. Come on in." She opens the door a little wider, and we walk through.

Sophie doesn't let go of my hand. "Is Dad home?"

"No, he went into work. What's going on?" she asks once we're standing across from her at the kitchen counter.

Sophie clears her throat. She glances wildly at me, and I can see it in her eyes. She can't tell her mom that she resigned because her ex-boyfriend revealed her secret pen name to her students.

Maybe her mom will find out anyway. But right now, she needs me to save her.

And so I do.

"Sophie and I have decided to move in together," I blurt.

Her mom gasps. "Sophie!" she scolds. "But what about Tyler?"

Soph clenches her jaw for a beat. "That's been over for a while."

"And now you two?" she asks, circling her finger between us.

I glance at Sophie, and she's looking at me, and when our eyes connect…

Oh boy. She's got that look in her eyes that I know so well but that I already know I need to brace myself for.

"Yes," Sophie says, and she pushes up to her tiptoes and presses a kiss to my lips.

Jesus Christ. Mary and Joseph. All the biblical names.

What in the holy hell is happening?

My mind goes absolutely blank for a moment as Sophie's lips form to mine.

It's brief. Too brief. Only a couple of seconds at most.

But holy fuck, is it filled with absolute fireworks. Intense, explosive fire.

Two seconds. Lip to lip.

Imagine sex. Jesus. I can't. I *have* imagined it, lots of times, and this one kiss for her mother's benefit doesn't do a damn bit of justice to my imagination.

She pulls back and settles down onto flat feet again, and I'm supposed to come out of it like it's no big deal. Like it wasn't my first kiss with the woman I have loved for years.

Oh, wait. Right. It's not supposed to be a big deal if we're at the point of moving in together. I clear my throat as I try to come up with something to say, but she speaks before I can. I'm supposed to be saving her, but I'm too caught up with that kiss to think straight at this moment in time.

"I quit my job, and we're moving to San Diego because Miller and I are together now." She turns to me. "Right, baby?" She slides her arm around my waist.

We're together now?

Oh, right. *Play along, Banks.*

I finally pull myself together enough to say, "Right." I sling a casual arm around her shoulders and lean down to press a kiss to the top of her head.

Her mom purses her lips. "Well, I can't say I'm surprised. You two always seemed to have a little thing between you."

We did? Wait a minute. What?

Sophie leans her head on my shoulder. "Definitely."

"But Sophie, this isn't like you." Her mom is definitely judging us. "You're in the middle of a school year. Just a couple more months until it's over…and you're just quitting and leaving? What about your students?"

She clears her throat, and then she blurts, "Miller and I are getting married." She slaps a hand over her mouth after the words escape.

Her mom gasps.

Hell, I think *I* gasp, too.

Are we really doing this?

Whatever I say, just play along.

Her mom's eyes dart to her ring finger, but she keeps talking, making the lie bigger and bigger with each word.

"We just want to get started on our future right away, and with him playing in San Diego now, it makes the most sense for me to move there." She shrugs at the end, and she waves a hand in the air. "He asked me last night on his thirtieth birthday, and we're going to pick out a ring soon."

"Oh, honey," her mom says, and she walks around the counter to hug Sophie. "I'm just—I don't know what to say. I just want you to be happy."

Her mom hugs me next, and my eyes meet Sophie's over her mom's shoulder.

"I am, Mom," Sophie assures her as she widens her eyes at me as if to tell me *thanks for playing along.* Did I have a choice? Her mom turns back to Sophie, who's still babbling…and I'm a little worried if she *keeps* babbling, she's going to blow this whole story. "I just wish Dad was here because I wanted to tell the two of you together. We need to get home. Miller's got some things to do, and he flew in last night and we're driving my car back."

"Congratulations to you both. And happy birthday, Miller," she says. "Oh, honey. We get to plan a wedding!"

"Don't get too excited," Sophie warns her. "We'll probably keep it low-key. Besides, he's got a new season coming up, and he'll be busy with that."

"Oh, of course," she says. "Didn't you two make a pact back when you were teenagers that you'd get married if you were both still single when you turned thirty?"

Sophie's eyes widen like she's been caught, and I turn and raise my brows at her that she shared that news with her mother.

Sophie clears her throat nervously. "Oh, did we? Anyway, we just wanted to stop by to tell you the news." Sophie hugs her mom. "But we really do need to get moving. I'll call you later, okay?"

Her mom looks a little shaken, and I feel like I got hit by a bus, but we say our goodbyes and head out to the car.

I pull out of the driveway without a word since her mom is waving to us and Sophie has her window down—likely on purpose so she doesn't have to answer any questions right away, and then we're out of her mom's sight as we turn the corner.

She rolls the window up, and I pull over to the curb.

"What are you doing?" she asks.

"What am I doing?" I ask, putting a hand on my chest. "What are *you* doing?"

She shrugs. "I don't know."

"Clearly."

"Are you mad?" she asks, her nose wrinkling up again.

I sigh. "No, Soph. You know I could never be mad at you. You just…kind of blindsided me."

"I know. And I'm sorry. I'll figure out a way to get us out of this mess."

I just don't know how to tell her that I don't really want her to get us out of this mess. I think I'm going to like being engaged to Sophie Summers.

Chapter 7: Sophie Summers

Call the Butler

The drive from Phoenix to San Diego is six hours, and we pass the time with the kind of music that was popular when we were in high school. I plug my phone in and start the playlist on random, and it's no surprise when Miller knows every word to every song.

These are the songs of our formative years, the ones we danced to at homecoming and the ones we still listen to today because they're classics to us.

It's a lot of boy bands…and I'm not ashamed of that. There's some country in the mix, too, and some alternative. Our tastes are eclectic, but they're similar, and boy bands will forever hold a special place in my heart.

We laugh as we talk about our memories with each song, and we reminisce as neither of us can believe we've been out of high school twelve years already.

He hasn't said a word about the *fake engagement*.

Neither have I.

We haven't spoken about the pact my mom brought up.

Maybe it won't come up.

Maybe it will.

I can't believe that whole thing slipped out of my mouth, but I had to come up with *something* to tell my mother, and the truth just seemed too far-fetched. This seemed more believable than telling her I broke up with Tyler, who exposed my secret romance pen name to my students, and I quit my job this morning because of it.

Besides, will it really be so bad playing house with Miller? We can put on the act, and it's not that big of a deal since we're moving to San Diego while my parents will be back here.

We stop halfway at a gas station to grab snacks and stretch our legs, and I forgot how much fun it is to spend time with Miller. It's been a while since we've had six hours uninterrupted together. Between my controlling ex and Miller's busy schedule, it's rare that we get to share this sort of time.

The six hours seem to pass in a flash. Suddenly we're stopped in southern California traffic, which is worlds apart from the kind of traffic we see at home.

Miller handles it like a pro, calmly and easily weaving in and out when he needs to, careful and polite as he never cuts anyone off even though everyone else seems to drive like a maniac. I'm in the passenger seat, pressing on my invisible brake pedal and swearing at everyone around us. Miller just keeps glancing over at me and laughing.

"What?" I ask after I yell, "Fuck you!" to the Tesla that just cut us off.

He laughs. "I forgot about your road rage."

"Me?" I ask dramatically. "I don't have road rage." I toss up a middle finger at the car next to us as I yell, "Asshole!"

"Be careful with that shit here. You'll meet your match when it comes to road rage, and they don't play here."

I take the warning to heart. We stop and go a little longer before we turn off and start climbing into the hills of San Diego.

The views are beautiful from here as traffic starts to thin, and I look out in the distance and see the ocean.

"I can't believe you opted for a house in the hills and not on the beach," I say.

"There are surprisingly few houses on the market directly located on a beach in this area. This was closer to the stadium and still offered gorgeous views, so Tanner and I agreed on it when we moved here."

"How far is it to the closest beach?" I ask.

"Fifteen or twenty minutes, depending on traffic. Or if I'm driving, closer to twenty. If you're driving, ten."

I giggle. "Where's the lie?"

He pulls into the driveway of a gorgeous mansion and clicks the garage door opener, and I can't believe I haven't been out here to see him since he moved to the area.

"This is gorgeous, Miller," I say.

He pulls my car into the roomy garage with a Ford F-150 Raptor parked in it, and he pulls to a stop and hands me my keys.

"New truck?" I ask, nodding toward the army green truck.

He nods. "I treated myself with my new paycheck." He wiggles his eyebrows, and I laugh. He always had a truck—his first vehicle was a used Ford Ranger. Mine was a Camry, and we just made the trip here in my little Honda SUV.

I follow him inside. We walk in through a laundry room, and that room alone should be my first hint that this house is a little nicer than the apartment I shared with Tyler. Even the countertops in the laundry room are quartz, while the laundry room at the apartment was down in the basement and shared with all the other tenants in the building.

From there, we walk into a gourmet kitchen that looks out over a family room with a beautiful couch and entertainment setup. I gaze at the kitchen table, which is where I seem to do the majority of my writing, and I can already see the seat that will be the one where I spend time dreaming up my next bestseller. I walk over to the slider doors to study the pool that's shimmering in the sunlight. Just beyond the pool, there's a view of the gorgeous valley peppered with beautiful homes, all looking out over a similar yet different view.

It's totally dreamy.

I glance over at Miller and see his blue eyes are lit with the natural light streaming in from the slider doors. My breath catches in my throat for a second as I realize yet again how hot he is. I am pretty damn lucky to have him in my life—not because he's hot, but because he's been such a good friend to me.

There's nobody else who literally would have left his birthday party in Vegas to be by my side during one of the worst moments of my life, but he did. And then on top of it, he bailed me out of that situation and offered me a chance to start over.

I feel tears pinching behind my eyes at the thought of what a wonderful friend I have.

He glances over at me. "What's wrong?" he asks.

He knows. He just always somehow knows. He can read me like a book, which is one of the many things I'm so grateful for in our friendship.

"I was just thinking about how grateful I am that you're in my life. You're such a good friend, Miller, and I don't know what I would do without you."

He tilts his head with a bit of sympathy and offers a small smile. "I feel the same way." He slings his arm around my shoulder and pulls me into a side squeeze, and I slip my arm around his waist.

Has he always smelled this good? Warm and clean and masculine all at the same time, and it makes me want to stay here a little while longer.

He shows me around the rest of the house, including the primary suite, which used to be Tanner's room, the same room Miller never moved into once Tanner moved out.

"Do you want this room?" he asks.

I glance around at the ginormous room. There's a built-in bench beneath one window where I can sit and look out the window over the view with my laptop perched on my lap and a blanket over my legs. The room is absolutely luxurious, and I think it might be exactly what I need as I move here temporarily to try to start my life over.

"This will do, I guess." I smirk at him.

"Yeah, I guess my job comes with a decent paycheck, so if you need anything at all—"

"Call the butler?" I interrupt, and he laughs.

"No, nothing like that, but I have considered hiring a personal chef to prepare my meals."

I raise my hand. "Let me earn my keep. I can be your personal chef."

"And my fiancée?" he teases.

I blush as I scrunch my nose up in apology, and I'm about to tell him how sorry I am about that whole mess when he narrows his eyes at me.

"Since when can you cook?"

"I'll learn for you."

"I think you have yourself a deal, but If I need to prepare my last will and testament, just let me know."

"Shut up." I smack him in the arm as we both laugh.

He helps me unpack the car and once again offers to get me anything I could possibly need. I really only took the essentials from the apartment I shared with Tyler, and maybe someday I'll go back to collect the rest, but I'm not worried about it right now.

All I'm worried about now is getting back into my manuscript so I can finish the book I've been working on since this is my full-time job now.

Chapter 8: Miller Banks

"He stuck his *what* into her *where?*" I ask as I saunter up behind my new roommate, who is busily tapping away at her keyboard in my kitchen.

She slams the lid to her laptop shut, and she whirls around, embarrassment in her eyes as her cheeks redden. "Don't sneak up behind me! Especially when I'm writing a sex scene!"

"I'm sorry!" I hold up both hands. "I wasn't sneaking, I swear. I just walked in to get dinner started."

"I thought I was your new personal chef," she says, pursing her lips.

"Oh, sorry. Did you start dinner?"

She rolls her eyes. "No. I've been writing."

I laugh. "Okay, then let me get dinner started." I open a drawer and pull out the takeout menus that they staple to the bag when I order food. I only keep the menus for the places I like, and this is an easier method than trying to remember restaurant names and locate their menus online. "What are you in the mood for?"

She lifts a shoulder. "I don't know. What's good around here?"

"There's a good sushi place not far, Italian, seafood." I flip through the menus. "We have it all, though fair warning, the Mexican is better back home."

"What about shrimp tacos? I really want shrimp tacos."

I pull out the menu for my favorite seafood place, and sure enough, they have shrimp tacos on the menu.

"Let's go out and celebrate your first night in town instead of ordering in," I suggest, and she nods.

She glances down at her black leggings and T-shirt with a stack of books and a cup of coffee on top, and something about those leggings makes her ass look absolutely phenomenal. "Let me just go change my clothes."

I chuckle as I glance down at my black San Diego Storm collared shirt and the khaki shorts I paired with it. "Don't do it for me."

"Give me five minutes." She takes her laptop with her, and I'm tempted to tell her she doesn't have to. After what just happened with her ex, I don't blame her. But I want her to know she can always trust me. I would *never* do something like that to her. I would *never* do anything to hurt her.

I'm sure she knows that after all these years. I'm sure she's just being a good roommate and cleaning up after herself.

But the thought still crosses my mind that there's a bit of psychology behind it for her.

I call the restaurant to reserve a table while she changes. She appears in the kitchen fifteen minutes later, and she looks…

Well, gorgeous.

She's wearing a simple black dress paired with black flat shoes, and her dark hair falls in loose waves around her shoulders. Her brown eyes seem bigger somehow, like she did some makeup to make them brighter. Her cheeks are pink and her lips are shiny, and *fuck*, I can't stop staring at them.

I can't stop thinking about that kiss in her mom's kitchen.

Pull it together, Banks.

I feel like I'm telling myself that a lot around her.

We climb into the truck and head toward the restaurant, and nerves climb up my spine. There's nothing to be nervous about, obviously. I'm just taking my best friend—my new roommate—out to dinner.

I just wish it were a date.

I force myself to shake it off, weaving easily through traffic as we make our way toward our destination. She turns up a song by Pink that comes on the radio, and we both sing along.

The restaurant is busy at dinnertime every night of the week, but I manage to find a tiny spot for my huge truck at the back of the lot. We walk toward the restaurant, and some dude in the parking lot does a double take when he sees her. Maybe it's for me—I don't know. I'm usually recognized around these parts since I play for the local pro football team, but it feels like he's looking at her.

I have the strongest urge to grab her hand. To mark my territory. To let everyone know she's here with me.

And physically, yes, that's true. But walking into a restaurant together isn't the same as *being* together.

I think back to a conversation I had with my brother just a few months ago. He told me he was going to shoot my shot for me because I did it for him.

I didn't, really. I just told the woman he loved that he needed her, and the rest is history. She showed up when he needed her most, just like I did for Sophie.

I know Tanner never really would do that, though. It's different with Soph and me, with our history and our friendship.

But sometimes I think the only way I'd ever take the shot is to let someone else take it for me.

We both order the shrimp tacos, and she orders a margarita, so I get one, too.

It's been years since I've had a margarita. Tequila is more my brother's drink of choice, while I usually lean toward whiskey or beer, but tonight we're celebrating Sophie. Her new job, her new home, her new city. Her new roommate.

And, lest we forget, her new engagement.

I did forget. Sort of.

I didn't forget that kiss. It's been right there at the forefront of my head since it happened. But like everything where she's concerned, I'm locking it into a little box and throwing away the key.

Except it doesn't really go quite that way.

We both just ordered a second round of margaritas when I hear a woman's voice. "Oh my God, is that Miller Banks?"

My head whips up at the sound of my name, which happens to be my first mistake since it's essentially admitting that yes, it's me.

"It *is* Miller Banks!" another woman beside her says.

I offer a small wave and a sheepish smile.

"Can we get a pic?" the first one asks, and I smile politely and glance at Sophie.

She holds up both hands. "Don't say no on my account."

I chuckle and nod, and the first one takes her friend's phone as the second one moves in beside me.

The first one holds up the phone and says, "Smile, San Diego's most eligible bachelor!"

"Oh, God, Chelsea, he's on a date!" the one who's currently leaning into my side for a picture says.

I don't bother to correct her, and neither does my *date*. And it's a good thing, too, because of what happens next.

"I know, but we can still have a little fun, right?" She snaps the picture, and then she switches places with her friend.

I smile for the second photo, trying my hardest to make the smile genuine and not stilted as these two interrupt my dinner with Sophie.

"Is he still considered a bachelor if he's engaged?" the one called Chelsea asks.

My brows dip together. "Huh?"

"Is this your fiancé? I just saw a snippet on Page Six."

"*Page Six*?" I repeat.

Why the fuck would *Page Six* be reporting that I'm engaged?

"Yeah, you know. The celebrity gossip column?" she says, defining it as if I don't know what it is. She looks between Sophie and me. "Oh, did they get it wrong? Are you not engaged?"

My gaze falls on Sophie, who's smiling like a pro while I'm getting a strong sense of whiplash.

"Oh, we're engaged," Sophie says smugly.

"Can I see the ring?" Chelsea asks.

"We're going this weekend to pick one out together, right, honey?" she says, her eyes moving to me and widening in that way that says *play along*.

I guess I don't have a choice. "Right, babe." I move over toward her and angle my head down.

Shoot your shot, Miller.

I press my lips to hers for the second time today, and for the second time today, I feel the wind knocked clean out of me.

I force myself not to open my mouth. Not to deepen the kiss. Not to do anything other than put on a show for the two women currently staring at our every move.

A margarita and a half in…and it's hard.

I have to go against every instinct telling me to give her the kind of kiss I've wanted to give her for the last sixteen years.

Maybe someday. Just not today.

Chapter 9: Sophie Summers

Cooling the Heat with Margaritas

After the two fans walk away with their pictures and gossip, we're left alone.

I try cooling the sudden heat I'm feeling with the margarita, but part of me thinks that's what's making me hot in the first place. The other part of me thinks it might be the kiss.

His hand came up to cup my chin, and it was such a chivalrous move. It was possessive and masculine, which are not two words I've ever associated with Miller, but here we are.

He's just leaning into playing the part of my fiancé, and I have to admit…I kind of like it.

Still, as we get back to our drinks, I can't help but wonder how *Page Six* picked up on our engagement when there was literally only one person we told.

How does the world suddenly know?

As I open my mouth to voice my thoughts, Miller's phone starts to ring. He glances at his watch, and his brows crinkle as he says, "I'm sorry, I better take this." He pulls his phone out of his pocket and answers. "Mom? Everything okay?"

I watch as his eyes widen a little. "Oh, um…yeah. I'm sorry." He listens to whatever his mom is saying, and I'm dying of curiosity over here. "She's living with me. We, uh…well, yes. We are. But it's new. We haven't had a chance to—"

He pulls the phone away from his ear a little as if she's yelling or something, and then he says, "I'm actually out to dinner with her right now, so can I call you back?"

He mumbles a little more, and then he hangs up. "Well, it's out there. *Page Six* official or whatever."

I gasp. "But how?"

He raises a brow and presses his lips together. "Your mother."

"My mother?"

He nods slowly. "Apparently she contacted the paper in Phoenix to have our engagement printed this weekend, to which they informed her that couples mainly do that via social media this century. She mentioned our names, and whoever she spoke with sold the story."

"I'm gonna kill her," I mutter under my breath.

Except…truth be told, I didn't hate the attention he gave me when those ladies asked if we were engaged. I didn't hate that his eyes moved off them and over to me.

And I certainly didn't hate that kiss. That's for damn sure.

She's just being my mom. It's what she does. She did the same thing when my older brother got engaged. She doesn't think about how she's announcing it to the world before we ever got the chance, but it was different with Chris and Marie. Chris isn't a football player. She asked them first before the notice ran, and I'm sure she would've asked me first as well, but she didn't stop to think that Miller's status as a celebrity might mean this situation is a little different.

She means well, and she's my mom. I love her no matter what—even if sometimes I want to metaphorically strangle her.

"What did your mom say?" I ask.

He smirks a little. "She wanted to know why she found out about our engagement from a headline on the internet and not from me."

I wrinkle my nose. "I'm sorry."

He shakes his head. "Don't be. We'll roll with it as it comes, right?"

Our shrimp tacos arrive, and we order another round of margaritas with them. I'm not used to drinking three margaritas in one night, and even with the food heavy in my stomach, I'm definitely tipsy by the time the meal is over.

And apparently, so is my fiancé. He calls an Uber so we don't have to worry about driving home, and he puts on a bit of a show while we wait for our ride out front, tossing his arm around me. I lean my head on his shoulder and reach up to link my fingers through his, giving into the show with him.

The weird thing about it is how natural it feels. I guess that's what happens when you're with someone you've been friends with for half your life. It's easy and comfortable, and we just fit together.

Which is why these weird new thoughts I'm having about him have to be kept at bay. I've never had a friend like him. Who else in the entire universe would leave their thirtieth birthday party in Las Vegas to be with an old friend? Nobody. The answer is nobody. Nobody has ever been so thoughtful and kind the way he simply always has been. He doesn't forget birthdays, or favorite songs, or the little things, and it's one of the many things I treasure about him.

So why suddenly am I breathing in his cologne? Why suddenly am I looking at him a little differently?

Because he's serving up my dreams on a silver platter, that's why. I'm misplacing my feelings of appreciation and gratitude as something more. He's comfort in the storm where I find myself, that's all. He's calming and reliable when my life has been thrown into utter chaos, and he believes in me in a way nobody else ever has.

I straighten and push off his shoulder so I'm not leaning into him so much. It feels a little dangerous as I start to lose myself there, and I'm trying not to let the romance author side of my personality interfere with my actual personal life.

Although…

If it's a book boyfriend I'm looking for, Miller Banks is a solid choice.

He's a pro football player.

He's strong and protective.

He's dependable and reliable.

He's kind and smart.

He's charismatic and funny.

He's hot as hell. Like *hot* hot. Hot.

He smells good.

When he looks at me, he makes me feel like I'm the only person in the room.

If my love language is acts of service, he delivers on that front.

We have a history together that gives us so much to reminisce over.

Oh…right. That last one.

Our history. It means so much to me, and the thought of losing that because I'm having weird feelings I've never felt before is so overwhelming that tears actually pinch behind my eyes.

It has to be the margaritas. It's definitely the tequila fucking with my emotions. Between that and the breakup and losing my job…it's definitely been an intense twenty-four hours.

I draw in a breath, and we slide into the Uber that stops in front of us. I keep my gaze turned out the window.

"So we're really doing this, huh?" he whispers as we make our way back to his place.

I turn back toward him with my brows pinched together in a silent question.

"The engagement," he clarifies.

Oh, right.

I offer a half-hearted smile. "I don't want to mess up your life, Millby."

He reaches over and grabs my hand. "You're not, Summers."

I blow out a breath. "I am, though." I glance up at the driver, and I lower my voice to make sure he can't hear us. "Those two girls back there, they would've gone home with you. But they saw you there with your fiancée, and they backed off."

He squeezes my hand. "I'd rather go home with you any day of the week."

My eyes find his, and I *swear* a heated moment passes between us.

It has to be my imagination. He'd rather go home with an old friend than some random stranger, and I can't really begrudge him that.

I flip my hand over and link my fingers through his. "You're a good friend."

He blinks, and the heat from his gaze seems to dissipate. He glances away from me and out the front of the car. "You are, too, Soph."

Whatever intense moment that coursed between us seems to have passed. I turn my gaze back out the window, too, sure I'm making a huge mistake by letting the world think we're engaged but, at the same time, incredibly grateful for the man by my side.

My fiancé.

Chapter 10: Miller Banks

Staring at My Abs

She went up to bed right after we arrived back home, and now her voice is in my head as I read *Married to the Enemy* for the third time. The story is great, but it's the sex scenes I'm flipping to, mostly so I can read one-handed and fist my cock in the other while I read the words that she wrote and hope for some insight into how she has sex.

On the one hand…I don't want to know.

On the other hand…it's all I want to know.

It's so conflicting, and I know this is fiction. Just because she wrote it doesn't mean she's tried it, and the enemies-to-lovers heat in this one is off the charts as these two finally give in to the strong feelings they're having only to have the hottest hate sex I've ever read in a book.

To be fair, I haven't read a ton of romance novels. I tend to read playbooks and nonfiction books about athletes and healthy lifestyles, but I do enjoy the occasional guilty pleasure of a Summer Love book.

And in this book, during the hate sex scene, he slips his cock into her ass, and fuck, is that scene hot.

Has she ever had ass play?

Could I break that barrier for her?

No. Pull it together, Banks. Jesus.

I was in the next room the night she lost her virginity. I know she's had sex, and she's told me about her previous partners—much to my distaste. Sometimes I hate knowing those things about her, but our openness with each other is one of the things I appreciate about our relationship.

Still, we've never discussed anal.

Maybe we *should* discuss anal, though the more I even *think* about anal, the harder my dick gets.

It's painfully hard as the hero thrusts into the tight ring of the heroine's ass, and the scene is from his point of view. I start to stroke my own cock as I read the words on the page.

It's so realistic as Sophie—or Summer Love—paints the picture of how it feels from a man's perspective. The pressure building up, the intense emotions, the heat tearing through his body.

How does she know how it feels? Did she interview someone, or is this just out of her imagination?

He inches closer and closer to his climax, and I feel it, too, as I stroke my hand up and down my cock.

He explodes into her ass, and I set the book down and close my eyes.

I picture Sophie bent over my bed the way the woman in the book is as I pound into her ass from behind. I tighten my fist over my cock, and I give in to that image that lives rent free in my brain.

I stroke myself faster as I sprint toward the finish line, my other hand coming down to cup my balls as I feel them drawing up. The same fire that the hero in the book just felt tears along my own spine, and my body contracts as pulse after white-hot pulse of come jets from my cock and onto my fist. I stroke myself through it, never letting go of the image I have in my head, watching it like a movie as she screams out in pleasure, too. As I finish and my body starts to come down from the high of an orgasm, I picture her turning around, those gorgeous brown eyes connecting with mine in a hot, intimate moment.

God, I want her.

But I can't have her.

And there's nothing I can do about it.

When morning dawns after a fitful night's sleep knowing she's in my house sleeping a few doors down, I get up, throw on some athletic shorts, and head straight for my home gym. Tanner and I worked hard to ensure this gym would have everything we need in it, and I start with a run on the treadmill followed by squats, lunges, and weights.

By the time I emerge two hours later, I'm ready for some fuel to start my day.

Sophie is up and working at the kitchen table when I walk into the room, and she slams the lid of her laptop shut again.

I watch as her eyes zero in on my abs, and she says, "Good morning. Have your abs always looked like that?"

I laugh. "I wouldn't say *always*, but probably since I started working with the pros."

"Damn, Miller." She wiggles her brows.

"What? If I had these abs in high school, you would've given me a chance?" I'm flirting, and she blushes.

I think she likes it, though we both know it's just harmless fun. Or it appears like it is, anyway, even if I'm serious about it.

She lifts a shoulder. "Maybe."

"Well, you had that same ass in high school, and I never had a chance." Her ass. Why did I bring up her ass? I'm still hot thinking about last night and what I was imagining while I read her book.

She scoffs as she rolls her eyes. "My ass is definitely bigger now than it was fifteen years ago."

"Just as hot now as it was then." I know she thinks I'm just being nice, but the words are true. Before it gets awkward, I change the subject. "I was just about to make some breakfast. You want anything?"

"Sure, whatever you're having is fine."

"Protein oatmeal with extra nuts?" I ask.

She wrinkles her nose. "I thought you'd say, like, scrambled eggs and toast."

I laugh. "I can do that. And a protein shake."

"Why all the protein?"

"I just worked out. Replenishing energy." I head toward the fridge to grab a bottled protein shake, and I take out the eggs while I'm in there.

"Hey, wait a minute. Wasn't I supposed to be cooking for you?"

I laugh and set the eggs down. I point to them. "I'm pretty good at scrambled eggs, but be my guest if you'd like."

"I'm actually right in the middle of a pivotal scene. Is it awful if I ask you whether I can finish typing while you cook?"

I laugh. "Not at all. I was planning to make food anyway."

I chug down my protein shake, and I wonder what our daily routine will look like. I'm quiet as I listen to the rhythmic tapping of her keys, and when it stops, I glance over at her.

She's staring at my abs.

I pretend like I don't notice, but then she moves her attention back to her document. I hear the typing stop again, and this time when I look over, she's staring out the window, seemingly lost in thought for a few seconds before she starts typing again.

It's a whole process, and I've never seen this side of her work. It's interesting to watch her stop and go, and ten minutes later, breakfast is ready.

She shuts the lid of her laptop as I set her plate beside her, and she grins at me. "This is awesome. Thank you so much."

I dig into my own plate, and truth be told, it *is* pretty damn awesome.

But I can't help wondering what she was just writing. Was it another sex scene? Was it from the man's point of view? Will I jerk off to it in a few months when it's published and I get to finally read it?

"What do you want to do today?" I ask, shaking those thoughts off.

"Well, I already hit my word count goal, so the rest is just bonus. I guess I could unpack a bit. What about you?" she asks.

"I was thinking I could take you ring shopping."

She sets her hand on her forehead. "Oh, God, I told those girls that, didn't I?"

"And your mom," I remind her.

She laughs. "Right. Look, I'll chip in some money on it. We don't have to do anything fancy, just something cheap to—"

I hold up a hand. "If you're playing the part of my fiancée, you'll wear a ring my fiancée would wear."

Her brows rise at that, but she doesn't challenge my words.

We each shower—separately—and I call Tanner to fill him in on what's going on before I head downstairs to meet her for our excursion.

"Hey, bro, what's going on with Sophie, and why did Mom call me asking me if you're engaged?" he answers.

I blow out a breath. "Because we *are* engaged."

"Holy shit. You did it?"

"No. I didn't."

"Huh?" he asks, clearly confused.

I glance at the closed door and wonder if she can hear me. Likely not. She's probably still in the shower, or maybe drying her hair, but I lower my voice anyway.

I tell my brother everything. He's more than just my best friend. But something stops me from telling him the specifics about *this*. Her secret pen name is not my secret to tell—even to Tanner, who I trust implicitly.

"Here's the short version. Sophie's ex posted something personal about her on her student message board, and it led to her being put on leave. She decided to quit, and I told her to come stay with me a while to get back on her feet. When she told her mom she was moving in with me, she blurted out that we're together, and it was one of those play-along-with-it kind of things. So I did, and she told her mom we were getting married. We left, her mom called the paper, and the news got out."

"Wait, wait, wait, wait, wait," he sputters. "Her mom called the paper?"

I blow out a breath. "She wanted to take out one of those engagement announcement things and was giving out our information. She meant well, probably wanted to book a date in a few weeks after we announced it, but as soon as she mentioned my name—"

"The jig was up?" he guesses.

"Yeah, something like that."

"So you're engaged now?" he asks.

"I guess."

"Figures you'd steal my thunder right after I got engaged," he mutters.

"I'm sorry. I really didn't think this was the way it was going to go. But we'll have a nice, long engagement, and—"

"And in that time you'll get her to actually fall in love with you?" he guesses, ending my sentence for me.

I press my lips together.

I wish that was the way this story was going to end, but I don't think I'll ever actually get up the courage to admit my true feelings to her.

Chapter 11: Sophie Summers

He Remembers Everything

What exactly is one supposed to wear ring shopping?

This feels sort of pivotal. I know we went out to dinner last night, but this feels like our first outing as a couple—or at least the first that might garner some attention.

Miller isn't just some average dude. He's Miller Freaking Banks, star running back for the San Diego Storm, number twenty-three, heartbreaker extraordinaire. He's made *People Magazine*'s list of sexiest athletes more than once. He's been approached to appear on dating shows. He's frequently featured on celebrity gossip sites and channels because people are curious about the hot bachelor twin brothers who've played together their entire careers.

And now?

He's my fiancé.

I, on the other hand…well, I *am* just an average girl. I'm a former teacher who likes to spend time with the characters I create rather than most people. I love animals and want to get a dog, but, as a teacher, I was always worried I'd never be home long enough to care for it.

I still dress up for Halloween, I prefer sour gummy candy over chocolate, I can't hide what I'm thinking, I love sparkly things, I burn popcorn every time I make it, and I adore boy bands to this day.

That's it. That's me in a nutshell.

Miller shares a lot of those same things in common with me, but there's a huge difference.

He's a professional athlete for arguably the biggest sport in the US, and since he's a star on his team and an attractive guy, that elevates him into a different stratosphere entirely.

Which means that I'm engaged to a celebrity.

I don't have any training on this. I don't know how to handle the media or people firing questions at me. I don't know how to smile on command for hours at a time or how to act like I'm happy if I'm not.

And I don't know what to wear when I go ring shopping.

I don't have enough clothes to play the part of a celebrity's girlfriend. Maybe I can go shopping this weekend and dig into some of my savings since I'm not paying rent right now.

I also need to learn how to cook, but I can only tackle one issue at a time here.

I settle on a long, flowing dress with flowers on it, and I pair it with a denim jacket. It's casual but trendy at the same time, and I slip on a pair of white sandals.

This will have to do.

Just before I head downstairs, my phone rings. I check it, and it's Brooke, one of the teachers in my department and my closest female friend.

Or…my former department. Maybe my former friend. God, this is complicated.

When I graduated from Arizona State University, most of my friends scattered. Over the eight years since we graduated, life moved on. Some of my friends got married and started having kids, and others moved on to one failed relationship after another. And by "others," I mean *me*.

Regardless, we grew apart, and we made new friends wherever we landed. For me, it was Cactus Valley High School, the place where I've spent my entire career teaching.

I made friends. Teachers came and went, but Brooke started the same year as me, and we've been through all the ups and downs of this career together.

Until now.

I glance at the clock. She's on her prep hour, and that's why she's calling me now.

I should've called her when it all went down, but I didn't. I called Miller instead.

"Hey," I answer a little weakly.

"What the hell is going on?" she demands. "Where are you?"

"It's complicated."

"Spill it, Summers."

I blow out a breath. The truth is, well…I haven't even told her about my secret pen name. Literally only Tyler and Miller knew.

I guess I'm good at keeping secrets.

"I broke up with Tyler." Best to start at the beginning. I'm not sure whether I want to admit the rest.

"So you took the day off? I gotta tell you, babe, rumors are *flying* about what's going on with you."

"I'm, uh…" I trail off, not sure where to go next, but ultimately I settle on the truth. "Can you promise you won't tell this to anyone?"

I have a feeling she'll say she promises but won't follow through, and I'm not even sure how much it matters at this point.

She's probably my closest girlfriend, but between my job and my hobby, I haven't exactly nurtured friendships the way I should have. But maybe she deserves the truth even if we aren't working together anymore.

"I've been secretly publishing romance books under a pen name for a few years, and Tyler knew. He posted about it on my student message board after I broke up with him. Elizabeth called me to let me know I was on administrative leave until they could investigate, and rather than sit through a lengthy investigation that would only out my pen name in one of the most conservative communities in the state…I resigned."

"Jesus, that's a lot to unpack." She's silent a few beats before she murmurs, "You resigned?"

"Yeah."

"Oh my God, Sophie. Are you okay?"

I feel the heat of tears pinch behind my eyes, but the truth is…yes. I am okay. And even if I'm not, I have Miller to be okay for me, just like he told me yesterday. "I'm okay."

"Where are you now?" she asks. "Can we grab lunch and talk this weekend?"

"I'm actually in San Diego right now. I called a friend, and he invited me to stay with him while all this blows over."

"He?"

I clear my throat. "My friend Miller."

"Banks?" she asks. She knows exactly who I mean when I say *Miller*. For as much as I've kept my pen name a secret, I never kept my friendship with the pro football player a secret.

"Yes."

"So have you gotten naked with him yet, or are you still waiting?"

"Oh my God, Brooke!" I yell.

She laughs. "Sorry. I have to keep things light. But really. Have you admitted you're in love with him?"

I roll my eyes even though she can't see me. We're just friends, and it's a conversation we've had a million times. "I need to go. I'm meeting Miller in a few minutes."

She sighs. "Give that dreamy butt a squeeze for me. And really, babe, I'm going to miss having you next door. Maybe you can un-resign and come back when all this blows over?" she asks.

"I miss you already, too," I say. "And we never know what the future holds. Maybe I'll be back after all."

"What's this secret pen name?" she asks.

"Ask the students. I'm sure someone caught it before I took it down."

She huffs out a breath. "Fine. Call me if you need anything, okay?"

"I will." I hang up, feeling a bit of nostalgia as I think about how even though I just told her that maybe I'll be back…something tells me I won't be.

I fluff my hair, put on a little more lip gloss, and head down to the kitchen to meet my fiancé for this outing.

He's standing in the kitchen wearing khaki shorts and a black shirt, and what is it about khaki and black that makes him look so hot?

No, Sophie. No. I need somebody to snap me out of this.

I blow out a breath, and his jaw slackens a little when he sees me. "You, uh…you look great, Soph. Really leaning into the part."

My brows crinkle together. "What's that supposed to mean?"

He lifts a shoulder. "Nothing. Ready?"

"Let's do this."

He navigates us toward downtown San Diego, and it's a tour of the town I wasn't expecting. We drive near the water, and then he cuts up a side street and slides into a parking spot. We walk a block until we find ourselves in front of a jewelry store.

"My brother recommended this place," he says, and I glance over at him.

"Your brother has a jeweler?"

"Didn't I tell you? He just got engaged."

My jaw drops. "What?"

He nods. "Yeah. He proposed the night of our birthday, actually."

I touch my forehead in embarrassment. "Two nights ago? As in the night I called you and you came running for me?"

He slings his arm around my shoulders and squeezes me in a side hug. "Trust me, he didn't need me there for whatever came after she said yes."

"I can't believe Tanner is engaged." I guess I didn't see him settling down first.

"Get this. She's seven years older than him and has two kids."

My eyes widen. Holy hell. Good for him. And her.

"I can't wait to meet her."

"She's amazing. She's a physical therapist. She helped him recover from his ACL injury last year. She's a great mom, too, and she and I have gotten close. Her name's Cassie. I'll ask Tanner when they're free, and maybe we can get together for dinner."

"I would love that. I haven't seen Tanner in years."

"You haven't missed much," he says dryly, and I laugh.

We walk into the jewelry store, and we're greeted by a salesperson who introduces herself as Charlene. "What can I help you with today?"

"We're looking at engagement rings," Miller says.

"Congratulations," she says warmly. "Did you have something in mind?"

We glance at each other and shrug, and Miller takes the lead. "Can we see what you have? This is our first time doing this."

He glances at me. "When we were in college, she and her friends all designed their dream engagement rings. She wanted a princess cut back then, one with diamonds all around the center stone and down the band."

"A fine choice. We have something like that over here," Charlene says, but I barely hear her because…*what?!?*

He remembers that? I hardly remember doing it, but he remembers everything down to the cut I liked.

Princess cut is classic. It's square and sparkly and lovely, and part of me wants to tell him that no…I want the princess cut for my *real* engagement. I want that to be the ring I wear forever, not for whatever it is we're doing here.

But I can't make myself stop this train.

"We have this gorgeous ring here with a three-carat princess cut diamond in the center. It has an additional two carats of diamonds down the shank and around the halo," Charlene tells us.

That's it. That's the ring.

My eyes widen and get a little misty as they fall on it.

It's the dream one, the one I created on a website all those years ago. It's the one I dreamed I'd wear forever when the man of my dreams slid it onto my finger one day.

But I haven't really met any dreamy men worthy of slipping a ring onto my finger. The only guy worthy of sticking a ring on my finger is doing it purely for show.

Is this just kicking my goals of being a wife and a mother down the road? We haven't talked about what this fake engagement really means. We haven't discussed how long we're going to keep up the act.

Hell, I don't even know how long I'm going to stay here in San Diego playing house with Miller.

He glances over at me, sees that I'm overwhelmed with emotion, and turns back to Charlene. "We'll take it."

Chapter 12: Miller Banks

I don't give her time to protest. Charlene sizes her finger, and she tells me she'll call me when it's ready to be picked up.

And that's it. Boom. Ring shopping—check.

Over the next few days, we fall into a routine that'll get thrown into upheaval once the season begins in a few months, but it's working for us for now.

I start the day with a workout while she works in the kitchen. She's always up already typing in the morning when I walk in. She keeps going until she hits her word count goal, and then she does her administrative work. If there's time left, she goes back in for more words.

She works until I make breakfast and shove a plate of food in front of her, and it's really anybody's guess if she actually ate meals before she moved in here or if she just grabbed whatever protein bar was handy in between her busy schedule.

We eat breakfast together, sometimes out on the back patio, and then she usually gets back to work while I sometimes swim and sometimes take a shower.

We eat lunch together, which is usually something simple like a premade salad or leftovers.

She works for a few hours while I do my own thing, which consists of meeting up with Tanner or some of my teammates, attending meetings, or doing little things for Sophie like setting up an LLC or looking into finding her an assistant.

When I get back, she's usually showered and ready to tell me about what she worked on.

It's one of my favorite parts of the day.

She's always so enthusiastic and excited to share what she was working on, almost as if she's bragging about her accomplishments because she wants to impress me. I guess I'm sort of an investor in her company, though to be honest, I'm invested in her as a person far more than in her business.

Today I'm meeting with my publicist, someone new I'm working with in San Diego. She was recommended by Ford, the backup quarterback to my brother, and I hired her midway through last season. We haven't had much opportunity to work together yet, but I have some plans I want to talk to her about, which is why I scheduled today's meeting.

I head to the office where Tara Holt works, and her assistant greets me with a bottle of water as she walks me back to Tara's office. She's sitting behind her desk in a pantsuit as she studies her computer, clear square eyeglasses perched on her nose and her chin-length dark hair pushed behind her ears.

She glances up when the assistant knocks on the doorframe, and she rises from her chair and removes her eyeglasses as she greets me with her hand stuck out over her desk.

"Mr. Banks, lovely to see you again," she says, no warmth in her tone as it's all professional. "Have a seat."

The assistant leaves, and I sit.

"What can I do for you today?" she asks.

"My brother is getting married," I begin. I'm not sure why I begin there, and she gives me kind of a funny look as I say it, so I backtrack. "We've always been a package deal. But he's doing his own thing now. He started up an after-school program for kids to learn how to play football. I guess I just…want my own thing, too. I want to work on my branding as an individual. Create my own programs. Do my own community outreach. You know?"

She squints a little and nods as she clearly begins to formulate some ideas. "Well, there are tons of ways we could tackle this, no pun intended. We could simply work on a line of endorsements or sponsorships. You could be the face of, say, All Pro Athlete Drink, or whatever offer comes your way that you feel is a good fit. That would help with the branding angle. As for program creation, what are you thinking?"

I shrug, and Sophie's face comes to mind. "I don't know. Something with high school kids, maybe?"

She nods. "Let's give it some thought. Are you thinking a business or a charity?"

"More charity, I think."

"Okay. An annual event, virtual or in-person, related to sports or something else…" She trails off after firing off all those questions.

"All great questions that give me things to think about."

"What are you passionate about?" she asks.

Another great question. "Football."

"Obviously."

I clear my throat. "Player health. Leadership. Giving kids the tools and open doors to be successful in this career—or even helping them figure out if this career is right for them because it isn't for everybody."

She nods. "By high school, I think most can recognize the potential a kid has and if they have any chance of making it pro.

So I think you're onto something. Let me do some research and see what similar programs are out there. But help me break this down. You want to run a charity event where you inform and instruct students on things such as player health, leadership, and a career in professional sports, and you want it to meet…weekly? Monthly? Annually for a week, like a boot camp?"

"Yeah, something like that. Let me do a little research, too, and let's touch base next week with what we've each found," I suggest.

We set an appointment a week out, and then I head home to find Sophie crying at the kitchen table.

"Oh my God, Soph. What's wrong?" I ask, rushing over and kneeling beside her.

She sniffles and wipes her cheeks. "Sorry. I just, ugh. God. Tyler called. He's breaking his lease on the apartment and said he needs my key back tonight, and I can't just magically make it appear. So I have to drive back to Phoenix tonight."

"Fuck him," I say. "Tell him to make a copy."

"I would, but he had my name on the lease, too, and I'll be on the hook for the deposit. And it's not just that. I left a few things there, and he said he'll trash them if I don't come get them."

I pull my phone out of my pocket. "There's a flight that leaves in an hour. We could hop that one, stay the night, and come back in the morning."

"Stop, Miller. You've been way too good to me already with this whole thing. I can't let you book me a flight on top of your generosity."

"I'd be booking it for both of us, not just you," I say with a smirk. I click the button to purchase two tickets before she can protest, and I flash my phone at her.

Her jaw slackens. "I swear to God, I don't deserve you."

"Go pack an overnight bag because we have to get to the airport," I say instead of responding to that. Of course she deserves me. I just wish she could *deserve* me in an entirely different way.

We rush toward the airport with an overnight bag for each of us, and if she left anything large at the apartment she wants, I figure we can leave it at her parents' house, or I can ship it home.

We get on the plane with plenty of time to spare, and I'm all set to listen to a podcast and think through this charity thing when she leans over onto my shoulder. I glance down at her.

"Thanks, Banks."

"Anytime, Summers."

She sits up and wraps her arms around one of mine, pulling it in close like she's hugging it. "You've been so helpful to me. I wish there was something I could do to repay the favor."

"Besides cooking for me?" I tease. We both laugh since we've been living at my place together for several days now, and she has yet to cook anything.

"Right. I'm going to learn, I promise. These things just take time."

I laugh, but then I turn thoughtfully toward her. "You know, there actually *is* something I need some help with."

"What is it?"

"I met with my publicist today, and I told her I want to expand my community outreach and branding. I told her I want to do some sort of program where I work with high school students to help them with some of the real shit that comes with being a pro athlete—leadership training, player safety, figuring out if they even want this as a career. That sort of thing. She asked me about a billion questions, and I need to come up with answers before our meeting next week. Want to help me?"

Her eyes light up. "Help you? Dude, this sounds like a job I was born to do."

I narrow my eyes at her. "You think so?"

"I know so. Let's back up. What were these billions of questions she asked?"

I start rapid-firing some of the things I need to make decisions on, and somehow…she's absolutely right. She was born to do this. She knows a lot about high school kids and their interests since she worked with them for eight years, so planning a curriculum for this is like second nature to her.

It's totally foreign to me, though. I know football. She knows curriculum design.

And together, we're one hell of a team.

The short flight is enough to get several of my questions answered, and when I meet with Tara next week, I'll be ready.

We hop into a rental SUV and pull in front of the apartment complex where Sophie lived until a week ago, and she sucks in a fortifying breath. I reach over and grab her hand. "You've got this, Soph."

She nods. "I know. Because you're here."

I press my lips together. I wish she knew how much I'd drop everything to be there for her at any given moment. I think I've started to prove that to her this week, but she's been hurt enough times that it might not be sinking in quite yet.

"Let's do this," I say.

"Let's do this," she echoes.

We get out of the car, and she grabs my arm and hugs it to her chest as we walk, just like we were sitting on the plane. She holds tightly to me, and then she lets go to let herself in. I walk in behind her.

"Tyler?" she calls.

No answer.

Good. I'm not sure exactly what I would do if I came face-to-face with that dickhead.

She sets the key on the kitchen counter, and then she heads off in search of the items she left behind.

"I'm going to use the restroom, and then I'll help. Okay?" I ask, and she nods.

When I emerge from the bathroom, I hear voices down the hallway.

"How could you do that to me, Tyler? I thought I meant something to you!"

"You ended things out of nowhere, so I just put the final nail in the coffin," he hisses back at her.

"What's going on here?" I demand as I walk in and throw a protective arm around Sophie.

Tyler rolls his eyes. "Jesus Christ. Of course you called in your best friend." He says *your best friend* with a healthy dose of mocking sarcasm, and I want to punch the dude in the face. "You two were probably fucking the whole time we were together."

Oh, how I wish that were true.

I want to finish that thought with my fist in his guts, but instead, I do what will hurt him far more. A punch would wear off after a couple of days. A week, maybe. But this? This he gets to play on repeat for as long as he fucking lives.

I turn toward Sophie, and I slip a hand around her neck. I pull her closer to me, guiding her into me with that hand. I tilt my head down and drop my lips to hers, and she leans into me, sliding her arms around my waist as I open my mouth to hers. It's a natural response, and I know she thinks I'm doing it for show, for his benefit—but it's everything I've wanted since I was fourteen.

I kiss her like he's not standing there watching us.

I kiss her like my life depends on it.

I kiss her like I'm finally free to do it, in a way that shows her just how deeply I love her.

Her tongue meets mine, and she kisses me back with the same sort of warmth, the same sort of adoration and love. And maybe it *is* for his benefit, too, but the way she's leaning into me, the way she moans softly, the way she grips onto my bicep as if she needs to hold onto me just to steady herself…it's all enough to make me think there's far more between us than just friendship.

She pulls back first.

Of course.

I would've kissed her all fucking night like that.

She turns toward her ex. "He asked me to marry him, and I said yes."

Fuck, I wish we had that ring, that we didn't have to wait for it to be sized, that she could shove it in his face right now.

But we don't.

So I lean down and press my lips to her temple as if to punctuate her words.

"I can't wait to spend the rest of my life with her."

It's a pretty goddamn easy act since every word I just said happens to be true.

I just wish her words were true, too.

Chapter 13: Sophie Summers

It Was Just For Show

Holy shit.

Holy shit.

That kiss…whoa.

Wow.

I'm without words, and words are my trade.

It was the stuff of romance novels, that's for sure. The way his palm came up to wrap around my neck, the way he pulled me into him, the way he kissed me like he needed my lips for his very survival.

Whew.

I'll be dreaming of that for a while, that's for damn sure.

I'm grounded back into reality when I realize *it was just for show.*

Tyler is still standing across from us, and my gaze edges to him for a second before I glance back at Miller.

Tyler is looking at me with some combination of rage and curiosity, while Miller is looking at me with pure adoration.

Man, he's a good actor. It's nothing short of totally believable.

"Well, we better get to packing," I finally say to Miller. I turn back to Tyler. "We do have a wedding to plan, after all."

He raises his brows. "And when, pray tell, is said wedding projected to take place?"

"Maybe before next season starts." The lie is out before I can stop it, and I feel Miller's heated gaze on me immediately after the words fall from my mouth.

"So, like…in the next few months?" Tyler asks.

I nod. "Yep. That's before next season." I smirk at him, and oh my God, why am I still talking? "If we can't make it work since there's so much to be done, then likely at the start of the offseason."

Miller clears his throat. "Nice seeing you again," he grunts toward Tyler, and then I spin on my heel and head toward the guest room to finish grabbing anything left in this apartment that belongs to me.

Miller makes eyes at me over the bed as if to say, "*Before next season starts?*"

I shrug and widen my eyes back at him as if to say, "*I'm sorry, but I had to!*"

He lets out a soft sigh as if he's relenting—maybe even *considering* a June wedding—and one of the things I can appreciate about our friendship is the fact that we can have these silent conversations where we both know exactly what the other one is thinking, no words exchanged.

Tyler isn't in the family room anymore when we emerge with the rest of my things, and that's it. We don't bother with goodbyes. Instead, we walk out, me with one box, Miller carrying two, and we head down to our rental SUV.

"Where to?" he asks once we're sitting in the car and the boxes are in the back.

"Same hotel we stayed at the night I broke it off with Tyler?" I suggest.

He nods, and we head in that direction.

"What do you want to do with the boxes?" he asks.

I lift a shoulder. "Drop them at my parents' house, maybe. Or, I don't know. I could just drive them back."

"Let me look at my schedule tomorrow, but that could work," he says.

"I meant by myself. I don't want to put more on your plate."

"Are you kidding?" he asks. "A road trip with my favorite author? It's not more on my plate. It's a dream come true."

A thrill lights up my spine when he calls me his favorite author. Something about his approval is just everything to me.

We end up in a room with two queens this time, and I'm not sure why I was hoping those rooms were sold out again.

Miller takes a quick shower, and when he emerges, he's just wearing a pair of mesh shorts.

No shirt.

Good Lord, those abs.

My eyes zero in on them for a second before they flick up to his, and he totally catches me staring.

My cheeks redden, but I don't let him see me sweat. "My turn?"

"Yeah," he grunts, and I practically run into the bathroom.

I take a minute to stare at myself in the mirror as I draw in sips of calming air. What the hell is wrong with me?

That kiss affected me more than I realized, I think.

I have to remind myself that he's just being a good friend. He dropped everything to be here for me. He's willing to drive me back to San Diego with my three boxes filled with what amounts to a bunch of meaningless junk.

His hand on my neck.

I'm his favorite author.

His lips on mine.

He's my best friend.

His tongue brushing against mine as butterflies raced around my chest and my stomach flipped.

God, this is so confusing. Why can't I stop thinking about the kiss?

Maybe I'm just horny. I wrote a sex scene this morning and a different one yesterday. Tyler and I hadn't slept together in a while before we ended things. Maybe I just need a quick orgasm to help alleviate some of this nonsense running through my brain.

I wasn't planning on taking a shower, but I find myself turning on the water, undressing, and getting in. I turn it to hot, and I stand under the stream of water, breathing in the steam as I bring my fingertips up to rub slow circles around my nipples. I grab one between my thumb and the side of my finger, rubbing it there and working overtime to quiet the moans I want to let out.

I let go with one hand and let my fingertips trail down my torso toward my pussy, and I slip a finger in, not wasting any time as I pump my finger in and out. I pull it out and slide it over my clit, rubbing myself there as I tug on my nipple at the same time.

I snag my bottom lip between my teeth and bite down hard as the pleasure starts to push me toward the peak. My fingers both start to move a little faster as I climb higher and higher, and I push my fingers back inside as I feel myself tipping over the edge.

His hand on my neck, pulling me closer.

I finger myself harder as I start to fall apart, my body thrashing instinctively as the pleasure ripples through me.

His lips on mine. His tongue brushing mine.

I pull my fingers out to focus on my clit as pulse after hot pulse throbs down low, and all I see is his face.

As my body starts to calm, I move over to the little shower bench and slump down onto it for a few beats as I let the warm glow fall over me.

And now I need to go out and face him.

He's in his bed, sitting up against the headboard and scrolling his phone when I emerge in a loungewear set. I feel his eyes on me, but I'm too embarrassed to look at him. It's like he'll sense that I just fingered myself in the shower while I was thinking about him, and that feels too heavy.

I've never done that before—thought of him while I did anything sexual. I've never seen him as anything more than a friend.

But suddenly…

What? Suddenly *what?* I wish I had the answer to that. All I know is that I want him to kiss me again.

And this time, I don't want it to be for show.

I brush away those thoughts and feelings, instead focusing on *him* for a change since it feels like everything lately has been very *me*-centric.

"Do you want to do more planning for your charity project?" I ask.

He glances up from his phone. "Funny you should ask. I'm actually looking up some things now." He flashes his phone at me, and I climb onto his bed next to him.

Dangerous, I know. I do it anyway.

I adjust the pillow behind me and lean against the headboard the way he is, and he settles his knee against my thigh once I'm comfortable.

"I wanted to plan out more of the curriculum for each day, and I liked your idea of doing a small chunk of information for a variety of topics each day," he says, his tone excited and enthusiastic. "If we do a weeklong camp, let's say we get eight to ten hours a day of instruction, plus up to a few hours for scrimmage or technique or whatever. We could be up and at 'em bright and early for workouts, do classroom stuff a bit, drills, break for lunch, more classroom, more drills, break for dinner, review film, bed."

"Is that sort of like training camp?" I ask.

He nods. He opens a note on his phone, and I can't read it, so I scoot closer to take a look at it. I'm so close I'm practically leaning on his shoulder, and his clean scent wafts to my nose, causing a pulsing, searing ache to land squarely between my legs.

Were his shoulders always this broad? I glance down beyond his phone at his thigh. Holy hell…were his *quads* always that thick? He's got this, like, massive quadzilla thing going on that's leaving me a little breathless. Those thighs are powerful and sexy and probably useful for more than just football games.

Oh God, Sophie. Get control of yourself.

It's just Miller. It's just my best friend. Why does the way he smells suddenly make me want to get naked right here in this bed beside him?

And the passion with which he speaks as he talks about this camp he's putting together…

It's hot.

Really hot.

And those quads.

God, this is getting confusing.

Really confusing.

And I don't even have anybody to talk to about any of it since *he* is the one I'd normally turn to.

Chapter 14: Miller Banks

Nothing Can Heal

Is there something between us, or am I completely off my rocker?

Either option is viable, if I'm being honest. She has always leaned her head on my shoulder. We've always been close enough that I could rest my leg against hers, and she wouldn't immediately move hers. It's easy. It's comfortable.

Three kisses have thrown the equation a little off kilter for me, though.

Or a lot.

Feeling her melt into me the way she did back at the apartment is something I won't soon forget.

She goes to her bed after we discuss the camp a little longer. We sleep in separate beds, the way it was always intended to be, but it feels somehow wrong.

I toss and turn all night—the exact opposite of what happened the last time we stayed at this hotel when I woke up with her in my arms and slept better than I had in a long time.

In the morning, we meet my parents at a breakfast diner before we head out of town.

It's nice to see my parents. It's low pressure despite the feelings that have coursed through me for ages, feelings really only my brother knows about—and even he doesn't really understand the depth and complexity of them.

I'm not entirely sure I understand it, either. All I know is that it's getting stronger. Somehow.

We have this shared history that bonds us together. We spend half our drive home talking about people I haven't thought about in years. When we're not chatting, we're singing, and when we're not singing, we're reminiscing or sharing inside jokes. No matter what the topic is, though, I know one thing for sure.

Everything feels so much lighter with her here with me.

When "Photograph" by Ed Sheeran comes on her playlist, we crack up about how she misheard the opening lyrics of the second verse in the song when it first came out and thought it was, "Nothing can heal." She belted out those words with such confidence at the time that even now, we both still sing it that way.

It's these little things that make the drive back to San Diego pass in a flash, and soon we're pulling into the rental car return even though I wish the trip could last a little longer. I spot Tanner's fiancée's SUV in the parking lot. They're here waiting for us, and they offered to take us out to dinner before they drive us home.

It feels like a double date.

To be clear, it's not one. But it still feels like one.

"Sophie Summers, how the hell have you been?" Tanner asks as he hops out of the driver's seat of Cassie's car as his fiancée gets out of the front passenger seat, her blond hair in a ponytail swinging behind her.

She gives me a quick hug as Tanner embraces Sophie, and my eyes edge over to the two of them. I wonder if either of them will say something about my feelings for Sophie.

Jesus, I hope not.

Maybe this dinner idea wasn't such a good plan after all.

I wonder if Sophie is attracted to my brother.

We're identical twins, but attraction has as much or more to do with personality as it does with looks. There have been plenty of women who went for me over my brother and vice versa. And there have been plenty of women who were gorgeous on the outside but showed their true colors on the inside.

There are huge differences between us. A couple of inches in height, for one. Tanner is taller and leaner, while I'm the shorter one with thicker and more defined muscles. A lot of it stems from our very different positions. As a running back, I need to be quick and able to break through tackles with my lower body strength, while Tanner needs stronger upper body strength to throw the football and manage plays.

I brush the errant thoughts from my brain. It doesn't matter who Sophie is or isn't attracted to. The fact is he's engaged to Cassie, and the other fact is that I'm hopelessly in love with Sophie and have exactly zero plans to act on it.

Except, of course, to play the game in public and shower her with as much affection as I possibly can since we're supposed to be *engaged.*

"It's so lovely to meet you," Cassie says to Sophie. *Do not say you've heard so much about her. Do not say you've heard so much about her. Do not say you've heard so much about her.* "I've heard so much about you."

Jesus Christ.

"Tanner says you're a high school teacher," Cassie says, her voice inflecting at the end like a question. She leans in a little conspiratorially and says, "My kids are about to turn eight and six, and I need you to prepare me for what to expect."

Sophie laughs, and Cassie laughs, and I feel like I dodged the first bullet of the night.

My brother catches my eye, and as I move over to give him our inside handshake where we slap hands forward, then backward, grab hands, shake once, fist bump, and hug, he quietly murmurs to me, "Everything okay?"

I raise both brows and nod as I press my lips together, and the secret look doesn't seem to be lost on him. I can't lie to him. He'd know anyway thanks to our twintuition.

He knows he'll get the full story later when we can talk.

But for now, we're taking our women out to dinner.

We head to our favorite steakhouse downtown, and we're seated at a quiet corner booth. Sophie slides in first, and I move in beside her. My thigh touches hers, and neither of us moves. I glance up and spot Cassie openly staring at the two of us, studying us as if she's coming to her own conclusions about what's going on here.

I tilt my head at her, and she glances back at her menu as if I didn't just totally catch her.

"What's everyone ordering?" Tanner asks.

"Surf and turf," I say immediately, setting my menu down. "And some whiskey. Anyone else need a drink?"

Sophie raises her hand. "Me. Margarita, definitely. And I'm looking at the salmon."

"Oh, me too! On both of those," Cassie says, and it's like they immediately bond because they want to order the same thing. "What about you?" Cassie asks, elbowing Tanner.

"The filet," he says. "And tequila, obviously."

"Straight tequila?" Sophie asks. "You still drink that?"

She remembers his signature drink? She leans across the table a little to tell this story to Cassie. "I remember this one time in high school, Tanner drank straight tequila until he puked in the bushes, and Miller had to drive us home." She giggles.

Tanner tosses a glare in her direction. "As I recall, you were watering the bushes yourself that night, and that's why you caught me."

She holds up both hands. "Guilty as charged. But my excuse is that I was mixing beer and rum. Ah, to be young again."

"Tell me about it," Cassie says. "But I'm seven years older than the three of you. Between mom brain and old age, my memory of that time of my life is pretty much shot at this point."

Tanner laughs as he tosses his arm around her. "My old lady," he teases, and she rolls her eyes as he presses a kiss to her temple.

"Call me old again, and you're sleeping on the couch tonight," she says with a glare, and Sophie and I laugh at their banter. She turns to Sophie. "So you've known these two since high school?"

Sophie nods. "Miller and I had freshman English together, and we immediately hit it off and have been best friends ever since." She leans her head on my shoulder, and I slip an arm around her.

"And now we're getting married," I blurt.

I glance around and see there's no one within hearing distance, and when I look at Sophie, she's looking at me. I give her a nod because I see the question in her eyes. *Is it okay to tell them?*

Sophie leans across toward Cassie again and lowers her voice. "You asked me before about teaching high school, and the truth is…well, the truth is a long story, but suffice it to say I'm no longer teaching, and instead I'm focusing on publishing romance books under my very secret pen name that only two people knew about until a few days ago."

Cassie's wide eyes are accompanied by a jaw drop.

"As my parents are conservative, I kept that little nugget from them and instead told them I'm moving to San Diego because Miller and I are engaged." She glances at me and then back at Cassie. "And then the envelope was pushed a bit when we went to my old apartment to pick up the rest of my things, and we told my ex we were getting married before next season begins."

"We?" I say pointedly.

Sophie giggles. "Yeah, that was all me." She puts a hand over her mouth in jest. "Whoopsies."

"So what are you going to do?" Tanner asks, his brows pushed together as he fixes his eyes on me.

I shrug. "Get married, I guess. But maybe wait until after the season."

"Dude, do you really think that's a good idea?"

I glance at Sophie. Yeah. I really do. I think it's the best goddamn idea I've ever had.

I let out a heavy breath, and just then, the waitress comes by with our drinks. I guess if we're putting on the act, now's as good a time as any.

"That's right. I can't wait to marry this girl," I say to Tanner, tossing my arm around Sophie and pulling her close.

She doesn't stiffen. She doesn't freeze. Instead, she seems to melt into my side again, as if we're the perfect fit. She sets her hand on my thigh, and I just need her to move about six inches up and a little to the left, and we'd be good to go.

"And I can't wait to become a football wife," she says. She looks up at me, and I look down at her.

As the waitress walks away, Cassie says, "Well, you two certainly have the act down."

Because it isn't an act.

She knows how I feel about Sophie. Tanner knows how I feel about Sophie. The whole *world* knows how I feel about Sophie.

Only Sophie doesn't know how I feel about Sophie.

And maybe if I drink enough whiskey tonight, I'll get up the nerve to admit the truth.

Tanner holds up his tequila, and the women each grab their margaritas while I pick up my whiskey.

"To marriage," Tanner says.

I guess I'll drink to that.

"And to family vacations," I say. "That cruise we talked about taking with the Nash family. Let's plan it. Let's do it before next season starts," I say. I'm not sure why it comes out of my mouth, but the thought of a vacation with all the people I'm closest to—including Sophie—is just hitting right. Maybe it's the whiskey.

Tanner glances at Cassie, who nods. "We're in. We're doing a July eighth wedding, and we wanted to do a Caribbean honeymoon anyway. What's twenty or thirty more guests? We can leave right after the wedding and be back before rookie camp."

"Are you sure you want us tagging along on your honeymoon?" I ask.

"The kids are likely coming along, anyway, so with the entire Banks and Nash family along for the ride, if everyone is in, that just means more babysitters," Tanner says. He wiggles his eyebrows at Cassie, who laughs.

"Oh!" she says. "Can I plan it? I *love* looking up vacations, and I was planning to book something for our honeymoon anyway."

We spend the rest of the meal chatting about cruises, where to go, and who might be able to join us, and I see the excitement in Sophie's eyes.

I guess we're really doing this.

I guess we're really doing this.

Chapter 15: Sophie Summers

Cassie already feels like my best friend, and I just met her an hour ago.

Maybe it's because she's marrying Tanner, so she already feels like family since these two boys have been like family to me for half my life.

Or maybe it's because we're part of this exclusive club—the only two women who've ever been engaged to the Banks brothers. It's quite a feat, to be honest. They're some of pro football's most eligible bachelors, and we managed to snag them.

Except for me, the only thing I *snagged* is a friend.

A good friend, but still just a friend.

But when he tosses his arm around me and looks down at me in that way he has, sometimes it feels like it could be more than just a friendship.

And when my hand lands on that huge thigh of his…my God.

I *want* it to be more than just a friendship.

But this is Miller Banks. My Millby. The guy who would show up for me at the drop of a hat. The guy who *did* do just that and invited me to live with him as he facilitated a way for me to give my dreams a real chance at being my reality.

And so I will carefully pack away these new feelings I seem to be having. I will continue resisting the running back…no matter how hard that may be.

Speaking of hard…good God, that thigh muscle.

I remove my hand from his thigh and toward my margarita instead because, yeah, tequila is a great idea when I'm already having inappropriate thoughts.

Dinner is served, and Cassie laughs as I fill her in on all the stories of the twins as teenagers. She asks me a million questions about the direction of my career change, and by the end of the meal, I slip a business card over to her so she can pick up one of my books.

And that's when Miller says, "She's an amazing author. You'll love her stuff."

Tanner turns to his brother. "I didn't even know she wrote, and you've read her books?"

"Every single one of them," Miller admits proudly.

And then I melt into a puddle. How the hell am I supposed to resist this guy?

The longer I sit beside him, the more real it feels.

By the time we're done, it's like we're two couples out on a double date.

We're photographed as we leave the restaurant, and Tanner drives us back to Miller's house. We say our goodbyes to Tanner and Cassie, and Cassie and I exchange numbers. She tells me she would love to meet up for coffee and show me around town since I'm new, and since I don't have any friends here, well, the truth is, I'd absolutely love to.

"Is it too soon to text her?" I ask as Miller shuts the door behind them.

He laughs. "Yeah, it might be a little on the early side."

"I don't care. It's not like a dating situation. It's a friend thing, and if she's marrying Tanner, then she's stuck with me being part of your lives." I say the words as I pull out my phone to send her a text, but then a question plagues my mind.

Will she be stuck with me forever?

Or will Miller eventually find somebody who he really *does* want to marry? Somebody who doesn't love the fact that his best friend is a girl that he's been engaged to, fake or not. Somebody who doesn't believe in platonic friendships between men and women. Someone who's jealous of the history we share. Someone who gets closer to Cassie than me because she's the one who gets to bond with her true sister-in-law.

I couldn't take him ending up with someone with those sorts of jealousy issues, and he doesn't seem like the kind of guy who would fall into that trap anyway.

Still, it's a very real and scary potential future for us, one where I'm written out of the story because I'm *just* the best friend.

What if I want to be more than that?

I can't say I've *never* considered it. But as we formed a close friendship, I forced the thoughts away. I'm the girl-next-door type. He could have any woman in any room. He's handsome, he's talented, he's smart, he's kind. He's frickin' hilarious.

And he's a good friend. The best friend I've ever had.

He chuckles, and the sound startles me from my thoughts. I glance up at him as I realize I've been staring at my phone as all of this has been racing through my mind.

All that time, he's been staring at *me*.

"Not sure what to say?" he asks. "Give it an hour at the very least."

I laugh as I try to mask my true thoughts. "You're probably right." I slip my phone into my pocket, and I sigh as I follow him into the house. "Tonight was fun."

"Cassie's the best," he says as he saunters over toward the fridge. "He really managed to meet his match in her."

"How's he with her kids?" I ask.

He lifts a shoulder. "Great, actually. He loves them like they're his own." He pulls a canned margarita out of the fridge for me and a beer for himself. "Want one?"

I glance at the clock. It's already eight, and to be honest, that's usually about when I go to bed. I'm used to my teaching routine where I get up at four to write for a couple of hours before I shower and head to school. I haven't fallen out of that habit yet, and besides, I'm exhausted after today's events. I don't really drink all that much, either, yet a drink with Miller sounds fun. "A margarita in a can?"

"Don't knock it until you try it."

I wrinkle my nose and eventually nod, and he cracks open the can like a gentleman before he pushes it across the counter toward me. He opens his beer and holds up his can in my direction.

I hold mine up, too, a little reticent about actually drinking a canned margarita, but I probably had enough at the restaurant that I'll barely taste this one anyway.

"To more fun nights," he says, and I tap my can to his.

We each take a sip, and I let the sour liquid swirl around on my tongue for a beat as I study the can. "This is good."

His eyes flick to my lips, and my chest tightens for a quick beat as an errant butterfly seems to take flight.

Pull it together, Summers, I berate myself. He's just looking at my mouth because I just tasted a canned margarita.

"I've never tried them. Cassie left them here when Tanner moved out, and she told me to give one to the next girl I brought home."

I giggle. "And whoever that was refused to drink a canned margarita?"

He shakes his head, and his eyes climb slowly up to mine. "No. You're the next girl I brought home."

Heat seems to sizzle through the air between us as our eyes stay connected a beat longer than they should, and I clear my throat as I tear my gaze away.

What the hell am I doing?

I chug my canned margarita.

That'll surely help.

"So Cassie's kids are five and seven?" I ask, trying to change the sudden charge of energy in the air. I lift myself up so I'm sitting on the counter, and he sits across from me on the island.

He nods. "Five going on fifteen, and the boy is turning eight soon."

"I never imagined Tanner as a father. You, on the other hand…you're such a golden retriever. I think you'd make a great dad."

He wrinkles his nose—and that's *my* signature move. "I'm not sure I really want kids," he admits.

My brows crinkle together. "No?"

He lifts a shoulder. "I go back and forth. Do you?"

"Want kids?" I ask.

He nods.

I lift a shoulder. "I guess I've always pictured a future with them, but it's not like I'm getting any younger. I'm turning thirty next month, and I still feel like I did when I was eighteen. And now I don't have stability, and I roped you into this engagement thing, and…" I trail off and shrug at the end.

It's a roundabout nonanswer, but honestly, I'm not the person who dreamed about being a mom my whole life. When I picture the future, I picture a kid or two…but I also picture a husband who's in love with me, not someone who's marrying me to help me get back at my shitty ex. I guess if it happens, it'll be a blessing, but if it's not meant to be for me, then that's something I'll have to make my peace with.

"Can I be honest about something, no judgment?" he asks.

I tilt my head. "You're my ride or die, Miller Banks. You know I'd never judge anything you could say to me."

"I know. But still…I feel like anytime this topic has come up with anyone else, there's judgment."

"Not from me. Ever," I say, my tone adamant.

He nods, and he glances down into his beer. He sighs. "When I found out the truth about Eddie Nash being our biological father, it changed something in me. I think I always wanted kids and thought I'd be a good dad because I had Charles to look up to, you know? But when I learned it was Eddie's blood running through my veins, a new era of self-doubt planted itself inside of me."

"Oh, Miller," I say, my tone changing to one of sympathy now. "You were raised by a great man, and it's the great nature versus nurture debate. Just because Eddie donated sperm to your mom doesn't mean you're going to turn out anything like him."

He makes a face like he's going to vomit at my choice of words, but I continue anyway. "Besides, the four Nash brothers turned out fine, don't you think? Some of them have kids, and they're great dads, aren't they?"

He lifts a shoulder. "I guess. I'm just the last one in a long line of six, and somehow it feels like because of that, I'm doomed to fail. I'm doomed to be the one most like him because the others were able to escape."

"Your feelings are absolutely valid. But I know you, and I know your heart. You're a damn good man, Miller."

He presses his lips together a little doubtfully, and as his ride or die, I suddenly realize it's on me to make him see what an amazing person he really is.

"You're sacrificing so much for me, and I'm just a friend. Imagine what you'd do for your future wife and kids. And besides, you don't need to decide anything right now, anyway. Playing engagement with me is just pushing those decisions further down the road." Something sparks in my mind that maybe that's part of his motivation for agreeing to it. He doesn't have to face reality for a little longer if he's tied up with me for however long we decide to do this.

He glances up at me, and there's something there in his eyes, but I can't quite put my finger on what it is.

You don't have to decide now. I'm just a friend.

I'm just a friend.

Sometimes when he looks at me like that…I wonder if I'm missing something.

Sometimes when he looks at me like that…I think maybe someday I could be more than *just a friend.*

Maybe I'm totally delusional.

But ever since I moved into his house with him, I think I'm starting to want to be more than *just a friend.*

Chapter 16: Miller Banks

"I don't know, man," I say to my brother. We're in his weight room at the house he shares with Cassie and her kids, and it's just the two of us. The kids are at school, and Cassie's working. "I keep feeling this *heat* between us, but I'm not sure if it's just because of my feelings for her or if there's something more to it," I say. I finish my set of squats and set the weight bar back in the rack as I think about that look we shared after we toasted last night in my kitchen.

"Are you taking her to the SDSYS event at the end of the month?" he asks, referring to the San Diego Storm for Youth Sports charity event happening on a Saturday evening. It includes dinner, live music, and an auction along with raffles and one-on-one experiences with pro football players for attendees.

"I RSVPed for one long before all this happened," I say.

"If you're doing the VIP experiences, I'm sure they'd be happy to amend that. Cass will be there and would love nothing more than to hear more embarrassing stories about me from high school," he says.

I laugh. "Well, Sophie has plenty of those."

"And I know you when you're around her, man. You seem…" He tilts his head as he trails off, and he squints at me a little. "I don't know. Happier."

"I *am* happier when she's around."

"I know. So are you finally going to tell her how you feel?" he asks.

I shake my head. "Fuck no. I'm not about to ruin the best thing in my life."

"Your friendship?" he guesses.

I nod.

"But if you're this happy just because she's around, imagine if there was more. Imagine if she felt the same way," he says.

"Look, I know you want everyone to be as crazy in love as you are, and that's cool. But maybe it's not meant for everyone." I don't believe the words as they come out of my mouth. I firmly believe that everyone deserves love.

I keep thinking eventually I'll get over these feelings for Sophie. I've tried. I've dated women. I've tried to fall in love. I even got close once or twice, but ultimately if they couldn't stand beside her on the pedestal she's up on in my heart, then I knew it wasn't right.

And nobody has ever even come close to standing beside her.

"Shoot your shot or move the fuck on," Tanner says. He sets a barbell back into the rack.

"It's not that simple."

He sighs. "I know it's not. I just hate seeing you stuck in neutral when you've been there for half your life, man."

"I've tried to get over her, and I can't." My voice is flat as I take a seat on a weight bench.

Tanner comes and sits beside me, and he bumps my shoulder with his. "I know you have, bro. But don't you think she'd be worth the risk?"

"Not at the expense of our friendship." I shrug.

"Dude, I've had some good friends in my life, but none I wouldn't give up for Cassie."

"So what if I take the shot and lose her forever?" I ask, staring straight ahead at the wall in front of me at a poster with Wayne Gretzky's famous quote: *You miss 100% of the shots you don't take.* "What if I fuck up our friendship and have to live with the regret when I could've just kept my mouth shut?" I nod at the poster. "What if I take the shot and fail anyway?"

"What if you don't?" he asks gently.

His question is ambiguous. I don't know if he means if I don't take the shot or if I don't fail.

If I don't take the shot, I'll never know the answer. But if I take the shot and don't fail…well, then I could have everything I've ever wanted.

I blow out a breath. "Fine. I'll ask if she wants to go to the SDSYS thing with me."

Tanner grins as he elbows me. "It's a start."

I guess it is.

When I get home, Sophie is typing aggressively on her keyboard as I walk into the kitchen.

"Damn, what did that thing do to you?" I ask, and she practically jumps out of her chair as her hand flies to her chest.

"Oh my God, you scared the shit out of me!" she says, and I chuckle.

"I'm sorry. You were really intense there."

"Sometimes the words fly out as if by magic, and I'm writing a really angsty, juicy scene I've been waiting for," she says, and her hair is pulled back in a messy bun, she's in sweats with no makeup on her face, and her brown eyes look twice as large as usual behind her clear-framed glasses.

She's as beautiful as ever.

"Don't let me interrupt you," I say. I grab a protein shake out of the fridge. "Need anything?"

"A break," she admits. She taps a few keys and closes her laptop lid as she stretches her arms above her head. Her shirt rides up, and I catch a peek of her stomach.

I'm instantly hard.

It's absolutely ridiculous.

It's a tiny peek of her skin. It's not even boob or side-boob. It's not ass. It's certainly not pussy. But it's a peek of something I don't usually get to see, and I want that shirt to keep going, going, going until it's off and she's naked and writhing beneath me right there on the goddamn kitchen table.

I chug my protein shake. "What's going on in the book?"

"No spoilers!" she protests, and I laugh.

"Not even for me?"

She shakes her head. "No one. Not even my editor." She opens her laptop again, and she pulls up an email. "I got this invitation to an event in Vegas. I've always declined these things since I was keeping my identity hidden, but now that I'm sort of exposed…"

"You're thinking about it?" I ask.

She nods.

"What kind of event?"

"There are around sixty authors, and we each get a table and can sell our books. All romance, and I've heard great things about it," she says.

"When is it?"

"February of next year," she says.

"That's a long way off."

She nods. "And I think by then I might even get up the nerve to admit the truth to my parents."

My chest tightens at her words. If she tells her parents the truth, does that mean our fake engagement is off?

Or was she serious when she told her ex that we were getting married?

"I, uh…have a question," I begin.

She tilts her head at me as if to tell me to go ahead.

"Were you serious about what you told Tyler?"

"About what?" she asks.

"About getting married either right before or right after next season."

She twists her lips. "I said it in the heat of the moment, and Miller, I couldn't do that to you. You have your own life to live, and I don't want to walk in and mess everything up."

I clear my throat. "What if…uh…" I trail off as I try to figure out how to correctly frame this. "What if there were some advantages in it for me, too?"

"How would it be advantageous for you?" she asks.

Because I fucking love you! "There's something to be said for wholesome football players who are in healthy marriages. My brother and I have sort of been branded as playboys, but if the twins got married within a year of each other, we'd be opening our sponsorships to an entirely new audience. Besides, if this helps you, then I'm all in. You know that." I sling my arm playfully around her.

She leans into me a little. "I do know that, and I can't thank you enough. But marriage? It's one thing to *write* about a marriage of convenience. It's another thing to actually do it."

"Can't write about it if you haven't experienced it." I shrug.

"I have a book with a threesome, and I've never done that," she points out. "And anal."

I choke on something in the back of my throat. "You've never done anal?"

"You have?" she asks, her brows pinching together.

"Hasn't everybody?"

"No!"

"Well, if you need my help with a marriage of convenience or anal or anything else…"

She smacks me on the arm, but I swear I catch another glimpse of heat.

Anal with Sophie?

Welp, now I'm hard again. Or still. Maybe always and forever around her.

Before I lose my nerve, I ask the question. "Oh! Do you want to make a public appearance with me at the end of the month?" *And have anal sex afterward? Or vaginal. I'm not picky.*

"Where?"

"It's a charity ball and a chance to show off my fiancée."

"I'd love to. Is it black tie?"

I nod.

"Mm, Miller Banks in a tux. I'm definitely in. Haven't seen that since prom."

I laugh. "Well, get ready for a treat."

As it turns out, I think I'm in for a treat, too.

Chapter 17: Miller Banks

It's Just a Story

We picked up her ring last weekend. I always sort of figured I'd only pop the question once in my life, and I didn't have the nerve to get down on a knee and ask her to marry me. Instead, I simply handed her the ring when we got into the car, and she slipped it onto her finger.

It's not exactly how I imagined proposing to Sophie Summers, and believe me…I've imagined it.

"Holy shit," she'd breathed as she held her hand up. The rock practically blinded me in the driver's seat, and it's gorgeous on her finger. It just *looks* right…which is why it's such a fucking punch to the gut that it's fake.

I locked that into a box in my mind as I plowed through the next couple of weeks, meeting with my publicist about the ideas Sophie and I have drafted about a summer camp and getting a move on with plans. Tara thinks if we plan it right, we could even launch the first camp mid-June. It's three months away, but she has an entire team ready to help plan this thing. With Sophie helping me on the curriculum, I think we have a shot at really launching it.

I put my all into planning it over the next couple of weeks with the help of Sophie, Tara, and some of the people on her team, and I find myself standing in my kitchen in my tux with a glass of whiskey while I wait for her on the night of the SDSYS charity event.

When she walks into the room, it feels like the wind is knocked clean from my lungs. It's a harder hit than the last time I was tackled by a linebacker when I tried carrying the ball into the red zone.

She's wearing a black dress that's sort of shaped like a heart over her tits. It has tiny straps over her shoulders and a ruffly skirt with a sky-high slit that nearly shows me all the goods but still manages to keep them hidden. Her dark hair is curled into waves that cascade down her delicate shoulders, and her big, brown eyes are lined with darker makeup than usual.

Fuck, she's hot.

And tonight, she's my date.

My fiancée.

And I will make damn sure everyone at the event knows it—especially with that ring on her finger.

"You look so handsome," she says softly when she spots me. She walks up to me and adjusts my tie, and I was pretty sure it looked fine before. I can't help but wonder if she's making up an excuse to touch me. Surely it's just my overactive imagination at play.

"You're gorgeous, Soph," I say. My eyes fall to hers, and that searing heat between us appears to be back.

Fuck, I have *got* to get control over myself. I grab my whiskey and chug what's left—probably a mistake given that I have to spend the night with her, but a little dulling of the nervous system seems to be exactly what I need right now.

"Thanks," she says.

"Can I get you a drink before we go?"

She nods. "I'd love maybe just a quick shot of your whiskey or something. I'm nervous to meet all these football players."

I laugh. "They're really just a bunch of disgusting overgrown boys."

She raises a brow. "Including yourself?"

I shake my head. "Of course not. But Tanner? Definitely."

She giggles. "I'll be sure to tell him you said that."

"Go for it. He'll agree." I slide a glass over to her, and I tip the bottle of whiskey over both our glasses. I hold mine up. "To another fun night."

"To all the football players," she counters.

I narrow my eyes at her. "To the only football player you'll be going home with."

She looks taken aback for a beat, so I backpedal.

"Because we live together. And, you know…because we're engaged."

She clinks her glass to mine, and her eyes meet mine. "Yeah. Because of that." Her voice is sort of an echo, but there's something in her eyes I can't quite read.

A limo takes us to the event, and a half hour later, we're pulling in. I get out of the car and rush around to her door to open it, and then we walk the red carpet. Her cold hand slips into mine as photos are taken and questions are fired.

"Miller, is it true you're engaged? Is this your fiancée?" someone asks, and I turn toward him.

"Yes and yes. Her name is Sophie Summers, and I'm the luckiest man in the world that she said yes." Even though I never asked. Technicalities.

"When's the wedding?" someone else asks.

"Soon," Sophie says, and there's more warmth and confidence in her voice than I was expecting.

We head inside, take some more photos, and get into the ballroom, where I spot Tanner near the bar talking to Spencer

Nash, our teammate and one of the four half-brothers we only learned about a little over a year ago when we learned Eddie Nash was our birth father. Eddie passed away at the end of last year before Tanner and I got the chance to get to know him, and it's something I've struggled with over the last few months, to be honest.

But having Sophie here has helped. I've barely thought of those struggles at all since she's been here. All I've thought about is her, and tonight is no different as I watch her walk, my eyes falling to the dangerous slit in her dress.

All I can do is imagine my palm sliding along that thigh until I get to where the slit ends, but my hand won't stop there. It'll keep going as I pull the heart-shaped neckline down with my other hand and suck one of her tits into my mouth.

I need to get a handle on these thoughts. I beeline toward my brothers at the bar, and Tanner and I share our typical secret handshake greeting. I turn to Spencer next, who bro-hugs me, and then I introduce Sophie.

"This is my fiancée, Sophie Summers," I say. "Sophie, my secret half-brother, Spencer Nash."

Spencer chuckles at my introduction as he shakes Sophie's hand. "It's nice to meet you."

She looks a bit awestruck as she says, "I'm such a huge fan of you and your brothers." Her cheeks are flushed, and I strike that feeling of jealousy right out of my chest as I wonder how I can make her cheeks flush like that.

"This is my wife, Grace," he says, and the women shake hands and exchange pleasantries while I greet Cassie.

"You doing okay?" Tanner murmurs only loud enough for me to hear him.

I nod. "Fine."

"You two look good together," he says, leaving a hint of suggestion in his tone. My eyes meet his, and I give him a *what-the-fuck-am-I-supposed-to-do-about-it* kind of look.

"We're just friends," I insist.

"'Just friends' don't look at each other the way you two do."

I roll my eyes, and I'm about to pop off about how she got all embarrassed when she started talking to Spencer, but we lose the moment as she returns to my side.

I glance down at her, and she's looking up at me, and is Tanner right?

Is she looking at me like that?

Because I know I'm certainly looking at *her* like that.

"Drink?" I ask, and she nods.

"Just a glass of wine. Something sweet."

"Oh, I know all about wine," Grace says, and she links her arm through Sophie's as she escorts her over to the bar. "I'll take a whiskey," I say after them, and Sophie turns and winks at me.

"She's not looking at me like that," I mutter to Tanner.

"You want to bet?" he challenges. "If only you could see it how I do."

"We keep having these moments. A couple of kisses, always for someone else's benefit. But it always seems like it's just the feelings I've always had for her at play," I admit.

"Have you ever thought that maybe she's got those same feelings?"

I shake my head because the truth is no. Until the last few days, I *never* once thought that.

"What's the worst that could happen?" he asks.

"I could lose her forever." I shrug, the motion minimizing the actual pain that slices through my chest at the mere thought of it.

"Or you could have everything you've ever wanted forever." He also shrugs at the end as he gives me a pointed look. He's not wrong, I guess. It's just two very extreme options, and right now, the middle, where I am, feels the most comfortable.

Because what if he's right, and we try, and I get to hold onto what I've wanted for half my life…and then it doesn't work out?

"Sophie's a good one, Miller. Don't you think she wouldn't let this come between you either way? Take the leap, man. Get over those fears in your head."

I glance at Cassie. "Like you did?" It's my turn to raise a pointed brow.

"Hey, it all worked out in the end." He sips his tequila, and then Sophie returns and presses a glass of whiskey into my palm.

I drink it faster than I should.

She walks with me as I introduce her to different teammates, and we take our seats for dinner. There's one player at every table, and this is part of the VIP experience. Fans bid on the chance to sit at their favorite player's table, and I'm thrilled that there are eight fans waiting for me as I pull out Sophie's chair first, then take my own seat.

A hush falls over the table as we sit, and I break the silence with my announcement. "Hey everyone, I'm Miller, and this is my fiancée, Sophie. Thanks for choosing to sit with us."

"Oh, congratulations!" one woman at the table says to us, and then we dive into a conversation about how Sophie and I met.

I'm dreading the moment someone asks how I proposed because I realize only now we never drafted a story for that.

I should really have more faith in my fiancée, the storyteller.

"So how'd he propose?" that same woman asks Sophie.

Without missing a beat, she starts to gush.

"Oh my God, I was just *waiting* for someone to ask so I could share the amazing story," Sophie says. "I was back home in Phoenix, and I'd just broken up with this guy who it had been over with for a long, long time. I called Miller because he's just always who I turn to, and he flew in immediately to just be there for me. The next morning, he took me to the high school where we met, and he held my hand as he pulled me into the classroom where we first met. It was empty, and we sat in the desks we sat in sixteen years ago when we were in that freshman English class, and he said the sweetest, kindest words to me."

She glances over at me, and I see the hearts in her eyes. Either she's a really, really good actress…or Tanner is right.

She reaches over and squeezes my hand.

Kiss her.

I do it. I lean down and press a gentle kiss to her lips before she continues, and she looks just the slightest bit dazed as she pulls back to finish the story. "Then he said, 'I don't have a ring, but it's always been you, Soph. Will you marry me?'" She lifts both shoulders. "How could I say no to that when I realized it had always been him for me, too?"

Jesus Christ.

I know it's just a story. It's just words for the benefit of these people at this table.

But she still said it. It's always been me for her, just the way it's always been her for me.

It's fake. It's a lie. It's pretend.

And yet…it's also the purest truth she's spoken tonight.

I blow out a breath as I slide an arm around her shoulders. "She said yes." I grin my goofy grin at the people at the table, and she leans in and lays her head on my shoulder.

"You two are *so* perfect together," the woman says. "You can just *see* the love you have for each other."

Really? Can you?

I mean, of course you can. It's true—we love each other. But there are different categories of love, and I fear mine falls into a different one than hers does.

I respond by kissing her again, and she slides her chilly hand along my jawline. I think about deepening the kiss. I want to feel her tongue against mine again.

But it's getting hot enough in here, and I can't exactly get indecent with her in front of a bunch of fans.

A little more whiskey and a little more time, though, and maybe I can tonight when we're back at home together.

Maybe tonight's the night I finally admit the truth after sixteen long years.

Chapter 18: Sophie Summers

The Dynamic Shifts

He kissed me twice, and each time, a new set of butterflies took flight. The first was just a sweet punctuation to my story, but the second felt different.

It felt like he wanted to give me more, but he held himself back.

Surely it's the wine talking, but maybe I want the wine to do a little more talking. I'm on my third glass now, and I think a fourth might give me the nerve to do something I never would've dreamed of doing a couple weeks ago with this man beside me.

Maybe I want to take this somewhere with him that we've never gone before, and maybe I want that to happen tonight.

I set my hand on that huge quadzilla thing he has, and a deep, dark ache has me clenching my own thighs together.

What the hell is going on with me? Is this because he's in a tux?

No.

I know that's a dumb question the moment the thought forms in my brain, though the tux certainly isn't hurting anything.

It's him. It's Miller Matthew Banks. It's the way he cares for me, the way he shows up for me, the way he believes in me. It's the way he chooses me, the way he makes me feel like anything is possible, the way he drops everything for me. It's more than friendship, and as I think back over the years, I realize he's *always* been this way.

Always.

And as I glance over at him with that realization only to find he's already looking down at me, something changes between us.

The dynamic shifts, and it's something I can physically feel.

I lean toward him, and I close my eyes as I press my lips to his. It's our third kiss since we sat down at this table, and while the first two were part of the story I was telling, this is my experimental one.

This is the one that means something. The one speaking to me in a language I didn't understand before, but as his soft lips press firmly to mine, it's a language I feel like I've known my entire life.

It's instinct. Pure and simple. And that instinct is telling me that for once, I'm getting this right.

His hand slides along my neck, warm and strong, and I pull back and lean my forehead to his for a beat as I feel a little dizzy, a little unsteady. My hand is still on his thigh, and I have exactly zero intention of moving it.

But then our first course is served, and the heat that was sizzling between us seems to dissipate as I pull back and turn toward my plate. His eyes catch mine first, though, and the heat fires back in full force.

I don't know if I can eat. I'm nervous and excited as thrills seem to race through my chest.

I want Miller.

The admission is scary, but the way he just kissed me makes me think maybe he wants me, too.

We can be friends who sleep together…right?

Maybe it'll turn into something more. Maybe I'm not at a point where I'm ready for that, or maybe I'm just realizing I've actually been waiting for this for half my life.

Whatever happens, we'll come out on the other side okay. We have to. He's my best friend, and I can't lose him.

But I also can't go much longer without knowing what it feels like to have him moving inside me, his fist tangled in my hair as his tongue glides against mine.

This is dangerous. *So* dangerous. I'm risking my heart here when maybe he's just putting on a really good act.

But as dinner ends and we find ourselves on the dance floor, he holds me close. He drops kisses on my lips. He makes me feel like the only person in the room despite the crushing crowd and the many fans who want just a second of his time.

"Hey, a few of us are heading to a bar once all our obligations here are fulfilled. You want to come?" Tanner asks as he bumps into us on the dance floor. "Spencer and Grace are in, and Spence said Clay, DJ, and Sam are all coming."

Miller turns to look at me, and even though I'd rather go home with him, I nod.

More time out means more drinks and more anticipation building between the two of us. It means a little more time to build up the nerve to tell him I want a night with those muscular thighs rubbing against mine.

I drink some water to try to cool down, and then we hop into Tanner and Cassie's car with them as we head to our next destination. Tanner sits up front since he's the taller of the twins, and while it's a luxury car, it's still tight with Miller in the middle between Cassie and me.

"That was fun," Cassie says, breaking into the silence in the car just as Miller's fingertips slide between mine so he's holding my hand.

I look up at him, and he's looking down at me again.

And holy shit, the absolute *fire* there makes me glad as hell that I'm already sitting because it's making me weak in the knees.

I think about tilting my face up so he can catch my lips with his, but there's nobody in this car we need to pretend for. There's no reason for me to kiss him other than the fact that suddenly *I want to*.

With everything inside of me.

With a passion that's leaving me breathless.

The driver hits a pothole, breaking up the intense moment between us.

He doesn't let go of my hand, and my brain is trying to reconcile that with the close friendship we share. Tonight, it's convincing me that this is a good idea—that we have the sort of foundation that will allow us to go the distance.

"Clay told me SDSYS is one of his favorite events," Tanner says. "I guess it's top-notch every year."

Miller and I remain quiet as I shift my gaze out the window.

It doesn't make the heat feel any less intense, though. I still feel him next to me, hard everywhere. I still feel his warm hand in mine. I still have butterflies flapping around in my stomach.

I still want to kiss him.

We listen as Tanner makes small talk with our driver, and we arrive at the bar a few minutes later. We're ushered back to a VIP area, and it's kind of fun being with these pro athletes and getting this top-notch sort of treatment.

I'm used to getting a discount at certain stores with my teacher ID. That's as close to VIP as I've ever been.

Bottle service and roped-off areas and security…it's all new to me, and it's a brand-new world that I'm starting to fall in love with already.

And I think it could be because I'm already in love with the man who brought me to it.

Chapter 19: Miller Banks

Can You Take Me Home

I've only had a few drinks, so I know I'm not drunk. I'm a big enough man that I can put down quite a few before I even start to feel it, but it's all the other things I'm feeling that are leaving me feeling a little drunk.

I couldn't help but hold her hand in the back of the car, just like I couldn't help tossing my arm around her shoulders as we walked into the bar, and like I couldn't help setting my hand on the small of her back to guide her toward our VIP section.

It all feels so goddamn natural with her. It feels like this was the way it always should have been, and every time I've looked down at her and found her looking up at me, I've felt more and more confident in that.

"So this is the fiancée?" Clay asks, sauntering up to us. He's a little younger than us and definitely single, and while he's a good dude, I still want him far, far away from my girl—I mean…from Sophie.

"This is the fiancée," I confirm, and I lean down and press my lips to Sophie's temple as I slide my arm around her waist this time and haul her into my side. She slips an arm around my waist, too. "Sophie, this is Clay."

"Nice to meet you," she says, and they shake hands.

A waitress comes by to take our drink order, and we each get another round of what we were having back at the event.

"When's the big day?" Clay asks.

We exchange a glance, and Sophie gives what's becoming our standard answer. "Maybe before next season starts, maybe just after it ends."

"Dude, that's only a few months off," he says.

I nod. "When you know, you know." And I've known since I was fourteen, not that I mention that.

"Do you have all the plans in place?" he asks.

Sophie shakes her head. "Not a single one, but it'll come together."

Clay laughs. "Right. I'm sure it will. Good luck to you both."

He moves along to another conversation, and I glance down at Soph.

"If we're going to do it before the season, we should probably get the planning underway," I point out.

"Do it?" she squeaks.

"The wedding."

Light seems to dawn in her eyes. "Oh! Right. Do it. The wedding." She giggles, and she seems a little…off. Nervous, maybe. It's probably just the wine—or maybe the fact that we're hanging out with good-looking, single guys like Clayton Mack, Sam Collins, and DJ Evans, three of the wide receivers on the San Diego Storm. "We should just keep it simple. Maybe we should just go to Vegas and do it there."

"Is that how you dreamed of your wedding?" I ask.

She lifts a shoulder. "No," she admits. "But there's a lot about this I didn't dream of."

I raise a brow. "Oh? Like what?"

It's dark in here, but not so dark I don't catch the fact that her cheeks seem to flush. Must be those other football players getting to her again.

She draws in a deep breath and seems like she's about to say something when our waitress interrupts by handing us our drinks.

Sophie immediately downs about half her wine while I slowly sip my whiskey.

"Is everything okay?" I ask her as I watch her nervously play with the stem of her glass.

She presses her lips together and lets out a little giggle, and then she draws in another deep breath. She snags her bottom lip between her teeth, and I tilt my head as I study her.

I lean in a little closer, and I ask her, "Is it the wedding? Are you having second thoughts?"

Her eyes flick up to mine. Her lip is still caught between her teeth, and she shakes her head as she slowly frees it. Her eyes hold mine captive as she rests one of her hands on my bicep.

My brows pinch together. "You're not having second thoughts? Then…what is it?" I press, and instead of answering, she sets her glass on the table beside us and turns back toward me.

When her eyes meet mine again, a strange sensation darts through me.

Her eyes flick to my lips, and she tilts her chin up as she rises onto her toes.

Her lips catch mine, and I lean down into her so she can settle back down onto her feet. I slide one palm along her neck as my other hand moves to her hip, where I haul her closer to me.

My mouth opens naturally as I deepen the kiss, and she's kissing me back with this newfound urgency that I wasn't expecting.

This isn't for show.

Strange sensations whip through me at the feeling of kissing this woman, sensations I never want to stop—and I won't be the one to stop it. I *can't* stop it.

I want to live in this moment with these feelings forever. It's warmth and history and friendship, sure, but it's also more. It's lust and need and want and heat, things I've always felt *for* her but never felt *from* her.

Until now. Until this very moment.

Our tongues tangle together, and she's grasping my bicep now where she had simply set her hand just a few seconds ago, grasping it as if she'll fall if she lets go.

I memorize every single thing about this moment—the summer garden breeze of her hair, the feel of her tongue as it brushes against mine, and the deafening sound of my heart beating in my ears as I can almost hear the blood rushing straight down to my cock.

The feel of her in my arms, the sharp angle of her hip under the itchy ruffles of her dress, the way she's leaning into me, her tits pressed against my chest as I rock my hips toward hers.

The sweet little moan that somehow makes its way through that deafening rush in my head.

Holy shit. Sophie June Summers is kissing me.

And I never want it to end.

It has to end, of course. All good things must come to an end.

But tonight, as this kiss *does* come to an end, it's only to briefly pause as she pulls back to ask me a question.

Her eyes are heavy with need. Her lips are swollen from our kiss.

And the single question that drops from her lips is the sweetest sound I've ever heard in my life. Her voice is breathless and throaty as she asks, "Can you take me home?"

I stare at her a few beats before I ask, "Are you drunk?"

She slowly shakes her head, and I don't answer with words. I don't bother with goodbyes.

I'm not doing anything to jeopardize this chance.

Instead, I grab her hand and lead her through the bar as I navigate the Uber app on my phone. The car is one minute away when we land on the sidewalk out front, and I don't dare let go of her hand as we wait.

A black car pulls up, and we slip into the backseat.

We greet the driver, and when I glance over at her, she's looking up at me. She sets her hand on my jaw and pulls me toward her, her lips catching mine again.

I could've justified the one back at the bar. I could've said she was only kissing me in public to further our plot of a fake engagement.

But here in the back of an Uber?

It's just the two of us.

My fingertips glide along her thigh where that gorgeous slit has been tempting me all night, and I rest my hand right at the top of the slit. She shifts a little, and it has the effect of pushing my hand up her thigh toward her hip.

She deepens the kiss as I let my fingers move up a little more, and it's as if she's giving me permission to touch her with the intensity of the way her tongue moves against mine.

I shift my hand down a little, and her legs fall open just enough for me to brush against the silky fabric snugly fit against her pussy.

My cock swells as I cross a line I've never crossed with my best friend.

There's no turning back.

Chapter 20: Sophie Summers

Are You Sure About This

I have no idea what this is, but I know I like it, and I know I want more.

The way he's kissing me…damn.

Has he always been this good of a kisser? I wouldn't know since my experience kissing him has been limited to a few for show over the last couple of weeks.

But as we make out in the backseat of an Uber holding only the two of us, there's nothing about this that's for show.

And it feels good. Better than I ever would've imagined. I never really thought about kissing Miller before, but I guess if I did think it, I would've thought it would feel weird.

It doesn't.

There's nothing weird about it.

In fact, I think this may be among the best kisses I've ever experienced in my life.

It's passionate and tender at the same time. It's as if he wants to give me everything but is holding himself back—maybe because we're in the back of someone else's car, or maybe because in the back of our minds somewhere, this isn't supposed to be happening. We're friends, just friends, something we've always both been so adamant about.

But kissing him is setting my blood on fire. My nerves are fully exposed, and my heart is racing in my chest as emotions plow into me.

I reach around the back of his neck and pull him closer, and his hand glides along my panties again, causing a throbbing, pulsing ache between my legs. I need him to slip his finger beyond the fabric, but instead, he's teasing me.

I cling on around his neck as the kiss somehow deepens and intensifies, and I'm not sure I've ever had such an all-consuming kiss before. My hand trails along the front of his pants, stopping when I find what I'm looking for, and I rub his cock over his pants.

Oh my God.

I'm touching Miller's cock. It's hard and thick and *long*. Longer than I was expecting it to be, and that throb pulses steadily as the ache starts to become unbearable.

It's only then that he pulls back from my mouth, and his lips drag along my neck. He whimpers, and the sound causes fireworks to explode down my spine as it fuels me to form a fist around the steel length.

I start to move my fist as best as I can, giving him a hand job over his pants while he continues to tease me beneath my dress. He fingers the edge of my panties, and I thrust my hips toward him as if it'll give him permission to keep going.

He softly bites my neck as I keep moving my hand over his cock, the feel of his teeth causing a little moan to escape from me. He grunts near my ear. "Fuck, Soph," he says, the hard *k* in *fuck* dragged out and hot as hell as he finally, blessedly slips my panties to the side. I allow my legs to fall open a little wider, giving him more space to work with as I continue rubbing his cock.

I'm a hot fucking mess of need as I wait for him to slip his finger inside, and that's when we both hear our driver. "We've arrived."

We both whip apart as if we're caught—because *we are*. We were so caught up in each other that we didn't even realize we'd arrived back at Miller's place.

He clears his throat. "Thank you." He reaches into his pocket and pulls out a hundred-dollar bill. He hands it to the driver, and then he gets out of the car, holding out a hand for me to get out next. I grab it, and then we practically run toward the front door.

Miller fumbles with his keys for a beat, and we both slip inside. The door is barely kicked shut behind me when his mouth is back on mine, but his hands aren't—not yet. He slips out of his tuxedo jacket and drops it on the floor behind us as he pins me to the front door with his hips. His tongue swirls with mine, and I simply hold onto his biceps for support because if I don't hold onto something, my knees are going to buckle purely from the way he's kissing me.

His hands aren't on me yet, but I feel his fingertip as he slips the strap of my dress down. He pulls back from our kiss to trail his mouth down my neck and across my collarbone to my now naked shoulder, where he leaves another tiny bite, and then he trails back up again to my mouth.

Good Lord, who ever thought kissing Miller would be this fucking *hot?*

I sure didn't.

And all of this heat and emotion I'm feeling for him is just from a *kiss*. I can't begin to imagine what *sex* with him will be like, but with him, I feel safe and protected and secure.

I want this. I want him like I've never wanted anyone else, and I'm not sure what's fueling this sudden change other than the fact that he's always been so, so good to me. It feels like he's been right here in front of me the whole time, but in the back of my mind I just figured he'd never want anything more with me than friendship. I'm the girl-next-door type, the one in the friend zone, the one who was always there but felt more like a sister.

There's nothing sisterly about this kiss, that's for damn sure.

He reaches down between us toward the slit in my dress again as he continues kissing me. He gets almost back to the same place where he was in the back of the Uber when he pulls back, his heavy eyes hot on mine. "Are you sure about this?" he murmurs.

I respond by grabbing his head and pulling him back down so his mouth is on mine again, and I reach down between us to grasp his cock over his pants again.

I'm definitely sure about this. Even if I wanted to, it's not like I could stop now.

Instead of fingering the edge of my panties like last time, this time he reaches for the fabric where it lays against my hip, and he gathers it into his fist. He yanks on it, and the thin material falls apart. The other side is still snugly between my hip and my dress, and he reaches across to that side and pulls until the now useless fabric falls down my leg.

I part my legs to give him space, but he's not quite done teasing me. He pushes his knee between my legs, and I'm so goddamn desperate for some friction that I start to ride it.

"Oh God," I moan as his lips move from mine down to my chest and into my cleavage.

My voice doesn't even sound like my own. It's all deep and throaty, hoarse from not being used while his mouth assaulted mine in the most beautiful way.

"There's still time to turn back," he says against my chest.

I shake my head, unable to form words but somehow managing a whispered plea. "I want you."

My words propel him into action, and he yanks the spaghetti strap on my other arm down and pulls down the front of my dress, exposing my naked breasts.

He immediately moves his mouth to one, latching onto my nipple and sucking it. I ride his knee a little harder as the feel of his mouth on my tit sends a dart of need straight to my pussy. I reach for his shirt, and I fumble with the buttons for a few seconds, but I can't seem to make my fingers work. He's still sucking on my tit as he bats my hand out of the way and rips open his shirt.

I hear the scattering of buttons on the ground, but it's no match for the sound of our moans as they fill the air. My hands move immediately to the cut, hard planes of muscle that span his stomach, and he groans as I slide my hands along his body. I wrap them behind his back, feeling his warm, smooth skin under my palms, wanting that body covering mine as he pushes me to heights of pleasure I've never known before.

I slow my hips as they rock against his leg, and I reach up and hold his head to my tit for a few beats. My voice is breathless when I say, "Take me to your bedroom."

I don't have to ask twice.

He grabs me up into his arms and carries me up the stairs as if I weigh nothing—and I'm grateful since I don't know if I could walk right now. He sets me gently on the floor near his bed, and he spins me around to pull down the zipper on the back of my dress.

It falls in a pool on the floor around my feet, and I stand naked with my back to him. He reaches around me and pulls me into a hug from behind, his hands moving up to grab each of my tits in one of his hands. He massages them, and the rubbing of my nipples against his rough palms is pure and utter bliss.

His hands move to trace along my torso down to my hips, and he gently glides those palms along my ass. I feel self-conscious as he inspects every part of my body with his hands, but his words immediately quell those thoughts.

"Jesus Christ, Soph. You are so fucking perfect."

His lips move to my neck, and I reach behind me to try to touch him over his pants some more. I land on his belt, and I undo it as he shifts back to give me a bit more space to work, his hands still gliding along my body.

"Your skin is so soft," he says as one hand moves back to my breast. "And your tits are perfection."

I get his button undone and his zipper next, and then I reach behind me to pull his cock out of his pants. He hisses as I fist him, and even though I want to see him so badly, I don't dare move as he pinches one of my nipples between his thumb and forefinger as his other hand moves along the curve of my ass.

I slide my hand up and down, a difficult feat since he's behind me, but I can tell by feel that he's big. Massive. I reach down with my other hand to cup his balls. They're heavy and big, and I have the sudden feeling like I want to suck on them. I've *never* had the urge to suck on somebody's balls before, but the thought crosses my mind that he'd like it, and I want to do whatever I can to make him groan and grunt for me as I push him to the brink of pleasure.

His hand on my ass finally curls around, gripping my hip for a beat before he inches his way toward my pussy. It feels like a lifetime passes as I wait for him to dip his finger into me. He trails slowly along my hip to my pubic bone. He moves down so he's fingering the lips of my labia, and then finally, *finally*, he slides a finger through my pussy, pushing it inside of me as I let go of his cock and lean forward to brace myself on the bed in front of me.

When I do that, I push my ass out without realizing it, and I feel his cock as he shifts to settle it between my ass cheeks. It's warm there, and he's mere inches away from pushing into me.

We haven't discussed condoms or birth control or any of it, but this is Miller. I trust him with my life.

And the thought of him moving inside of me bare is nearly enough to push me into an orgasm.

What the hell is happening to me?

He pulls his finger out as he shifts his hips so his cock moves along my slit but not inside of me.

"You're so fucking wet," he hisses.

"It's you, Miller," I moan. "You're making me wet."

He moans at my words, and he shifts his cock again. "Fuck, I want to slide inside of you so goddamn badly," he groans, but instead of doing that, he pulls back. "Don't move," he demands.

I'm still leaning over the bed, and I see him out of the corner of my eye as he moves toward his nightstand. When I felt how big he was, I didn't know how he'd look.

He's sheer perfection.

He opens a drawer and pulls out a condom, and he rips it open and glides it on before he rushes back over toward me.

He moves exactly back into the position he just vacated, but he leans over me as his lips find my neck.

As much as I want him to fuck me from behind, this is our first time together. I want the intimacy of looking into his eyes the first time he pushes into me.

So even though he told me not to move, I do. I shift my hips back toward him, and then I straighten. He moves along with me and stands, too, and then I turn around to face him. I sit on the bed, eyeing his cock for just a second, and then I lie back and pull him down on top of me.

His lips fall to mine as he gets into position, and he pulls back as his eyes find mine.

God, the passion there. There's something there I've never noticed before when he's looked at me, and it's so, so beautiful.

It's addictive.

And as he leans down to kiss me, I can say with certainty that his lips are addictive, too.

As if he can sense I need his eyes on mine, he pulls back from our kiss. "Are you okay?"

I nod. "I don't think you're going to fit," I admit, my voice a little nervous.

"You can take it."

He reaches down between us, aligns himself, and pushes into me as his eyes move to mine.

I see everything I need to as we connect in this erotic, intimate moment.

My body adjusts to his size as he fills me slowly at first. He pushes all the way in, and it's a wonderful, full feeling as he glides out before pushing back in.

"Fuck, Sophie. You have no idea how long I've wanted this," he murmurs, and maybe those words will mean something later, but right now he's got me in a lust-induced haze where words are incomprehensible as he pushes into me over and over, pushing my body closer and closer to a climax.

He's right. I can take it. I can take *him*. All of him. And I *want* all of him.

I answer him with moans, and his lips catch mine.

I'm lost to everything as I lose myself in the feel of him, and if I thought his lips were addictive…well, they've got nothing on his cock.

He rocks into me, and as we have sex on his bed, one thing is certain.

Things will never be the same again.

Chapter 21: Miller Banks

I Can't Help It

Did I really just admit that I've had feelings for her for a long time?

I might have, but I'm not really sure what the hell is coming out of my mouth.

Strings of words. Filthy phrases.

Your cunt is so fucking tight, Soph.

You feel so good.

This pussy was made for my cock.

I'm not stopping until this cunt is dripping with my come.

I don't know where that last one came from. It doesn't even sound like me, and it's impossible right now anyway since I'm wearing a condom, but I just muttered those very words as I slammed into her over and over.

Her response only spurs me on. "God, yes, Miller. Wreck my pussy."

Fuck. I'll wreck the shit out of it.

"Your pussy is even tighter than I imagined," I say, more words that should stay in my brain but are slipping out as if her pussy holds some sort of magic truth serum.

God, I love you. I keep that one inside.

I hold it because I don't want to go overboard our first time together.

I don't want to scare her away.

She's too tight. It's too good. Too hot, too slick, too wet, too perfect.

As much as I want this to last forever, I know it can't.

I drop my mouth to her neck as I feel my body start to tighten with need. I'm close, and I feel her pussy clenching onto me. She's close, too. I slam into her, picking up the pace. "Wrap your legs around me," I demand, and I feel her legs move around my torso as I continue slamming into her.

Fire burns at the base of my spine as the pleasure starts its ascent. "Fuck, I'm gonna come," I grunt.

"So am I," she cries back at me.

I give her a few more powerful thrusts before my body betrays me. A guttural growl rises up from my chest as I start to come, and her pussy is like a vise on my cock as her body gives way to the pleasure.

My drives slow as we both ride out the wave, but she keeps her legs locked around me even as we both start to come down from the high of a brutal, all-consuming climax. I collapse on top of her, pulling out of her and sliding down a bit, careful not to put my full weight on her even though I'm physically depleted after that release.

She holds me against her as we both fight to catch our breath after that rigorous workout, and I rest my head on her chest as her legs unlock and she drops them back onto the bed. I feel her pussy on my lower stomach, warm and wet and still pulsing after her release, and I'm not sure I've ever felt more content than I do in this very moment.

We're both quietly lost in thought even though we're still lost in each other when she finally speaks.

"Miller, that was—" She cuts herself off as she searches for the right word.

"Unexpected?" I guess.

She chuckles a little. "Yeah. And amazing."

I move off of her and settle in beside her, pulling her into my arms so her back is against my front. "It really was," I murmur.

I'm nearly asleep when I hear her playful voice. "You imagined my pussy being tight?"

I jolt awake, and I lean up, bending my arm at the elbow as I rest my face on my palm. I pull on her shoulder until she turns in my direction, and I stare down at her gorgeous face.

We already crossed the line. May as well leap right the fuck over it.

"From the day I met you, I wondered how tight it was."

It's dark in here since we bumped our way in without bothering with the lights, but I left the door open, and light filters in across her face from the hallway. I see her cheeks redden.

"That's just fourteen-year-old Miller talking," she says.

I shake my head. "Twenty-year-old Miller wondered, too. But it was thirty-year-old Miller who got to find out."

"Lucky guy."

I raise a brow. "You have no idea."

She looks like she wants to say something, and I have a feeling I know what it is.

To be honest, I'm wondering, too. What does all this mean? How will it affect our friendship? How will it affect our new living situation?

Will we do that again? And…when?

They're all questions I want the answers to, but we also have all the time in the world stretching out before us. We can talk tomorrow.

Tonight…well, tonight I just want to kiss her again.

I lean down and press my lips to hers, and she seems to melt into me. Damn if I'm not raring to go already.

I hold it together. I can't literally wreck her pussy even though I'm tempted to get right back in there.

"Do you want to shower?" I ask quietly. Most women I've been with seem to want to freshen up after sex, and I'm never opposed to slippery, wet tits covered in soap bubbles.

"I do, but I also don't want to move. You really did wreck my pussy with that enormous dick. How do you walk around all day with that thing?"

"That thing?" I ask, feeling a little defensive.

She chuckles, and she glances down between us. "It's like…" She holds up her hands to exaggerate my length.

So I've got a big cock. I can't help it.

I push her hands a little closer.

"What's that, like…ten inches?" she asks.

"Right around nine when it's hard," I admit.

"Jesus Christ," she mutters. "And how do you know that?"

"Rulers. Men are idiots," I say with a playful shrug.

She giggles. "And, what, like Coke can girth?"

"No. A Coke can is eight inches in circumference. The average dick is closer to four."

"How do you know this?" she asks.

"The internet. Teenage boys are also idiots."

"And yours is…?" She trails off as she waits for me to fill in the blank.

"Above average."

"In basically everything you do," she says flatly.

"You're one to talk."

"What's that supposed to mean?"

"Oh, I don't know…your books are bestsellers, for one thing. Not everyone who publishes a book can say that."

She purses her lips and narrows her eyes at me. "Okay, go on."

I chuckle. "You have the most perfect pussy I've ever been inside, and your tits fit perfectly into my palm." I grab one in my hand to prove my point, and she laughs. "Never mind that sexy laugh of yours."

"My laugh is *sexy*? Since when?"

"Since always," I say.

I'm giving myself away. I *know* I am. But I can't seem to stop.

"Have you always been this sexy?" she asks.

I lift a shoulder, and she twists her lips before she tilts her head and moves to catch my lips with hers. "About that shower…can we do a bath instead?"

"We?"

She nods and ducks her head a little. "Baths for two are way better than baths for one."

"That's the wine talking, but I'll take slippery, soapy tits wherever I can get them."

She giggles as she sits up, and then she turns back to look at me. "Bring a condom. Just in case."

She scampers toward the bathroom in a fit of giggles, and I grab another condom *just in case* before I follow her in.

Chapter 22: Sophie Summers

For the last sixteen years, Miller Banks has been my best friend. In one night, he managed to change into something else completely, but it's still something I can't quite define.

We're beyond the boyfriend/girlfriend stage, we're fake fiancés, and now we're apparently having the hottest sex of my life.

The wine has worn off, though when he asked me if I was drunk and I told him no, that was the truth. I'm not a huge drinker, but a couple glasses of wine wear off pretty fast when you're dancing and eating. And, apparently, having sex.

And bathing.

We're in the tub in the master suite since it's much larger than the one in his bathroom, and he's sitting behind me with his arms wrapped around me. Bubbles surround us, and each of his hands rests on one of my breasts as I rest my hands on his quadzillas.

I'm glad I told him to bring a condom, because the more I feel that enormous cock digging into my backside, the more I want to feel it inside me again. Though I'm not sure logistically how you slide a condom onto a wet dick. I didn't think this through.

When I dumped Tyler and called Miller hysterically crying, never in my wildest dreams could I have imagined *this* is where we'd end up. In a bathtub, soaking after sex and ready for round two. Having a casual conversation with his hands on my boobs after we just tenderly washed each other.

The mere thought of it would've been crazy to me a few weeks ago, yet here we are.

I don't know what tomorrow will bring. I don't know how this will affect our friendship. I don't know if it will continue on, or if we'll revert back to being just friends tomorrow. I don't know much of anything except how very *right* this feels despite how *scary* it also feels.

I don't want to lose him. I can't imagine not having him to call on when I need a shoulder to lean on, just as I can't imagine not being there for him when he needs me. But maybe I'll still have the same shoulder, and it'll just fill a new exciting and unexpected role.

Or maybe I'm delusional, and it's just drunken sex. Maybe he'll want nothing more than a friends-with-benefits situation.

I'm too scared to ask.

But the way he looked at me, and the things he said to me…all of it leads me to believe he wants more than just benefits with a lifelong friend.

I want to ask what this means, but I don't think I have the nerve.

I shift my ass a little, and he groans in my ear.

"Don't do that unless you want me inside again," he warns softly.

"What if I do?" I ask, doing it again so my ass is rubbing along his cock. I may have only had him inside me once so far, but it was pretty damn addictive that first time.

"Mm," he moans, and his lips drop to my neck, where he gives me a little nibble. That nibble sends a shockwave right to my core.

There's no simple or sexy way to turn around and straddle him in the tub, so instead, I stand and grab the towel. I climb out and hand him a towel, too, and he follows suit. When I'm dry enough, I snatch the condom from where it sits on the side of the tub and carry it with me back to the bedroom.

He follows me in, and he pulls me into his arms, dropping his lips down to mine. I take charge this time, turning us and pushing him back until he falls onto the bed with a grunt. He's sitting at the edge as I rip open the condom and roll it onto his cock, and then I climb onto his lap, straddling his legs as I get into position. He wraps his arms around my back, his palms flat on my skin as he pulls me close to him, and I reach between us, fist his cock, and slide down on top of it.

"Fuck," he hisses as I push my body as far down over him as it'll go, and I moan as his hands move down to my ass.

Even though I'm on top, he starts to move us, setting the pace as we fall into a slow, luxurious rhythm. I cradle his face in my hands, and I lean down to kiss him. It's intense, kissing him as I move up and down his cock, feeling the pleasure radiating between us as I push all the emotion I'm suddenly feeling for him into this kiss.

It's somehow tender and sweet, just like him, and sexy and erotic at the same time. Usually after I take the top with a guy, my legs are sore the next day from the position of using them to move us toward our climax. But the way Miller uses his strength to move me up and down over him allows me to focus solely on the pleasure of this act with him. I don't know if I've ever been so in tune with the pleasure a man is giving me as I am with him, and I think that's what's so addictive.

It's like I can see clearly for the first time. I can feel the way he cares about me in the tenderness of his kiss, and I can feel how much he wants me in the passion with which he moves beneath me.

I pull back from the kiss, my hands still cradling his jaw as our eyes connect, and the intimacy we share in that second is beyond anything I've ever experienced before. It's as if two souls are entwining together, and as crazy as it sounds, I think a piece of me realizes how I've always loved him.

I just didn't know we could unlock *this* sort of love.

It's passionate and carnal, tender and volcanic all at the same time. It's explosive and sweet. All contradictions, but all part of this new equation we're sharing.

As our eyes connect, I see his start to cloud over. He shifts our rhythm to pick up the pace, and I slam down over him as I feel him start to tense beneath me.

Just seeing the way he's about to fall apart—knowing it's *me* making him get there—is enough to push me into my own release.

"Oh, God, Miller!" I yell as my body races toward the breaking point. "I'm coming!"

"Fuck," he hisses again, and he growls as he starts to come, too, pulling my mouth back down to his as we both grunt and moan our way through our orgasms together.

I've never been this in sync with a man before. I think maybe once in history I came during the act of sex rather than afterward, as either the guy I was with or I rubbed my clit until my body fell apart.

But this, coming while he's inside me, coming *together* with him as we both hit our peak at the same time, it's so different. So magical. So beautiful. So addictive.

And all that only tells me that I want to have a lot more sex with Miller Banks.

Chapter 23: Sophie Summers

Miller Poked Something Inside Me

Morning dawns, and as I wake to a new day, I feel a little…out of sorts.

Miller's arm is under me as he sleeps soundly on his back, and I'm lying on his chest, one arm tossed across his abdomen.

We've slept in the same bed before, but not after a night where we had sex. Twice. And not when I woke up snuggling him.

I can't put my finger on what it is that's making me feel out of sorts. I only know what it's *not*. It's not a hangover, and it's not regret.

I glance at the clock. It's already after seven, and usually I've been up for nearly three hours at this time of day. Usually I've hit my word count goal, and I'm already showered and ready to face the day.

But that was all back when I was a teacher. Now, I'm a full-time author and the fiancée of Miller Banks.

Life has sure changed a lot over the last few weeks.

That *has* to be what has me feeling all out of sorts.

I stare up at his face as he breathes his even breaths. I wonder if he's dreaming. I wonder if it's about last night.

It *felt* like a dream.

Maybe we shouldn't have done what we did. Maybe we shouldn't have crossed that line.

I think it might be fear that seems to be plowing into me this morning.

I'm scared that we just altered the course of our friendship. I'm scared I'm going to lose him.

I'm scared I'll never be enough for someone like him, someone who can have any woman they want at the snap of a finger. He's the total package—a great personality, dangerously good looks, money in the bank, and a secure job doing what he loves. Oh, and he has a big cock that he certainly knows how to use.

And what am I? An unemployed teacher whose new paychecks are unstable at best. A roommate mooching off the guy who offered me a place to stay. I promised to cook for him. I still haven't.

I'm scared of commitment. I *just* got out of a relationship, and my ex hurt me. Badly.

But it was Miller who was there to pick up the pieces when Tyler tried to ruin my life. It's Miller who's giving me a shot at my dreams.

It's Miller who I *should* resist. I *need* to resist him. But I'm just not sure that's possible after the kind of night we shared.

I slip out of bed and pull on some sweats. I brush my teeth and head down to the kitchen, make a cup of coffee, and sit at my computer.

And then the words seem to pour out of me as if by pure magic mixed with caffeine. Words are flowing in a way they haven't flowed in months, and it's like Miller poked something inside me with that cockzilla of his.

Whatever it was would love the pleasure of being poked again.

I finish the scene I'm working on and plot out the next few chapters, and then I get started on the next one. Miller saunters down a little after nine.

"Good morning," he says, and I'm sort of expecting him to stop and press his lips to that little crook between my neck and shoulder.

He doesn't, and a wave of disappointment passes through me.

"Morning," I say, and I continue tapping on my keys until I finish the sentence I'm working on.

He walks over toward his little coffee station and makes himself a cup as he pulls out the stuff to make breakfast.

"Want some?" he asks.

I save my file and close my laptop, and then I say, "I'd love some. Can I help?"

"I got it."

"Will you show me?" I hop down from my chair and head over toward him.

"Of course." He pulls the ingredients out of the pantry as he explains that these are steel-cut oats, and he stirs the oats into the boiling water and milk combination he started on the stove.

It's small talk. Meaningless chatter about breakfast as neither one of us acknowledges what happened last night, and I hate that suddenly things feel awkward between us.

"We can't leave it. It's been known to boil over," he warns, and he keeps stirring the mixture. He sets a timer for twenty-five minutes, and he leans on the counter beside the stove, folding his arms across his chest once he's comfortable with the simmering level of the oats.

"Now we wait?" I guess.

He lifts a shoulder. "Now we stir every few minutes so it doesn't stick to the pot, and we stand by to keep a close eye on it."

I nod, and I lean on the kitchen island that's behind me. I mimic his posture, folding my arms over my chest as if it'll protect my heart from the conversation we should likely have.

"How'd you sleep?" he asks.

"Really good. You?"

"Good until you left," he admits.

We're both quiet, and my eyes are down on the floor. I glance up at him, and he's looking at me. "What?" I ask.

He presses his lips together. "I want to kiss you."

I'm not sure why relief seems to filter through me at his words, but it does. "Then do it."

He closes the gap of a few feet between us with one long stride, and I look up into his eyes.

"I probably have coffee breath," I admit since I'm already on my third cup of the day.

He chuckles. "So do I." He moves down until his lips collide with mine, and as our lips touch, it's as if any awkwardness I felt this morning disappears into thin air.

Instead, lust takes hold as he kisses me so sweetly and tenderly. It's unexpected from him and from our relationship, and I feel like I'll never get enough.

We both hear a hiss at the same time and jump apart, and he rushes over to the stove to lift the pot and turn down the heat after the oatmeal boiled over as advertised.

"Shit!" he yells. He sets the pot back down and stirs it, and we both review the clumpy mess that we'll have to deal with once the stove is off and cools down.

"I mean, honestly…that kiss was worth it." I shrug, and he laughs. "It's time I start making myself useful around here, anyway, and I can clean it."

"Making yourself useful? I'll tell you what, Summers, you sure made yourself useful last night." He turns back toward me and loops an arm around my waist. He hauls me against him and rests his forehead against mine for a beat.

"By offering my very comfortable bed for sleep?" I tease.

His lips connect with mine for a brief moment. "I think you know exactly what I mean."

That familiar, delicious ache is back in full force between my legs at his words. I clear my throat. "Well, to be honest, I'd like to make myself useful again." I nip a kiss at his lips as he bucks his hips toward me, letting me know that *he* is also ready to make himself useful as well. "After the oatmeal is done cooking, of course."

He laughs, and he pulls back to stir the oatmeal before it boils over again.

And honestly? I sort of need the space to cool down a bit. This is my best friend. I'm not used to having these raunchy and inappropriate thoughts about him, but maybe they're the exact right thoughts I should've been having about him all along.

Maybe we were both missing what was right in front of us this whole time, and maybe we're on track to correct that now.

Once the oatmeal is ready, he adds peanut butter, nuts, chia seeds, banana, and some protein powder to his, and I sprinkle a few nuts on mine. We sit at the table with our oatmeal and coffee, and he asks the first question.

"What's on your agenda for the day?"

It's a Sunday, and when I was a teacher, I'd always spend the morning grading papers and the entire rest of the day writing—as long as Tyler didn't make other plans for us, which he often did. I never wanted to take weekends off since it was the only time I really had to write.

But now I have unlimited time thanks to Miller, and part of me wants to take the day off and spend it with him.

I never felt that urge with Tyler.

"Usually I spend my Sundays writing," I admit. "But that was before when I had a job to go to, and weekends were my only time to get words in. What about you?"

"Since last night was a late night out for everyone I usually meet for early morning workouts, I don't have any plans for the day. Want to do something together, or do you need to write?"

I glance up at him, and I surprise even myself when I say, "Let's do something."

"Got anything in mind?" he asks.

"Well, we could plan our wedding," I deadpan, but he doesn't take it as a joke.

"I was thinking about that, actually. It would be nice to have a date in mind, maybe even a location—you know, for when the media asks."

"Do you really want to set a date when it's not even real?" I ask.

His gaze moves from my eyes down to his oatmeal, but I don't miss the little dart of something in his eyes before he moved them.

Is he…is he *upset* that I just said it's not real?

Why am I getting the feeling he is?

He clears his throat. "Right. I don't know. I just figured if we're doing this for the media, it would look more believable if we had some plans."

"We could do it here. Do they have chapels for quickie weddings in San Diego?"

"I would assume every major metropolitan area has chapels for quickie weddings, but is that what you want?" he asks.

He asked me that about Vegas, too.

And the answer is no. No, it's not. Not for my real wedding to my forever husband.

But that's not what this is.

Still, it begs the question.

What exactly is this, then?

And are we really going to go through with it?

159

RESISTING THE *Running Back*

Still, it begs the question.

What exactly is this, then?

And are we really going to go through with it?

Chapter 24: Miller Banks

Serious as a W2

I'm not sure how to pretend like it doesn't hurt to have her say it's not real after what we shared last night.

But the truth is…she's right.

She mentioned once many, many years ago that she wanted a destination wedding. She had mentioned a cruise or a beach, and like the design of her dream ring, I remembered.

But this isn't real. It's not meant to be special and meaningful the way her dream wedding should be.

Still, I want to make all her dreams come true…even if it isn't me as the groom she dreamed about walking down the aisle toward.

It felt like something shifted last night, like maybe I could finally admit the truth about my feelings to her—that I've loved her since the day I met her.

I got close to admitting it last night, even blurted out some truths that probably should've stayed quiet, and the sex definitely only made those dreams closer to reality.

But this is a cold wake-up call back to reality.

I'm getting confused by the mixed signals flying between us in this kitchen this morning. And maybe it's stupid of me to even consider what I'm thinking, but I've said it before, and I'll say it again.

I will do anything for this woman.

"It's not exactly what I want, but I think we could make it easy on ourselves and just do something in Vegas."

"Then let's go to Vegas today," I suggest.

She looks up at me. "Are you serious?"

"As my half-brother Spencer would say, serious as a W2."

"Does he really say that?" she asks.

"He does," I confirm.

She laughs. "Well, then I guess my question to you is whether you really want to go through with this. I keep thinking I can't do it to you, can't actually get you involved in this sham, but then you keep saying it's fine."

"If I can do this to help you out and find my own benefits from it, then why not? I'm the last of the Nash and Banks boys to find someone, and…" I trail off.

I stop myself before I say the words that are on the tip of my tongue.

I actually found my other half long before any of my brothers found theirs, but I was too stupid and scared to act on it. And maybe this is my way in. Maybe that's why I'm so set on agreeing to help her out because it isn't just about helping her. It's me finally getting the one thing I've always wanted, even if I'm coming by it in a nontraditional way.

It's probably better to just admit the truth to her, especially after last night. The truth is always the right road to take, but I haven't done it in the sixteen years I've known her, so why start now?

"I know what I get out of it. I get my parents off my back. I get to make Tyler seethe with jealousy. I get to prove what I said was true. I even get to try something I've written in my books. But what do you get out of it?" she asks softly. "I know you said it opens doors to sponsorships, but I just…I don't know. I need you to convince me that this is a good idea."

"Because I love you, Soph," I say simply. She assumes I mean as a friend. "I'll do anything for you, even if it's some crazy experiment to help you come out on top after what that dick did to you."

"I love you, too, Miller." She presses her lips together, and she lets out a breath as she pauses to think things over for a few seconds. "Okay. Let's go to Vegas."

I sit back, surprised. "Yeah?"

She nods. "Let's find a place and a date to do this thing."

"What place?" I ask.

She lifts a shoulder. "The Bellagio is nice, isn't it?"

I nod. "Very. But it's also sort of Tanner's place with Cassie."

She taps on her phone and flashes me a picture of a room set up for a wedding. It's sophisticated and elegant with a high ceiling and large windows on either side of double doors opened to a garden.

"Where's that?" I ask.

"Venetian."

I pick up my phone, and I find the next flight to Vegas leaves in less than two hours. I book us each a seat. We pack a few essentials in case we decide to stay the night, and we take off for the airport.

I text my half-brothers who live in Vegas on my way to the airport. I always try to see them when I'm in town. Lincoln is out of town with his wife and their kids, and Grayson is at the bakery he owns with his wife, Ava, all day, but Asher is in town and free to meet up with us for a late lunch.

We spend the most time with Spencer since we're on the same pro football team, but both Tanner and I are developing relationships with all four of our brothers. It may be a strange dynamic, but it's working for us. And since our biological father died, I feel like that's brought me even closer to my brothers. It made me realize that while I didn't get the time with our father, maybe we never really needed it. He wrote us off, but the second our brothers learned about us, they welcomed us in.

And that means something to me.

It's a brotherhood nobody else could understand, and I enjoy bonding with them as we get to know one another and make new memories.

We board the plane, and as we settle into our seats, I'm sort of expecting her to just slip in her earbuds and watch a show for the short flight.

Instead, she turns to me and asks, "So are we going to talk about last night?"

My eyes widen as I freeze for a beat, and I glance over at her. She looks nervous, as if she were bracing herself to ask the question, and it becomes my only priority to make sure she feels comfortable. "It was one of the best nights of my life," I admit. My voice is low, and she shivers a little at my words.

"Mine too," she whispers. "And I want to do it again."

Holy shit. It was?

All it makes me want to do is take her into the bathroom and make her a member of the mile-high club, but these thick-ass thighs of mine won't fit in one of those bathrooms with another human being.

Instead, I study her, our eyes meeting in the middle with a heat I'm used to *feeling* but not used to seeing back from her.

"Then we should do it again," I suggest, my voice low and raspy. "Tonight."

She snags her bottom lip between her teeth as she nods her agreement.

I book a hotel room at the Venetian before the plane even takes off, and now I sit with a giant erection until I can get her to our room so we can take care of it together.

Chapter 25: Sophie Summers

We Have a Date

I don't know what this is. I don't know where it's going. But I'm following my feelings for once, and they're leading me straight toward Miller.

It's terrifying, but I can't stop thinking about how great last night was.

I tilt my chin up, and he lands a soft kiss on my lips. Why does this feel so right?

I've never kissed Miller before, but now that we've started, I don't want to stop.

The flight is quick, and we land in Vegas and head straight for the Venetian. On the way there, he makes a call, and we're able to get in with one of the wedding planners to view the chapel I showed him on my phone.

It all comes together as if it was meant to be. We find ourselves looking at a calendar with Jamie, our wedding planner, and choosing the date of our wedding.

It's becoming so real, and that should make me nervous. It doesn't. All I can think about is finishing up here so we can check into our room and get naked.

I've *never* felt that way with a man before. I write about it in my books, the passion and excitement of ripping each other's clothes off because we can't get enough of each other…but I've never experienced it in real life.

I guess Miller is giving me more than one book research experience.

Maybe we'll even try anal someday.

Though the thought of that cock entering the no zone seems slightly terrifying.

Still, if there's anyone I'd try it with, I suppose that would be Miller. He'd figure out some way to take care of me.

He always does.

If there's one thing I can count on in life, it's that.

We look at the dates the Venetian has available as Miller checks his own calendar. He has a lot of obligations as the season draws nearer, and I…well, I got nothing.

Literally.

My calendar is totally and completely open, and it's a very strange sensation.

"We have space on these two Thursdays in June. Or this Sunday at the end of the month," Jamie says, showing us the openings.

"Those feel close. What do you have for the end of February or beginning of March?" I ask, glancing up at Miller.

"Valentine's Day is full, but the weekend after is wide open if you want something there," she says.

I keep my gaze on him as he looks at his calendar, and then he looks at me. His eyes are full of warmth as he says, "February twentieth."

We have a date.

Now I just need a dress, flowers, rings, and about a million other things to prepare us for this momentous event.

If only it were real.

Thank goodness for Jamie, who has it all under control. So much so, in fact, that she asks a few more questions, takes payment from my rather generous future spouse, and then we're done.

We have our date. Our venue is booked, and now we just have to figure out whether we're actually going to go through with this.

But now? We celebrate. After we check in.

There's no line, thankfully, and we get our key and our room number. And then Miller practically runs through the lobby to find the elevators. We race up to our suite with him carrying both of our overnight bags, and as soon as we've entered the room, he drops both bags on the floor in the entryway and turns toward me. The look in his eyes is intense, and I take a step back, finding myself bumping against the back of the door.

He stalks toward me, and he boxes me in as his hips press to mine. He leans one arm on the door above me as he tilts his head to look down at me, and we're both already breathing heavy—maybe from the exertion of practically running here, or more likely from the intense need suddenly present between us.

I search between his eyes, and I get the sudden overwhelming feeling like I'm home. I'm safe. Whatever happens next, we'll be okay. I'm not sure I've ever felt so secure with someone before, but there's this level of trust that exists between us that really can only be formed by knowing someone as long as we both have, by experiencing life and laughter and tragedy together as we have.

And now…this.

We're experiencing something new and wonderful, something forbidden and different. Something beautiful and magical.

His lips move to mine, and it's a soft, gentle kiss that nearly immediately intensifies. One of his hands trails down until it lands on my hip, and his fingertips dig in there for a few seconds as his tongue starts to move more urgently against mine.

It's as if he's hitting his frenzy of need, and I feel it, too. My knees are shaky again, and I wrap my arms around him in part to hold myself up and in part to smash my body as closely to his as I possibly can.

Out of nowhere, he sweeps me up into his arms, and he stops the kiss to carry me through the suite toward the bedroom.

I don't have the luxury of time to look out at the gorgeous view outside our window and down below, but maybe later. Right now, there's only one thing in my line of vision, and that's Miller Banks.

He sets me down on the bed and climbs over me, and he kisses me some more. His hips move against mine so he's humping me on the bed, both of us still fully clothed. I buck my hips back at him, meeting him in the middle each time, and I wrap my legs around his body as we keep moving like this, his tongue brushing mine as if we have all day even though the frenzy is building between us and pushing us into needing more. Now.

He pulls back from my mouth, and his lips trail down my neck.

"Fuck," he mutters against my skin. "You taste so good." He nips at my neck, and he keeps driving his hips to mine. He starts to moan, and I shift a little so I can feel his length through my jeans against my clit. I need him inside me, but my God, I don't want this to stop.

I cry out as I feel the edges of an orgasm start to close in on me. I'm not quite there yet, but I'm getting closer as he keeps slamming against me.

I've never come just from humping, but I feel like I'm seconds away.

He slows his drives, and I feel his teeth along my collarbone.

I shift my hips toward him again, trying to angle for some more of that delicious friction, but he stops.

"Don't stop," I pant. "Keep going."

"If I keep going, I'm going to come," he admits.

Holy shit.

Just the words send another pang of need straight through to my core. He's so turned on that he's about to come?

"So am I. I need you," I plead.

He pulls back, and his eyes meet mine.

"Fuck me like you did last night," I beg. "Fuck me so hard I can't sit without thinking of you."

His eyes seem to darken with lust at my words, and he springs from the bed. He runs through the suite, and I shimmy out of my clothes while he's gone.

When he returns, he's holding a condom in his hand. He doesn't look surprised that I'm lying naked on the bed even though he was only gone a few seconds, and he tosses the condom on the bed beside me as he races to get undressed as quickly as I just did.

I grab the condom, tear it open, and pull it out as he moves over me. He's straddling my legs, kneeling over me, and I take his very hard cock in my fist and pump it a few times.

"Unless you want my come all over your tits, you better stop," he warns.

"What if I do?" I challenge, my eyes gleaming as I keep pumping my fist along his shaft.

"Then I won't be able to fuck you until you can't sit without thinking of me," he warns, and I let go of my grip on his cock.

I reach down and palm his balls for a few beats, and then we both shift into position until he's aligned with my body. He reaches down and fists himself as he slides that big, beautiful cock into me, and I close my eyes and let out a sigh of contentment as I feel him inside me again.

It's that same big, full feeling. It's bordering on pain, but there's so much pleasure in it that it's a delicious, addictive sort of pain that I never want to stop.

He starts to move, and that's when I hear the demand fall from his lips. "Open your eyes."

He stops moving as he waits for me to follow his instructions, and when I do, I'm rewarded with absolute lust staring back at me. His eyes are heavy and hooded as he stares down at me.

"That's my girl," he says, and my God, why are those the hottest words I've ever heard?

That's my girl.

I *want* to be his girl with everything inside of me. I want this to be more than just two friends fucking. I want this to be more than just a marriage of convenience between two friends.

I want a life with him. It's sudden, and it's out of the blue, and it's an absolutely terrifying realization.

But it's a realization that's going to have to wait, because he's moving inside me, and I can't think with any sort of coherence.

At first, he moves slowly, with precision, but he slams into me as deeply as he can go, and that's what's going to give me that beautiful ache that'll make me think of him every time I sit later.

I'm not sure my body is healed yet from last night's activities, and here we go again. He thrusts into me with a force that's both brutal and immeasurably sexy, and every time he drives in, I feel closer to my climax.

He must see it in my eyes.

He starts to pick up the pace as my body begs for him, and just when I'm about to tip over the edge into oblivion, he pulls out.

"No," I cry.

He moves beside me and lies on his back as he reaches over for me. "Get on top," he pants, and I climb over him as he holds his cock up for me to slide down on top of him.

We both groan at the new angle, and he holds onto my hips as he moves us into a rhythm from beneath me. I claw at his chest as I hold myself up, and he hisses with every scratch I don't even realize I'm making.

"Fuck, Soph, your cunt is so goddamn tight for me," he mutters, and my eyes move to his.

"I've never had anything as big as your cock in there," I admit.

He chuckles, and his eyes seem to light up a little at the compliment. He bucks his hips harder into me, and all I can do is hold on for the ride.

My body starts to tighten, and this time, the orgasm doesn't give me any warning. Instead, I spring right into my release, screaming my way through it as my hips gyrate of their own accord over his body. I think I say his name, and I think there might be a string of curses, but I find myself in another galaxy for a few seconds, so I can't really be sure. This place is a land of pure pleasure and bliss, and I never want to leave it as my body contracts over and over, my legs squeezing together as I buck wildly over him, the climax brutal and intense.

I come back down to earth when I hear his own string of curses along with my name, and that's when he starts to come, too. I ride it out along with him, nearly feeling myself pushed into a second orgasm as I experience his pleasure through my own.

I collapse on top of him, both of us panting, and I start to wonder how we ever lived without this.

I'm not sure I can ever go back to how we were before—not now that I know how good he is at this.

And that thought is more than a little terrifying.

Chapter 26: Miller Banks

Cat in a Cowboy Hat

She's standing by the window wrapped in a blanket, and I can't help but wonder exactly how we got here.

My life went from pining for this woman over the last sixteen years to having her naked in a hotel room in Vegas as we plan our nuptials.

I realize the nuptials are for show, but there's still something in the back of my mind that makes me wonder if I could somehow win her over and make her see that we were always meant to be.

My cock has been doing a lot of the heavy lifting for me, that's for sure. And watching her come as she rides on top of me is some sort of dream come to life. She's so fucking gorgeous, and she's all fucking mine.

Except…she's not. It's a painful reminder.

I should tell her how I've always felt. Sometimes it's right there on the tip of my tongue, but then I worry she's going to run, and I swallow down those words instead.

I don't know if I could handle it if she ran.

"We need to meet Asher in a half hour," I say absently as I walk up behind her and wrap my arms around her. I'm still naked, and I know she is under that blanket, too. My dick wants to play some more, but she could probably use a break.

"I'm hungry," she says, leaning back into me. It's comfortable here, as if we were always meant to stand just like this.

"So am I. And thirsty."

She tilts her chin up, and I press a kiss to her lips. I keep it light and simple even though every urge in my body is telling me to deepen it.

I pull away first, and we both stare out the window for a few seconds.

"I've always wanted to go to Hell's Kitchen," she says. "My mom and I used to watch that show back when I was in high school, and she would get so uptight about the language."

He chuckles.

"But I always loved the drama and the dynamics. I always wanted to eat at one of his restaurants and order all the delicious food they cook on the show."

"Let's plan another trip and make sure that place is on the agenda," I say. I'd suggest changing the place we're meeting Asher for lunch, but I'm guessing he's already on his way.

I hunt for my clothes, and she follows suit. We chat as we get dressed.

"Is there anything else you want to do while we're in town?" I ask.

"Let's see a show. Maybe go to a club. Do it up Vegas style," she says.

I nod. I didn't bring club clothes, but we'll worry about that later.

We head down to the restaurant in the hotel that Asher said he'd meet us at, and his wife, Desi, is with him.

I eye Asher's shirt, not surprised he's wearing a button-down, probably designer, shirt with a cat wearing a cowboy hat on it. I chuckle as I greet them both with hugs and introduce Sophie to them, and then we head inside.

"We're thinking of seeing a show tonight. Do you have any nearby recommendations?" I ask.

Desi names off a few, and I search them on my phone. I find one with some tickets still available, and I flash my screen at Sophie. She nods, and she glances at Asher and Desi. "Would you two like to join us?"

"We'd love to, but we're already committed to dinner plans with my mom and dad." Desi makes a face. "Next time you're in town, maybe?"

Sophie nods. "Definitely."

The two women get to chatting about the best clubs in town, and I glance over at Asher.

"How've you been?" I ask. Of the six of Eddie Nash's children, Asher was definitely the closest to the man.

"Pretty good. My mom's been in town, which has been great since it means another babysitter nearby. We've been traveling a bit this offseason, but it feels like it's going fast. Too fast. You know?"

I nod. We're only a month out from the draft, and that's sort of the kickoff of the next season. A few weeks later, organized team activities begin, and then minicamps will start, and then we'll be at training camp before we know it.

We chat about football and what we're looking forward to about the upcoming season, and then our food arrives. By the time we're done, Sophie has agreed to head to their place to ransack Desi's closet for a club dress to wear tonight, and Asher has agreed to loan me something to wear as well…though I've seen Asher's clothing choices, and I'm not sure I want to go through his closet.

"I promise, I have shirts that are more your style," he assures me, and I laugh and shake my head as my eyes fall back to the western cat. "Though I can't guarantee my pants will fit over your quads."

We head toward their house with Desi and Sophie in the backseat, chatting away about books.

"I'm in a spicy book club with my best friends, and one of Asher's teammates owns a bookstore with his wife, Victoria," she says.

"Ooh, what spicy books do you like to read?" Sophie asks.

"All. The spicier, the better. Last week we did this hot doctor romance that was amazing." She names off a few other authors and books, and then she says, "And last month we read the new one by Summer Love called *Second Chances.*"

Sophie gasps, and my ears perk up as I eavesdrop on their conversation.

"Have you heard of it?" Desi asks her.

"Uh, yeah," Sophie says. "What did you think of it?"

I brace myself for the answer. It's brave of her to ask. What if she didn't like it? And why am I bracing myself? It's not like *I* wrote the damn book.

"The spice was—" Desi kisses her fingertips. "Chef's kiss. She's become one of my favorite authors, actually. I keep telling Victoria to get her into the bookstore for a signing, but Victoria said this author doesn't make appearances."

"She didn't," Sophie says. "She was a high school teacher and didn't want her identity getting out. But she's not teaching anymore, so maybe if your friend reaches out to ask again, she'd say yes."

"Wouldn't that be amazing?" Desi asks. "So you know of her?"

Sophie clears her throat. "I do." I wait for it because I have a feeling she's ready to let the world know, and then she does it.

"Actually, this is the really crazy thing, and, God, it's such a small, small world. I'm actually, um…well, I'm Summer Love."

My chest tightens for her as she reveals her identity for the first time.

Desi gasps. "What?"

I hear a zip, and when I glance back, I see Sophie handing Desi a business card.

"Tell Victoria to get in touch. I'd love to visit her bookstore."

"Oh. My. God!" Desi yells, punctuating each word. "I can't believe I just had lunch with *Summer Love*! You're a freaking rock star! Oh my God, I can't wait to tell Victoria! I can tell her, right? Are you still keeping a secret?"

Sophie clears her throat. I know she still doesn't want word getting back to her parents. It's part of the reason why we're getting married, after all.

But I also want this for her. She deserves the recognition for the incredible accomplishments she's made, and if I can help with that in any way, I'd love to.

"You can tell her," Sophie says.

I let out a tiny sigh of relief as I realize how Sophie just fits like a puzzle piece into yet another part of my life. She has her own identity, but she's able to slide right in as if she were always a part of things. Because she is. She always has been. She's a part of me, and I'm a part of her.

Now if I could just figure out how to admit the whole truth to her, maybe we really could have it all.

Chapter 27: Miller Banks

We take an Uber back to the hotel with the garments in hand. Asher had a button-down black shirt and gray slacks for me to borrow. Admittedly, the pants are a little tight around my thighs, but so long as I don't try to bust a move on the dance floor, it should be fine.

I'm not sure what Desi lent Sophie since it's in a garment bag, but I have a feeling it'll be hot as fuck on Sophie no matter what it is.

I don't know how I'm supposed to keep my paws to myself when I just want to get her naked, but we do have show tickets in an hour, so we don't have a ton of time to kill. We get back to our hotel, and she locks herself in the bathroom with her makeup bag and a curling iron as I change clothes. I'm ready in about twenty-three seconds while she takes over half an hour to get ready.

When she steps out of the bathroom, it was well worth the wait.

She's wearing a black and gold metallic long-sleeve short dress with a deep V-neck down the front that's cut so low I'm going to have my eyes on her tits all night to see whether they're spilling out of her dress or not. She has black heels on that give her five inches of height, and she's still a couple inches shorter than me, but fuck if I don't want those legs wrapped around me with those heels on while I slam into her.

Her makeup is dark and edgy for a night out, and her hair is pulled back into a dramatic ponytail with long curls cascading down.

How the hell am I supposed to keep it in my pants when she looks like that?

Fuck, man.

"Wow, Soph," I breathe, finally able to make my mouth work. "You look gorgeous." I want to walk across the room and pull her into my arms, but I'm not sure we're there. We're fucking, and we're getting married, but the act of pulling her into my arms while I drool over how beautiful she is feels more intimate than the level we're at.

It makes no sense.

She shakes her head back and forth, playfully swinging her ponytail behind her, and she winks at me. "You look pretty handsome yourself, Mr. Banks."

I glance at my watch. "You ready? And can you walk in those shoes?"

She laughs. "Get me enough vodka, and my feet will numb to any feeling."

We head down the hallway, and she links her arm through mine to hold onto me for balance. I smell her fresh, fruity, summer garden scent just as I feel her tit brush against my arm, and my already hard cock takes notice as an ache pings through my entire system.

I press the button to call the elevator, and she doesn't move from my side where she's still clutching my arm. I lean down and press a kiss to her temple because I need my mouth somewhere on her, and she glances up at me. She catches my lips with hers, and my chest seems to light up with anticipation for this night.

It's like we're on a date. It's like we leapt over a few levels of dating straight toward the aisle, and I'm so goddamn confused about where we are and what we are while I'm trying to just live in the moment and get the fuck out of my head.

I'm not a *get out of my head* kind of guy, though. I'm analytical, and so I'll analyze the fuck out of any situation. It's one of the things I share in common with my half-brother Spencer. Well, that and the fact that I'm an adult who enjoys building Lego sets, though I have nowhere near the collection Spencer and Grace do, and I tend to donate my sets after I build them.

We arrive at the theater where our show is, and we swing by the bar first. The lady asked for vodka to numb her feet, and she orders a Moscow mule. I get a Jack and Coke, and then we head inside the theater.

We're seated on the second level right in the middle of a row, and as the theater lights go down, I reach over and set a hand on Sophie's thigh. She shivers as she leans into me a little, and I glance over at her.

"Are you cold?"

"A little chilly," she admits, and she holds up the ice-cold drink in her hand. I take it and set it in the cup holder, and then I set my hand back on her thigh—just a little higher this time, and I try to cover more of her exposed leg with my hand to give her warmth.

She wraps her arms around my arm and pulls it into her chest, and I feel her tits brush against me again. I chug down my Jack and Coke. I can't sit beside her with all this heat flying between us and not fucking do something about it.

It's dark up on our level. Nobody would see if I slipped my hand beneath her dress…would they?

Nobody's watching us. All eyes are focused ahead on the stage as the show begins. It's one of the Cirque du Soleil shows, a contemporary visual arts circus with dancing and acrobatics, and it's somehow also sexy as we watch a woman pining for her man through the art of dance.

But how the hell am I supposed to pay attention when all I can focus on is how Sophie smells beside me? How she feels against my arm as she clutches it to her chest? How much I want to rip that hot-as-fuck dress from her body, pull her on top of my dick, and fuck her until neither one of us can see straight?

I inch my palm up a little more along her thigh, and I glance over at her. She's watching the show intently. I should be, too.

There will be time later for the things I want to do to her.

She glances over at me and offers a warm smile, and I let out a small breath.

Later, Banks. Pull yourself together.

I manage to sit through the show without moving my hand, but it's all I can think about. It's a pure obsession with the woman beside me, and I know how dangerous this is.

But I can't stop how I feel. I'm finally getting to act on the way I've felt about her, and it's overwhelming.

The show comes to an end, and everyone around us moves to a standing ovation. I don't want to get up. Getting up means I'm breaking the connection my palm has with her thigh and her arms have around mine, and I'm not ready to give that up.

When I look over at her, she lets go of my arm and instead sets her hand on my jaw. She leans toward me and presses a soft kiss to my lips, and it's the reassurance I need that this is real.

Somehow, it's real.

She pulls back and offers me a small smile, and then we both stand and clap for the performance. People start to file out of our row, and we follow suit. She's right behind me, close enough that I can feel her heat, and I like having her so close.

Scratch that. I *love* it.

We move out into the aisle, and she grabs my hand. I'm not sure if it's because she wants to be physically close to me, too, or if it's so we don't lose each other in the crowd. Either way, I'm not complaining.

We make it out into the lobby, and it's a mass of people all moving toward the exit. And that's when I hear my name beside me. "Are you Miller Banks?"

I glance over to see a man close to my age, and I nod as I reach out a hand to give him one of those universal bro-shakes. "Nice to meet you."

He grins. "I'm a huge fan of you and your brother. I've been following your career since the college days. I played for the U of A," he says, naming the university in Tucson that was the biggest rival of the university we attended in Tempe.

"Ah, bitter rivals. Were you there when we were at ASU?"

He nods. "Jason Dale," he says, giving me his name. "I was a senior when you two were freshmen. I was a linebacker, and I got a good tackle in on you once. But you were so goddamn fast, I had a hard time bringing you down. Congrats on all your success, man. You both deserve it."

The name isn't familiar, but I don't remember the name of every opponent I faced once over my entire career. "I appreciate that. Are you still in Arizona?"

He shakes his head. "Chicago now, and I don't play anymore. But I've enjoyed watching you two. This is my wife, Carly," he says, slinging his arm around her as we continue our slow crawl toward the exit.

"Nice to meet you," I say, nodding at Carly. I wrap my arm around Sophie and introduce her next. "My fiancée, Sophie."

"Hey, would you two want to grab a drink?" he asks.

I feel bad declining, but honestly I don't know this guy, and I don't owe him anything.

Besides, I'm on the lookout for a dark hallway or bathroom or *somewhere* that I can take my *fiancée* for a little one-on-one private time.

"I wish we could, but we have plans," I say, and he nods.

"Of course, man. It was great meeting you," he says.

"You too." We split up at that point as we head out a different set of doors than they do, and I continue to hold onto Sophie as I glance around the casino. "You mentioned a club. You ready?"

"Let's do it," she says, and I get the feeling she's not talking about going to a club but that we're on the same page about finding a dark hallway.

As it turns out, the club is the perfect place.

Sort of.

It's dark in here, the flashing lights contained mainly to the dance floor. Since money talks, we wind up in a private corner booth with tall walls. Our drinks arrive quickly, and we toast to the night and guzzle a bit before I lean over and press my lips to Sophie's neck.

"Mm," she moans. The sound is soft and eaten by the loud music, but I still hear it, and it sends a shot of need straight to my cock.

I trail my lips up her neck until my mouth is on hers, and suddenly we're making out in the dark corner booth at a club.

I slide my hand up her thigh, and nobody will see since a tablecloth drapes over our table on the other side.

I move up her thigh toward her hip in search of panties I can rip from her body, but I can't find the fabric.

I move my hand lower and between her legs, forcing her legs to fall open a little, and all I feel there is skin. That's when I pull back from our kiss, and my eyes meet hers.

"Are you…not wearing panties?" I ask, my voice hoarse and low.

A gleam lights up her eyes as she snags her bottom lip between her teeth. "Haven't been all night, and I kept wondering when you'd make that discovery."

"Jesus Christ," I mutter, and my mouth falls back to hers as my fingers move down. I slide one finger into her, and she squeaks into my mouth. I shove that finger in again and again, grateful for the darkness, grateful for a little alcohol, grateful that I'm here with her.

She reaches over and runs her hand along the outside of my pants, and I shove my hard cock at her, the need for release tearing through me as we do this private act in a public space.

This isn't me. I've never been the guy who fingers a girl in a dark booth in the corner of a club, but I've also never been with someone who ignites my passion the way Sophie does.

She drops her head to my shoulder, and she kisses the side of my neck as I hear her whispered pleas. "Oh God, Miller, yes, yes! I'm coming!"

Jesus. Her needy voice is low in my ear as she rubs my cock, and I feel her sweet pussy drenching my hand is too much. It's overwhelming in the best way, and I do everything I can to hold off the inevitable, but it's impossible.

As I feel her pussy clench tightly around my finger and she comes on my hand, I lean down to kiss her, and then I give into the feel of her hand on the outside of my pants, rubbing me the way she is. I pull back and drop my head to lightly bite her shoulder as I start to come.

I growl near her ear as I rasp, "Fuck, Soph, you're making me come so hard for you. I only wish I was inside you right now."

She pulls back, surprised and definitely a little dazed as she rubs harder along my cock, and I close my eyes and lean my head back on the booth as I give in to the sheer perfection of having this woman's hands on me in any way I can get them.

"God, I want that again, too," she murmurs near my ear as my body starts to slip into the warm tingling that comes with the euphoric feeling after a climax.

I sit up and open my eyes, and I lick the finger I just had inside her as her eyes zero in on what I'm doing.

"Did you just…?" she asks.

I nod and lean in toward her. "And it was fantastic." I hold my finger up. "Want to try?"

She shakes her head. "No, but why is seeing you do it making me need sex with you immediately?"

I grab my whiskey. "Give me ten to fifteen minutes."

She lets out a small chuckle. "What is it about you that I can't get enough of?"

"My charm?"

"That and the cock," she says.

God, I love her.

Is this perfection? Because it feels an awful lot like it.

Chapter 28: Sophie Summers

Finish What You Started

Is it fake?

Is it real?

We're teetering some line in between where we're both scared to admit it's more than something casual because of how that could impact the friendship that's so important to both of us, but I think it's safe to say there's no going back to how things were before.

So for now…does it matter? Do we have to define it?

My heart doesn't want to. My gut says we don't. So I'm sticking with that.

For now.

I'm also sticking to the addiction that is Miller Banks. Good Lord, he's good with his hands. His cock. His mouth. His body.

I want him in a way that terrifies me.

I want him now. I want him always. I want him any way I can get him, whether it's his finger inside me under a table or up in our hotel suite.

I feel positively *giddy* that I just made him come the way I did under the table. I got him so worked up that he came in his pants without my hand ever physically making contact with his cock, and I've never had that sort of power over someone before. I was touching him, sure, but it felt like him getting me off was enough to get him off. How damn sexy is that?

Very. Incredibly. Ridiculously.

We sip our drinks and watch the dancers on the dance floor, and I turn toward him. "Do you want to dance?"

He glances down at the spot where I just had my hand on him, and he turns toward me. "I need to use the restroom first."

I get his meaning, and honestly, I could use a clean-up myself—in particular since I'm not wearing panties. We finish our drinks, then head down the darkened hallway toward the restrooms. It's crowded here—too crowded to sneak into a stall to have sex, that's for sure.

I meet him back in the hallway, and he takes my hand and leads me toward the dance floor.

We're smashed together in the crush of people, and I love it. I love being close to him. I love smelling his clean scent, and I love when he slides one of his legs between mine so I'm practically riding his leg.

I'm so hot for him that I'm certain I'm leaving a wet mark on his pants, but I'm beyond the point of caring. I feel his cock as it presses against my hip, and he's hard again, which means he might even be ready to go again.

Suddenly the only thought in my mind is finding somewhere to have sex with him.

I lean forward and move my lips toward his ear. "I need you. Now."

He glances around at the crush of people, and he grabs my hand and leads me back to our booth. He reaches into his wallet and pulls out a condom, always prepared like the good boy he is, and he unbuttons his pants. Our server comes over to ask if we want more drinks just as he's about to pull his cock out, and we both know we need to say yes to keep our table.

"Another round," he says, somehow composed despite the situation in which we find ourselves.

I glance down to see him sliding the condom on as the server walks away, and then he reaches for me.

"Sit on my lap."

"Right here?" I squeak.

His eyes glint in the flash of light from the dance floor, and he doesn't look like my Miller. He looks like this dangerous, sexy beast who probably has the ability to break my heart, but underneath all that, I know he won't. It's Miller.

He would *never* hurt me.

With that in mind, I climb over and sit on his lap as requested. He lifts my dress as I move into place, and he slides himself inside me.

Oh. My. God.

It's that same full, beautiful feeling that I've already become hooked on, that same feeling of pleasure that makes me wonder how we lived without this for as long as we have.

He stills inside of me, careful not to move just yet as we look around to be sure nobody is watching us, trying to act casual like I'm not impaled by Miller Banks's enormous cock right now.

I can't act casual. Are you kidding me? He's seated fully inside of me, neither of us moving, and it's hot as hell.

And I feel him twitch inside me.

It's nearly my total undoing—again. Already.

I moan as I shift over him, not meaning to but also sort of needing to, and he grips my hips to still me as the server drops off our drinks, barely giving us a second glance.

Does she know what we're doing? Does she see this sort of thing all the time?

"Fuck, you're so tight over me," he murmurs close to my ear after she leaves, and he reaches forward to pick up his drink.

He's just casually drinking a Jack and Coke here in the club as his enormous dick fills me.

I pick up my drink, too, and my hands are shaking. He chuckles as he sees my trembling, and that's when he starts to move. I slam my drink down a little harder than I mean to, and I grab onto the edge of the table for balance.

I'm lost to the world as he sets a slow, tender pace, and I close my eyes and lean my head back on his shoulder.

"Sit up," he demands.

Oh, right. We're not in the privacy of a home or hotel room, and I need to act like I'm not getting fucked under a table right now.

I sit up, and I'm still gripping the edge of the table. I'm not sure how we're supposed to do this without being completely obvious since I can't exactly bounce up and down over his dick, but he's moving us slowly.

He reaches over my leg and brushes my clit with his fingertips, and *God*, it feels good. I groan, and he buries his face in the crook between my neck and my shoulder for a few beats as he shoves up into me and continues to finger my clit.

I start to unravel as he picks up the pace on my clit, and I let go of the table to grip onto his arms as the edges of a climax start to curl into me.

He pulls his fingers away from my clit as he feels me starting to get close, and I whimper over him as I lean back.

"Don't stop. I'm so close."

"I know you are, and I'm saving that one for later," he says. He still moves slowly inside of me, and the throbbing need to release pulses through me.

"Don't you dare," I hiss.

He chuckles as he lifts me off his lap. "Oh, this is going to be a fun little game."

I fold my arms over my chest. "This is not a game. Finish what you started."

His eyes gleam as they connect with mine. "Oh, I plan to. Believe me."

I'm not sure what that means, but the anticipation of it rolls through me anyway.

He puts his cock away and chugs what's left in his glass, and I follow suit.

He scoots out of the booth, his cock still wrapped in a condom in his pants, as he sets his hand out to help me out of the booth—ever the gentleman despite leaving me panting and breathless.

"Let's get back to our room, shall we?" he suggests, and I take his hand and allow him to lead me through the club toward the exit and back to our hotel room.

The second the door is closed, he reaches into the front of my dress, takes one breast out, and latches his mouth onto it. "Fuck, you taste so good," he mutters against my skin, and then he lifts me and tosses me over his shoulder, carries me to the bed as I kick my legs and yell at him to put me down, and finally sets me down.

He pushes the bottom of my dress up around my hips, and he dives face-first into my pussy.

I wasn't expecting that. I would've freshened up for him a bit first, but from the way he's growling as he starts to lick through me, I guess he's okay with whatever shape it's in down there.

He sucks on my clit, the feel of his mouth sending shockwaves through me. I grip onto the breast that's still hanging out with one hand in some attempt to give attention to more than one erogenous zone, and I clutch the sheets with the other.

His tongue starts to move in and out of me, and all I can think about is how his cock is still in a condom in his pants and how very badly I want it in my mouth. But it'll have to wait because my body tightens as the orgasm plows into me, as if I was so close back at the club and I stayed right there on the precipice waiting for him to take me over it.

My legs press together around his ears as my body unravels, and I grip onto my breast so hard that I'm likely going to have a bruise tomorrow, but I don't feel the pain right now because of the pulse after pulse of pure pleasure he's delivering courtesy of his very talented mouth.

The tremors start to slow as bliss plows into me, and my entire body relaxes as I let go of my own breast, the sheets, and the hold I have with my legs around his head until I'm lying flat on the bed.

"Do you need a minute?" His voice is soft a few moments later.

I'm in some orgasm coma, not really sure what he means by the question, and my answer is, "I only need you."

He slams into me at my words nearly unexpectedly, and my eyes pop open as I feel him start to move. My body is still tight as hell after coming down from that climax, and he feels it.

"Fuck, yes, Soph, you're so wet and tight for me," he groans, and my body immediately warms to him even though I just had that brutal climax.

I feel like I can barely move, so I let him do the work. He holds me still anyway as he pumps into me, thrust after delicious thrust. I've never had the kind of foreplay where he gets me off with his hand, and then his mouth a little while later, and then he fucks me, and it feels like our bodies were made for each other.

And it's a powerful feeling as I listen to the grunts and groans that are getting him off, too—the ones that are bringing him into the same place of bliss where he just brought me. I feel myself being taken on yet another ride as he pushes my body to intense heights it has never been before.

He picks up the intensity of his drives as he pulls closer to his release, and when he hits his peak, he shoves in still harder as he murmurs my name over and over.

Heat spreads through me as the knowledge that my body did this to him takes hold of me, that our bodies together create this frenzy and this crazy connection I never expected in a million years.

He did indeed finish what he started back in that club, and I don't think I've ever been this sexually satisfied in my entire life.

And yet he keeps proving to me time and again that he can take me one step further into the land of bliss.

Chapter 29: Miller Banks

What a night. It was incredible, the stuff dreams are made of. The type of night I'll think about when we're apart in a few months when I'm at an away game and missing the hell out of her.

I'm not sure how we got here, but I never want to leave.

I realize I have to.

I have to get home tomorrow. I have to meet with my publicist and finalize our plans for summer camp, which is only two and a half months away now. We need to start advertising it and getting the word out to fill seats. Most of the back-end work is done thanks to her team, but that doesn't mean I don't still have plenty of shit to do to prepare.

And we have a wedding to plan. It's mostly Sophie making those decisions with the wedding planner, but we have invitations to send and people to notify. We need to discuss who we're telling the truth to and who we aren't. There are tons of things to decide and not enough hours in the day to decide them all, so I bring it up over breakfast.

"So February twentieth, huh?" I begin.

She chuckles, and then she grabs her phone. "Oh! I saw this amazing tux that would be perfect. Let me just find it."

She opens her email, and I wish she wouldn't have.

"What the hell is this?" she asks. It's an article from *Page Six* forwarded to her from a friend, and she clicks a link.

A picture of the two of us from last night appears on her screen. It's grainy, but it's definitely us. She's sitting on my lap, her head leaning back against my shoulder, and it's pretty damn clear what we're doing.

We thought we were being so sneaky. We were also a little drunk, but that's beside the point.

The headline reads, "San Diego Storm Running Back's Wild Night Out in Vegas."

"Oh my God, I am completely and totally mortified," she says, and I study the picture for a second before she flips through the slideshow. There are others of us kissing in the booth, another of her probably when I was getting her off with my fingers.

There's one of me where my head is tipped back. I look like I'm climaxing, and it's probably when she was rubbing me over my pants, and I actually *was* coming.

"It's not a big deal," I say, trying to minimize her embarrassment. "As far as the press knows, you're my fiancée, so there's nothing wrong with what we were doing."

"Miller," she says flatly. "Come on." She lowers her voice so only I can hear her. "We were having sex in public, and someone caught it. There's a *lot* wrong with what we were doing."

"Nobody saw anything. It was dark, and we were in our booth. It's fine."

I glance at the first few lines of the article attached to the images, though, and it's pretty damning.

"Who would've taken our picture and sent it in?" she asks.

"Probably someone out to make money," I say. Who knows who it was? It could've been anyone. Maybe it was that Jason dude who I declined drinks with. Maybe he was angry at the rejection, and this was his way of getting back at me. Or maybe it was just someone who recognized me and decided to make a buck from it.

"So someone took our picture in an intimate moment, and then they *sold* it? Like…they profited from it?"

I shrug. "It happens all the time, and there's not really much I can do to stop it."

"Except, you know, *not* having public sex."

"Well, yeah, there's that. But where's the fun in that?"

She huffs out an annoyed breath, and then our breakfast is served, effectively ending that part of our conversation. Still, I bring it back up mid-meal.

"Are you okay?" I ask, a little worried about how this sort of thing might affect her long-term.

"I don't like it, but I can't change it. I'm just trying to force my eggs down over the nausea I feel."

"From the vodka?" I guess.

She shakes her head and nods at her phone. "From those pictures of us."

"I'm sorry," I say quietly.

"It's not your fault."

"Yeah, it is. People do this. They see an athlete or celebrity, and they take advantage of the situation. I thought we were protected in the dark. It was a corner booth. People were occupied with their drinking and dancing. But I've been in this field long enough that I should've fought the instincts I had to be with you in that moment. I should've warned you that something like this could happen."

She presses her lips together and sets her fork down. "Is this what it's like being with you?"

"It is," I admit. "But it's not all bad." I lift a shoulder. "We could use it to our advantage, you know."

Her brows dip together. "How?"

I hold my hands up and look into the distance as I make a sort of rainbow with my hands to indicate the new headline. "San Diego Storm Star Running Back's Fiancée Has a Secret Identity as Bestselling Romance Author Summer Love."

Her brows that were already close together seem to pinch a little tighter. "Are you saying we should reveal my identity to the world?"

I shake my head. "Not if you're not ready for it. But I have a platform, and I'd be more than happy to use it to tell the world about my favorite author."

"You'd do that for me?"

I reach across the table and grab her hand. I squeeze it gently, and my voice is quiet as I say, "Don't you know by now that I would do anything for you, Soph?"

She blinks a few times as her eyes shine at me, and then she swipes at her cheek with her thumb. "I do."

"Good. Don't forget it."

Chapter 30: Sophie Summers

The Friday we get back from Vegas is my thirtieth birthday, and honestly, I haven't spent much time thinking about it.

I see the pictures on Facebook of my high school friends who are getting married and having babies, and I feel a twinge in my chest that they're getting that while I'm pushing that life further down the road as I do whatever it is I'm doing with Miller. We're getting married, sure.

Babies?

No. He's pretty convinced he doesn't even want kids, and I was never really all that sure. But the more I see photos of my friends holding their newborns moments after giving birth, the more I think I want that life, too.

I want a baby I can post pictures of. Not just to post pictures of, but to create a legacy with another person out of love, to be a mother who loves another being so selflessly and unconditionally, to give myself a new purpose and meaning as I shift into an entirely new role.

And I want a husband who adores me—who's marrying me because we're in love, not because he's trying to help out an old friend.

More and more, I think we could get there. This *feels* like more than friends with benefits, and I already had a deep love for Miller because of the strong foundation we built over the years.

I'm not sure I can go through with a wedding that isn't real when the feelings I'm starting to feel for him are *very* real.

But I'm also not sure I'm brave enough to have that conversation with him.

I guess turning thirty is affecting me more than I realized.

It's making me want to start a family, which wasn't really something I was worried about in my twenties. It feels like time is starting to close in on me a little, but I push those thoughts from my mind, close Facebook, and get back to writing.

"Happy birthday. I'm taking you out to celebrate," Miller announces on Friday morning as he sets a breakfast plate in front of me. It has a bowl of his famous oatmeal on it along with an assortment of fresh fruit. "I thought maybe we could go to a club and reenact last weekend's shenanigans."

I roll my eyes. It's still a little bit of a sensitive subject for me, I guess. "No public sex, but I'm game for going out." I nod toward the plate. "Thanks for this, by the way. What do you have in mind for tonight?"

"Just a little something. Pack an overnight bag," he says. "We're leaving at noon. We'll grab lunch on our way."

"What sort of clothes should I wear?" I ask.

"Whatever you want."

"Casual? Dressy?"

He shrugs, and he's really giving me exactly nothing to go on here.

"Oh my God, Miller! Tell me what to wear!" I demand.

He laughs. "Shoes comfortable to walk in and an outfit that gives me easy access." He wiggles his eyebrows.

"I already said no public sex."

"You didn't say no public fingering," he says innocently, and I pick up a grape to throw it at him, but he runs out of the room before I get the chance to toss it, laughter following behind him.

That effectively ends my writing session for the day, as now I can't stop thinking about where he's taking me, so I head upstairs and rifle through my closet to find the right outfit to bring. I decide on a long skirt that I can wear sneakers with and a cute top to match. I throw everything I need for an overnight trip into a bag, and there's still a solid three hours to kill before we leave.

I field some calls and texts from my parents and friends back in Phoenix, and I work on a few graphics for some things I have going on next week. The clock seems to slow to a crawl, but eventually it's time to go, and Miller appears in the kitchen with a duffel bag and a sly smile.

I snag my bottom lip between my teeth. "What are you up to?"

"Creating birthday memories." He shrugs, and I follow him out to the car.

I have no idea where we're going until he pulls into a parking spot at the San Diego Zoo.

"The zoo?" I ask, and he just smiles. We head inside, and he treats me to lunch at a grill where we both order burgers and fries. Once we're stuffed full, he grabs my hand and leads me to the penguin exhibit, where we have a private encounter where I get to interact with my favorite animal.

When we're done, he takes me through the gift shop and stops at the register, where the clerk pulls out two wrapped boxes and hands them over the counter for me.

I open them to find a stuffed penguin and a beautiful necklace with a diamond penguin pendant, which he immediately fastens around my neck.

It's such a sweet, thoughtful surprise.

After our penguin encounter, he leads me back to the car.

"That was so fun," I say with a contented smile.

"The day is just beginning," he says with a gleam in his eyes, and then I lean back into the seat and get ready for whatever's coming next.

We arrive at the airport next, and we board a plane heading to Vegas. Of course it's Vegas. We're getting married here early next year, and we had a lot of fun here last weekend.

When we land, we head straight for Caesar's Palace, and we check into a gorgeous suite in one of the towers that gives us a view of Las Vegas Boulevard.

I'm staring out the window gazing out at said view when Miller saunters up beside me.

"What are we doing here?" I finally ask, curiosity getting the better of me as I glance over at him.

"Celebrating your birthday."

I chuckle. "Well, I mean…I know that. But this is all so extravagant, Miller."

"I just wanted you to feel special on your birthday. You're always working so hard, and you hardly ever take time for yourself. Tonight is just for you."

I melt at his words, and then he proves it's just for me by giving me my first orgasm of the night with his tongue.

I'm about to reciprocate when he says, "We have dinner reservations we need to get to."

Truth be told, I'm already hungry after traveling and that climax he just gave me, so I freshen up, and we walk toward our destination, which turns out to be Hell's Kitchen.

When we're seated, I'm surprised to find Tanner and Cassie already at the table.

"What are you doing here?" I ask.

"You said you wanted to do dinner with these two again, and I've heard good things about this place," Miller says with a twinkle in his eye as he obviously remembers me telling him I wanted to eat here less than a week ago.

They both stand and give me hugs as they wish me a happy birthday, and I sit and have an absolute *experience* for my meal.

I order all the things I've seen the chefs make on the show, and it's undoubtedly the best meal I've ever had in my life as we talk about the family vacation Cassie ended up booking a few weeks ago.

She discovered the entire Nash clan has the week after her and Tanner's wedding off, so with some rearranging of schedules considering the sheer number of people we're doing this with, she booked a weeklong cruise for mid-July. We will return the weekend before the oldest of the Nash brothers, Lincoln, needs to be back for rookie camp, and even though some of the men will have a bit of work to do on the cruise, mostly it'll be a time for the entire family to relax together and build a bond only in the way traveling together can.

I shove a forkful of scallops into my mouth, and I think I might be moaning. Miller is looking at me like he wants to eat his beef Wellington off me.

I think that could probably be arranged, but only if we take it in a to-go container—which we can't since we apparently have plans after dinner.

The four of us walk over toward the Coliseum here at Caesar's, and I see the banners advertising the act playing here tonight.

"No way," I whisper as we get in line at the will call ticket booth.

Miller angles his head down to look at me. "You want to see Backstreet Boys tonight from the front row?"

I think I might pass out.

Are you kidding me?

How is this real life right now? This man is literally the stuff book boyfriends are made of. Miller Banks is everything Tyler Boyd was not. He's everything every single one of my ex-boyfriends was not, to be honest.

He's everything I've ever wanted, and he's been right here in front of me the entire time.

I'm done resisting him. Now I just have to figure out how to hold onto him.

Chapter 31: Sophie Summers

I'm in Love with Miller

The next few weeks are a blur of sex, words, and planning. Time flies when you're having fun, and I'm having so much fun that time is rocketing by.

My muse must be working overtime, because the book I'm working on is absolutely pouring out of me. I sit at the keyboard, and it's like magic happens as the words flow out of my fingertips. I wish every book felt like this, and maybe it will going forward—if Miller and I keep doing what we're doing.

If my muse keeps *inspiring* me.

So I'm enjoying the best writing of my life and the best sex of my life as the heat builds between Miller and me. He continues to be the book boyfriend of my dreams, and I know things will change once the season is underway and he can't be at home as much as he has been, but I'm enjoying the routine we've fallen into.

The draft comes and goes, and we find ourselves in May, a month out from Miller's summer camp program. Organized team activities, or OTAs, start at the end of the month, and they give us a little taste of what life will look like when he has daily practices to attend. With that in mind, I start to look for my own community here in San Diego.

Cassie is busy with her two kids and the physical therapy business she owns, but she still makes time to meet me once a week for lunch. We talk about the upcoming cruise pretty much nonstop. I've also started talking more to Spencer's wife, Grace, who takes Mondays through Wednesdays off from the winery she runs in Temecula, and sometimes we grab lunch while the boys are at workouts.

It's a Friday afternoon at the end of May, and Miller is still at OTAs when an email comes through on my author account from a bookstore in Vegas. I open it the second I spot it because I already know what it is based on the subject line: *An Invitation*

Dear Summer,

My name is Victoria Woods, and I'm the owner of Harts and Harps Book Nook in Las Vegas. One of my good friends and book besties, Desiree Nash, told me to get in touch with you because you may be interested in making an appearance in our store. We would be absolutely delighted to host an event featuring you and your books. We have several ideas for various events if you're interested, such as a single day event with you, a romance book crawl that would include other authors, or even a launch party for you in store for your next book release. If you're interested, please reply back and let us know what potential dates would work for you along with your headshot, Instagram handle, and the ISBNs of the books you'd like us to feature.

Looking forward to hearing from you!
Victoria Woods
Owner, Harts and Harps Book Nook

Excitement rushes through my veins. I take a look at my calendar, and since Miller will be at training camp after we get back from the cruise, I give her a list of dates starting toward the end of July. It'll be perfect timing for me, too, since I have a book scheduled to release at the end of the month. I let her know I'd be interested in both the launch party and the romance crawl, and I also let her know that I don't actually have headshots since I've never put my face anywhere.

It's probably time to fix that.

I'm both nervous and excited about this opportunity, and when Miller gets home, I'm practically bursting with excitement to tell him.

And the longer we live together, sharing in each other's victories and spending time together, the more I want it to be real.

Whatever is happening between us is powerful enough that this is the strongest muse I've ever had. I go with it, and we plow through another month. Edits are done on my book releasing at the end of July, and I start writing the next one.

Miller and I run his weeklong camp together. He managed to rope most of his brothers into making an appearance and either teaching a session or running drills on the practice field.

I help organize things behind the scenes all week, and I find it's yet another place for us to work together and bond. Because of that, the program is a huge success, and Miller has decided to make it an annual event that he can build into something bigger and better every year.

In between it all, I'm getting ready for the cruise, and before we know it, it's a Tuesday and we're flying to Vegas for Tanner and Cassie's wedding. We'll spend two days in Vegas before we fly with the Banks and Nash clan down to Florida for our cruise leaving out of Miami on Friday, so I had to pack for eleven days.

I think I probably packed enough for twenty.

In fact, I brought so much stuff that I had to borrow some space in Miller's suitcase.

He's a guy, so he has like three pairs of shorts and some dress pants. His tux is waiting for him in Vegas since he's the best man in his twin brother's wedding, and we're excited to be here tonight for the joint bachelor and bachelorette parties.

And this cruise is going to be something for the books. Literally. Just like every experience in my life, I'm going to use it for book research, and I can only imagine the sorts of things I'll see over the week we're on the ship with a group of thirty-two relatives. All six of the brothers will be there, some with kids, some with in-laws. It's a huge event—so big, in fact, that Cassie started a Facebook group so we had an open place where we could communicate, and I feel like I'm bonding with this family every single day in one way or another.

It's a little scary, if I'm being honest.

My engagement to the member of this family isn't real. It *feels* awfully real, though, and I'm wondering if the cruise might be the right time for us to actually talk about our feelings.

I'm in love with Miller.

I haven't told him that, and he hasn't said it to me, either—at least not in the meaningful way as more than a friend.

But I'm there. I've been there for quite a while at this point, and I think it's time to clue him in on it.

Maybe there was something to that pact all those years ago. Maybe the fake wedding we're planning could turn into a real one.

A girl can hope, anyway.

Chapter 32: Miller Banks

The Truth

Tanner and Cassie wanted to keep it simple, but that's not exactly how things panned out.

How can it be when you have four half-brothers you didn't even know were related to you a year and a half ago?

They've become actual brothers to us in the short time we've had together, and since we're all heading out on a cruise in a few days, this is just an extension of the party.

So the bachelor and bachelorette parties are a joint affair with the six Banks-slash-Nash brothers in attendance along with our dates—plus Cassie's maid of honor, her cousin, Jess.

I've had the pleasure of meeting her a few times, and in truth, Cassie once tried to set us up, but I politely and respectfully declined since my mind was on Sophie.

I can't say I've *always* declined invitations because of Sophie. I never *really* thought we had a chance, but something made me say no to every opportunity that came my way with the fairer sex over the half year before Sophie broke it off with her ex, and somehow that felt right. Like I was saving myself for her, and then she happened to come along.

I've been waiting for the right time to tell her that I'm in love with her. It's not as easy as it sounds.

It's a secret I've kept hidden away for more than half my life, and to admit it to the one person I've worked hardest to keep it from feels like it would be quite the shock.

I know I should just tell her.

Losing Eddie before we got the chance to know him should've been a clear reminder about how short life really is, but instead I let it fuck with me in other ways.

Regardless, I'm thankful that it connected us to the four brothers we didn't get to have growing up. Tanner and I always liked our small family, but I still wanted more—something like this, where I walk into a room and immediately find five close friends who share interests and blood even if we didn't share a childhood.

Everything that's happened over the last year and a half has only bonded the six of us, and the next eleven days will only bring us even closer together. In fact, I'm not sure why we didn't come up with the idea to take a family vacation sooner. Leave it to the women to come up with this plan.

Our group of thirteen meets at the restaurant in the Bellagio that Tanner and Cassie chose for tonight, and we begin the night with drinks, naturally. It's a party, and we're here to celebrate.

Sophie is caught up in a conversation with Cassie about how she's doing an in-store event with one of the Vegas Aces team members' wives when Jess smiles at me from across the table.

"Congratulations on your engagement. You seem really happy," she says, angling her head between Sophie and me.

I slip an arm around the back of Sophie's chair. "I am."

"I'm happy for you. Is this why you and I never…?" She trails off with a question at the end, and I lift a shoulder as I glance at Sophie.

It seems like she knows about my feelings for Sophie, and it makes me wonder whether she knows the truth about the engagement, too.

Though to be fair, I'm not sure I even know the truth about the engagement at this point.

I guess I'm just living in the moment and hoping for the best. It's not the greatest plan, but I'm trying to manage all this the right way. I want to continue being there for Sophie as the friend I've always been, but I want to explore this new side of things more and more with her without scaring her off.

And sex. I want sex. With her. Now. All the time.

I glance back at Jess and give her a small nod. I don't want her saying anything I'm not ready for Sophie to hear, so I turn to my other side and join in on the conversation with my brothers about some of the offseason coaching changes around the league.

Dinner is served, and more drinks are, too. Our large table gets louder with laughter the more drinks are served, and once the last dessert plate has been cleared away, Tanner stands and tugs on Cassie's hand. She stands, too, as he begins a short speech.

"Thank you all for spending this night with us. Now before we have *too* many drinks and my future bride gets mad because we're all hungover tomorrow at the wedding, I think we're going to call it an early night."

The twinkle in his eye gives him away—to me, at least, since I know him better than I know myself sometimes. He's probably had his hand up her skirt all night, and now he's ready to take it to the privacy of their hotel room, so he's making an excuse and skipping out on the plans he had for all of us to go to some club after dinner.

And it's fine. Really. I'm not much of a club guy anyway, and getting Sophie up to the privacy of a hotel room sounds pretty damn perfect to me.

"To the bride and groom," I say, holding up my nearly empty drink, and everyone at the table holds up their glasses as they repeat my toast.

I'll have a longer, more meaningful speech tomorrow night, but I can see Tanner is antsy to get the hell out of here, so I leave it at that.

They head out first, and I look around the table as everyone starts to make plans.

I glance at Sophie. Her eyes are warm when they meet mine, and I lean in a little closer and murmur, "Do you want to go to the club, or do you want to head upstairs?" I press a little kiss just under her ear, and she shivers.

"Upstairs." Her voice is a whispered plea.

"We're going to head up, too. Best man duties bright and early tomorrow," I announce, and Grayson gives me that old *yeah, bro* kind of look that tells me everyone knows I don't have any early duties tomorrow since it's an evening wedding, but we're all grown adults here. I bet every single dude at this table is itching to get his significant other somewhere private.

Except Asher. He strikes me as the type to just do it right here.

Sort of like we did at that club that one night.

I guess that was a little out of character for me, but intimacy with Sophie will do that to a guy.

And tonight, I'm ready for some more of that intimacy. So is she, and I'm loving getting to know this side of her.

She squeezes my hand as we walk toward the elevator. She lets out the softest little sigh when she sees we won't be alone on that elevator, and she lets go of my hand and moves closer to me as we wait. I toss my arm around her shoulder and squeeze her into my side as she slips an arm around my waist, and we walk to the back of the elevator that way.

Once we're in place, her hand trails down, and she squeezes my ass.

I let out a soft chuckle as I look down at her, and she's looking up at me, the warmth that was there just a few moments ago replaced now with a heat that tells me exactly what's about to go down when we get into our room.

My hunch is correct.

As soon as the door latches shut behind us, I flip the bolt and push the swing lock over. I turn around, and she's standing mere inches from me. She lifts onto her tiptoes and runs her fingertips along my jawline, and then she tilts her head back as she moves toward me. I drop down to press my lips to hers, and she opens her mouth immediately to mine.

Our tongues swirl as she moves her hands down to my torso, and I pull her into me as the urgency between us seems to kick up a few notches.

She pulls back, and for just a second, I think maybe it's because the intensity is too much. But then she pulls her dress over her head and drops it to the floor, and she stands in front of me in a black bra and thong. All the blood in my entire body rushes straight to my cock, and I'm nearly lightheaded because of it.

Jesus, she's beautiful.

And she's mine.

Sort of.

Chapter 33: Sophie Summers

More Than Enough Man for Me

His eyes sweep over my body, and they seem to brand me in every place they land.

It's hotter than any scene I've written, and I once wrote a scene with three guys and one girl.

Not that I'd want that in real life. Miller is more than enough man for me.

But in fiction? Hell. Yes.

He rushes toward me, and I reach for his shirt. I pull it over his head, and I wrap my arms around him as I slide my hands along the smooth, warm skin of his back.

He plants his lips on my neck as his hands move achingly slowly down my torso and around to my ass. He cups both my cheeks in his palms and gives them a squeeze, and the ache that was already centered between my thighs intensifies at his touch. The fabric of my thong is pulling against my clit, and I push my ass back into his hands as a way to try to draw out the friction.

I'm too wet for it to move, though. I'm soaked, and I fully blame Miller for that.

All night he's been finding little reasons to touch me. A light hand on my thigh. An arm around the back of my chair while his fingertips lazily brush my shoulder. A quick kiss on the cheek, or the neck, or my lips.

I arch my back, and he grabs me up into his arms and carries me across the room. He sets me down on the bed and is on top of me a heartbeat later, his lips pressing against mine and his hips slamming against me as he draws me closer and closer to a climax without ever taking off my underwear.

The very second I have the thought, he backs off me and moves to a stand. He's panting as he removes my bra, then yanks me by my hips to the edge of the bed, and he peels my panties from my body. He kneels to the floor, sets my legs on his shoulders, and moves his face toward my pussy.

I nearly fall apart the second I feel his tongue on my clit, but I clutch onto the sheets because I'm not ready to give in. I'm not ready for the pleasure to stop. I can't buckle to it when I've barely had a chance to enjoy it, and I know that what he's doing will be next-level enjoyable.

He slides his tongue through my slit, and my hips buck up off the bed as I concentrate on every sweet movement of his tongue. He hums against me, the vibration sending me to another level, and I let go of the sheets to clutch onto his hair.

"Oh, God, Miller, yes!" I cry out, and hearing his name from my lips like a prayer seems to only spur him on. He sucks on my clit, then moves his tongue back inside me, moving back and forth before he concentrates on my clit a while and adds his finger inside me.

He pumps his finger in and out as he showers my clit with attention, and he reaches up with his other hand to massage one of my tits. It's his endurance at work as he pleasures me in three separate zones at once, and as he tweaks my nipple, he sends a shot of pleasure right through to my core.

It seems to collide with the same feelings coming up from my pussy, and I fall headfirst into an intense ride of pure pleasure.

I scream and moan my way through it as it hits me with brute force, and he licks and laps his way through me as I come all over his tongue.

He moans as if he's pulling his own pleasure from mine, as if he can hardly take how good I taste, and it makes me feel like the most powerful, most beautiful, most loved creature in the universe.

And *that* is ultimately what Miller Banks does for me. He makes me feel like I can do anything, like I can *be* anything, simply because he's by my side. Or simply because his finger is inside me and his tongue is sucking on me, as the case may be.

I very nearly say the words. *I love you.*

Because I do. This is so much more than just the friendship we've both come to rely on. It's what I want for my future, too.

I just don't know how to tell him that I don't really want this engagement to be fake anymore.

And so I don't let the words slip out despite how close they are.

Instead, after he climbs up the bed and collapses beside me, I get onto my knees, move between his legs, and pull the button of his pants. I lower the zipper, and I reach in and pull his cock out. It's heavy and hard as he waits patiently for me, and I don't draw it out.

I slide my fist along his length a few times before I bend down and suck him into my mouth. His hands are immediately in my hair as he guides my head up and down his cock. I suck him in, and he holds me there in place a few beats. Just when I think I might choke on him, he lets go, and I draw in a deep breath.

Listening to the moans he's making as I suck him back is enough to spur me on to take him all the way to the back of my throat again. I slide my fist along his shaft as I go, and I move down to take his balls into my mouth as I continue to jerk him off.

"Fuck, Sophie," he groans as I gently suck on his balls, and I feel them tighten and draw up, the sure signal he's about to come.

I let go of his balls so I can suck his cock as he starts to come, and the hot jets hit the back of my throat. I swallow as he fills my mouth, and as the pulsing throbs start to slow, I suck the head of his cock to clean him off, and he shudders as I let go.

"Jesus Christ, that was hot," he murmurs as I move up the bed and settle in beside him.

"Let me know when you're ready to fuck me."

He groans. "How the hell did I get so lucky?"

I lean up on my elbow and look at his handsome face, and a replay of the last four months runs through my mind. It all started with a breakup and a phone call, and here we are. "I was just wondering the exact same thing."

The last four months have been full of ups and downs and even more ups, and I can't help but wonder what the next four months and the four after that have in store for us.

Chapter 34: Miller Banks

"Are you nervous?" I ask, mainly because I feel a strange, unfamiliar dart of anxiety, and I can't help but wonder if it's *my* anxiety or *his*.

I'm not sure what I have to be anxious about. I'm here with Sophie, we're about to embark on a cruise for the next week with thirty of our closest family members, and my brother is getting married today.

"Maybe a little. Not for me, but for her. What if she realized she can do better than me and decides not to show up today?" my brother asks, and it's a rare show of vulnerability from someone who is normally overly confident, bordering on cocky.

But it's me. I'm the one person aside from his bride who he shows that vulnerable side to.

"You two are perfect together. You know she won't realize that." I try to give him the calm reassurance he needs.

"You know, we never did the twin switch thing," he says.

"Where we swap places on some poor, unsuspecting woman?"

He lifts a shoulder and gives me a wry nod of his head. We thought about it once back in high school, but I was too far gone over Sophie to agree to it.

"We still have time," I tease. "You're not married yet."

He narrows his eyes at me. "Are you saying you want to take a crack at Cass? Because the answer is—"

"Fuck no," I finish for him, interrupting him. "And I'm not giving you a crack at Soph, either. Though she'd know the difference between the two of us. Wouldn't Cassie?"

"For sure. Especially the cock. She'd know as soon as she saw how much smaller you are."

I narrow my eyes at him. "I may be two inches shorter than you, but I more than make up for it everywhere else."

We both get a good laugh out of that, and the rest of our brothers show up to the room at the Bellagio where we're hanging out until the ceremony.

"Okay, all four of you are married," Tanner says. "So hit me with your best marriage advice."

Lincoln goes first, and his words are very much in line with his personality as a leader and a coach. "You've got a teammate for life, and as long as you put in the work and adjust your strategies when you need to, you'll be fine."

"Thanks, man," Tanner says, and Grayson slaps him on the back next.

"Keep her happy, man. That's all that you need to know for a successful marriage. And if you fuck up, which you will since you're a dude, fight your ass off to make it up to her."

Spencer just laughs at Grayson and says, "What he said. Or, you know…don't fuck up in the first place."

And Asher is last with advice that's right in line with what I'd expect from him, too. "Keep her on her toes so she doesn't get bored with you."

I laugh at all four of them and think how incredible it is that we're all one big family now.

I hear a knock at the door, and I open it to find our mom and dad standing there.

"We'll head out to give you all some time. Good luck out there, man," Lincoln says to Tanner, and the four Nash brothers head out to the courtyard with the fountains where the ceremony is set to begin in about twenty minutes.

Mom walks over and grabs Tanner into a tight embrace. "I'm so proud of you, my boy. It feels like just yesterday I was holding you for those twelve minutes before your brother came along, and I remember thinking that no woman would ever be good enough for my sweet boys. But then Cassie came along, and I saw how she healed the things in you that were broken right from the start. You always deserved the very best, and I think you found her with that woman."

I feel emotional with her words, and those words weren't even directed toward me.

Of the two of us, I've always been the more emotional twin. Tanner always lived by the theory that emotions just get in the way—until he met Cassie, anyway. As for me, I always found emotions to be the very things that direct our lives. They help us survive, they motivate us, and they connect us. Without them, we'd be reduced to robots.

It's easy to say that now since I'm happy where I'm at with Sophie. But for a long time, they were a nuisance that did nothing but cause me pain and distress.

Still, I channeled that into motivation, and look where I am now.

Okay…fine. It's not the *best* place to be considering she still doesn't know about how deeply my feelings for her actually run, but we'll get there. Someday. Definitely.

"Thanks, Mom," Tanner says softly.

Dad claps me on the back, and I'm glad we're back to where we always were. It was a long road getting here considering the fact that both Tanner and I felt lied to when we found out that our biological dad was Eddie Nash, not Charles Banks, but part of learning that life is short is also acknowledging the fact that sometimes people act in ways that protect the ones they love.

Like me not telling Sophie about how long I've been in love with her.

Our parents head out first, and then it's just Tanner and me—much like it has been our whole lives despite always having people surrounding us, rooting for us, and wishing the best for us.

"You got this, bro," I say to him, and he nods.

"So do you, you know."

"Yeah, I know. I think I'll probably admit the truth on the cruise. Depends how drunk we get." I duck my head a little as if I'm joking. I'm not.

He chuckles, but it's meaningless small talk. We stare at each other for a beat, and then he says, "You know this doesn't change anything."

I nod. "I know. It's you and me. We're just adding someone into the mix. And some kids to keep you on your toes. They'll come first now, as they should, but I know you're there if I need you."

He presses his lips together. "Always." He holds out his hand so we can do our secret handshake, and I slap his hand with mine. We move back to slap hands backward, grab hands, shake, fist bump, and hug.

It's the last time we'll do this as two single men. A year and a half ago, I'm not sure either of us could possibly have seen that this is where we'd be today.

Tanner getting married to a woman seven years older than him with two kids. Our four new half-brothers present at the wedding. Sophie here as my date. The two of us living and playing in San Diego. Gaining and losing a biological father.

What a change a mere eighteen months has brought. It kind of makes me wonder what sorts of changes the next eighteen months will bring.

Or, you know…even the next eighteen days.

I escort Jess down the aisle just after Cassie's two kids, Luca and Lily, who are playing the parts of ring bearer and flower girl, and we take our places. I seek out Sophie in the crowd, and I grin at her when our eyes connect.

My brother walks down the aisle next, and then the music changes, and Cassie appears on the arm of her father.

Twenty-three minutes later, my brother is married. He kisses his new wife with the officiant's permission, and everyone laughs at the "Ew!" from Cassie's eight-year-old that forces the bride and groom to break apart.

"Introducing Mr. and Mrs. Tanner and Cassie Banks!"

It's official. They walk hand-in-hand back up the aisle, and Jess and I follow with Cassie's parents ushering the kids behind us toward the conservatory at the Bellagio, which I guess means something to Cassie and Tanner since they wanted the wedding photos done in there.

A million pictures later, we head for the reception, where we eat, drink, and dance the night away.

And the more we drink, the closer we dance. When the parents start to leave a little after ten, the close dancing turns into downright grinding, which eventually we take upstairs to do naked.

When morning dawns, my head is pounding, and we have to get up to get ready for brunch at ten at Lincoln's house.

I need to have a serious talk with whoever planned brunch the morning after the wedding. None of us should be forced to get up this early.

Okay, fine. Ten isn't that early. But I'm thirty now, and I can't party like I did when I was in my twenties. It's like something happened overnight that changed everything, and I'm sure I don't like it.

But waking up with Sophie by my side…now *that* I like.

Chapter 35: Sophie Summers

Something's About to Go Wrong

The wedding was beautiful. Life itself is beautiful. I have no complaints as I wake up to a bright and beautiful morning in Miller's arms.

Tanner is married, Miller and I are getting married, and my entire life has been flipped upside down. They say things always work out how they're supposed to, and it feels like this right here is how it was supposed to happen.

Which gives me that weird, ominous feeling like something's about to go wrong.

It can't be this great, can it? Someone's going to get sick, or something will cause problems for Miller and me, or the cruise ship will get swallowed up in a hurricane.

Okay, it's all worst-case scenarios, but I have to allow them to play out in my mind, or else they'll chew at me.

And once they play out in my mind, I need to voice them. Usually I voice it by writing it into a book, but this time I don't have that luxury since we need to get to brunch. So instead, I push it off the plate of my conscience and onto good ol' Miller's.

It's after I get out of the shower and he's standing at the sink next to me brushing his teeth while I'm applying some makeup that I say, "Hey, so you know how when things are going *too* well, you sort of just expect it to all come crashing down?"

He glances over at me in the mirror, and I can see the haze of sleepiness still surrounding him that tells me it's too early for this conversation.

"Huh?" he asks, his voice muffled by the toothpaste in his mouth.

I plow ahead anyway. "Like, oh, I don't know. Like something bad will happen on the cruise. Someone will get a tummy bug, and it'll pass through all thirty of us, or a hurricane will hit the boat. I don't know."

He spits and rinses his mouth before he glances up at me in the mirror. He wipes his mouth with a towel and tilts his head a little. "Babe, I don't think it's hurricane season."

I lift a shoulder. "Well, what if one just forms out of the blue? They can hit when it's not in season, can't they?"

"I think that's only ever happened, like, twice."

"What if the third is while we're on the boat?"

"Have you been on a cruise before?" he asks.

I shake my head, and he walks over and wraps his arms around me. "Listen, Sophie. There are tons of precautions in place these days. It's not like the days of the *Titanic* when they hit an iceberg. They can track that kind of stuff now, and they can reroute if they need to. Nothing bad will happen."

"What about the tummy bug thing? Or food poisoning? What if I get food poisoning and you have to share a bathroom with me and you're so grossed out by me that you don't even want to sleep in the same bed as me let alone have sex with me?" I ask, and I hear the ridiculousness of my own question, but I still feel that it bears asking anyway.

"Jesus, Sophie. I promise you, nothing will *ever* make me feel that way about you." His eyes drop to mine, and when I see the sincerity there, I feel a whole lot better.

I draw in a deep breath and let it out slowly, and he drops a quick kiss to my lips. "Now get ready, or we're going to be late to brunch, and everyone will eyeball us walking in late and assume it was because I was having my way with you."

"What if it was *me* having my way with you?" I shoot back, and he chuckles.

"Do you feel better?"

"I just get a little nervous before big trips. I know everything will be fine."

We pack up our stuff, check out of the hotel, and head to Lincoln and Jolene's place for brunch. Tanner and Cassie are opening their gifts when we walk in. Jess is keeping track of who got them what, and the kids are fighting over who gets to pick the next present. Jolene's baby, Joey, who's somewhere around six months old, is crawling all over the place while his big sister Josephine—who's three and a half—is playing mom to him as she babbles in toddler talk about where he can and can't crawl. It's a little bit of chaos, and it's actually sort of adorable.

But then Lily starts to cry because Luca picked the next gift out of turn, and Cassie decides it's time to eat rather than continue opening gifts as a way to distract the kids from their current fight with each other.

Whew. I am *so* not ready for that sort of life. I'll just take my books and Miller for the moment, thank you very much.

We're halfway through the meal when Miller leans over and whispers, "What if *I* am the one who gets the food poisoning and you're grossed out by me?"

I giggle. "Okay. I get it. I was being ridiculous."

He's not laughing. "I'm serious."

My eyes widen. "Oh, shit. I'm sorry. I didn't mean to offload my own worries onto you. I just needed to get them off my mind."

He twists his lips. "You're right though. Things are going well. Too well. Something's going to snap."

I wrinkle my nose a little nervously, and he taps it.

"Whatever it is, we'll be okay. Right?" I ask. Actually, it comes out as far more than an *ask*. It's more like a *beg*.

"We'll be just fine," he assures me, but there's something there in his eyes that tells me he's not so sure about that himself. Food poisoning and hurricanes aside, though, what *really* could go wrong? It's probably a question better left unasked—especially now that I've passed some of my anxiety onto Miller.

I let it go as we finish eating, and then the newlyweds finish opening their gifts. We spend the day at Lincoln and Jolene's house with the Nash clan, and Tanner and Cassie duck out early to do whatever it is newlyweds do while we stay with the rest of the family and start a poker tournament. We have to end it early since some of us have an evening flight down to Florida—Miller and I included—and we hitch a ride with Grayson and Ava over to the airport.

I haven't had the pleasure of spending much time with Ava, so I'm excited to get to know her better. All I know is that Grayson is hilarious, and Ava seems like his perfect match.

"So how did you two meet?" I ask on the way to the airport as I sit beside Ava in the backseat.

"He's my brother's best friend," she says.

"Oh, come on, babe," Grayson says from the front seat. "That's sort of leaving out the entire story, isn't it?"

"You tell it," she says petulantly, and he barks out a boisterous laugh.

"We hadn't seen each other in a decade when I was traded to the Vegas Aces. I went out to a bar to celebrate and ran into her. I didn't recognize her. We spent the night together, and I won't bore you with the details, but eventually we ended up married and running a bakery together."

"That's adorable," I say. "Who's manning the bakery while you're on vacation?"

"Oh, my best friend, Kelly. She works on and off for me, but our staff there is totally incredible. What about you two? How did you meet?" Ava asks.

"Miller and me? We go back to high school. We met in freshman English class, became best friends, and—"

"And only recently admitted how we really felt," Miller says.

Oh, okay. So that's how it is…keeping up with the ruse.

But where's the lie, really?

I guess it's in the fact that we haven't *exactly* admitted our feelings for one another, and maybe it's because I'm not even really sure where we stand. I know one thing for certain, though.

I can't get enough of Miller Banks.

I just don't know exactly how he feels about me, but we'll be in tight quarters together for the next week. I can't think of a better time for the truth to come out.

The only problem is that there are just a whole hell of a lot more truths that emerge over the next week than I ever thought possible.

Chapter 36: Miller Banks

This really is the goddamn life.

I'm sitting on the balcony of our room as I stare out over the ocean. We just boarded and found our stateroom, a suite that's luxurious for two, and for the record, the bathroom is big enough and far enough away from the bed that even if one of us does get food poisoning, the healthy person won't have to listen to every detail of the sick person's bathroom shenanigans.

Sophie wanted a piña colada, citing it as her official *cruise drink*, so I got one for myself as well. The straws aren't paper like we've become accustomed to in California, but instead happen to be made of some sort of edible substance. I take a bite, and I take a sip, the sunshine warm on my face as I sit back and relax.

In two weeks, all hell will break loose as training camp kicks off a new season, but right now, that's the last thing on my mind.

At the forefront is definitely sex with Sophie, and somewhere just behind that is figuring out where to order my next drink from.

We thought about exploring the ship, but we have an entire week to make that happen. Right now, my only interest is sitting on this balcony with my girl and our piña coladas.

Everyone else in the family is boarding, too. It's too big a group for us to have planned boarding the ship together, but we have a standing dinner reservation for thirty-two, and I assume we'll have an entire section of the restaurant where we can meet and sit with various groups within our party. I called the guest service desk and asked if they could do something to spoil the newlyweds, too, and it sounds like Tanner and Cassie ended up with a pretty kickass suite.

Not that we have anything to complain about. We're up toward the top of the boat, and the views are incredible from up here. Endless ocean in front of us, and I hear my girl let out a soft sigh as she slips into the chair beside me.

"This is amazing," she says, and she leans her head back as she sucks down some of her piña colada.

"A whole week of this? It's paradise."

"A whole week with Miller Banks? Definitely paradise."

My lips lift into a smile. "Now that's something I thought I'd never hear."

"Should we test out the bed?"

I laugh. "Fuck yes, we should." We abandon our piña coladas, and it sounds like whoever is next to us is breaking in their own bed, too.

As we find out about an hour later when we exit our suite to start exploring, it's Grayson and Ava, who are exiting their suite at the same time.

They tell us Grace and Spencer are on our floor, too. Tanner and Cassie have the presidential suite two floors up from us, Lincoln and Jolene have a family suite with their three kids near the kids' club a few decks below us, and parents are scattered everywhere on the ship—including mine, Sophie's, Cassie's, and most of the clan of Nashes and Nash-in-laws.

At least Sophie's parents didn't end up in Grayson's room. That would've been awkward.

We're up on the top deck playing a game of mini golf with our stateroom neighbors when the ship's horn blasts a few feet away from us. Sophie jumps at the sound, and I can't help but laugh...until it blows again, and this time I'm the one who jumps.

I guess that's the signal that the ship is about to start sailing, so we head over with everyone else toward the railing to watch as we start to move away from the dock.

My arm is around Sophie, who's leaning into my side, and I breathe in the slightly humid, warm, sea-salty air as I memorize everything about this moment. The scent of her summer garden shampoo wraps around me, mixing with the sea air as the wind starts to lightly kiss our faces.

I lean down and press a soft kiss to her temple, and she glances up at me with a smile playing at her lips. I can't see her eyes hidden behind her sunglasses, but I can still read her like a book. I lean down and find her lips with mine. It's just a quick, tender kiss, but it's the kind of kiss that tells me she's as content as I feel.

Maybe this really will work out for us.

A moment later, Grayson is recognized, and then me. Word is already out that the Nash and Banks families are on board, and it's fine. Let's get this over with because once people have their pictures, they'll leave us alone. I guess that's the advantage of being on a cruise ship—eventually everyone will get a turn since there's a limit to the number of people on board.

I take a few photos and do my best to be polite. I know I work in an interesting profession, and people are either fans or they're not.

Everyone here seems to be cordial, which is really all I could ask for.

The four of us head to the bar, where we grab another round of drinks, and we explore the various pools the ship offers before we head back to our staterooms to get ready for dinner. Sophie changes into a flowery dress that's perfect cruise attire, and I throw on a pair of khaki shorts and a white shirt with sailboats on it—crazy for me, but downright demure compared to Asher's tropical shirt with neon flamingos plastered all over it.

Our group of thirty-two is divided into three tables of ten with a few high chairs, and tonight we're sitting with Tanner and Cassie, Cassie's parents, Sophie's parents, and our parents— after we take some more photos with strangers who seem to know us, of course.

We're all quiet as we peruse our dinner options, and once we order, Tanner carries the conversation as we all chat about how wonderful their wedding was. Sophie's parents weren't in attendance, so they're filled in on all the details as Mom shows off photos from her phone. I glance at Sophie's dad, and I can't help but notice how quiet he is. It's not a conversation he has much to contribute to, I guess.

My dad is sitting to my left, and he nudges me a little. "So you two are next, huh?"

I press my lips together and nod. "February twentieth at the Venetian in Vegas."

Sophie's mom glances up, and she looks surprised. "You set a date?"

Sophie clears her throat. "Oh, uh. Didn't I tell you?"

Her mom purses her lips and shakes her head, the look of disapproval evident in her eyes.

I know that look, and I know it's exactly why Sophie doesn't want to tell her the truth. She quit her stable job teaching to pursue a career in publishing. Her mother would never understand.

Sophie drops a small smile that doesn't reach her eyes. "I'm sorry. We chose February twentieth. I hope you can all make it."

The drinks are served along with a couple baskets of dinner rolls, thankfully diverting both the conversation and the attention.

But now Sophie is quiet, too, and I can't help but wonder whether her mom shut her dad down like she just did to her daughter.

It's only the first night, but I already feel a little stuck on this boat with so many family members. Maybe this wasn't such a good idea.

And maybe that's because of the ominous feeling Sophie passed onto me. Maybe it's not paradise after all.

Chapter 37: Sophie Summers

I don't know why I didn't tell my mom we picked a date. Maybe because I wasn't sure whether we were really doing it, so I didn't want to get her hopes up when it might not actually happen—regardless of the fact that I *want* it to happen.

And I'm still sort of feeling shut down by all that when Cassie turns to look at me, and I realize about two seconds too late that I never told her that my parents don't know about my books.

"So what's next for our famous friend?" Cassie asks me.

My eyes widen, but I glance at Miller to try to play it off. "Oh, training camp, I suppose," I say, my voice an octave higher than is natural.

"I mean you, silly," she says, not getting my hint.

"Famous friend?" my mom repeats, and *fuck*, of course she heard.

"Her books," Cassie says, smiling at my mom. "I read *Married to the Enemy*, and I *loved* it. Please tell me there's more of the Hendrix clan coming our way soon."

I'm frozen to the spot as I try to come up with something to say, but I'm at a total loss. I don't know how to get out of this one.

"Her books?" my mom says.

Cassie finally seems to put it together, and she slaps a hand over her mouth as her eyes widen. "Oh my God," she murmurs. "Do they not know?"

I close my eyes as I slowly shake my head.

"I'm so, so sorry. I had no idea. I just—"

"It's okay," I interrupt. I glance over at my parents, who look…confused.

Well, my dad does. His brow is a little furrowed, and his head is tilted. My mom, who always looks a little judgmental, on the other hand, has her lips puckered up so tightly it looks like she just sucked a lemon.

"What's going on?" she manages through those puckered lips.

I clear my throat. "Mom, Dad, it's time I tell you the truth. I'm thirty years old now, which means I've been an adult for a long time. You've always been so conservative that I've felt the need to keep some things from you."

Okay, so I'm not being *fully* honest even with those words. The truth is…I don't want my parents reading my books. They've always been supportive, and I'd know they want to read them. But knowing they're reading my words might make me write them differently, and that was never a risk I was willing to take.

Silence envelops our table as all eyes are on me.

I keep my eyes down on my dinner roll as I finally admit the truth. "For the last four years, I've been secretly publishing romance books under a pen name."

My mom gasps, and I peek up at her. She's back to sucking that lemon, but my dad's eyes are sort of lit up.

They are completely opposite reactions.

"You…you—" my mom begins, but my dad interrupts.

"Sophie June, that's incredible. I'm sorry you felt like you had to keep it from us," my dad says.

"You're writing pornography under our noses?" my mom demands, her voice a hushed whisper.

I blow out a breath. "This is why I didn't tell you. I knew this would be your reaction. No, it's not pornography, Mother. I write stories that explore complex themes about people finding love even in unlikely situations." I lift a shoulder, hating that I need to defend what I do to *anyone*, most of all to my parents. Or my mom, anyway. "It allows readers to find a connection to someone who might be like them. It helps people see that there can still be happily ever afters even after the darkness, and don't you think this world could use more happily ever afters?"

My mom opens her mouth to shoot back with something most likely nasty, but my dad stops her. "Judy, enough." He turns to look at me. "I'm proud of you, sweetheart. You're really going for it, reaching for those dreams, and that's all I ever wanted for you."

"Is this why you left your job?" my mom asks, clearly not on board with things the way my dad is.

I shake my head. "No. I left my job because my ex posted about my books on my student message board as me, and there was going to be a huge investigation that would've only publicized my pen name. So I quit before that became public consumption." I glance at Miller. "Miller swooped in and saved the day. He showed up for me, and he took care of everything."

His arm is already draped on the back of my chair, and he moves it a little to wrap his hand around my shoulder in solidarity.

"And before you ask, that is why I'm marrying him. Because he does that. He shows up for me. He takes care of me. He saves the day every day, and he supports me. He encourages me. He believes in me." I glance over at him, and I hope he can see how much I adore him from those words.

"Supports you how? Financially?" My mother snorts.

Miller jumps in to tackle that one. "We're a couple that's planning to get married next year, Mrs. Summers. I will support her in every possible way I can."

My dad looks beside himself with happiness for me, but my mom just isn't having it. She's sputtering and pursing her lips, and then she says, "So you quit your job to write porn and live with yet another man you're not married to. Did we teach you nothing?"

I clench my jaw before I say something I'll regret, and Miller jumps in to…well, to save the day, as he does.

"Mrs. Summers, I would really appreciate it if we could continue this conversation privately later. Let's celebrate the bride and groom, shall we?"

He turns toward Tanner and opens his mouth to ask a question, but my dad interrupts him before he can get it out.

"Since we're dropping truth bombs here tonight, I have one."

Everyone at the table turns their attention to my dad. I have no idea what he's about to say.

My mother is glaring at him, though, so whatever he's about to say, he's saying it without her express written consent.

She tries to stop him. "John, do you really think this is the time?"

He shrugs, and truthfully, as I study him for a few seconds…he looks more relaxed than I've ever seen him. Maybe it's the cruise.

Or maybe it's his truth bomb.

"After thirty-six years of marriage, Judy and I have decided to get a divorce."

I hear a variety of gasps all over the table, and I feel eyes on me as everyone awaits my reaction.

I'm not sure *how* to react, exactly.

I'm a grown woman. It's not like I'm a kid who is going to have to split time between Mom and Dad.

Is it weird? Yes. But they're both here on this cruise—sharing a stateroom, no less, which means cramped quarters together—so they must be on decent terms despite the news.

Before I say anything, my dad adds, "I figured the news would come out some time on the trip, so why not just get it over with the first night so we don't have to pretend?"

I'm not sure if he's saying that to me or to my mom, but suddenly heat rolls over my body from the top of my head down to the tips of my toes, and I have the strongest urge to get the hell out of here.

I take a sip of water to try to calm whatever that feeling is, but it doesn't help.

"I'll be right back," I mutter, and I stand, toss my napkin on my chair, and bolt out of the room.

Tears pinch behind my eyes. First my mom's disapproval, then my dad's announcement—and all when we're supposed to be here celebrating Tanner and Cassie with the Nash family.

Why did we invite my parents along on this cruise?

Oh, right. It was supposed to be a fun family vacation. Chris and Marie couldn't make it work, but it would sure be nice to have my older brother here so we could talk about the news. I wonder if he knows.

I feel like I should be upset. Like I should be crying.

Instead, I just feel…panicky. Thirty-six years, and they couldn't make it work. They stopped fighting to make it work.

Will the same thing happen to me and my own future husband? Will it be Miller, or will we both jump ship before February?

Will I lose his friendship? Will I lose *him*…forever?

I wish I could skip ahead to the end to see how things pan out, but I can't. Instead, I'm stuck on a boat with my parents, who are divorcing, my fake fiancé, and my fiancé's entire extended family.

In fact…I don't think it's panic at all. I think it just might be claustrophobia.

But then a hand slips onto my shoulder, and it's like things are immediately better. I know who it is without even turning around. It's the clean, familiar scent, the warmth, the love that radiates from something as simple as a hand on my shoulder.

This is what I meant by support. He's here for me even when I don't know how to ask him to be.

I turn around.

"Hey. You okay?"

"This boat suddenly doesn't feel big enough," I admit. I turn into him and rest my forehead on his chest, and he clutches me with his arms tightly around me.

"Do you want to go to dinner somewhere else?" His voice is quiet and soothing.

"Can we, like, just have a parent table and a kid table?"

He chuckles. "Maybe tomorrow night."

I blow out a breath and don't move my forehead from his chest. "How weird is it that they're getting divorced?"

"Any weirder than finding out my dad isn't my biological dad?"

I can't help a laugh at that. I pull back, and I wrap my arms around his waist as I look up and catch his eyes. "Same sort of lane, I think."

"Yeah," he murmurs. "Parents are people, too. They're human, and I guess that's what I've learned over the last year and a half. Take it for what it's worth."

"Thanks, Millby."

"Anytime, Summers. You know that."

"I do." I tip my chin up and press my lips to his.

"Do you need to talk about it?"

I twist my lips and shrug. "I don't know. I need to process, I guess."

"Then let's process, let's eat, and let's go for a walk tonight and talk. Sound okay?"

I press my lips together and nod. "Sounds good."

When we return to the table, the food has arrived. Everyone is quiet as they dig in, and I'm debating whether they're quiet because of the situation or because the food is here.

I've lost most of my appetite, but I force myself to eat some of the salmon. It's delicious, and I guess what I've heard about the food on these cruises is true—it's top-tier.

When our server comes by, I think about ordering a piña colada, but instead I settle on a dark and stormy—stronger to dull the nerves faster.

It feels like a lifetime passes before dessert arrives, and my mother excuses herself early. I don't know where she goes, and frankly, I'm not sure I care right at this moment in time.

Everyone is involved in their own little side conversations over dessert. My dad is to my right, and I lean over toward him as he digs into his key lime pie. "So when is all this happening?"

He clears his throat. "It's in progress. We've filed all the paperwork, and it should be finalized in the next month or so."

"What made you decide to give it all up?"

He tilts his head, and I swear I see a little sympathy in his eyes. "Truthfully? It was you, sweetheart."

My brows push together. "Me?"

He nods. "You up and moved to San Diego in the middle of the school year to be with the person you love, and it just felt so…" He trails off, and I wait for him to fill in the word. "Brave. And now we find out you're giving your dreams a shot, doing this writing thing you felt like you had to keep from us. I'm sorry you felt that way."

"You know how Mom is," I mutter, and I don't want this to turn into a me and him against her thing, but part of me feels like that's just the way it's always been.

And a bigger part of me is starting to realize that's the reason that likely fueled this whole thing between them.

"I do," he confirms, and then he goes a step further to confirm the rest of my hunch. "And I got to a point where it just felt like we were too different to stay on the path we were going down. We grew apart, and it's as simple and as difficult as that. As you get older, you get more and more set in your ways, and rather than growing in the same direction…well, we didn't."

We're both quiet as we take a bite of our pie, and then he adds, "Every marriage is a little different. Some can go the distance, and others can't. So I don't want you to think you're doomed to failure."

I nod, and I glance over at Miller as I think about how well my dad knows me.

I wonder what my dad would think about knowing the entire reason we're even engaged was due to an elaborate lie to Mom.

I'm about to admit the truth when he says, "But it's you and Miller. You have a strong foundation of friendship. You'll figure things out."

I hope he's right, but since I'm not even sure if we're actually going to go through with this, I guess there's no way of knowing.

But I do think that's something we need to talk about— maybe tonight on our walk.

Chapter 38: Miller Banks

After dinner, we head to the promenade to walk the loop that circles the outer edge of the entire ship. Her hand is clutching mine. The air is cooler at night without the hot daytime sun beating down on us, but it feels balmy and comfortable.

"How are you feeling about everything?" I ask.

She sighs. "I feel like I should have stronger feelings than I do. You know? Like I should be upset and crying, but it sort of just feels like it is what it is."

"I get that. Did you know Missy Nash and Eddie got divorced after forty years of marriage?"

"I guess I'd heard that. Doesn't it kind of make you feel like we're all destined to fail?" she asks.

I squeeze her hand. "Nah. If anything, I think it makes me feel like it's never too late to start over."

"But Missy's here by herself. Is that starting over?"

I lift a shoulder. "Who knows what she's up to. Maybe she and your dad will find their way to each other."

She lets out a little cackle. "Oh my God. Could you imagine?"

I chuckle. "Whatever happens, don't you think your parents are better off apart if they're unhappy?"

"I think maybe that's why I don't feel all that upset over it. I haven't been close with my parents in a long, long time. Probably since high school, and then I moved out during college and never looked back. But maybe I won't feel this pressure to be the perfect girl anymore now that they know the truth."

"You're pretty damn perfect to me, Summers." I let go of her hand and slip an arm around her shoulder.

She leans her head on my shoulder as we continue walking. "You're pretty damn perfect, too, Banks."

We make our way past one of the pools, and I spot a row of vacant cabanas in the back row that are hidden beneath the shadows. It's sort of a daybed with a wicker frame and a retractable canopy with a shade on it that's meant to block the sun. A big cushion that's almost like a mattress is calling us to lie down, and the pillows across the back look like a great place to lean back as we chat about anything and everything.

I walk over toward one, and we both sit and scoot back, putting our feet up as we lean back into the pillows.

"This is nice," she says. "It feels like we can't get any privacy with both our families on this boat unless we're in our stateroom."

"Watch this," I say, and I flip the retractable shade screen on top of the cabana. At night, it becomes the perfect place for privacy.

She giggles, and we settle back in.

"I have a question," she says.

"Go for it."

"We haven't really talked about this, and I feel kind of weird even asking, but…" She trails off, and a pulse of nervousness darts down my spine.

"But?" I prompt.

"But when February gets here, are you, uh, planning to actually walk down the aisle?"

It's everything I've wanted since I was fourteen, Sophie.

I blow out a breath without saying those words even though they're on the tip of my tongue.

And then maybe because of the salty sea air, or maybe because of the piña coladas and the rum drink…or maybe because something unlocked in her tonight when she found out about her parents' divorce, she says, "Because I am."

A sort of grunt escapes me at her admission, and I'm left without words for a moment.

"And not because we just told my parents about it or whatever. Because I want to."

She turns a little on the cabana cushion, and then it's like she makes a snap decision. She moves over me, straddling my lap, and she drops her lips to mine for just a few sweet seconds before she pulls back. She takes my face between her palms, and I can hardly see her in here with the shade screen in place.

Maybe that's what's fueling her confession—the darkness.

"Because the last few months have been the greatest of my life, and I realized that you're everything I've ever been looking for, Miller. You're the ultimate book boyfriend. You're always there for me. You care about me. You make me laugh. And I want to marry you because I've fallen in love with you."

Holy shit.

Am I fucking dreaming right now?

Did she just say—

I let the words fall unfiltered from my lips. "I love you, too, Soph."

Her mouth moves back to mine as we seal that pledge with a kiss. I didn't get the chance to tell her that fuck yes, I want to marry her. I didn't get to answer her question. I can do it later, though. Right now, passion has taken over, and as her hips start to rock against mine, I know we're both too far gone to even consider making it back to our stateroom.

We have all the privacy we need right here—and all the supplies, too, since I slipped a condom into my pocket before we left the room.

She reaches for my belt. She unbuckles it, and she pulls my cock out. She pumps her fist up and down my shaft a few times, and I hiss as I give into the feel of her hands on me.

I lift my hips to grab the condom out of my back pocket, and I tear it open and slide it on.

And then before I know what she's doing, she's lifting her dress up to her hips, yanking her panties to the side, and sliding down on top of me.

Holy fuck.

It's heaven as I enter her from underneath, and her pussy grips greedily onto my cock.

She arches back as she continues to rock on top of me, and there's no way I'm going to last. This woman just told me she wants to spend her life with me because she's in love with me. If I thought sex with her was good before, it had nothing on this moment. It's pure trust and adoration moving around us as we give into the very things I've pined for.

I just wish we could do this with nothing between us. No barrier, just skin to skin, me inside her as we move together in this rhythm that's ours and ours alone.

"Oh God, Miller," she whispers—or she tries to whisper—but it comes out as kind of a moan. I know we should be quiet. We're going to get caught if we're not, but sex with her is such a moving experience that grunts and growls I cannot seem to control emit from me. I'm drawing closer and closer to the finish line, and I reach under her and hold onto her ass as I control our movements from underneath her.

I'm sort of sitting up, and she drops her head to my shoulder. I feel her bite me there over my shirt just before she leans in and whispers close to my ear, "I'm coming."

I feel her pussy as it squeezes my cock, the feeling sending me into my own climax. I pump up into her as her body continues to contract around me, and I let go, too, with a loud moan that anyone on the outside of the cabana could surely hear.

It was deserted when we walked up here. I'm not sure it still is. I'm not sure I care, either.

I pump into her a few more times as I ride out the wave of my release, and once the condom is full and my body is sated, I let go of her ass and wrap my arms around her. She collapses down onto my chest, both of us fully relaxed. I'm still inside her, and even though we both just came and the warm glow of satisfaction is rolling over each of us, I'm not sure I ever want to move.

We have to, eventually, of course. And when we do, I'm reminded of her words.

You know how when things are going too well, you sort of just expect it to all come crashing down?

I hope it doesn't.

Chapter 39: Sophie Summers

I Can Totally Keep a Secret

Our first stop is Cozumel, and we get off the ship to check out the port. There's plenty of shopping, bars, and more shopping. It was a tough decision not to book an excursion since there are so many available, but ultimately we wanted a day to just bum around the port and get back to the ship for a little private stateroom time.

We weren't able to secure our romantic cabana during the daytime, but I have plans to check it out again tonight.

Maybe every night.

Since we found out my parents are getting divorced on the first night of the cruise, I can only imagine what secrets will be revealed on night two.

As we arrive at dinner, I see that tonight, there's a *parents* table, for which I'm grateful. Seated at it are my parents, Miller's parents, Cassie's parents, Grace's dad and grandmother, Desi's parents, and Missy Nash. The next table is Lincoln, Jolene, their kids, and her parents, along with Luca and Lily, who have become fast friends with Lincoln and Jolene's kids.

So that leaves our table—the three younger Nash brothers, their wives, and the two Banks brothers and their significant others, along with Asher's son.

The parents place their orders first, and I spot the servers as they bring over the drinks. It seems like all of the parents ordered wine, and their table is already getting loud with laughter. My mom is sitting next to Miller's mom, and my dad is on the other side of Miller's dad—which makes sense since we've known their family for years, and it's probably better to split my parents up given their impending divorce.

On my dad's other side is Missy Nash, and she's next to Grace's dad. Missy is telling some story about her four children, and everyone at the table is in stitches.

Sort of like our table. Grayson is leading the conversation, and everyone is laughing. This is a much more relaxed atmosphere than last night when I had to sit at the table and listen to my parents talk about their divorce after Cassie blew my little secret on night one.

These were not things I was expecting to deal with on this cruise, but I guess if you get enough family members together in the same room, secrets are bound to come out.

I'm next to Cassie again. "I'm so, so sorry about last night," she says to me once Grayson finishes his story. Miller turns to Asher on his other side, and Cassie and I talk while he chats with his half-brother. "I had no idea your parents didn't know."

"It's fine. It's better that it's out in the open. Really." I reach for my water since tonight's dark and stormy isn't here yet.

"I'm usually really good at keeping secrets. In fact, I can *totally* keep a secret, so please don't hold it against me."

"Promise," I say, holding up a pinky. She links hers through mine, and I love that we've become real friends over the last couple of months. If Miller and I are truly going to get married as we said we were last night, then Cassie is going to be like a sister to me.

And that's something I'm really, really excited about.

Our drinks arrive, and I glance around the table. The men all ordered different beers, and the women are all drinking daiquiris—except me with my rum and ginger beer concoction and Cassie with her margarita.

We're through the first round before our food arrives.

"I'm starving," Cassie says to me. "Tanner made me go snorkeling today when I just wanted a day at the beach, and we didn't eat lunch. Now I'm half-drunk since that was the strongest margarita I've had in a while."

I giggle. "We just hung around the port…and then our stateroom." I wiggle my eyebrows, and Cassie laughs.

"I'm so happy for you two. Tanner told me how Miller's been in love with you forever, so to see you two finally together is just so amazing."

Wait…what?

What the hell did she just say?

"What?" I ask.

"How Miller's always been in love with you," she repeats.

Miller's head swings over in Cassie's direction, and I catch the look of horror he gives Cassie, who's totally oblivious to it.

"Always?" I repeat.

"Yeah, since, like high school or whatever."

I clear my throat as this feeling of being totally blindsided overwhelms me. I'm looking at Miller when I say, "He's been in love with me since *high school?*"

Is Cassie drunk?

Well, yes. A little. She just admitted to that.

Have I really been that blind?

If he's really been in love with me that long, why did he wait until last night after I said it first to tell me he loves me?

Did we just waste half our lives searching for the *wrong* thing when the *right* thing was within reach the entire time?

"Yes," she says, and her eyes finally move over to Miller. She slaps a hand over her mouth. Her eyes are wide as her hand slides down. "Wait. You didn't know that."

"Does this look like the face of someone who knew?" I ask.

She shakes her head as she looks up at the ceiling. "Dear Lord, this is really making me look like a terrible secret-keeper."

I turn toward Miller. "Is this true?"

I watch as he thinks quickly. He swallows, his throat bobbing up and down for a second, and he presses his lips together. And then he turns toward me, and he nods. "Yes. It's true. I think I fell in love with you the second I met you."

My chest tightens as I think back over the years we've known each other, all the way back to when we first met.

I thought he was cute, but I was fourteen. I thought everyone was cute. And when he slid so easily into the role of my best friend, he just sort of stayed there.

He cheered me on when I started dating Bryce McDaniels, but at the same time, he was noticeably absent from many of the events Bryce and I attended together for nearly two years.

When Bryce and I broke up, he was right there for me, but he was dating Mandy. They broke up, and I was with Liam. We broke up, and he was with Jamie. They broke up, and we headed off to college.

Our timing just never seemed to work out.

We always said *I love you* to each other, but I always thought we meant as friends.

I didn't realize he was saying it from a totally different place. And the more I think about the love I feel for him, the more I realize how totally unmatched it is in every aspect and every relationship of my life.

I would do anything for him, and I know he would do anything for me.

And suddenly, just like that, my heart seems to swell for him as I think about how very much I want this love to last a lifetime.

And with Miller, it feels possible. *Anything* feels possible when I'm with him because he's the kind of guy who *makes* anything possible. Because he loves me.

I always just thought he was a really, really good friend. I didn't realize his acts of service were because he was in love with me.

How stupid I've been. How much time we've wasted.

How very, very much I love this man beside me, and how lucky I am that he loves me too.

All this darts through my head in the space of a second, and I finally draw in a breath and lean toward him. I press my lips to his, and then I whisper, "I love you, too."

And after dinner, we rush right over to our private cabana to celebrate that love.

Chapter 40: Miller Banks

We Almost Got Caught

Our third day on this ship is a day at sea, and it's strange how one person's slip of the tongue could result in me feeling completely and totally free today.

I'm no longer harboring some secret from the one person who means the most to me, and at the same time, the one person who I don't want to find out.

But she knows, and the feelings I associate with that are elation and freedom and so, so much love.

Cassie, however, *cannot* keep a secret, and it would probably do me some good to remember that since my new sister-in-law and my future wife are apparently best friends who share pinky promises now.

Every other day on this trip is a day at sea, and what's great about those is the fact that we can spend the entire day naked in our stateroom. We leave for meals, and we hang out in the pool with Grayson and Ava a while. Tanner and Cassie are probably busy bumping uglies, and I have no idea where anybody else is, but it seems like everyone is having a great time. All in all, this cruise was a great plan despite the secrets that have been revealed so far.

We're getting ready for dinner when Sophie asks, "Is tonight the night Tanner and Cassie are having their own romantic dinner for two?"

"Yeah," I say. I'm lying on the bed in my boxers. It'll take me twelve-point-two seconds to get ready since all I have to do is throw on some clothes and run a hand through my hair, but my girl said she needed at least an hour.

She's currently doing something with her hair as she makes conversation.

"Good, then maybe no new secrets will be revealed tonight," she says with a giggle.

I laugh. "I never knew Cassie couldn't keep a secret."

"Get a little liquor in her, and she can't keep things to herself." She lifts a shoulder, and there's a twinkle in her eye. "But can I ask you a question?"

I nod. "Anything."

"If you've had feelings for me since high school, why didn't you ever say anything?"

I duck my head. "I guess we just got comfortable as friends, and I wasn't willing to risk that."

"I know you're quiet with your feelings, and that's okay. I'm glad I know now. And Miller?"

"Yeah?" I ask, raising my brows. My chest tightens as I wait for her words, but I should know by now that I don't have to worry when it comes to Sophie.

"This whole engagement has felt pretty damn real to me since pretty much the start."

Relief washes over me at her words, and I drop a kiss to the top of her head since she's sitting on a stool doing her makeup. "Same," I murmur.

As it turns out, there aren't any secrets revealed at dinner.

But Sophie and I do happen to catch onto a secret *after* dinner.

We head to our cabana, and I close our little privacy shade. We're kissing, and I'm about to slide my hand under her dress when we hear some voices outside the cabana.

"There's no one up here," a female voice says. It sounds familiar, and since seemingly half the guests on board this ship is related to me in one way or another, it very well could be someone I know. "Since we almost got caught last night, I don't think we should go back to my room."

Sophie pulls back from our kiss as we both freeze, neither of us wanting anyone to catch us out here when we're about to get naked and fuck in a cabana.

"Well, we can't go to mine," a male voice says. "We could just…*talk* in one of these cabanas here."

We hear a little rustling and some footsteps, and I think whoever is out there might be kissing, but it's hard to tell kissing noises from anything else in a closed cabana over the sound of the wind and general sailing noises.

I move as slowly and quietly as I can, and I peek out through a little gap on the side of the shade, where I spot a man and a woman in a passionate embrace.

The man's back is toward me, and he's blocking the woman as he pulls back. "We shouldn't do this out here," he says.

"I know," she says.

He turns to look around as if he hears someone approaching, and as he turns in my direction, I see who it is.

It's Grace's dad, Steve.

I force myself not to react despite the surprise weaving its way through me.

But when he moves out of the way to gesture toward the cabana he can sit in with his lady and I see who that lady is, I can't help the breath of surprise that heaves from my chest.

Holy shit.

I lean back in the cabana, my eyes wide, and Sophie tilts her head.

"What's wrong?"

"It was Steve Newman," I begin in a whisper as low as I can manage.

"Grace's dad?" she asks, her whisper as soft as mine.

I nod.

Sophie's eyes get wide with excitement that she's in on the family gossip. "With who?" she asks. "Someone we know?"

I nod again.

"Who?" she repeats.

"Missy Nash."

She gasps. "Oh my God!" she nearly squeals.

I widen my eyes and nod toward the cabana beside ours, angling my head in that direction. "They're in there."

"Having sex?" she whispers.

I make a face. "I'm not sure I want to know. We should go and let them have their privacy."

"What if they're doing it in there?"

"Well, at least it isn't either of our parents in there."

She giggles softly. "Thank God for that. But it *is* Grace's dad with Spencer's mom, right? Like mother-in-law with father-in-law?"

I nod.

And that's when we hear it.

Distinctively and decidedly a feminine moan.

"Let's get the hell out of here," I whisper, and we quietly but quickly bolt the fuck out of there before Missy and Steve know that we're onto them.

We rush away from the cabanas and only slow to a walk once we're on the other side of the pool, where we both promptly burst out laughing.

And as we round a corner, both of us still laughing and really not paying attention, Sophie bumps right into someone who's rounding the corner from the other side.

"Oh! I'm so sorry!" she exclaims as she backs up and recognizes the person she just literally walked into.

It's Spencer.

Spencer Nash.

With his arm around his wife, Grace. You know…the woman whose dad is currently making her mother-in-law moan right this very moment in a cabana about a hundred yards away from where we stand.

"Uh…Spencer. Hi. Sorry. And oh, uh, hey, hi there, Grace," Sophie says, and I think it's some attempt at being casual after we just discovered what we just discovered, but it's a complete and total fail.

Spencer narrows his eyes at us. "What are you two up to?"

"We were, uh, just…" Sophie looks wildly at me as she clearly needs some saving, and let's be honest. Saving Sophie is what I do best.

"Taking a walk. What are you two up to?"

"We were going to take a walk, too," Grace says, looking at us as if the two of us have lost our minds.

"Nice night for it. Want to walk with us? We were just heading this way," Sophie says, nodding away from the cabanas, and honestly, taking a walk with these two right after we caught their parents about to do it in a cabana seems like the worst possible idea at the moment, but she offered, and if they take us up on it, at least we can direct them away from the cabanas.

"You're welcome to join us," Spencer says. "We were going to sit in the lounge chairs by the pool and look up at the stars."

The lounge chairs by the pool are mere feet away from the cabanas, but if we go with them, at least we could direct them *away* from the cabanas.

Except if we're over there, they could see his mom and her dad emerging from a cabana together.

They said something about almost getting caught tonight. Well, they did get caught…and they don't even know it. But we'll do what we can to keep their secret safe until they're ready to share it.

We follow them as we walk right in front of the cabanas at one point, and I start talking loudly to clue in whoever might be in there that there are people nearby.

"So, Spencer, are you ready for training camp?" I practically yell to him even though he's just a few yards in front of me.

Sophie snickers beside me, and I shoot her a look.

"I'm ready. You?" he asks. These two are clueless about what's going on in the cabana to their right.

"Nope. Never am, but even worse this year now that it's Sophie I'll be leaving behind." My chest tightens as I really think about that. Sure, she'll be waiting at home for me, but things are about to change, and I'm not sure yet how this new phase of our relationship will react to that.

"Cassie and I will be close by to help her manage it," Grace says with a smile, and we're past the cabanas and on the backside now, so hopefully my loud voice was enough to clue Missy and Steve in on the fact that they were very nearly caught *again* tonight. "It's always a weird transition, but you have your own thing, and that'll really help those days and nights when he's away. It'll be new for Cassie, too, since Tanner missed all of last season."

"True," Sophie says, and she and Grace walk a little ahead of us as Spencer and I talk about our plans for the week between when we return from the cruise and when training camp is set to begin. He's already got plans to work out with the other wide receivers, and I assume our team trainer will put together a plan for the running backs, too. I just haven't taken much time to look into any of it since I've been wrapped up in Sophie.

But it's almost time to return to reality.

I'm pretty sure I'm not ready for it, but it's coming whether I'm ready or not.

I guess the same can be said about a lot of things in life, but at least training camp is expected to come for me whether I'm ready or not.

Chapter 41: Sophie Summers

We stayed out with Grace and Spencer later than we'd intended to, and Cassie booked excursions for the entire family at the final two ports of our trip. Today it's a park in Honduras with something for everyone, and we're all up and at 'em nice and early with a meeting time of seven in the morning.

It's far too early for vacation, but Miller and I force ourselves out of bed anyway since we don't want to be the ones to ruin it for everyone else.

I take a short nap on the forty-five-minute drive from the port to the excursion, and our adventure begins.

There's an area with "jump on your shoulder" monkeys that has most of the kids crying in fear, so they head to the pools where they spend the rest of the excursion. Miller and I walk a suspension bridge with Tanner and Cassie, and we take in the gorgeous views all around us. We have encounters with macaws and parrots as well as plenty of iguanas, and we're all sun-kissed and exhausted by the time we're back on the ship with just enough time to shower ahead of dinner time.

It feels like I've hardly had a moment alone with Miller, but I'm hopeful that'll come after dinner.

In our cabana.

I skip the dinner drinks since I'm already tired and rum will just put me to bed early, and I go for a lighter dinner so I'm not too full for the cabana shenanigans we've affectionately titled our *cabanigans*.

It's near the end of the meal, and I've just dug into a delicious lemon tart when Miller leans over and whispers, "I missed you today. Cabanigans?"

I raise my eyebrows. "Now?"

He nods slowly, and I giggle.

"Yep, definitely too full for this lemon tart," I announce, setting my fork down.

He glances at his empty plate, and he looks around the table. We're at the adult-kids table with all the brothers again, and this is my favorite group to sit with at dinner. We laugh through the whole meal, and Miller is more relaxed with his parents and mine at another table, which makes me feel more relaxed, too.

He slides his chair back and pushes to a stand, and he pulls my chair back, too, to help me up. He makes a big show of rubbing his stomach. "Stuffed after that amazing meal. We're just going to head to the promenade. See you all around," he says, and we take off before anyone asks any questions.

I'm already kissing his neck before he even gets the privacy shade down on our cabana, and I have no idea what the hell sort of magic is in this thing, but it's the exact right combination to make me horny as hell.

I slide down into the pillows the second he has the shade tied into place. He moves over the top of me and bucks his hips against mine as his lips drop to my neck.

"God, I missed you today," he says. He kisses me.

"We were together all day," I remind him between kisses.

"Not like this," he says, and his tongue starts to batter mine as his hips rock wildly against me.

We didn't get a chance to have sex last night here in this cabana since we were interrupted, and then we were out late with an early wake-up call.

We haven't *been together* since I found out that he's been in love with me since high school.

And there's something different between us. It's a new intimacy, a new understanding that wasn't there before. We're closer and more connected than we've ever been, and it's downright sexy.

He backs up and pulls the top of my dress down so my breasts are exposed, and he dives face-first into them, sucking my nipples into his mouth as my hips seek out his for some friction and the ache between my legs grows unbearable.

He teases my nipple with his tongue, and then he licks his way up my neck until his mouth is back on mine.

He kisses me as he uses his thumb to continue the intense pleasure he's giving my tits, and then he lets go of me there to let his hand trail down to the hem of my dress. He reaches beneath it and seeks out the edge of my panties only to find that I went without them tonight. Again. For him. To give him easier access. I knew that this moment was coming and that eventually I would be, too.

He growls softly into my ear as he slips a finger inside me, and it takes everything in me not to cry out with the intense feel of his finger when it's all I've needed all day.

"Fuck me, Miller," I whisper.

Maybe it's the illicit nature of being in this cabana rather than in the privacy of our stateroom, but there's something so hot about being in here with him where really anybody walking by could catch us.

They won't. Nobody would actually open a closed cabana. But they could, and I think it might be the thought of that exhibitionism that's so hot to me.

He pulls a condom out of his pocket and fumbles with his pants as he mutters. "Always prepared."

"Just like a boy scout," I murmur with a little chuckle.

"There's nothing boyish about what I'm going to do to you."

"Oh, trust me, I know. Now give it to me like the man you are," I beg, and he laughs this wild, maniacal laugh as he pushes into me.

I've never been in a relationship where sex could be as *fun* as it could be *serious*. It was always so serious. But Miller somehow makes everything fun, too, and I think that's part of what's so addictive about being with him in this way.

He's driving into me in this cabana, and it's all I can do to lie back and take it quietly in case anyone is walking by outside.

And just as I have that thought, we both hear voices.

"Quick, before someone sees," a female voice says, and I'm almost positive it's Missy.

Miller stills inside me, and we both freeze so we're not caught.

Honestly, I was too caught up in the moment to think that maybe another couple would bolt from the dinner table as quickly as we did.

We're quiet as we listen to the sounds beside us, and it just feels…*wrong* having sex somewhere where two older people so close in relation to us are doing who knows what in there.

It would be one thing for one of Miller's half-brothers to catch us. Parents? That's another story.

"Let's go to our room," I whisper, and he slips out of me as he nods.

The ache between my legs is downright unbearable as he pushed me so damn close to release, and Miller must be suffering, too, as he zips himself back into his pants.

I cross my fingers that we don't run into anybody we know as we quietly but quickly exit our cabana and start the long, long walk back to our stateroom.

The coast is not clear.

We have to walk right past the casino that Lincoln, Jolene, Asher, and Desi are all standing out in front of with drinks in their hands and no children with them.

"Kid-free date night!" Jolene tells us as we walk by them. "Want to join us? We're going to play blackjack and get drunk!"

Miller laughs as he says, "Kid free and you're going to the casino with your brother instead of taking your wife up to your stateroom for some privacy? Good score, man." He punches Asher lightly in the shoulder and elbows Lincoln, and I don't know how the hell he can be so casual as he teases his brothers with a condom-encased, very hard cock that's likely also pretty wet since he was just inside me and I was wetter than a water slide in peak season.

But here we are.

His brothers laugh at the ribbing, and they're still waiting for us to answer if we want to join them.

"We have plans," Miller says to Jolene. "But thanks for the invitation."

Jolene nods with a knowing smile, and we barely get a goodbye out over our shoulders as we continue making our way toward our stateroom.

It feels like it takes fifty years to get there, and maybe it's because he stops halfway down our hall, pushes me up against the wall, and plants his lips on mine. It's a steamy, passionate kiss—the kind that just couldn't wait until we got back to our room. His hips buck to mine, and I let out a little moan, which seems to be the signal that we need to get moving.

He grabs my hand and practically runs down the hallway toward our room.

I walk in first, and he's right on my heels as I peel off my dress while I beeline for the bed. I lay down on it as he fumbles with getting his cock back out from his pants. He drops those to the floor, and his shirt is somehow already off. He's on top of me a second later, shoving his way back inside me, both of us naked now as we finally get the chance to alleviate the powerful ache we both feel that only the other can alleviate.

He slams into me, both of us grunting at the feel of picking up right where we left off. He's still hard. He's still wearing a condom. I'm still wet. And my body is begging for release.

I cry out—something I couldn't do in the cabana—as we find our rhythm together. The rhythm is slow and intense as he drives into me with a force that's stronger than before. Every thrust against me feels harder than the one before, and it's sending me into another level.

After all these months, my body is used to his size, but when he slams into me the way he is, it feels like he's reaching a new place inside me. It's hard and intense, a little edge of pain riding along with the powerful pleasure as he penetrates me in a hot, new way.

"Oh fuck, Soph," he grunts. He pushes into me again and stays there a beat, his cock twitching inside me as he holds still, my walls clinging against him as I lift my arms above me and clutch onto the pillow.

"You feel so good," I moan. He pulls back and pushes in hard again, holding himself still.

"I love when your cunt grabs onto my cock like that. So fucking greedy," he says.

I can only moan in reply as he pulls back and slams in again, my eyes rolling back as I grip harder onto that pillow, the feeling like I'm going to come mere seconds away.

He leans down and sucks one of my tits into his mouth, and that's it. That's everything I need to shatter into a million pieces beneath him on the bed. I cry out his name as I start to come, and he helps me ride it out by picking up the pace, slamming into me over and over and over as I fly over the edge of bliss.

"Fuck, yes, yes, yes," he groans as he starts to come, too, keeping up that wicked fast pace as he drives into me, and we ride out this climax together.

I'm still clutching onto the pillow as my body starts to calm down, and he's still slamming into me as he comes. It feels so good as he keeps up the pace, his growls and grunts enough to spur me into a second orgasm.

"Oh, God! Miller!" I scream, and I let go of the pillow to clutch onto him, my nails digging into his skin as the second one hits me harder than the first. I think I might black out for a second from the pleasure as it falls over me like a blanket, enveloping me and surrounding me everywhere. I don't know which way is up. All I know is that Miller is still inside me, still thrusting into me, still pushing my body to these heights I've never known before.

God, I love him. I love what he does to me. I love how connected we are. I love the intimacy between us. And I really, really love coming while he's inside of me.

Twice.

I've never been with a partner who made me feel like this, and I never, ever want to let it go.

It's when he moves to pull out of me that something feels wrong.

It's always wrong when he pulls out and leaves a chill in his wake, but this time, I feel not a chill but a warm heat as something drips out of me.

"Oh fuck," he says, and there's something urgent in his tone, but I can't quite get a handle on what's happening with the fog my brain is currently under.

"What?" I ask.

"Condom broke," he mutters. "Shit." He stands and walks over to the bathroom rather than lying beside me as has become his habit after sex, and I try to sit up, but a rush of dizziness plows into me.

I lay back down.

The condom broke?

I feel like I should stand, or go clean up, or *something*, but I can't seem to make myself move. I'm some level beyond exhausted and sated after a double orgasm, and everything is a total blur.

Did he just say the condom broke?

The condom broke.

I've never had sex without a condom. I'm not on birth control.

I try to think rationally about my cycle and where I might be in it, but I'm in a sleepy, orgasmic brain fog. My last period was…a couple weeks ago? I think. I should be fine. We should be fine.

Except…what if we're not?

Miller has told me he doesn't want kids.

The reality of the situation is starting to hit me as I continue to feel his come dripping out of my pussy.

I guess it probably wasn't the *smartest* move for him to fuck me in the cabana, tuck his cock away, and pull it back out with the same condom on to fuck me in the stateroom twenty minutes later.

Yet here we are.

And I have no idea what this is going to mean for the two of us…but I'm already scared based on his reaction that it's not going to be good.

Chapter 42: Miller Banks

Fuck. Fuck! Why do things always have to go wrong just when they're getting good?

It's the goddamn story of my life.

A happy family life? Great, let's tell the kids about their real dad when they're nearly thirty.

Playing for your own hometown pro football team? Awesome, let's set up a trade initiated by the twin brother who wants to get out of town even though I really didn't want to leave.

Finally sleeping with the woman you've been in love with since you were fourteen? Cool, let's break that condom and see how things blow the fuck up.

I blow out a shaky breath as I stare at myself a little nervously in the mirror. So the condom broke. It probably means nothing. The risk is minimal.

But it's still a risk.

Why didn't I just switch to a different condom when we got back to the room? I know better. It was a dumb move, but it was fine before, so I didn't think twice about it.

What a disaster.

I think through our options, but it's her body and her call. I don't even know if we could get something like Plan B on this ship, and I doubt she packed some just in case.

I blow out a breath and exit the bathroom to give her a turn, and she's still lying on the bed as if she hasn't moved in the two minutes I took in there.

Maybe she's asleep.

Maybe she doesn't realize what happened.

I'm not sure I'll sleep again until I know we didn't just do something totally irreversible.

Fuck.

When she finally stands to use the bathroom, her eyes are averted to the floor rather than looking at me. My chest feels like it might collapse in on itself.

I sit on the bed and try to draw in deep breaths to help with the pain in my chest, but it's not moving. It's like a rock is stuck in there, and I'm helpless to do anything to make it go away.

I'm trying not to freak the fuck out, but it's futile.

I don't know if I've ever wanted kids, but I've always wanted Sophie. What do we do if I just put a baby in her without even realizing it?

We talked a little about kids and the future. She knows where I am on it. Learning that my parents lied to us for our entire lives really kind of fucked me up, but it was one of those things I could easily tuck away.

Now, though, faced with the potential of what just happened…I can't really tuck that away.

A baby turns into a kid, and a kid turns into a lifelong responsibility. Some people want that. Some aren't sure. Some don't. I'm thirty, and I have no idea where I fall on that spectrum.

She emerges from the bathroom, and she still isn't looking at me.

"Is there anything I can do?" It's my polite way of asking her if she wants me to head down to the shops and see if I can find some Plan B or whatever.

She lifts a shoulder. "We should be fine, but it probably wouldn't hurt to see if we can find some emergency contraception. Do you know much about it?"

I shake my head. "Never had to use it."

"Neither have I. I don't know how I feel about it."

I grab my phone and pull up a website that explains what it does. "Sounds like it prevents ovulation and makes it harder for sperm to reach the egg. It's best to take it within seventy-two hours." I glance at the clock. It feels like a timer has started.

"Should we see if they have any at the souvenir shops?" she asks.

"Sure." We both put our clothes back on, and we take a slow walk toward the shops.

Things feel suddenly awkward between us.

I've *never* felt awkward with Sophie before, but we've also never been here before. This is uncharted for us, and truthfully, I don't like it.

I'm torn. I'm not sure I want her to take this thing.

But I also don't know if I want kids.

I want to be responsible for whatever we just did. But a child isn't like a dog. You can't just drop it off at boarding when you go on a weeklong cruise. I've been watching Lincoln and Jolene at dinner with their brood of three. I've caught Asher and Desi with Jacob.

They're parents now. They were celebrating a night away from kids tonight with a trip to the casino with each other.

They're exhausted all the time. They can barely fit in time for anything that isn't their kids when they're not at work. Is that the life I want?

What happens to *us* if there's a kid in the mix? We've barely had time to be together. Even if I did decide to eventually have kids, it would be far down the line. Not today—or nine months from today.

We arrive at the shop, and my chest tightens as she finds the pharmacy section. Ibuprofen, acetaminophen, and an assortment of seasickness medications.

Tampons. Condoms. Lube.

She flicks an empty bracket and reads the tag. "Plan B. All out."

"Let's ask at the desk," I suggest, and we head up to the clerk. There's a line, naturally. We wait patiently…sort of. She's got her arms folded over her chest. I'm tapping my foot impatiently.

This isn't us.

I hate this.

It feels like there's already this *big thing* between us.

How much worse would that be with a baby in the picture? There'd be an *actual* thing between us.

We finally make our way to the front of the line. "Are all of your products on the shelves?" I ask.

"What are you looking for, sir?"

I lean in and whisper, "Plan B."

"Ah, yes. We're sold out. Sorry. It's best to bring it with you if you think you may need it. You can try at the next port."

I clear my throat, that rock in my chest growing a little bigger. "Thanks."

We bolt from the store.

Tomorrow is a day at sea. That puts us at nearly forty-eight hours before we can get our hands on anything, and Cassie planned another group excursion, so I'm not even sure we'll be able to break away to shop. Then we have another day at sea, and by the time we're back in the US, we'll be past the seventy-two-hour mark.

Right. So we'll just wait this one out and see where we land in the next few weeks.

As if that won't be the longest few weeks of my life. Of *both* of our lives.

She blows out a breath as we stroll aimlessly along the deck with all the shops, both of us quiet. It feels like we've been hit with something I'm not sure we can recover from, and the thought pulses a fear in the pit of my stomach. We can't let this come between us. We have to pull together.

I glance at the window beside me. They have a sequined jacket for women in twelve different sizes in the window, but no fucking Plan B on this boat.

"I'm sure it'll be fine," she says quietly. "If they're out of it…I guess it wasn't meant for me to take."

I nod as I try to be supportive. "I'm sorry. I should've changed to a new condom. It's my fault."

She shakes her head. "Don't blame yourself, okay? It's fine. We're fine."

I just wish she was as convincing as she thinks she's being.

We eventually end up back in our stateroom. We both stare at the bed for a moment as if it's the bed's fault.

It's not. It's my fault for not changing the condom.

"I'm going to take a quick shower," I say, and she nods. I should invite her in, but it feels like that would only lead one place, and I'm a little too freaked out at the moment to consider more sex.

And a little too spent. She is, too. She must be exhausted.

I do my best thinking in the shower, and I need a minute to just think right now.

"Okay. Can I just wash my face real quick?" she asks.

I nod, and she gets ready for bed first. By the time I emerge from the shower, she's asleep. I didn't have any big revelations while I was in there. Now I guess we just play the waiting game.

I slip into bed beside her. She doesn't move. She's facing away from me, where I soon learn she'll spend the night.

We're closing in on training camp. Sophie has work to do, too, with a book release coming up. As fun as this vacation has been, we're careening toward reality, and this is a wake-up call that neither one of us was expecting.

It feels like the condom is suddenly a symbol of everything that was hanging in the balance for us, and when it broke, so did whatever we were starting. It's early to call that, I know.

But she's facing away from me, and I'm nervous, and as much as I want to turn in and figure out how we can get through these next few weeks together, I'm not quite sure how to do that when we both have other obligations and feelings and fears that are driving us away from each other.

The answer should be simple.

Eventually the season would start, and we'd be apart simply because of my career. By then, we should've been more certain about what this is, and that certainty would've been enough to help us get through it.

We don't have that certainty. Instead, we just have more fears piled on top of fears, and I'm starting to do what I always do.

I've always been the quieter twin. I've only opened up to a few people in my life—Sophie being one of them, of course. She knows the real me, the one who doesn't always hide behind silence.

Yet here we are, silence spanning between us and causing a chasm that feels like it's widening by the very second.

Chapter 43: Sophie Summers

What's Meant to Be Will Be

Neither of us talks about the condom that broke when morning dawns. Neither of us brings up what that might mean about our future. It's not just me withdrawing into myself. He is, too.

And I have no idea how to get him back.

It felt like we were so close to having it all, and now he's retreating. The problem is that I don't know how to deal with a retreating Miller when he's running scared. That's the thing. He's *never* retreated *from me* before. I've seen him do it to others, but I was always the one he turned to when he ran from someone else.

I don't know how to erase all this and go back to how things were. I'd already made my peace with the fact that we *couldn't* go back to how things were, but never did I think we'd wind up with a scare like this so early on.

I think the reason I feel so awkward about it all is that we've talked about how he doesn't really want kids.

What do I do if I'm pregnant? How do I even tell him? Do I just do this on my own? Do I give it up?

I'll admit that while he was in the shower last night, I set my internet search on fire with my rapid questions.

How soon can I find out if I'm pregnant after a condom breaks?

A week after my missed period. A *week*. A week *after*. I have to *miss a period*.

Okay, fine. *When am I due if I got knocked up on July thirteenth?*

April twentieth.

Great. Four twenty. I'm sure a child born on four twenty won't be teased mercilessly.

I threw my phone on the nightstand when I heard the shower turn off, and I closed my eyes and pretended to be asleep because I didn't know what else to do.

The scariest part of all of this is that if we did create something out of what we did last night…I'm not certain I want to give that up. It feels like fate that the shop was out of Plan B, like whatever happens is meant to be now.

Maybe I've been unsure about whether or not I want kids, but it might be because I've never been faced with having to make that decision. I've never been engaged. Never really had to worry about having kids even though I've had an active sex life. I've been safe and protected.

What if this was meant to be? What if Miller and I were destined to come together in this way?

We used a condom. We were being safe, and still…it managed to get through.

If we made a baby, it feels like that baby fought awfully hard to be here.

We're both quiet as we head to breakfast, and we find everyone else already seated. We're the last to arrive.

We jump right into the conversation, him with Tanner and me with Grace and Ava as we pretend like we're not fighting through something strange.

We're putting on an act for the family.

But we're also putting on an act with each other, and that is completely new territory for us.

The plan for the day is for the women to have a spa day. I don't know what the plan is for the men, but I do know they're participating in some poker tournament tonight at the casino, so basically Miller and I will be away from each other all day.

I think about talking to Cassie about this, but we've all seen how loose her lips get with a drink or two in her. I think about confiding in Grace, but we're surrounded by too many people. I don't want everyone finding out about our little drama, and truth be told, it's a little embarrassing that we're thirty years old and are dealing with an accidental condom break.

Besides, I'm not sure anyone here would really get it. They're all married. Some of them have kids, and I'm not part of this family—yet. And maybe now I won't be.

The thought has tears pressing hotly behind my eyes.

Did we just screw everything up?

I hide behind my cup of coffee so nobody sees that I'm on the verge of a breakdown, and I manage to swallow it down by chugging my coffee.

Which reminds me…if I *am* pregnant, can I even drink coffee? I know literally nothing about being pregnant or having kids or how any of this works.

We sit at the breakfast table chatting with everyone until it's time to get up and head to our spa appointments, and Cassie booked the works for all of us. We have manicures, pedicures, facials, and massages, and we're supposed to plan on being here at least three hours today. I booked an extra blowout for my hair and some professional makeup since tonight is formal night at dinner, but things feel so shaky with Miller at the moment.

And now we have to spend the day away from each other while we're both stuck on this ship since it's a day at sea.

Cassie is getting a pedicure at the same time as me, and we're sort of all on a rotation for who's getting what services when.

"Where are Luca and Lily?" I ask.

"Kids' Club."

"Do they like it?"

"Lily loves it. They do all sorts of arts and crafts activities. Luca likes it because there's some video games, but he doesn't love it like she does."

I wrinkle my nose. "Is it weird having kids?"

Cassie chuckles. "It's not weird, exactly. What's weird is how it's the most exhausting, hardest work I've ever done, but it's also the most rewarding, most incredible thing I've ever done." She shrugs a little as she gets this faraway look in her eyes.

"Do you want more?"

She twists her lips. "I mean…I'm not getting any younger. A pregnancy at this age is considered geriatric."

"Geriatric?" I repeat. "Aren't you, like, thirty-five?"

"Thirty-seven, but thanks. Anything over thirty-five is considered geriatric."

"They actually use that word?"

She nods. "That or *advanced maternal age*. I'm not sure which is worse."

"What an insult pregnant women don't actually need." I wrinkle my nose.

"Tell me about it. But to answer your question…yes. It would be a blessing to raise a baby with Tanner. What's meant to be will be."

What's meant to be will be.

I hold those words in my hands.

"What about you? Do you want kids?" she asks.

"I was never the girl who dreamed of being a mom, but I also never really saw a future without kids in it. But I don't really think Miller wants kids." I lift a shoulder.

"How does that make you feel?"

I think about what happened last night. I think about confessing it to Cassie since it seems like the perfect time to do it.

But I chicken out.

It's too early to really know anything yet, and besides, we have a port tomorrow where we might be able to find that emergency contraception. It's still on the table.

It's exhausting and hard, but it's also rewarding and incredible—according to Cassie, at least. She seems to really have her shit together. She just married Tanner Banks, formerly one of pro football's hottest bachelors. She has two kids who adore her, she's running her own physical therapy practice, and she still has time for things like pedicures and massages and coffee dates with her future sister-in-law. She was strong enough to leave a man who treated her like shit, and she made it out on the other side even when it was just her and her two kids.

This parenting thing…it can't be *all* bad, can it?

I lean back into the massage chair and give in to the lovely feel of the rollers moving across my shoulders. They're tight with tension both from sitting at a table on my laptop all the time and from the stress of whatever's happening with Miller and me.

"I'm not sure," I finally murmur.

But even as I tell her I'm not sure how Miller not wanting kids makes me feel, I think I know the answer.

If he draws the line at having kids…I don't think we can continue down this path. Because even though it's just a minor scare of a possibility at this point, the more I think about it, the more I think having kids is exactly what I want out of life.

Chapter 44: Miller Banks

Brotherly Competition

I stare up at the ceiling as I lie on the bed.

This was the scene of the crime.

I feel like shit. I feel awkward with Sophie, and that's one zone our friendship has never fallen into. I hate it.

It feels all wrong.

This trip that felt like paradise just a few days ago has turned into some weird sort of hellish prison. We can't even get off this fucking boat today because it's a day at sea, and suddenly I feel some strange combination of homesick and seasick.

I think it's just nausea from the condom breaking and the uncertainty surrounding that, but I force myself up off the bed and over to the Dramamine anyway.

I pop a pill, and I think about calling Tanner, but I'm not sure I'm ready to confess any of this to anybody just yet. Besides, we're meeting for a game of basketball in an hour anyway.

One half of me wishes today of all days wasn't the day that we were forced to be apart. But the other part of me is grateful for the isolation.

It gives me a chance to sit with my thoughts.

Obviously if our accident last night results in a pregnancy, I'll be there for her.

I just never imagined *this* is how I'd finally get my shot with her. Everything was going so well for us, and now it feels like we ran into a wall.

My biggest fear in her finding out that I've loved her since high school was that it would somehow change our friendship. It didn't. But I think this might.

Tanner will know something's up with me. He'll dig and dig until he gets to the bottom of things.

And that's why I should probably avoid him. I'm not ready for him to give me his big brotherly advice.

He's twelve minutes older than me, and somehow that makes him wiser than me. Fuck that. He doesn't know fuck about shit, and apparently neither do I.

I blow out a breath.

Who the fuck even am I right now? I'm insulting my brother in my own head. This isn't me.

I need to shake it off, and with that in mind, I head toward the fitness center.

I shouldn't be surprised to find Asher, Spencer, and Tanner already in there. There's nobody else in here, just those three men who are all prepping ahead of the looming training camp.

"Where are the other two?" I ask when I walk in.

"I think Grayson is taking a nap, and Lincoln said he wanted to get some work done before basketball," Spencer says as he runs on a treadmill.

Tanner is lifting weights, and Asher is doing squats.

I hop on one of the treadmills a few down from Spencer to give us each some space. I slip in my AirPods, turn on some indie rock, and I start immediately with a sprint.

"Whoa, dude. You okay?" Asher asks as he moves to stand in front of my machine.

"Fine," I grunt.

"An immediate sprint? Don't you need to warm up first?"

I shake my head. "I need to fucking run. Anybody else feel stuck on this boat?"

Tanner sets down his weights and moves to stand beside Asher. "You okay?"

"A bit of seasickness, I think," I say. It's a lie, and Tanner will see right through it.

As predicted, he studies me for a second, but he doesn't say anything in front of Asher and Spencer. Instead, he'll corner me later and try to get me to talk, but I've become pretty damn good at keeping my feelings to myself.

They leave me to my run as they get back to their own workouts, and I increase the incline and slow my pace. I run for thirty minutes, music blasting in my ears as I push everything out of my mind and focus on the task in front of me.

It helps.

By the time I'm done, I'm a panting, sweaty mess, but I do feel a little better.

Except the moment I stop, it all comes rushing back.

What if I got Sophie pregnant last night?

It feels like it'll be the *only* thing on my mind for the next month until we know one way or the other.

I can't have this weighing on me while I'm at camp. I'm a starter, sure, but that doesn't mean the team will play me if someone with more speed or better reflexes proves himself over me.

I need my focus. Last year, when Tanner lost his focus, he tore his ACL in the first regular season game. It took him out for the entire season.

He'll be back this year, and I refuse to let anything else come between us. This will be the first full season we'll get to play together on the San Diego Storm.

Our reservation time for the basketball court is quickly approaching, and the four of us finish our workouts around the same time and head together to the courts, where we find Grayson and Lincoln already waiting for us.

They're all relaxed while the four of us just finished an intense workout. We *may* have pushed it a little harder than necessary since we were working out with our siblings. Not that we have any sort of sibling rivalry, really, but let's be honest. It's six brothers who all played professional football at various times. Three of us play on the same team. Of course there's some sort of brotherly competition at play in the background.

And that only comes flying to the surface as we take the basketball court. I can't imagine what other places it might come to the surface. The five of them are all married already. Some have kids already. I guess those things aren't a competition, but if they were, I wouldn't be winning.

It's sure to prove an intense game of three-on-three—Tanner, Lincoln, and Spencer against Grayson, Asher, and myself.

It's fairly balanced in terms of size and speed, and before tip-off, I glance at the fence surrounding the courts.

People have gathered. They already knew the Nash and Banks brothers were on board this ship, and they're about to witness the six of us playing a game in the same space together.

This has never happened before, but we're six pro athletes. There's no way in hell this isn't about to get vicious as fuck.

It's probably a terrible idea given the fact that we need to be in tip-top shape in less than two weeks, but fuck it all. Let's fucking go.

Grayson manages to snag the ball first, and even though basketball isn't our sport, it's still one we all tried out at some point. Grayson is the tallest, and I'm the fastest with Asher just behind me, so we easily make our way back and forth across the court.

People are taking pictures and cheering for their favorites. Tanner and Asher seem to be the most popular names I'm hearing, though I hear everyone's at some point, including my own.

It's a tight game, and we only reserved the court for an hour. We decided we'd play to the end, and with less than ten seconds left on our game clock, the score is eighty-two to eighty-five. Tanner's team is winning.

Grayson tips Lincoln's shot, and somehow, I end up with the ball. I could sprint across the court for an easy layup, which would give us only two points—or I could try for a three-pointer to tie up the score.

My quick thinking pushes me to opt for choice number two, and I find myself at the three-point line as I square up. I hear my brothers running toward me from behind, and I shoot. The ball seems to pause mid-air, and then it hits off the backboard. It bounces to the rim, on the backboard again, around the rim, and finally drops through the net.

The crowd gathered around the courts goes wild, and Asher holds up a hand for a fist bump on his way by.

We're tied up with three seconds left on the clock, and somehow this game of pickup basketball with my brothers feels as important as a playoff game.

I realize it's not. It's just for fun. But the pride of winning will stay with us for the rest of this cruise.

Or the rest of the day, at least. Until lunchtime, maybe.

Lincoln throws the ball in to Tanner, and I'm right on top of my twin, making sure he has exactly zero space to move. He's struggling, and that's when Asher comes out of nowhere, steals the ball just as Tanner is dribbling, and runs it to the hoop for a layup right as the buzzer—a small bell, actually—sounds.

The crowd is cheering, and I'm yelling with Grayson and Asher as the three losers look on at us, all six of us panting as we try to catch our breath after the strenuous exercise of the last hour.

We all slap hands as good sportsmen do, and then we agree to meet up in a half hour for lunch so we all have time to head back to our rooms for a quick shower.

It was another hour that I didn't think about what happened last night.

I needed that.

Maybe the more time passes us by, the less I'll think about it.

I take a quick shower and head down to the dining room. I arrive first, and Tanner shows up just after me.

"What's going on with you?" he asks.

My brows dip. "What do you mean?"

"You know you can't hide shit from me, so stop pretending." He sounds exasperated.

"Nothing."

"You and Sophie barely looked at each other during breakfast," he says.

"You were watching?"

He lifts a shoulder. "Just quietly observing. Is everything okay?"

I chew the inside of my cheek for a beat before I say, "I'm just worried we want different things, and I'm not sure how we can make it work if that's the case."

"What different things?" he presses.

"I don't know. Different futures. Like maybe she wants kids, and I don't think I do."

"Is that something you have to decide right now?" he asks.

"I guess not," I mutter. "But shouldn't we be on the same page for that kind of shit? If we're not now, we might never be.

And now we're in this place where if we don't move forward together, then I might be losing her forever."

"Get out of your head, man. Enjoy it. You *finally* landed her, and now you're sabotaging things before you ever even get off the ground."

"It's what I do." It feels like it, anyway. It feels like things are always going fine or at least in the direction of fine, and then I look ahead, see the potential problems, and shut it down before I have to deal with those problems.

And nobody knows that better than Tanner.

"It doesn't have to be." His voice is gentle, and I guess it gives me something to think about.

Chapter 45: Sophie Summers

The massage is wonderful, the facial is lovely, and the spa in general is great.

It doesn't change anything. It only serves as a brief distraction.

How the hell am I going to get through the next four weeks?

I meet the ladies for a late afternoon tea time. I have no idea where Miller is at.

In fact, I don't see him at all until dinner. He isn't even in the room before dinner, so either he's avoiding me or he's out with the guys.

Our dinner conversation consists of what we did separately today, and it sounds like the basketball game was quite the event—at least from Grayson's perspective it was. Spencer seems less enthused about it.

"You okay?" Miller asks me quietly somewhere around dessert.

I press my lips together and nod, but the truth is…I'm not sure if I am.

Regardless of what happened last night, I'm not sure whether there's a future ahead for the two of us if we don't want the same things.

And the longer I sit with the idea that I *could* be pregnant, the more I think about how that is *definitely* something I want in my future.

And he doesn't.

It's better to figure this out now, truthfully. We can't go ahead with a wedding next February and mean the vows as we both said we would the other night if we want different things for our future. And kids? That's a big one. It's not like I want a cat and he doesn't.

This is a lifelong commitment, and regardless of whether I am or I'm not pregnant right at this moment, if he doesn't want that commitment and I do…then it's never going to work between us long term.

And that thought breaks my heart.

Mostly because I can only see this as the end of the road for us. I don't know how we go back to being friends after everything we've been through the last few months. I don't know how future partners are going to feel about me being so close with someone who's my ex. And I don't know if I can share the same kinds of things with someone knowing he's been in love with me as long as he has.

After dinner, the men participate in the poker tournament hosted by the casino. The ladies are invited, too, of course, but none of us want to play. It's more fun to watch, anyway.

Miller's doing well, and he's still in it when the clock strikes eleven. I'm exhausted, and I don't even know why. It's not like I did anything strenuous today, but the massage was so relaxing that I think I'm just done for the day.

I lean in toward Miller after he wins another hand. "I'm going to head up to bed," I say quietly.

He turns and looks at me. "You okay?" It's the second time tonight he's asked me that, and just like the first time, I lie.

"I'm fine. Just tired."

He puckers his lips for a kiss, and I give him one even though it feels like it's more for show for everyone around us than it is for us.

I push that icky feeling away and head up to our stateroom alone.

The alarm wakes us bright and early for another early meeting for an excursion. Today we're doing ATVs and ziplining with the six brothers and their significant others. Kids and parents are staying behind, and if I didn't have all this other stuff weighing on me, I'd be excited for the day.

We take a quick glance in the first shop at the port, but they mainly sell alcohol, not Plan B.

This isn't a quiet, romantic excursion where we can talk and work things out, but instead it's active, and we're surrounded by other people all day.

Our excursion runs late, which means we don't have time to look in the shops because we have to haul ass back to the ship.

I'm starting to believe Cassie's words more and more. *What's meant to be will be.*

If we can't get our hands on Plan B, then maybe I'm not meant to take it. Maybe I won't be pregnant at all…or maybe I will be, and that baby was meant for me.

When we get to dinner, I realize we only have one more night together on this ship. We'll go home, and things will return to normal.

Kind of.

Except…not really.

A week after we get back, training camp will start, and I don't know what our new reality will look like. He may not even be home the first time I take a pregnancy test. I might have to take it alone.

I might have to deal with the results—positive or negative—alone.

And I might have to sort through whatever feelings come with that…alone.

I've never felt abandoned by Miller before, but I've also never been in the role I'm currently playing with him. I always knew he had different obligations during the season, so of course I'd see less of him.

I didn't think about what implications that would hold as his fiancée or girlfriend or *whatever* it is I am to him now, and I'm already starting to feel that. Maybe he's pulling away because he's mentally preparing for the season. And I can tell myself to justify things between us all I want, but I know it's because he's going through whatever feelings he's harboring, and whatever they are…he doesn't want to talk to me about them.

And that hurts more than it should.

"Today was fun," Asher says, making casual conversation once the table is filled with the rest of us. Desi holds their one-year-old, and he glances at the two of them before he says, "And tonight will be fun, too."

"We have an announcement," Desi says. She turns Jake so we can all see his shirt.

Big Brother.

"Big brother?" Grayson says, reading the shirt. "Wait, are you—" He points a finger between Asher and Desi, and they're both laughing as the rest of us put it together.

"We're having another baby," Desi says. "We just told Mom and Dad a few minutes ago, and Missy, too." Our heads all swing to the parents' table, where Bill and Sue Dixon are beaming at their daughter, and Missy is wiping her eyes.

"But your daiquiris all week—" Ava begins, and Desi laughs.

"Virgin!"

"Unlike her, apparently," Asher says, wiggling his eyebrows.

What follows can only be described as a chorus of joyous "Congratulations!" and excitement.

So another baby. We're seemingly surrounded by them.

Desi's pregnant, and this enthusiasm and love and happiness around the table is what a pregnancy announcement *should* be met with.

Not the fear and retreating of a broken condom.

I draw in a deep breath and wipe the corner of my eye. I'm happy for them, truly. They're a lovely couple, and they deserve everything they want.

"When are you due?" Ava asks once everyone sits back down.

"February tenth," Desi says.

"Oh, cool. Maybe the cousins will be born on the same date," Grayson says.

"The cousins?" Asher asks.

Grayson and Ava look like they're about to burst with excitement.

"Oh my God, you're pregnant?" Desi asks Ava, and she's grinning as she nods.

The same excitement rolls around again, and everyone gets up to hug Ava and Grayson—including Missy, who heard everything and rushes over from the next table to congratulate her son and daughter-in-law.

Two babies, both due around the same time.

And maybe another one coming two months later.

I feel Miller's gaze on my profile, but I don't dare turn to look at him.

It suddenly feels like we're surrounded by babies.

"Guess that just leaves you and me," Grace teases me as we all sit back down.

I nearly choke on my water, but I force a quick recovery. "Guess so."

But maybe not.

Chapter 46: Sophie Summers

Cheering for Offense

It's our last day on the cruise, and it's a day at sea. We decided on a pool day for thirty-two, but there are another five thousand or so people on the ship who *also* decided on a pool day for their last day of the trip.

We're alternating between sitting on lounge chairs in the water with Spencer and Grace to sitting on lounge chairs out of the water with Spencer and Grace.

I sort of pushed the fact that I caught her dad with her husband's mom out of my head, but it's back right there at the forefront as we hang together all day.

There are no less than twelve times that I think about telling her what's going on, but then I remember it's not my story to tell.

Still, it's the two of us for lengthy amounts of time. I guess the others have more to talk about than we do. Ava and Desi are busy comparing pregnancy symptoms while Grayson and Asher talk about fatherhood and their own symptoms that come with a pregnant wife.

Miller hasn't mentioned anything about Missy and Steve to Spencer—or to anyone else, for that matter. Maybe he forgot about it in the broken condom scandal anyway.

Is it a scandal? It feels like one.

"Do you want that someday?" Grace asks me, angling her head toward her two pregnant sisters-in-law.

I lift a shoulder. "Sure, someday. You?"

"Yeah, sure. Someday. But right now, things are so crazy with the wineries, and I'm only twenty-seven. I feel like I've got time."

I nod. "Definitely. I just turned thirty and feel like I have time, too. But we're not getting any younger, you know? What's meant to be will be, I guess." I repeat Cassie's sage advice that I can't seem to stop thinking about.

"When it's meant to be," she agrees.

We both lean back in our chairs. I'm in the shade despite the SPF 50 sunscreen I lathered on this morning, but laying out by the pool on a cruise ship is nearly enough to help me forget my worries.

Nearly enough.

Not quite.

We head to our room to take showers before dinner, but before I get in, I join Miller out on the balcony for a quick chat.

Or…I *think* it'll be quick.

"I feel like you're pulling away, and I hate it." My voice is firm and direct, and if we can't communicate about this stuff now, what will life be like when he's actually gone for days at a time because he's in season?

He looks surprised at my combination accusation and outburst, but he turns his eyes back to the water as he says, "I'm sorry. You're right, and I hate it, too."

"Then let's figure this out. Whatever happens happens."

He nods. "You're right. We need to lean into each other, not pull away."

"I get being a little reluctant to hop back into bed, but you're also making me feel like you don't want anything to do with me."

His brows dip as he looks at me with surprise. He stands and pulls me into his arms. He's not wearing a shirt, and his chest is warm and cozy. "Nothing could be further from the truth. I love you, Sophie." His chest rumbles with his words against my cheek, and his arms are tight around me.

"I love you, too. We'll figure this out, okay?" I pull back and look up at him, and he looks worried.

I get it.

I'm worried, too.

But the last thing we should be worried about is where we stand with each other.

It's been a strange few days, but hopefully we can climb out of it as we focus forward together.

We don't have time for makeup sex, so we'll save that for later. We head to dinner, where we plan to spend a little extra time together with the family since it's the last night we'll all be together.

The wait staff has rearranged the tables so we're sort of in a triangle and can talk with more of our group, and part of me wonders why it wasn't like this the whole time.

I glance around at everyone gathered here. Come February, will they be my family? I have no idea.

Marriage was always part of my eventual plan—pending finding the right person, of course. And honestly, I thought Miller was the right person until this whole thing happened. Now I'm left questioning so many different things, and I hate how that makes me feel.

Later this season, the Storm will face the Aces, and Miller, Tanner, and Spencer will face off against Coach Lincoln and Asher, and that's about the closest we'll get to being in the same room all together in the foreseeable future. And I don't even know if I'll be there.

"Hey Missy!" Tanner yells from our table over to the parents' table.

"Hm?" she asks, turning away from Steve, who she was just talking to *and* who she's sitting next to *again,* and toward Tanner.

"When the Aces and the Storm face off this season, who are you cheering for?" he asks.

The three tables between the thirty of us fall silent as we all wait for the answer.

"Since my one defensive boy has hung up his cleats," she says, glancing at Grayson pointedly, "I'll be cheering for offense." She shoots him a wink.

"Good answer," Steve says beside her, and he's laughing and not really hiding that he's got a thing for the Nash matriarch. Maybe I just see it because I *know.*

They're both drinking wine, and I have to admit, even if we *hadn't* caught them red-handed, I might've put it together tonight.

I wonder if they'll say anything. I wonder if anyone else caught them. I wonder who *almost* caught them that first night.

I know Steve is sharing a stateroom with his mother, so that's likely why they couldn't go to his room. As far as I know, Missy has her own room. But the ship's capacity is only around six thousand. I mean, that's like an entire half a percent of the passengers on this boat that are related in some way to the Nash family. That has to increase the chances of them getting caught, even if it's just because someone else's room is close to hers.

"That's great news to this offensive coordinator's ears," Desi's father, Bill, says.

"Not as much for this head coach," Lincoln yells from his table, and we all laugh.

I realize my parents are here, and my brother is not, but this is still what I want out of my future. I want to be a part of this big family, of these celebrations of love and excitement for each other. Even if I've basically avoided my parents this entire week except for a few interactions at meals or near the pool.

I want to have Cassie, Ava, Grace, Desi, and Jolene as my sisters-in-law. I want to have a huge Nash-Banks family Christmas where we each pick a name or exchange a white elephant gift.

I love this family and the feelings I have here. But most of all, I love Miller, and I want to figure out how to make it work with him.

Maybe that means working harder to find that Plan B. Or maybe this is the reality he's going to have to face, and together we'll figure out how we're going to make this work. He was teetering, anyway. He said what happened scared him off from having kids. He didn't say he never wanted them.

So maybe this was meant to happen. Maybe this was the thing that was always meant to help him figure that out.

Or maybe it was the very thing that was always meant to break us.

Chapter 47: Miller Banks

The Hardest Week of the Year

It's strange waking up to a cruise director announcing groups that need to get the fuck off this boat, but I guess the crew needs to turn this place around so it's ready for the next group of people boarding later this afternoon.

Part of me doesn't want to get off the ship. I think about our first day here, sitting out on the balcony with the week in front of us, feeling like we were in paradise as we sipped our piña coladas with edible straws, and now here we are, a week later, and everything has changed.

We shouldn't let it, and deep down, I know this. Maybe it's just me bracing for the season. I don't really know because I've never been in a serious relationship as I looked toward training camp. I've never felt like I was leaving someone behind, but I do this time.

The other part of me is ready to face what's coming next. We've had a nice, long offseason, and life sure looks different than it did in January when our season ended. I'm ready to get to work. The competitor in me has missed the hell out of the game I love so much, and I'm ready to get back on the field and do what I was born to do.

We meet the rest of the family at the buffet for a quick breakfast, and then we disembark. It's pretty much pure chaos, and Soph and I end up sharing an Uber with Tanner and Cassie to get to the airport. We catch our flight back to San Diego, and then I have a week to prepare for camp.

To me, that doesn't mean we have one more week off. That means I need to fix what I fucked up on the cruise—meaning instead of having a dessert after every meal, I need to eat right. I need to work off any extra body fat I picked up over the last six months. I need to run drills for agility and footwork.

In short, I have a week to get ready for the season, and it'll be the hardest week of the year for me as I put all my focus back into my sport.

And it starts now.

It's late by the time we get home, so we unpack and head to bed.

Sophie missed a week of work while we were on the ship, and she's diving back into things there as I plan to meet with the other running backs at Coach Cook's house on Saturday morning. He'll coach us through some drills, and it'll give the three running backs returning from last year a chance to meet with Jalen Jones, the rookie we picked up in the draft, along with a couple of the guys from the practice squad.

The practice squad guys benefit the most from this since they're all leaving everything on the field when it comes to training camp. It's their shot to make the active roster, and I know how much they want it. But the three of us coming back from last year and our rookie are all pretty solid, so I'm not sure any of them will get the chance.

When I get to Coach Cook's house, I see I'm the last one to arrive. It feels like it's not a good look.

If I want to be the leader of this position, it's up to me to show up on time and ready to work.

I'm not late—but I'm not early, either.

Coach Cook has dedicated his entire life to the game and specifically this position, and his kitchen has the perfect setup for a team meeting while his backyard is the perfect place to run drills.

He lets me in the front door when I arrive, and I join the others already sitting at the table. Everyone here was at mandatory minicamp last month, so it's not like it's the first time we're meeting as a group. But this feels different, anyway. We're meeting now as a group of men working toward a common goal, yet we're still battling it out for who's going to start, who's going to sit, and who's going to even make the fifty-three-man roster.

It's always been such a strange dynamic to me. We're forming a brotherhood and a bond no one can break, but next season, we could all end up on different teams where we're battling against the men who were brothers the year before.

I guess it's why I've learned to focus on the present rather than what lies ahead. We don't know what lies ahead, and we certainly can't predict it. Just ask my brother, who sat on the sidelines all of last season with his ACL injury.

It could happen to any of us at any time, and I'm always hyperaware of that fact.

"Miller Banks," Isaiah Lowe says as he stands and holds up a hand for a shake. I clap my hand against his, and we hold on as we lean in for a hug. We got close last season, and while I was in the starting position, he was close on my heels, often stepping in for plays and making his mark on each game.

Drake Hawkins greets me next, and then the rookie Jalen, and finally, the two practice squad guys, Roman and Byron.

Coach stands at the head of the table and starts talking.

"Now that we're all here, I just wanted to touch base on what you can expect in camp. The coaches have met, and we decided we're going to put a big focus on fundamentals this year. For our position, that means a few different things. Our stats improved with ball carrying, but we can always practice keeping the ball secure. We'll run footwork drills and spend a lot of time with tape studying defense and analyzing how to read it. But before we start all of that, I thought it was important to work through some team-building drills, which is why I asked you all here today."

I hear a series of groans from the athletes gathered at the table. Team building usually means something that's going to be a waste of our time when the real team building takes place on the field.

"What is it, a blindfolded obstacle course?" Isaiah asks, and we all snicker since that's what Coach Cook had us do last year in his backyard.

"You'll see," he says. He checks his phone. "Our ride is here."

"Our ride?" I repeat quietly to Jalen, and he gives me one of those *are we supposed to be talking* kind of looks. Leave it to a rookie, I guess.

There's a party bus waiting out front, which is kind of nice since we all have rather thick legs and we each get our own seat.

The wide receivers are already waiting on the bus as we step on.

Spencer holds up a hand for a fist bump as I walk by him, and I spot Clayton Mack and one of our new guys, Madden Bradley. He's on the older side in his thirties, and we acquired him in a trade deal from Chicago. I don't know much about him other than the fact that he's from the Bradley family, a name as well-known throughout the league as the Nash name.

The other wide receivers on the team—Zach Moore, DJ Evans, and Sam Collins—are there, too, and we all share in greetings as we take our seats on the bus.

We head through town and pull up in front of Laser Zone.

"Laser tag?" I ask, and we tumble out of the bus and through the front doors.

Coach Cook and Coach Clark, the wide receiver coach, booked one of the courses for the next two hours, and we gear up and head out. Both coaches are playing, too, and for the next hour, we run around like a bunch of little kids, playing each for ourselves.

You'd think we'd just play for fun, but the competitive spirit is alive and well as we race around the course dodging fire and navigating obstacles. We have to constantly be aware of who is where if we want to get the highest score, and it's easy to spot the weaknesses in my teammates as Jalen is predictable, Roman is slow to react, and Isaiah always hides out in the same place.

In the end, Madden surprisingly emerges the victor, but I'm a close second. Very close.

I wish I wasn't so competitive, because I'm actually kind of pissed off that I lost.

For the second hour, we're divided into teams, and the coaches don't play along but instead watch and observe.

My team wins, but I'm still bitter I wasn't the winner of the first round.

I'm quiet on the way back to Coach's house, and he has lunch waiting for us when we get back. We're dropped first, and the wide receivers must go off to their own coach's place for similar meetings.

We talk a bit about how the fundamentals of what we just did relate to our position—agility, speed, and situational awareness were all part of it, and in the second hour, teamwork and communication became more important because we weren't just playing as individuals anymore.

All in all, it was a fun morning, but after lunch is when we put in the work.

We're at Coach's place until dinnertime. I decide to surprise Sophie with dinner since I've been away all day, but to my surprise, when I get home…she's not there.

I guess communication is important to more than just laser tag and football.

Chapter 48: Sophie Summers

The Same Heat and Passion

"It's new for me, too," Cassie admits. "I guess I didn't really think about how I'm not the only one going through something.

"Last season, I was helping him recover. We had unlimited amounts of time together. This is going to be a totally new chapter in our relationship," she says.

"Ours too," I admit. "I'm glad you invited me to dinner because I was going nuts at the house wondering when he'd be home."

"He didn't tell you?" she asks. She sounds surprised.

I shake my head. "I don't know if he knew."

"Tanner's meeting was a dinner meeting, so at least I knew that." She lifts a shoulder. "My parents wanted the kids for a double sleepover, so they're there tonight and tomorrow night. And then they start school the week after training camp begins, so we need to start supply shopping and all that stuff." She rolls her eyes.

Supply shopping.

It takes me back to the days of being a teacher. As much as I hated when summer was coming to an end, there was nothing I loved more than school supply shopping.

"I can take them," I volunteer.

Her brows dip together. "You don't want to do that. Really?"

"I *love* supply shopping."

"The last few years, I've just ordered everything online. But Lilypad wants to pick everything out at the store, and Luca is desperate for the newest Minecraft backpack. After being gone the last week, though, my schedule is full at work, and I have no clue when to take them."

"I'm serious, Cassie. Let me do it. I used to be a teacher, so trust me. This is my jam." I offer her a grin, and she relents.

"Okay, but only if you're sure. And let me treat you to dinner because trust me, taking both kids to the store at the same time is a feat I wouldn't wish on my worst enemy." She purses her lips at the end, and I laugh.

"Oh, come on. It can't be that bad, can it?"

She raises her brows as if to say, *just wait and see for yourself.*

"So they're at a double sleepover, but are they free, say…Tuesday around lunchtime? I can get them Happy Meals and take them to Target." Target was always my favorite for supply shopping.

"They'll be back from my parents' house by then and ready to shop. If you're sure."

"Stop saying that. You're scaring me." I make a face of horror, and she laughs. But the truth of it is that I want to be around kids. I want to see what it's like—not that taking kids shopping is any indicator of what being a mom is actually like, but I just want to see how I am in the situation. If I keep my patience, if I have to wrangle, if they're acting out at lunch. Any and all of it.

When I get home, Miller is on the couch with a tablet in his hand. It looks like he's watching a football game.

He clicks it off and sets it beside him as he glances up at me. "Welcome home."

"Thanks. I didn't know when you'd be back, and Cassie invited me to dinner."

"Fun. Did you have a good time?"

I nod. "You?"

"Actually, yeah. It was a good day."

I plop down beside him on the couch, but the tablet is sitting between us, so I don't get too close. It feels symbolic, like football is already coming between us.

Even though I suspect there's something far deeper coming between us.

"What did you do?" I ask.

"Coach Cook, the running back coach, took the running backs to play laser tag."

I flatten my lips and narrow my eyes at him. "So I was sitting here working all day feeling bad for you that you were also working all day, when you were actually…playing laser tag?"

He chuckles. "It wasn't exactly like that. It was a team-building activity. He drew parallels to the game—being aware of our surroundings, thinking on our feet, communicating with our teammates."

He leaves it at that, but that word—"*communicating*"—feels like it sits heavily in the air between us.

I nod. "Sounds fun."

"I brought dinner home for you. I didn't realize you were out."

I clear my throat. "You could've texted." I only realize how bitchy I sound as the words fall from my lips.

"You're right, and I'm sorry."

I shake my head. "I know you're busy. It's just an adjustment already. I'm used to you being here."

He moves the tablet and scoots a little closer to me on the couch, and it doesn't escape me that we haven't had sex since the night the condom broke.

More and more it feels like the symbolic thing that broke *us*, too. It's one thing to *write* about symbols as I plant them in a story. It's another thing entirely to keep having to face them.

He moves his arm around me, and I lean into his chest. "I'm used to being here, too. I missed you today. Hell, I've missed you since cruise night four."

I turn and look up at him. "I've missed you since then, too."

He leans forward and presses his lips to mine, and that same heat and passion are still there.

The urgency kicks in as his mouth opens to mine, and suddenly he's leaning me back onto the couch, hovering over me, his hips seeking out mine as they thrust against me. I'm moaning as I wait for him to do it again, and the ache is back, growing unbearable as the need for him to alleviate it burns bright and hot inside of me.

Maybe we're not broken after all. Maybe things are just a little bent right now, and all we need is some time to straighten them back out.

He moves his mouth from mine and toward my ear as his hips slam to mine again, and then he murmurs in a deep, raspy voice, "I need to fuck you."

"Do it," I beg. "Please."

He pulls off of me and pushes to a stand. "Be right back."

He disappears, and I lay there for a few seconds where he left me. I wonder where he went as I sit up, and eventually I stand and head over to the kitchen, where I grab a bottle of water from the fridge and drink some down.

He returns, and he was only gone a minute, tops—probably less, but it felt like forever.

He's holding a condom between his fingertips, and he wiggles his eyebrows as he shows it to me. I stifle a giggle as he starts to saunter over toward me, and a moment later, he has me pinned against the refrigerator.

His mouth falls to mine, open and hungry, and he kisses me like he wants to devour me whole. And I want him to. I crave the intimacy that so easily came to us once we finally crossed into the territory we'd been fighting against. I crave *him*.

He lifts me into his arms, and I wrap my legs around his waist as he thrusts up toward me. My back is still against the fridge, and he's holding me around my thighs now as he kisses me like his life depends on it.

His tongue thrashes against mine, the passion new and different while still familiar, and I meet him thrust for thrust, thrash for thrash.

He spins me around and sets me on the counter of the island that was behind him only a second ago, and he breaks the kiss to move back. He reaches for my shirt and pulls it over my head, dropping it on the floor, and he slowly unhooks my bra and tosses it aside.

I tug at his shirt, too, and he pulls it over his head and lets it drop as well. He moves in toward me, pulling me into a hug as our chests meet in the middle. It's warm and cozy here, and it feels like the sort of place I never want to leave. He pulls back enough to press his lips back to mine, and I sigh into him as I feel like I could stay right here in his arms forever, kissing him just like this.

He reaches into my jeans with a sudden movement I'm not expecting, and he isn't playing. He isn't teasing. Instead, his finger moves right inside my pussy, and he hisses when he feels how ridiculously wet I am for him.

"Jesus, Sophie," he mutters, and as he pulls back, his eyes are glazed with lust. "Lay back."

I do what he says, and the counter is cold as ice against my back. I don't care, though. I know he'll make enough heat between us that I won't even feel it in another minute or two.

He yanks my jeans off along with my panties and my shoes once he gets far enough down, and I'm suddenly lying naked on the kitchen counter.

"Mm," he murmurs, and he moves toward my tits first. He sucks one into his mouth, and heat sears through me. He seems to get an idea after a few moments of sucking on each of my nipples as he moves away from me.

He opens the freezer and grabs some ice cubes, and then he returns to me.

He circles one of the cubes around one of my nipples as he sucks the other one into his mouth. The heat of one and the ice of the other make the ache between my legs throb with need for relief. My hips start to sway as they search out something, anything, to give my pussy some friction and relief, but there's nothing there.

He chuckles as he watches me, and then he takes one of the ice cubes and slides it down my torso and over my clit.

I cry out at the sting of cold, grateful to finally have some friction there even if it's ice.

He moves his mouth to follow the trail the ice just made from my tits to my pussy, his tongue heating up the spaces the ice touched, and when his tongue moves against my clit, my hips buck up off the counter and toward his mouth.

I grip onto his head with my hands as I wrap my legs around his neck. I start to grind against his mouth, and he gives me that magical tongue of his as he slides it from my clit down into my pussy. He moves it back to flick against my clit, and every time he does it, my hips jerk off the counter.

His fingertips are cold as they move up to my nipples, but I don't even feel the sting of the cold anymore because what he's doing to my pussy is making me hot absolutely everywhere.

I cry out his name as he continues his assault with his mouth, and he pulls back just enough to say, "I want this pretty cunt to come all over my tongue."

His breath is hot against me, and he slides his tongue back inside me before he moves his finger down to replace it. He sucks on my clit, his tongue moving back and forth over the bundle of tight nerves, and that's when I lose it.

I shatter into a million pieces with this orgasm as he continues to suck on my clit while his finger moves in and out of me, and my legs clench around his ears as my body rides the intense wave of pulse after pulse of pure pleasure.

I scream my way through it, some string of incomprehensible words like, *Oh my God, Miller, fuck yes!* coursing out of me, and when the rolls of pleasure start to slow and I come down from the clouds, I realize how tense my entire body is. I relax back onto the cold counter, not feeling much of anything except the warm glow of satisfaction as it takes over all the other senses.

He kisses my pussy sweetly once he sees me visibly relax, and then he moves his lips to my hip and my stomach and up toward my tits.

Even in this moment of pure satisfaction, I can't help but wonder if those things will change, if I'll grow and swell over the next nine months.

We won't know for a while, but suddenly I feel that connection back with him in the way we'd been missing for the last few days.

It feels like a relief, like a weight has been lifted from my shoulders.

He kisses my lips, and then he pulls back and whispers, "I took care of that sweet cunt first with my tongue. Now I'm going to wreck it with my cock."

Oh. My. God.

Yes, please.

"God, Miller, yes. Give it to me." My own voice sounds whiny to my ears, but I'm not in a state where I currently much care.

He pulls that beautiful cock of his out and rolls on the condom, and then he yanks my body so my ass is right at the edge of the counter. His eyes are on mine as he slides into me, both of us moaning at the feel of his entrance—for me, the gorgeous, full feeling of having him back inside me, and for him, the tight, sweet feel of my cunt pulling him in.

He moves slowly at first, and I wrap my legs around his torso since I have nowhere for them to go. He holds onto my thighs as he slams into me, and something about this angle is different and hot as hell. He's looking down at me with so much love and adoration as he pushes as deep as he can, and I hope he can see that same feeling reflected back at him.

It's in this moment that the shakiness of the last few days seems to pass, and the feeling like we can conquer anything as long as we're together washes over me.

The only problem is that over the next six months, we won't really *be* together. Not as much. Not like we have been.

I don't know the solution, but I do know that right now, this is what I want. Miller. Us. Intimacy. Connection. Love.

"Fuck, you're so tight, Soph. God, I love you." He's gritting out his words through his thrusts, his voice raspy and passionate as he gives in to the beautiful feeling growing between us.

His words of love are everything I need to push me into another climax.

"Oh, God, Miller, I'm coming," I yell out in reply, and as my body starts to contract over his, he grits out a loud *fuck* as he starts to come, too.

He slams into me, his movements slow as we both fly over the edge of bliss, and he pumps a few extra times before he holds himself still inside of me as we both ride out the release to the very end.

He stays inside me and bends over me as he moves to kiss me, our tongues tangling together as we express our love in a tender way after the intensity we just shared. I taste my own tang still on his tongue as he kisses me, and somehow knowing that's me on his breath is intoxicating.

Eventually he pulls out of me and straightens. He disposes of the condom and pulls his pants back into place, and then he picks me up from the counter and into his arms.

He carries me through the house and up the stairs, and he sets me on the bed. "Do you want a shower or bath?" he asks.

"Mm, shower," I say.

He nods, and I hear the water turn on a moment later. He returns naked and carries me to the shower, and he sets me on the bench in there. He takes care of me, washing my body with the loofah and rinsing me with the shower head. He washes my hair, and then he washes himself, too, and I never have to lift a finger. I don't even have to stand. He brings me a towel and dries me next, and eventually I force my exhausted body to stand so I can comb out my hair and put on some clothes for bed.

And when he climbs in beside me, for the first time in the last few days, I finally feel like maybe, just maybe, everything's going to be okay.

Chapter 49: Sophie Summers

I take Cassie's kids supply shopping, and apparently kids are better behaved for people who aren't their mom. I have a great time with the kids, and Luca ends up with everything Minecraft while Lily ends up with cute little Squishmallow things for the upcoming school year.

Miller is busy all week with various workouts and meetings, but he's been better about communicating, at least. We do dinners together, and things mostly seem to be back on track. He's back to being the book boyfriend of my dreams…for the most part.

There's just one big problem.

Neither one of us has addressed the rather large elephant in the room.

It's sometimes all I think about, and other times I'm able to push it out of my thoughts so I can focus. I'm almost finished writing the first draft of my next book, which is perfect timing since advance copies of my new release are going out Monday— the same day Miller starts training camp, and then the marketing for the new release begins, and I won't have as much time and energy to focus on getting new words when I'm in marketing mode.

Except Miller won't be here. I won't have anything else to focus on, and I'll be going stir-crazy as I wait to get my period or miss my period or figure out when I can take a test to find out if that broken condom actually means anything at all for our future.

And even if I *do* find out either way…when do I tell him?

A negative is easy. I can do that over the phone. Over text, even.

But a positive?

I have no idea how to handle it.

So I count the days and wait for my period to come, trying my best to put the whole idea out of my head even as I stand at the grocery store staring at the different pregnancy test options on a Thursday afternoon by myself.

I should buy one. Right? I should have one at home for when I'm ready to take it. This box says it has results six days sooner. That test says it's ninety-nine percent accurate. That one has a line. That one has a digital screen that says *pregnant* or *not pregnant.*

And it's as I'm standing in the aisle at the grocery store staring at pregnancy tests on a Thursday morning that I hear my name.

"Sophie?"

I turn and gasp. "Cassie! What are you doing here?"

"Uh, shopping," she says, nodding to her cart. "What are you doing?"

I glance at the row of pregnancy tests in front of me, and my eyes widen as I suddenly feel very caught. "Um…" I trail off, and I grab a box of condoms. "Fresh out," I say, holding up the box with a cheesy smile that I hope is good enough to pass the test.

It has to be good enough. I already know Cassie can't keep a secret, as proven on the cruise, and I don't need her spreading the news all over town that Sophie was shopping for pregnancy tests at the grocery store.

I should've ordered these online. Doing this in person in a store when I'm with someone as high profile as a pro football player was a dumb move—and that's without thinking I might run into someone I know. Someone who can't keep secrets.

My act must be good enough to pass the test because she starts with casual conversation. "The kids can't stop talking about their shopping and lunch date with Aunt Sophie. They want you to take them to lunch again."

I laugh. "It's because I let them both order large fries at McDonald's. They said you never let them."

She narrows her eyes at me. "Yeah, maybe on second thought we shouldn't do that again." She giggles to let me know she's just kidding, but it still pulses a thought inside me that was never there before.

Should I not have given two kids large fries?

I don't know how kids eat. They wanted fries, so I got them fries. I guess logically, I know fries aren't healthy, but I also know kids can be picky eaters, and I didn't want to bring them back home to Cassie hungry.

The more I think about it, the more I realize I don't know anything at all about kids. It's not just their eating habits—it's everything.

I didn't have baby cousins I took care of when I was little. Instead, I was the youngest.

I didn't take up babysitting when I was an adolescent. I didn't even read the popular books about babysitting when I was that age, instead opting for semi-age-appropriate books that introduced me to my love of romance.

I really didn't even have many friends who had kids before me. I was busy between teaching and secretly publishing books, and I had a boyfriend. I didn't make much space for friends who were in a totally different phase of life than me.

But standing here in this aisle with my potential future sister-in-law staring at me as I stand in front of a variety of different tests makes me realize how incredibly unprepared I am for any of this.

And I don't even have the luxury of leaning on my boyfriend since he's about to dig into a new season, and we're going to have to spend time apart.

I suddenly feel a little lonely and a lot scared.

I think about confiding all this in Cassie, but ultimately, I realize her allegiance is to Tanner, not to me. She's married to him now, and he's a twin. Word will get back to Miller through some other source, and if I'm feeling these feelings, he should hear it from me.

I just don't want to pile on top of him when he's already going through his own stuff with the start of the season. I want to try to be there for him the best way I can, only…I have no idea what that looks like right now, either.

There's just a lot of uncertainty in my life right now, and I guess all I can do is ride the wave until things settle down.

I just don't know when that will be.

It's not in the next few days, that's for sure.

Training camp is here in San Diego. The team uses the stadium for practice, but the first week is meant for team bonding, so barring emergencies, players are asked to stay at the team hotel for the first two weeks of training camp.

Then they return home, and they start regular practices that aren't quite as intense as those first two weeks of camp. That's also when preseason games begin and the roster is finalized.

It'll be an intense couple of weeks for Miller and the rest of his teammates, and I already sense a bit of a change in him as he packs his bags the Sunday night before camp is set to start.

I'm sitting on the bed in his room while he works. I've asked if there's anything I can do, and his request was just to sit with him while he does what he needs to do.

It's like he wants us to spend every last moment together that we can before this shift in our relationship.

"I'll try to call you every day, but things get pretty intense," he says.

I nod as I try to be as understanding as possible. I can't imagine a job that's so intense that I can't make time for a one-minute phone call, but I let it go.

"If you remember, drag the black trash to the curb on Mondays. Organic is collected on Tuesdays, and recycling is every other Wednesday," he reminds me.

I nod. "Anything else around the house you want me to take care of?"

He shakes his head. "The pool pretty much takes care of itself, but my guy is scheduled for the first week of next month for monthly maintenance. The landscapers will be here on Thursday as usual, and I called a house cleaner one of my teammates recommended to come in weekly on Thursday mornings so it's all done at the same time."

"You didn't have to do that. I can clean." My protest is weak since—let's be honest—having someone clean the house sounds like a dream.

"I know, but I want you to have that time for writing."

I press my lips together and tilt my head. "That's really sweet of you. Thank you."

He nods without looking up from his pile of clothes. He counts everything out, and then he mutters, "Fuck it," as if he's not really all that worried about what he's packing. I'm sure they have laundry access anyway since they're gone two weeks.

He sits beside me, and he sighs. "This is weird. I've never had to leave you as my…whatever this is…when I'm starting a new season."

"I was just thinking that, too. And to fill in the blank, you could say girlfriend. Fiancée. Lover."

He laughs. "I like *lover*. That's how I'll refer to you. Surely they'll ask questions on media day. *Who'd you leave behind at home? Oh, me? Just my lover.*"

I giggle, but the truth is that the giggle is hiding a deeper fear.

Will he be able to say the same thing next season when he's asked that question? Or will his answer be different? He's leaving his *wife* behind. And his *baby*.

And we're talking about what days the trash is collected instead of any of that.

It's just because he's focused on the season. He should be. And I should be focused on my book coming out in a couple weeks.

I'm not.

We have sex, and I force myself to be present in the moment. To concentrate on every caress of his fingers, every slide of his tongue wherever it lands, every thrust of his hips into me.

It's the last time we'll get to do this for the next two weeks, so I memorize every second of it.

And when it's over, and I'm lying in his arms warm and sated, I memorize those moments, too. The way he smells, the way he feels, the warmth he exudes.

I hold onto those feelings as tightly as I can.

After we kiss goodbye in the morning, and I wave to him as he pulls away for the next two weeks, I can't help but burst into tears as I wonder whether life will be any different when he returns home to me.

331

Chapter 50: Miller Banks

The *Quiet* Brother

I want to be excited for the season ahead, and I'm trying to be.

It's hard when I realize everything I'm leaving behind.

It's even harder when I think about how much longer I even want to play.

I turn off the street where I could still see Sophie waving at me in the rearview mirror, and I pull to the side of the road. I draw in a deep breath as I grip the steering wheel with both hands.

It feels different this season.

I *love* playing this game. I have always loved playing football since I first picked one up.

It's always been everything to me, and getting to play it with my brother has been the highlight of my life.

But life is changing. Things are different now. Tanner is married. He has a wife and two stepkids, and maybe he and Cassie are trying to have a kid of their own. I wouldn't know since Tanner and I haven't had the same kinds of heart-to-hearts we were able to have back when we lived together.

I felt myself pulling back from Sophie as the season drew nearer. It wasn't really because of the condom. She hasn't been exhibiting any new or different symptoms, and I feel fairly confident that it was nothing more than an accident. I managed to push it to the back of my mind.

I wasn't pulling away on purpose, I guess, but I started getting busier. Workouts and meetings meant less time at home, and it's a semi-realistic picture of what the season will look like for us.

But I guess I was drawing back because I was scared, too. I felt her pulling away, maybe because of the condom, or maybe because of her book release coming up, or maybe because I wasn't home as much…but whatever the case, it's always been my habit to get ahead of problems before they become issues.

I just never thought I'd have problems *or* issues when it came to Sophie.

I always knew the gamble of getting involved with her could lead to my worst nightmare, which would be losing her as a friend or losing her completely from my life.

I feel like I'm leaving her behind as I pull away to a new season, but I don't have a choice.

I'm leaving things in a precarious position, but I have no clue how to fix it.

I just hope that this two-week pause isn't enough to break us.

I try to categorize these feelings. I try to push them aside.

I need to focus, and I pull back onto the road as I do my best to leave those fears behind on the side of the road where I allowed them into my conscious thoughts.

I arrive at the stadium and see the parking lot is already full of the vehicles my teammates drive—lots of trucks and luxury SUVs. I figured I'd be one of the first to arrive, but it looks like I'm one of the last.

Maybe I pulled over to the side of the road a little longer than I thought.

I'm already in my practice clothes, but I grab my duffel anyway and haul it into the locker room with me. I spot my practice jersey and some other gear, and I settle onto the bench inside my locker as I glance around the locker room that's already bustling with activity this morning. Loud rap music pours from the sound system as we all get pumped up for today's activities, and I glance at the locker to my left where Isaiah is changing his shoes.

"Are you ready?" he asks.

"Do I have a choice?" I shoot back.

He laughs. We both feel pretty secure in our positions. I'll start, but he'll get plenty of time on the field. Sometimes we run plays with two running backs, and other times I need to rest or sit out a play. I glance at the locker on the other side of Isaiah and spot Drake, who will get a little less time than Isaiah. Next to him is Jalen, who will have to prove himself at camp before we know what his season will look like. Roman and Byron are here, too, but they don't have lockers by ours. They're on the practice squad, so they get a shared space to store their equipment on the other side of the locker room.

Tanner walks by, and I stand as we do our twin handshake.

We haven't lived together since he and Cassie moved in together, and I miss seeing him all the time. We lived together the majority of our adult lives, and while we're still close, the dynamic has definitely shifted.

Still, he's my best friend, and if there's anybody I could talk to about the shit I'm going through with Sophie, it's him.

And maybe I will at some point over the next two weeks. Maybe I won't.

We start with a big team meeting to introduce the themes of the next two weeks. The new players are introduced even though we've already met, and then we break out into smaller groups with our position coaches.

It's all so predictable.

Our goal is to win games. We'll do that by focusing on fundamentals.

It's literally the same regurgitated speech every season from every coach who I've ever played for, from high school to college to two different teams at the professional level.

And this year…I'm just not sure I'm feeling it.

I know what happened last season when Tanner wasn't feeling it, though he was in a much different place than I was. And it led to a torn ACL. He was out for the season. It gave him the time he needed to focus on his new relationship.

I don't need that time, though. It's not like Sophie would be the one to rehab me if I got injured.

And I have gotten injured. Of course. I get injured nearly every time I step onto that field. But I've never sat out an entire season, and I don't plan on doing it now.

Even so, it doesn't feel like my heart is in it this year, and I don't know what to do about that.

We get out on the field after lunch and start with some drills, and then we head back in for more meetings. We review tape. We eat dinner as a team. We watch more tape.

It's after ten by the time I get up to the room I'm sharing with Tanner, and I'm fucking beat. I was up early, and between the emotional pull that's back home with Sophie and the feelings I'm experiencing here so far, I feel completely out of sorts.

"The fuck's going on with you?" Tanner asks when I walk into the room.

"Well, hello to you, too," I say dryly.

"Look, I know you're the *quiet* brother," he says, tossing air quotes around the word *quiet*, "but whatever's eating you is affecting me, so get it together."

"I'm fine." I don't sound very convincing.

"Is it Sophie?" he asks. "What's going on with the two of you? Cassie said she ran into Soph at the grocery store the other day, and she was acting strange."

I plop onto the queen bed that'll be mine for the next two weeks and lie back. I stare up at the ceiling. "When we found out Eddie was our biological father, something shifted in me. I was scared I'd end up like him."

He blows out a breath as he knows that's my intro to the rest of what's bothering me.

"I know I have the power to break the cycle and all that bullshit, but it doesn't matter. The five of you escaped it. You're all married, and most of you have kids or you're having them or you're a stepparent. And then there's me. You escaped it, but what if it lands on the youngest? What if I'm destined to be the most like him?"

"Meaning what?" he asks, clearly confused.

"Meaning being a shit of a human and not being the kind of father any kid would deserve."

"We got Charles, bro. We lucked out. You'll be like him. Sacrificing for your kids rather than giving up on them." He pauses before he adds, "You're a good person, Miller. You're not like him."

"How do you know that?" I ask quietly.

"Because I had the privilege of growing up with you. When I fell off my bike when I was eleven, who ran and got help? Who helped me with chores when I was out late? Who drove me home when I had too much to drink? Who was there for me every step of the way as I fell in love with Cassie? Spoiler alert, all of those were you. You're a good dude with a heart of gold, and finding out who gave us life has no bearing on any of that. So where is this coming from?"

"It's coming from that. It fucked me up, man. It made me think twice about having kids, and then—" I cut myself off, not entirely sure I want to confess about the broken condom. I thought I'd mostly pushed that out of my head.

But I have two weeks in a hotel with my brother. I'm not sure I can keep that to myself those entire two weeks without him pulling it out of me anyway. May as well get it out of the way.

"And then?" he prompts.

I blow out a breath. "A condom broke when we were on the cruise."

"Oh, shit. Is she…" He trails off, not saying the word.

I sit up and shrug. "No idea. Too early to tell."

"What if she is?" he asks carefully.

"Then I guess it doesn't matter if I don't want kids because I'll be having one."

He presses his lips together. "Is this the attitude you gave her?"

"To be honest, we haven't talked about it much at all."

"So you're running scared, she's presumably freaking out, and rightfully so since you're backing away, and your entire friendship is at risk. Sound about right?"

I raise my brows as I bite my lip. "Yeah, that about sums it up. But don't forget the whole chestnut about starting a new season and not really being sure how much longer I've got in this game."

His brows dip together. "Why would you say that?"

"We're thirty now, bro. Who's the oldest running back in the league?"

"Frank Gore played to thirty-seven."

"Yeah, and Jim Thorpe played until he was forty-one in the twenties. Those are outliers, man. *I* am a fucking outlier at thirty, and you know the game has changed even in the last few years." I lift a helpless shoulder.

"So sit out more. Don't take as many hits. Let the younger guys prove their worth." He lifts his shoulder back as if that's the answer. But it's not.

"You know I can't get out there and not leave it all out on the field."

"Yeah," he sighs. "I know." He's the same damn way. It's bred in us—from our biological father, most likely. It's a case of nature versus nurture, and that's why I've arrived at the conclusion that there's still a chance I'll end up like him no matter how hard I fight against it.

"Look, whatever happens, you've got to get your head on straight. Have you talked to Sophie about any of this?"

I shake my head.

"Do you really think you can plan a future with someone when you can't be bothered to talk to that person about what's going on in your head?" he asks.

I know he's right, but that doesn't make it magically easier to fix any of this. I don't even know how to fix it when the future is so unknown.

I thought coming here would help immerse me into the game. I thought it would help me focus and leave my fears behind.

As it turns out, it's not quite that easy to run away from my problems. They followed me here, and now they just feel like they're looming in front of me with no easy solutions.

I should call her. We do need to talk…but this isn't the kind of conversation I want to have when I'm beat after a day at camp.

It's also not one I want to have with my brother staring at me from the next bed over.

And so I'll wait for another day.

I send her a goodnight text while Tanner calls Cassie and hope that's good enough.

Chapter 51: Sophie Summers

One Word

Miller: *I'm exhausted after a crazy first day. Heading to bed. Will try to call tomorrow.*

That's it.

No "Love you!"

No "Miss you!"

Nothing. Not even a check-in on how I might be doing. He left exactly zero room for conversation, and the thought leaves me feeling hollow and alone.

I've never dealt with feeling alone and abandoned by Miller. He's always been my rock, but we've never been in a situation like this before.

I push those feelings aside and try to be the understanding girlfriend back home. But it feels an awful lot like in doing that, I'm simply being nothing more than a doormat.

And I hate that feeling.

I have to push it aside, though, because I'm releasing a book in three days. In four days, I'm appearing at the Harts and Harps Book Nook in Las Vegas, which means I need to get packed up and ready for my short trip. I'm flying in Friday morning, signing in the afternoon, and staying one night before I fly back home on Saturday.

I'm not entirely sure why I booked the trip that way. I could use an extra night or two away. It's not like I have anything waiting back here for me with Miller gone.

Cassie's busy with her patients and her kids. Grace is busy with her vineyard. I should be busy writing.

But it's like when Miller left, so did my muse.

I stare at the blank screen for far too long before I give up. I close the lid to my laptop and head up to bed, and I lie there staring up at the ceiling as I convince myself that tomorrow I'll be brave enough to go back to the store and pick a test so I can finally learn the answer to the question that has been on my mind for the last two weeks. Is two weeks enough time? Do I need to miss a period?

I have no idea, so I Google it. Apparently I could end up with a false negative…but I could also potentially see a positive.

I'm going to give it a try anyway. I can't stand not knowing for a second longer.

I toss and turn all night, and I force myself to stay in bed until seven. I get up, throw my hair in a ponytail, and head to the store before breakfast.

I pick the one with the electronic readout so there's no room for questions. I head home. I tear open the box without reading the directions, and I pee on the stick.

And then I sit there on the toilet staring at the screen as an hourglass blinks at me. I should've read the directions. I have no idea how long I need to wait. I don't even know if I peed on the stick right. Maybe I'm supposed to do something different.

I set the test on top of the box, finish up in the bathroom, and wash my hands. I keep my eyes on that blinking hourglass the entire time.

I sit on the edge of the bathtub, and I'm just about to reach for the box with the instructions when the hourglass stops blinking.

My heart leaps into my throat, and a single word appears on the screen: *Pregnant.*

I exhale as tears pinch behind my eyes.

I'm not sure what to think. I'm not sure what to feel.

My first thought is that apparently two weeks is long enough for a positive. I wonder if I could've tested last week. I wonder if I could've known sooner—known when he was here so we could be together to learn this news.

Instead, I feel like I'm keeping a secret from him the very second I know the truth.

It's early. Things could still happen.

But right at this very second, I'm growing Miller Banks's baby in my stomach, and that's a thought I never in a million years thought I'd have.

How will this change my life? How will this change things between us? How do I even tell him about this when he's been pretty upfront about how he feels about having kids?

I slide off the edge of the tub and onto the floor as I start to cry.

What if he resents the baby or resents *me* or resents our relationship? What if he feels forced into a future he never wanted because of an accident?

How do we get past those very real and very scary issues?

I have none of the answers, but I'm starting to panic as I continue to stare at the single word on that screen.

My chest squeezes tightly as I start to pant.

My stomach rolls over.

I think I'm going to be sick.

I run to the toilet and heave, but nothing comes out. I haven't eaten yet. I don't know if I can ever eat again. I have to eat. I'm growing a baby.

I can hardly take care of myself some days. I can't cook. How do I feed a baby?

How do I take care of another human?

How do I do any of this…alone?

I sit on the bathroom floor for a few seconds as I gasp and try to heave in gulps of air.

I finally draw in a long, steady breath.

I need to call Miller. I know I can't tell him this over the phone, but I need to hear his voice. I need him to tell me everything's going to be okay even though he has no idea what's going on.

I press his contact, and the phone rings. And rings. And rings. It goes to voicemail after six rings.

I don't bother with a message. It's probably better he didn't answer. It's better he doesn't hear the panic in my voice right now. I need to calm down.

A cup of coffee will help.

I run down to the kitchen, start the Keurig, and breathe in the heavenly scent of a fresh cup of coffee.

I tip the mug to my lips, and that's when I freeze.

Fuck. I never got the answer to the question of whether it's okay to drink coffee when I'm pregnant.

It's one more thing I have no idea about. One more thing I may potentially have to sacrifice. One more thing that makes me feel helpless, clueless, and overwhelmed.

I need to make an appointment to see a doctor.

I need to research.

I have a book releasing in three days.

Oh, God. I think I'm going to throw up.

Chapter 52: Sophie Summers

Bonding

Since I've only lived in San Diego since March and my annual appointments all take place in January, I haven't taken the time to find doctors here in town. But I know someone in the medical field who has lived here her entire life, which means I have the inside track.

I text rather than call.

Me: *Hey, my annual is coming up. Do you have a local GYN you'd recommend?*

Cassie writes back immediately with a name and phone number, and I've never been more grateful that I have a friend here. And then she sends another message.

Cassie: *She's the best around, so she fills up quick. I'm not sure if she's taking new patients, but I can ask.*

Me: *I can just call and find out. Thanks.*

Before she replies, I dial the number.

"Primrose for Women, please hold."

Of course.

I hold and hold and hold some more before she comes back.

"How can I help you?"

"Hi. I think I might be pregnant, and I'm new to the area. A friend recommended your office. Are you taking new patients?"

"Drs. Maddox and Thorpe are not, but I can get you in with Dr. Kacey this Thursday at nine fifteen."

Dr. Maddox was the one Cassie recommended, but that's okay. This Thursday is my book release. I don't go to Vegas until Friday, so that should work.

Great, birthing a book and finding out more about birthing a kid all on the same day. Just what I was planning when I picked July thirtieth as my release date.

"That would be great, thank you."

She takes some of my information down, tells me to complete the new patient packet on their website, and we hang up.

I immediately run to my computer and fill out the paperwork, and I realize I'm absolutely starving—as if the rolling over of my stomach has ceased and now it's angry for food.

I make some eggs and munch on cheese while I wait for the eggs to cook, and I stare at my phone as I will it to ring.

I wonder what Miller's doing right now. Is he in a meeting? At practice? Sleeping in?

I'd know if he called or communicated with me in any way, but all I have to go on is that one text from last night.

And that's how I spend my day.

I shoot him a text around lunchtime, figuring at the very least that he's awake.

Me: *Hope today is going well. I miss you.*

I don't get a reply for hours, and when it comes, it's another vague one.

Miller: *Sorry I missed your call. My phone stays in my hotel room during practice. Today is going well. Miss you too.*

I take the text back as my sign that he's available to talk, and I hit the call button. I really just need to hear his voice.

But I get voicemail.

I tell myself maybe he just hopped in the shower or something after he clicked send. I can tell myself all I want, though. It doesn't mean I believe a second of it.

I hate being this whiny girl obsessing over her man, so I decide to text Cassie.

Me: *You around tonight?*

Cassie: *I've got baseball practice with Luca. You're more than welcome to come hang out with Lily and me.*

Yeah, no thanks.

I try Grace next.

Me: *Are you around tonight? Want to grab dinner?*

Grace: *I'm not! Sorry! I flew up to Minnesota for a few days. Next week?*

I reply with some vague response, and I sigh as I let that sting of loneliness wash over me.

Is this the kind of life I want? Chasing after Miller, who can't be bothered to communicate more than a few words at a time. Raising a baby largely on my own as I wait for him to come home.

No. It's not the life I want. It's not the life I dreamed of.

I miss the Miller who was my book boyfriend. I miss the guy who performed acts of service without me ever having to ask him because he just knew how to speak my love language.

And so I take that loneliness, open my laptop, and channel all my feelings into my characters.

I find myself with great intentions to work, and instead, I'm navigating away from my document and opening a browser.

I search *two weeks pregnant* to see what comes up.

I start to study and learn. I start to feed the part of myself that feels clueless. I start to feel even more overwhelmed, but being equipped with knowledge is one small way to try to combat that overwhelm.

I spend the day doing none of the tasks on my *to-do list* and instead try to learn everything I can about the first few weeks of pregnancy.

I realize I have graphics to make, posts to schedule, and ads to run. But all of that seems to take a backseat to the fact that I'm going to be a mother in thirty-eight weeks or less.

The very thought of that causes the panic to rise once again in the back of my throat like bile. The urge to talk to Miller overwhelms me, and I think it's because I need to hear his voice to make me feel like we're going to be okay.

And so I try calling him again after dinner.

"Hey!" he answers. He sounds…jovial?

"Hey. I miss you."

"Same. It's been a wild forty-eight hours, but Coach just gave us an hour to bond with our teammates."

I hear laughter in the background, and a male voice mocks Miller. "Yeah, we're bonding all right."

"What are you doing?" I ask.

"Bonding." His answer is short.

"What does that mean?"

I hear a group of people cheering.

"I should go," he says. "I'll call you back in a bit, okay?"

He ends the call, and I fling my phone onto the table. I just wanted to hear his voice to help myself feel a little better, and instead, hearing it just made me feel worse.

It made me angry. It made me lonely.

He's never given me any reason to feel that way, but not being able to share this news with him is tearing me apart. The truth is that he *won't* always be available for me. He'll always have to put his work ahead of me.

Ahead of *us*.

And that just leads me full circle back to the scary question. How am I supposed to do this alone?

Chapter 53: Miller Banks

Better Off Without Me

I glance at Tanner and shake my head.

This was the exact wrong moment to pick up a call, but I've missed so many from her today that I don't want her to think I'm purposely ignoring her even though that's not the case at all.

The truth is that I've been working my tail off since I got here. All of us have.

The media is here this evening, and we just sat through rounds of interviews. The organization let some fans in for media day, and they were all yelling when my phone started ringing.

I duck into the tunnel since it's quiet in there even though I'm not supposed to leave the field, and I call her back.

She doesn't answer.

I decide to send a text message to try to clear things up.

Me: *Sorry, fans were yelling when I picked up.*

It shows as delivered, but I have no clue if she read it or not.

She doesn't call me back, and I'm not sure my text was very clear—the very problem with trying to communicate over text versus on the phone. Does she know it's media day? Does she even know what media day is?

Probably not because I haven't taken the time to inform her. It's like I have two different lives—the football life and the personal life, and they're suddenly not merging together the way they should be. Maybe because Sophie has been a part of my life for so long, but she was never really a part of my football life, barring the times in high school when she was a cheerleader for our team.

But a new fear pulses in me as I think about the fact that this is really our first time away from each other since we got together, and we're already struggling. It's not like it's going to get easier the more time we spend apart.

I think about my penchant for getting ahead of problems before they become issues.

I can't help but wonder if she's better off without me. I feel like all I'm doing is hurting her, and that's the last thing I want to do.

I blow out a breath as I return to the seat beside my brother.

"Did you talk to her?" he asks.

I shake my head.

"Maybe tonight," he says.

I lift a shoulder. "Yeah, maybe."

"What's going on, man?"

"What if she's better off without me?" I realize this is neither the time nor the place for this conversation, but Tanner usually has a way of making me feel better.

Usually.

Today is not one of those times.

"What if she is?" he asks.

What the fuck, bro? I was waiting for him to calm my nerves and tell me there's no way that could possibly be true.

Does he really think that?

I don't get a chance to ask because he's called back to the media table for more interviews.

But now it's a thought swirling around my mind, and it's going to send me into a spiral.

I would do anything for her…and that includes leaving her if I think she's better off without me.

I don't know what that looks like. She's living in my fucking house, for one thing. I'm away for two weeks. I've been gone less than forty-eight hours, and I'm already questioning whether she deserves better.

Of course she does. She deserves someone who can be present for her. Who can show up for her.

She deserves the guy I am in the offseason, not the guy who travels from city to city playing a game every week. Not the guy who's gone for two weeks at training camp, leaving her back home.

I only get to be that guy for half the year. The other half, I'm a football player first. I have to be. I have teammates relying on me to be.

But…so does Tanner, and he managed to strike a balance. Or not. This is his first season *playing* with Cassie in his life. Maybe they're struggling, too, and maybe that's where his words are coming from.

The difference is that he's married now.

This was never an issue in previous seasons, but I've also never had to leave someone behind who I was so deeply in love with.

And sometimes that deep kind of love means sacrificing the things that you want in order to give the other person what they need.

And I think Sophie needs someone who can be present for her.

Spencer slides into the seat beside me. "You doing okay?"

I lift a shoulder. "Hanging in there." I glance over at him. "How do you manage to keep the balance between your career and your wife?"

His brows dip. "I don't know if I do. I think it's more her understanding what this job entails than anything special I'm doing. Why do you ask?"

I lift a shoulder as I start to bare my soul to my half-brother. "It suddenly feels like I'm choosing between Sophie and this career. I know that's not the case. She would *never* make me choose."

But in a lot of ways, that's what it comes down to in my own head.

"But you're making yourself choose?" he guesses.

"Kind of, I guess." I blow out a breath.

"Why can't you have both?"

It's food for thought, I guess.

"How are things going for the wide receivers?" I ask, changing the subject.

"Madden Bradley is giving me a run for my money, man. He's a couple years older than me but fast as hell." He shakes his head like he needs to get his shit together to keep his place on the team. "But he's also got his father breathing down his neck to take over the family business when he retires, so he's got a lot of pressure on him. I'm not sure how long he'll stay in the game, but he's a hell of a player, and we're lucky to have him."

"We got quite the acquisition in that trade deal," I murmur.

He nods. "Chicago got rid of an all-star, that's for sure. It'll be a battle."

"May the best receiver win," I say, meaning it as a joke because surely it's Spencer, but I'm not sure it lands that way since he's currently worried it's not him at all.

This is a serious business. Any number of guys would give up anything to be in our position—including relationships. Family. Careers.

I guess I just thought I'd have a stronger base with Sophie going into the season considering the foundation of friendship we were building upon, but that doesn't seem to be the case. Instead, it's missed calls and misunderstood texts and a general lonely feeling.

She has a book releasing in a few days and that event at the bookstore in Vegas after that. I should be there supporting her. I'll call her on release day and check in with her, but will it just be another series of missed calls?

I try calling her once more before I climb into bed. Tanner is in the shower, and he still hasn't clarified his statement from earlier.

She doesn't answer.

I decide to leave her a voicemail message.

"Hey. I'm sorry we keep missing each other. What you heard earlier—it wasn't how it sounded. It was media day, and they let fans into the stadium. That's all it was. I feel like we need to talk. Call me, okay?"

I hang up and realize too late that I didn't tell her I love her. I miss her. I need her.

Maybe I didn't say those things subconsciously on purpose. Maybe I don't want to continue down a road that's leading straight to nowhere.

But despite leaving that message, my phone doesn't ring.

Chapter 54: Sophie Summers

I can't bring myself to listen to his message. I'm too scared, to be honest.

I'm sure he'll offer some explanation as to who was screaming his name and *woo*-ing in the background, but I don't really care to hear that explanation right now.

He made it sound like training camp is two weeks of hell, and the first chance I get to hear his voice, he sounds like he's at some goddamn party, most likely with half-naked women screaming his name.

I hate this for us, but I think the pregnancy hormones are sending me these different emotions that I've never felt before. It's one part rage combined with one part fear.

And then there's the exhaustion. It didn't seem to hit me until I saw that word on that stick, and now I just want to lie in bed and never get out of it.

I can't bring myself to write. I can't bring myself to do any of the tasks on my list.

My book releases in two days now, and I have so much to do. I have another book to finish writing. I have one chapter left plus the epilogue, and I'm not sure how I'm supposed to gush about their happy ending when I feel like mine was just within reach before it was ripped away.

I'm living in his house, sleeping in his bed, showering in his shower, and I have no idea where we stand right now.

Maybe I'd have a better idea if I picked up the damn phone, but a piece of me is too scared.

A piece of me thinks that message he left is letting me down gently.

The very thought of a life without Miller makes my stomach turn over, but it's right there at the surface, pulsing in a very irritating way every time I think I've pushed it out.

He tries calling me in the morning. I don't answer.

I turn on my computer. I'm behind on my deadline. I told my editor I'd have this book to her yesterday, but I can't write when I'm thinking about the strange place where Miller and I have landed. I'm really, really scared that this is going to spell the end for us.

So where does that leave me and the baby?

I have to tell him, obviously. I just feel like I need to do it in a way that will give him the option to walk away if this isn't the life he wants.

Babies are a big commitment, but the more I've sat with this over the last twenty-four hours, the more I know that this is what I want. I can do this. And if I have to do it alone, well…so be it. I will.

I will be everything this baby needs if it's up to me to be the sole provider. I will raise him or her knowing that she or he was created out of love.

I hope Miller will be there by my side for all the highs and all the lows.

But if he's not, I'm going to be okay.

I just have to figure out *where* I want to do this—in particular if it's just me.

It would be easier to move back home, to be close to my parents despite their divorce, to have some help nearby. It would be easier to be back in my group of friends, though I think I lost most of them when I quit my job.

It's only now I realize I haven't even spoken to Brooke in months. I've been so busy trying to build my life in San Diego that I neglected my life in Phoenix. Maybe it wouldn't be so much easier to move back home after all.

At least here, I have Cassie and Grace…

Who I realize now are part of *Miller's* family, not mine.

If he opts to walk away once I tell him, he'll get them in the fallout. Not me.

It feels like my entire life is slipping away before my very eyes. I should channel this angst into my books, but I'm not at that part.

I head to Miller's workout room, and everything in here reminds me of him.

I get on the treadmill and start a slow walk. I read that exercise is good for the baby, and maybe it'll be enough to jog my brain out of this fog so I can get some work done.

Truth be told, I need some coffee. I have a splitting headache from avoiding it for the last two days, and I need *something* to help alleviate it.

I run a quick search and learn that one cup a day is okay, so I treat myself to that after a half hour on the treadmill. I sit out on the deck in the backyard and look out over the view. The house is in the hills of San Diego with a gorgeous view of the rolling hills with houses down below. In the distance I can see the ocean, and it's peaceful and serene from here.

Will it still be that way in nine months? Or will the crying from inside be enough to pry that serenity right from my fingertips?

Will Miller run upstairs and check on the baby?

Or will I be somewhere else, doing it alone?

I won't know the answer to that until I talk to him. I need to talk to him.

I take a shower after my cup of coffee, my nerves suddenly feeling like steel.

I have to tell him.

I jump in the car and drive through town to the hotel where the team is staying.

I head to the front desk. "I need the room of Miller Banks, please."

"I'm sorry, but I can't give you that information."

"I'm his fiancée," I say, flashing my ring.

The clerk purses his lips. "Then you should be able to get in touch and ask him his room number."

I roll my eyes, but I guess it's not this guy's fault that he has to uphold the hotel's policies. It's probably safer for players anyway.

I realize the team probably isn't even at the hotel right now, so I get back in my car and head toward the stadium.

I'm not exactly sure what my plan is, but when I get there, I walk up toward the doors where fans enter.

Not shockingly, they're locked.

I walk around the building to every possible door. I try them all. They're all locked.

There are no workers out here for me to ask. Nobody to direct me anywhere.

I open my phone and search for the stadium's information. I find a phone number, and I dial it.

"Thank you for calling the SDS Stadium box office. We are currently closed."

Fuck. Fuck!

I head back to my car and slide into the driver's seat.

What the hell did I think I was going to do?

Like he'd magically walk out and spot me there, and he'd rush to me, and I'd tell him I'm pregnant and he'd sweep me up into his arms and kiss me and tell me we'll be a little family?

I think I've written one too many romance novels.

I blow out a breath as I start the car and navigate back toward home as I hope and pray that this will still be my home after these next two weeks are over.

Chapter 55: Miller Banks

"What the fuck was that?" Tanner yells at me. He doesn't usually yell at me, but I dropped an easy handoff. Twice. I probably deserve to have him in my face.

It's Friday morning. I tried calling her yesterday on her release day, and she never answered. Maybe she was busy. Maybe she doesn't want to talk to me.

I texted her instead. I wished her good luck on her release day. I texted her again later in the day to celebrate that her book hit the bestseller charts after I pulled it up to check it.

I told her I can't wait to read it. I said I love her and miss her.

She didn't reply.

I think she's really angry with me, and I don't know how to fucking fix it when she won't pick up the goddamn phone and we're forced to be apart.

I fucking hate this.

"Sorry," I mutter.

When it happens a third time, he walks away and heads toward Coach. A minute later, he's guiding me off the field and toward the locker room.

"What the fuck are you doing, bro?" he asks me.

It's just the two of us in an empty locker room, and I sink down onto a bench.

"I'm distracted. I slept like shit the last couple nights, and shit's hanging in the balance with Soph, who won't talk to me, and it feels like my life is falling the fuck apart and there's nothing I can do about it." It feels like a weight off my shoulders to confess all that to my brother.

"Do I need to remind you what happened to me last season when I let a woman distract me?" he asks through a clenched jaw.

"No, I remember. You got a year off to fall in love."

"Fuck off with that. You know that's not what happened." He sits beside me.

"Maybe not, but it was the result, wasn't it?" I shoot back.

He sighs. "This isn't about me. Don't you see that you and Sophie belong together?"

"Then why aren't we together?" I ask.

"Because you're being a fucking idiot."

"Thanks, man," I say dryly.

"Go get her, Miller," he says quietly. "Tell her how you feel before it's too late."

"I'm here another week," I remind him. "I can't just walk out."

"Coach always says family comes first. You know that. You're already a starter. He will understand. You know where you stand on this. You're just too fucking stupid to see it for yourself, so I'm here to tell you. Go fucking get her."

"She won't talk to me, man. She doesn't want to see me," I protest. "I need to be here."

"You said she released a book yesterday, right?" he asks, and I nod. "Then isn't it plausible she was just busy yesterday? Maybe she had an interview and couldn't pick up. Maybe she was on Instagram Live. Maybe there are a thousand reasons she didn't answer that have nothing to do with you—the same way you not answering has nothing to do with her."

I know he's right. But it's easier to believe the negative. It's also easier to live in the what-ifs than to be disappointed with the truth. There's still a chance she'll walk away from this. From us.

There's always that chance.

But what if I'm letting her do that without fighting for her?

This is all I've ever wanted. *She* is all I ever wanted. And she's right within my grasp. All I need to do is reach out and cling to her.

"Did you ever think that maybe she took that test?" he asks quietly. "Maybe she knows the answers you so desperately want to know, and she's too scared to tell you that over the phone."

The thought never occurred to me. I figured she'd wait and test when we were home together.

But maybe not.

Maybe she took it. Maybe it was negative.

But maybe it wasn't.

What if it wasn't, and she's had to live in loneliness knowing that for the last few days?

What if it wasn't, and she thinks I don't want kids?

I blow out a breath. That last thought stabs me like a knife.

"What if she did and it was positive?" I finally whisper. Tanner is the *only* person in the entire world I'd feel comfortable having this conversation with. I don't do vulnerability, but for some reason, with him, I can.

"What if it was?" he repeats.

Is that just what he does now? Repeats my questions back at me?

Well…it's pretty goddamn effective, that's for sure.

I never was the guy who was adamant about not wanting kids—at least not until I found out Eddie was my father. That changed a lot for me, but the truth is, Tanner could be right. Maybe I'm not destined to be anything like him despite having his blood in my veins.

I don't want to be like him. He abandoned us and paid our mother off to ensure we'd never know he fathered the two of us. The only reason we found out was presumably because he no longer wanted to pay her off and decided he'd slip the news to his youngest son, Asher…the one who orchestrated telling the two of us just after he informed Lincoln, Grayson, and Spencer.

What if I'm more like Lincoln, the man who took on a ten-year-old kid as his stepson and has two beautiful children with his loving wife?

Or maybe if I'm more like Grayson, who loves his wife so much that he gave up the game to help her run her bakery.

I could be more like Spencer, who is quietly logical and helps run the books at his wife's vineyards.

Or maybe I'm more like Asher, who had a baby with his wife, and now he's about to have another one.

I could even be more like Tanner, who married a woman seven years older than him and is the greatest stepdad in the world to her two children.

Or what if I'm just me…the guy who will do anything for the woman I love?

Anything for the woman I love…and any future we create together.

Anything.

Maybe we did make a baby together. It was meant to happen if it did. We tried using protection. But sometimes, what's meant to be will be. Sometimes these things are out of our control, and we're powerless to stop them.

Maybe I *want* to have children with her. I've been so blinded by the thought that I'd be just like Eddie that I never stopped to think that maybe I wouldn't be a damn thing like him.

Maybe I'm just me.

"Look, you made things happen when Cassie and I were apart," he says. "This is me paying it forward, okay? You need to see her. You need to work this out."

He's right.

I need to see her.

It's Friday. She's going to Vegas today for her book signing at the Harts and Harps Book Nook—the shop owned by a player on the Vegas Aces and his wife.

I know Travis Woods. I have his number. I can get in touch with him, see if I can launch this plan that's suddenly coming together in my mind…

"Your wheels are turning," Tanner says. "I can see it. I see the fire in you, man. Don't bother with Coach. I'll cover for you. Go fucking get her, and then get your ass back here and get your head back in the goddamn game."

I nod, and I can't help when a grin breaks out across my lips. "Thanks, man."

He smiles back at me, and he punches me in the shoulder. "Anytime, bro."

Chapter 56: Sophie Summers

Love Conquers All

"It's so lovely to finally meet you," I say. I'm putting on a brave smile even though it feels like my heart is breaking on the inside.

I haven't spoken to Miller since the call three nights ago. He's tried calling. He's tried texting. But I'm too scared I'm going to spill the beans that I'm pregnant. I tell him everything, and I can't keep this big of a secret from him.

I just never imagined telling him like this. I never imagined him staying with me out of obligation. I never imagined any of this, to be honest, and I'm a goddamn romance author. Imagination is my entire jam.

The doctor's appointment yesterday was good. It's confirmed. I'm pregnant. They said I'm due April tenth. It's anyone's guess if I'll have Miller there by my side in the delivery room or if I'll be by myself.

I can do hard things.

I'm here alone today, right? I'm about to sign books in public for the first time ever.

Victoria hugs me and nods to one of the chairs in front of her desk. "I can't believe you're really here! And engaged to a pro football player. Did we just become best friends?"

I giggle as I sit, and she perches on the edge of her desk in her office at the back of the bookstore. There was already a line out front when my Uber pulled behind the building to drop me off, and I'm suddenly a little nervous.

All these people are here to see me?

But why?

I'm just a girl who likes to make up stories.

"I think maybe we did," I say, forcing the nerves away.

"If only he played for the Aces instead of that silly team in San Diego," she laments.

"Maybe Travis should come play for the Storm," I suggest. "You know, summers in San Diego top out at like eighty. How are the summers here in the desert?" I ask knowing full well their temps rise above a hundred.

"Drier than yours," she teases.

"Yeah, the humidity really does nothing for my hair." I fluff the bottom of it.

"As much as I want to talk weather with one of my most favorite authors, can you please, please, *please* tell me what you're working on next?" she begs.

I pretend to zip my lips.

"Oh, come on!" she says. "You know everyone in line out there is going to ask you. Oh, that reminds me. Are you still okay with a little Q and A before you take your seat to start signing? Maybe you could read a passage from *The Accidental Roommate*!"

I nod. "A short Q and A is fine, but reading a passage?" I pull a face. "I don't know about that."

"I marked a few I thought could work, but if you don't want to…"

I blow out a breath. "Fine," I relent. "I'll do it."

She punches a fist in the air. "Yes! And thank you so much for being here, Summer…I mean *Sophie*. I'm just thrilled to meet you. You're welcome back here any time."

"That's really kind of you. I appreciate it."

"Have you seen the line out my door? I already love my new bestie, but there are definitely selfish reasons driving that offer." She laughs, and I laugh along with her. "You ready to get started?" she asks.

I nod.

"Can I get you anything? Water, coffee…"

"Some water would be great," I say, my throat suddenly dry as nerves climb up my spine.

"You got it." She opens a small fridge behind her desk and hands a bottle over to me.

I suck down half the bottle in a few sips, which does nothing good for the nausea in my stomach, and then I draw in a deep breath and follow Victoria out to the makeshift stage.

Rows and rows of chairs are set up to listen to me talk about my newest book. Every chair is taken, and people stand behind the rows of chairs and along the sides to see me.

Me.

I'm still in shock that people would show up here on a Friday afternoon to meet me.

This is absolutely beyond my wildest dreams.

It feels like an out-of-body experience as I sit on one of the chairs on the stage and Victoria stands at a podium with a microphone. "Welcome to Harts and Harps Book Nook! I'm Victoria Woods, the owner of the store, and today I'm beyond thrilled to introduce you to Summer Love." She reads my biography from a sheet of paper. "Bestselling author Summer Love has loved making up stories since she was a little girl, and her debut novel, *Just the Two of Us*, is a testament to her belief that love conquers all."

I freeze at that line.

Is that even true of me anymore?

I used to believe love conquers all. I used to believe love was enough.

I'm not sure I still do after everything we've been through over the last few months.

She continues reading, but I tune her out as I think about Miller.

"Ladies and gentlemen, Summer Love!" she says, and the applause snaps me out of my thoughts.

I smile and wave to the crowd.

"We'd love to begin with Summer reading a short passage from *The Accidental Roommate*, which is now available right here in this bookstore!" Victoria nods at me, and I stand and switch places with her at the podium.

"Hi," I say awkwardly to the room. It's a sea of unfamiliar faces. I can do this. I used to teach high school kids. I'm used to speaking in front of large groups. This shouldn't be scary or intimidating.

Except…it is.

For so long, I kept my identity a secret. Now it's out.

People know it's me.

And that's a little scary. It feels like I'm exposing myself and my innermost thoughts to the world.

I open to the tabbed passage Victoria chose for me, and I remember writing these words. The memory washes over me like a warm blanket.

I'm about to start reading the passage when I glance up at the crowd. "Victoria chose the passage, and before I start reading it, I just want to give a little background if that's okay." I glance at Victoria, who nods. "I remember writing this exact scene. It was ten o'clock at night. I needed to go to bed since I had to get up and teach a class full of high school juniors the next morning, but I was engrossed in the story. I was engrossed in the characters. I couldn't make myself slow down. I couldn't stop. And really, that's my favorite part about crafting stories. When I'm so into what I'm doing that everything around me seems to disappear." I lift a shoulder, a little embarrassed about baring my soul that way, and then I look down at my book.

My book.

This is my twelfth book.

Four years ago, I threw one out there as an experiment. Now I have *twelve* of them.

Life is sure magical and crazy and strange.

I think about that moment when my fingers were flying over the keys and I couldn't stop writing these characters until I got them through the conflict in this scene. I stayed up until three in the morning that night. I was exhausted at school the next day, but it was worth the pain for the result on the page.

Will I still be able to do that with a child?

I force the thought out of my mind since I have a room filled with people staring at me, waiting for me to read the passage.

I do it, and my face is bright red as I get through the words that my brain created in private and I'm now sharing in public.

This book is selling well. It's hitting the charts. It's doing everything I ever could've imagined.

I just wish Miller was here to celebrate in this joy with me.

After I'm done reading the passage, I return to the chair I was sitting in as Victoria heads back to the microphone.

"Whew!" she says, fanning herself dramatically. "Did it just get hotter in here, or was that Summer's words?"

The crowd laughs at that.

"I'm going to open the floor for a few questions before we head over for Summer to sign copies of the book. Who would like to start?" She points to a woman in the audience.

"What inspired you to write this book?" she asks.

Victoria hands me a microphone so I can answer the questions without having to get up.

"Honestly, I was reading another book about accidental roommates, and I loved the idea of that forced proximity. But I wanted to spin it into a fake engagement, so I took that inspiration and ran with it."

"Are your characters inspired by people in your life?" another person asks.

I think about the book I'm working on now, and I think about how I wrote the two characters first getting together. He was always there for her. He showed up whenever she needed him. He performed these acts of service that spoke to her love language.

He's Miller.

And *that* is why I've been blocked writing the end of their story. I don't know what the end of my story with Miller is yet.

The realization dawns as it also dawns on me that she's waiting for an answer to my question.

"Some have some characteristics of people in my life, but none are direct copies of anyone I know." *Except the hero in the book I'm working on now.* I don't dare say those words.

"Is it true you're doing this full time now?" another person asks.

I nod. "Long story short, I quit my job teaching, and I'm a full-time author now."

The crowd cheers for that, and I field a few more questions before Victoria says, "We can take one more question, and then we'll move over to the signing area."

Half the crowd starts to scramble over that way, but there was already a decent line waiting in that direction.

I answer the last question, and then Victoria leads me from the back of the stage over toward the table where I'll be sitting and signing. I see another bottle of water, a stack of Sharpies, and more stacks of books for sale in case anyone in line doesn't have one. Desi is there, too, to help me out with anything I might need, and it's a welcome relief to spot another friend.

There's a row of workers ahead of me who are selling the book while I sit at the end of the table. One worker will write the next person's name on a Post-it so I know how to spell it, and another will push the books over to me in order.

On the other side of the table are two more workers—one who will take photos and the other one who will direct the line. The one directing the line is currently blocking my view of the line, which is probably a good thing so I don't get intimidated.

Victoria is running around taking photos and videos already, and as the organized chaos begins, she stands across from me to take video of the first book I will sign today.

The worker with the Post-its passes the first book to me, and I open it up and gasp when I see the name at the top.

Miller.

I glance up at the worker, and she's smiling. There's writing inside the book, and I recognize it immediately as Miller's scrawl.

Tears heat behind my eyes.

Congratulations on your twelfth book. I'm so proud of you, and I will always be your biggest fan. I love you. I've always loved you, and I want to be by your side cheering you on for your thirteenth book, your thirtieth book, your hundredth book, and every book in between and beyond. Forever.

Whatever happens, I promise to be by your side forever. Not out of fear. Not out of obligation. Simply out of love. I have never loved anyone the way

I love you, and I want to spend the rest of my life showing you how much you mean to me.

"Oh my God," I murmur, and when I finish reading, I glance up to find Victoria to tell her I need a minute before I start signing.

But instead of Victoria standing in front of me, it's Miller Banks.

And he's kneeling on the floor in front of my table.

I have no idea *how* he's here.

All I know is that those words on that page? That's what I want, too.

Forever.

Chapter 57: Miller Banks

Adopt a Penguin

I know we have an audience, so I do my best to keep things fairly quick—and fairly vague since we don't need all these people knowing every intimate detail about our personal life. "I'm sorry the last few weeks have been strange, but I promise you, Soph, whatever happens, I'm here. I want this. All of it, the surprises and the excitement and the possibilities. I want a future with you. I want a life and a family with you. I have loved you for more than half my life, and I promise to love you for the rest of it. I can't wait to marry you in February. Will you marry me?"

I hold my breath as I wait for her answer. My hands are trembling. Hers are, too, as they fly to cover her mouth.

We're already engaged…technically—something I can see as I look at her hands covering her mouth. She's wearing the ring I got her when we decided to go through with a fake engagement.

We already agreed we were going to go through with the wedding.

But I never got down on my knee to ask her.

Then things happened that changed our course, and this is my way of letting her know that nothing has changed for me.

Regardless of what happened in the last few weeks, I'm here, and I'm not going anywhere.

Tears are splashing onto her cheeks, and I'm still kneeling even though every instinct in me is telling me to get the fuck up and dry her tears. I can't, though. I'm frozen to the floor as I hold my breath and await her answer.

"Yes, Miller. Yes. Of course I will." She stands and moves around the table as I push to my feet, and I pull her into my arms. I lean down and drop my lips to hers as I hear cheering behind us.

I finally pull back and rest my forehead to hers. "I love you."

"I love you, too," she whispers.

I catch her lips one more time with mine.

"What are you doing here?" she asks, pulling back. "Aren't you missing camp?"

I nod. "Tanner's covering for me. I need to get back, but I couldn't go another second without seeing you. And, you know, I couldn't miss your first book signing, could I?" I ask with a cheesy smile.

She giggles. "You're too much."

"And I'm yours. Forever. I swear to God, Soph, whatever happens, I'm here. And in the last few days, I've really been thinking about things, about the future, and I want whatever is meant to happen for us. Kids or no kids, a dog, a cat, a fish…fuck, a hamster. Any of it and all of it."

She wrinkles her nose. "A hamster? No to the hamster. And no guinea pigs, too."

"Deal." I laugh. "Ooh, what about a penguin?"

She nods. "Yes! We can adopt one through the World Wildlife Fund! Oh, and also, there's one more thing I need to tell you." She pulls back, and more tears are falling from her eyes. She wipes them away, and she leans in toward me. She moves to my ear, and she whispers, "I took a test. It was positive."

My eyes widen and my stomach turns over as my chest tightens. "It was?" I whisper as she moves back, and my eyes search hers.

She nods. "I hated keeping it from you, but it's why I couldn't pick up when you called. I didn't want to slip it over the phone, and I had to know you wanted this no matter what before I told you."

I hate that I made her feel that way.

Never again. Never again will she question my love for her.

"Of course I want this." I pick her up and twirl her around before my lips slam to hers again.

An unfamiliar feeling falls over me like this is what was always meant to be. It feels *right*. We're getting married. We're having a baby. Maybe we'll have more. That uncertainty about whether I wanted to have kids or not seems to have vanished into thin air as a new feeling takes its place: anticipation.

Holy shit. We're having a *baby*.

I'm going to be a *daddy*.

I knocked up the woman I've been in love with since I was fourteen.

Goddamn, I'm one lucky man.

We have a lot to talk about. We have a lot to work out. We have a lot to celebrate.

And now it feels like we have a lot of *time* where we can do all those things.

We hear a throat clearing behind us over the whoops and cheers of the people gathered here to get a book signed by my fiancée, and I pull apart from the woman I'm going to marry.

"So sorry to interrupt," Victoria says, "but we have a lot of people waiting to meet Ms. Love."

We both laugh at that.

"Yes, of course," Sophie says, and she kisses me one more time. "How much time do you have?"

"I have to get on a flight back to San Diego in a few hours."

"Will you hang out here with me?" she asks.

"I'd love to." I move into place behind her as the workers pass down the next book for her to sign. "Wait a minute," I say, and she turns back to look at me. "You didn't sign my copy."

"Oh, I'm keeping that one," she says with a grin. "Forever."

I smile, too, as warmth fills my heart. This is really, actually going to work.

The next two hours are madness as she signs books, smiles for photos, and answers questions. Some of her readers want my photo, too, and some even want my signature. I laugh when they ask if I've tried out any of the spicy scenes with her, and I make sure everyone leaves knowing I'm the man who inspired all the best ones.

Sophie just rolls her eyes and laughs. Considering she wrote most of them before we got together, it's not true. But I can still pretend it is, and all the ones going forward definitely will be.

I don't want to go, but I do need to get back to camp. There's a meeting tonight I can't miss even though I missed most of today's practice.

It was worth it. If I get fined for ducking out, so be it. It's worth every damn penny to know that Sophie and I are back on the track we were always meant to be on.

When the two hours scheduled for the signing are up, there are still a few more people in line. I was hoping I'd get a few minutes alone with Sophie, but I can't take away from her first event like this.

I snap photos of her and take some video footage that she can use for social media content, and when the final person is through the line, Victoria thanks us both for being here today.

"Are we still on for dinner tonight?" she asks Sophie, who glances at me.

"My flight back is in ninety minutes. Don't let me hold up any of your plans," I say, holding up both hands.

Sophie nods. "I need to run back to my hotel to change, but I can meet you here at, say…six?"

Victoria nods. "Perfect."

We head through the bookstore and out the back door, and there's already an Uber waiting there for us.

Sophie glances at me. "Can you make a quick stop with me?"

"You should know by now that I would do anything for you."

A smile lights up her entire face, and then we're on our way toward her hotel.

Chapter 58: Sophie Summers

Nothing Between Us

He kisses me lightly when we get into the back of the Uber after our driver confirms our destination, and the kiss turns into an actual make-out session.

His hand is sliding up my thigh, and if anyone in the world thinks I asked him back to my hotel to chat…well, they'd be wrong.

There won't be much chatting when my eyes are rolling back into my head in the kind of pleasure only Miller Banks can give me.

And since I'm already pregnant, why not just skip the condom?

I've never had sex without a condom. He says he hasn't, either.

And the thought of him moving inside of me with nothing between us is pulsing a quaking ache unlike anything I've felt before squarely between my legs.

We finally get to the hotel. I checked in earlier, and my bag is already here.

We race up to my room. We're not alone in the elevator, but his hand is on my ass on the entire ascent up anyway.

We practically run down the hall. Neither of us wants to waste a second when we have mere minutes before he has to leave.

Once the door closes us into privacy, he pulls my dress over my head.

And that's when he pauses.

I'm standing in my bra and underwear, heels still on my feet, and he stares at me for a few beats. He closes the gap between us and runs his hands down my sides, stopping to pause on my belly. It's still mostly flat for now, but in a few months, it won't be.

What will that be like?

I'm finally *excited* to know the answer to that rather than *terrified*.

He bends down to the floor and kneels before me, and he presses kisses to my stomach. It's sweet and intimate, and I wish I knew what was going through his head. I have a feeling we'll have lots of time to talk about it when training camp is over.

We don't have that kind of time right now. We're lucky we have any time at all.

He yanks my panties down my legs. I kick my heels off when he gets my panties around my ankles, and I wrestle out of my bra as he slides them the rest of the way off.

He grips my leg at the calf before he pulls it up over his shoulder, and he dives face-first into my pussy. He licks his way through me, his tongue moving inside me before he adds in two fingers and sucks on my clit. "God, you taste good," he hums against me, the vibration filling me with still more need for him.

My fingers thread into his hair and hold his head in place as he gives me everything I've needed for weeks.

He doesn't stay down there long, though. Instead, he pushes to a stand and lifts me into his arms. He carries me to the bed, where he sets me down gently, and then he proceeds to get undressed in what has to be record speed.

He moves over the top of me, hovering as he settles between my legs, and I feel his cock as it lies heavy and hard between us. He reaches down between us and fists his cock before he pushes it up against my clit. The feel of his bare skin against mine is overwhelming in the very best way.

He slides his cock through my slit before he moves it back up to tease my clit some more, and I start to thrash around a little beneath him as the need to feel him moving inside of me takes over.

"My girl wants my cock inside her," he murmurs.

"Yes," I beg. "I need to feel you inside me. Nothing between us."

He growls, but he doesn't push into me yet, though.

Instead, he lets go of his cock and runs his hand along my torso, stopping to massage my breast. "I need to taste your tits first." He dips his face down and sucks on the nipple of the breast he's gripping, and I arch my back off the bed as pleasure zings through to my spine.

It's like everything is heightened right now. Everything feels more intense. I'm concentrating on him and this moment and how good it all feels, how *right* it all feels with the heady contrast of how wrong everything felt when we were apart, hovering on the outside of where we find ourselves now.

His lips move back to mine, and our tongues are tangling when he reaches down between us once more. This time he aligns his cock with my pussy, and he pushes in.

I let out a long, low moan at the feel of him entering me unsheathed for the first time. This is different from when the condom broke. This is a conscious choice, the two of us doing this intimate act that we've never experienced before with other people. It's sexy and erotic, and it feels so different from sex with a condom.

He glides in and out of me, the chorus of our moans getting louder and more intense with each passing thrust as he drives us both closer and closer to release. He drops his head and buries it in my shoulder as he continues moving inside me, and I wrap my legs around his waist and my arms around his torso as I memorize him—the feel of him as he hovers over me and moves in and out, his fresh scent even after being at practice this morning with the need to return soon, the sounds he makes, and the sounds of our bodies rocking together in pleasure. Everything.

"Fuck, Soph. I love fucking you," he says as he hammers into me.

"I love when you fuck me," I say, my voice whiny as it comes out in a moan.

The climax hits me out of nowhere right after that, and maybe that's the singular thing that's *most* different about sex without a condom. It's brutal and intense as I'm already wrapped around him like a vine. I tighten everywhere as my body seems to explode all at once, and he growls before he says, "Fuck yes, baby. Give me your orgasm."

"Give me yours," I cry, and he does. Just as I say the words, I feel him pump harder into me, the sure signal I recognize as his breaking point, and he thrusts a few more times with a loud, mighty roar that seems to rumble out of his chest before he comes to a still and spills inside of me.

My pussy is greedy for his come, and I close my eyes as I feel a totally different sensation. It's like a warmth spreading inside me, and as he finishes his release and slowly pulls out, I feel the hot drip of his come as it oozes from my body.

He moves beside me and reaches down to play with his come, moving it around in gentle circles over my clit as the scent in the room changes to one of sex. I groan as he massages those wet circles over and over, moving slowly and with intent as he starts to pick up the pace. When he leans in and starts to suck on my nipple at the same time, that's it. I'm done.

I roar into a second orgasm that is even more intense than the first, my body contracting over and over again as I cry out. "Oh, holy fuck, Miller, yes! Oh my God, yes, yes, yes!"

As my body starts to come down from the ridiculous high, I'm sated in a way I'm not sure I've ever felt before.

He's given me two orgasms before, but there's something so much more intimate about having him make me come by using his own come to get me off. The mere thought of it has me wanting him to do it again.

We don't have time.

He has to get back.

I have dinner plans.

And that's life. We'll make time when we can. We'll make each other a priority always. But we both have interests outside of our relationship, too, and those are the things that make us strong individuals who come back to each other with something new and exciting to contribute.

We lay together for a few peaceful moments in silence, and eventually he gets up and uses the restroom. He gathers his clothes and starts to get dressed, and I still haven't moved from my spot on the bed.

"I need to get going," he murmurs.

"I know. I was just thinking that it's good we have interests outside of each other, but that doesn't mean I have to like it when you leave."

He walks over and plants a kiss on my lips. "My thoughts exactly. I don't want to go, and I have to be honest, Soph. I've thought a lot about the future of my career over the last couple weeks."

"You have?"

He nods. "It's unusual for running backs to play very far into their thirties. I don't know how many years I have left before this game takes its toll on my body. But we're having a baby. We're getting married. I don't know exactly when I plan to retire. It may be after this season, maybe after next. But I know exactly where I'll be."

I sit up, trying not to feel awkward that I'm completely naked, that my boobs are hanging out, and there's still come dripping out of my pussy while we have this serious conversation. "Where's that?"

"With you."

I can't help the smile that lifts my lips. He presses a kiss to those lips.

"I can't wait," I say.

Chapter 59: Sophie Summers

Bedazzled Jerseys and Celebrations

A Little Over a Month Later

I'm wearing a totally bedazzled Miller Banks jersey and sitting with Cassie, who's wearing her matching bedazzled Tanner Banks jersey.

We snagged front row seats in the end zone for the first home game of the season even though we were invited to sit in a suite. I don't want to sit in a suite miles away from the field when I can sit right here practically on top of the action.

And the best part? During warm-ups, Tanner ran over to Cassie just as Miller ran over to me.

I bent over the railing as he climbed up to kiss me. "Score some points for me!"

"Only if you promise a private score later."

"Promise." I giggled and leaned closer to him. "Maybe I'll even let you penetrate the backfield."

He wiggled his eyebrows before he laughed and ran back out onto the field.

Cassie and I laughed about the two of them coming over to say hi, and then we headed up for our first round of game snacks.

Admittedly, it may be hard to see from this angle when the plays are on the other side of the field, but which team is running into which end zone changes each quarter, so we'll get the second and fourth right in front of us.

Cassie has bitten most of her nails off as Tanner takes the field. It's his first regular season game since he got hurt exactly one year ago today—during the first play at the first home game of the season.

It's been a long road to recovery, and this is the first game where Cassie is sitting in the stands as a fan watching the quarterback, who is now her husband.

A year ago, she didn't even know who he was. And now? He's the stepfather to her children.

What a difference a year makes.

I remember watching that game last year on television at the apartment I shared with Tyler—a man I haven't even spoken to since I went back to give him my key. I remember seeing Miller and thinking how much I adored him. I remember watching as Tanner went down, and I remember watching Miller rush out to make sure his brother was okay.

He wasn't okay.

But Miller was there by his side through it all, and now look where we all are.

I never would've guessed when I was watching that game that I'd end up sitting next to Tanner's new bride—the physical therapist who nursed him back to health after his ACL injury— and that I'd be carrying Miller's baby and planning a wedding with him.

What a difference a year makes for us, too.

Cassie and Tanner know about the baby. Miller told Tanner the night he went back to camp after he came to see me in Vegas, and I told Cassie a few days later when we met for lunch.

She's like a sister to me, and Tanner is like a brother to me, and I just want the very best for the two of them.

On the first play, Tanner throws a pass to Spencer for a seventeen-yard gain, and I see Cassie visibly relax after that.

Cassie is drinking beer, and I'm drinking Sprite. We're eating nachos and having a great time as the first quarter gets underway. The Storm puts the first points on the board as Tanner tosses the ball to Spencer again midway through the quarter, and Cassie and I go absolutely crazy as we cheer for our men. The Cowboys come back with a field goal on the next drive, and the Storm answers with a field goal of their own, putting the score at ten to three at the start of the second quarter.

The direction of the field switches, and the Storm has the ball as they move closer and closer to us. Cassie and I cheer as they hit the red zone, and now I'm the one biting my nails as I keep an eye on Miller and the defender who's been on top of him the whole game so far.

He's had a couple of carries, but I can tell he's eager to get his hands on the ball. I hear Tanner call the play, and then Miller runs across the field behind him. The ball is snapped, and Tanner hands it off to Miller. The fullback blocks the defender coming after Miller, and he's able to break away and run straight up the middle toward the end zone.

Somehow he's absolutely wide open, and I'm screaming like crazy as I watch him close the gap. He crosses the white line into the end zone, and the crowd goes crazy as he scores a touchdown. He drops the ball as Tanner races toward him, and they celebrate with a shoulder bump as they both jump high into the air back-to-back.

Miller runs out of the back of the end zone with his brother hot on his heels. The two of them race for the stands, and they both jump the wall at the same time—Tanner toward Cassie and Miller toward me.

It's a common celebration to jump the wall after scoring a touchdown, and having these twin brothers celebrating with the women they love at the opening game of the season is a picture-perfect moment in their careers.

He's wearing a helmet, and I'm still screaming as I cling onto him for a few beats. The guy next to me is slapping him on the back, and the same thing is probably happening on Tanner's other side, but it all happens so fast that I can barely register that they actually just did that.

Cassie and I are both laughing as they jump down and head back to their team. We high-five each other as we continue cheering for our men.

The Cowboys throw an interception right to one of our guys, and he makes his way down the field toward us before he's tackled at the thirty-yard line.

Cassie and I get to watch up close again as Tanner hands the ball to Miller. He doesn't score on this play—instead, he's taken down pretty quickly by that same defender, but he gained a couple of yards.

Tanner throws to Madden Bradley next, who does score, and we go wild again.

I don't know why I spent so much time resisting the running back. Maybe I couldn't have predicted what life would be like today when I looked ahead a year ago, but I sure love this little life that's mine.

Epilogue: Sophie Summers

April's Birthstone

Eight Weeks Later

"Wow, Sophie. You look incredible," Cassie breathes as I step into the room.

"Thank you," I say, and I twirl for everyone in the room.

When the options are getting married at seven months pregnant after the season is over or getting married before I start to show even though it's during the season…we opt for the latter.

I suppose we could've waited and tied the knot after the baby arrives, but I didn't want to wait another second. I just want to be Miller Banks's wife.

And so it's during the bye week that we decide to move up our wedding.

Miller is off for ten days—from the moment the game ends on Sunday night until the following Wednesday, and since Tuesday is the common denominator for the football players we'd like attending our wedding, we opt for the first Tuesday in November.

It's not traditional to get married on a Tuesday, but the Venetian happened to have an opening that day, so we moved our original date. It feels like everything fell into place just how it was meant to be. Cassie's words continue to play in my head—*what's meant to be will be*. And each passing moment makes this feel more and more inevitable.

I wasn't the girl who doodled *Sophie Banks* in my notebook in high school. But I sure as hell am the girl doodling that now.

We agreed not to find out the gender of the baby until he or she is born, and I'm not sure why I agreed to that since a part of me is dying to know. We're trying to figure out names now, and so far, I'm drawing a complete blank for either gender.

I'm sixteen weeks pregnant, and my flat belly isn't really all that flat anymore. I don't have a bump yet, but my boobs are bigger, and I feel pretty bloated. I chose a dress that made me feel gorgeous—a sleeveless, flowy empire waist with a gorgeous lace applique along one of the layers. And it makes my boobs look like utter perfection—something I'm sure my future husband won't be complaining about.

Speaking of my future husband, I'm still sitting here in awe that this is really happening. Cassie, Grace, Ava, Desi, and Jolene are all in the room with me now, and they've really become like actual sisters to me.

Chris and Marie are attending the wedding, and my parents are here. Miller's parents are here, too, and Missy Nash, who is basically a second mom to Miller at this point, and she's here with a date…Steve, Grace's dad. I guess things are public now.

And that's it.

We're keeping it small and intimate. Family only. I didn't even invite Brooke, my old friend from Cactus Valley High School. I haven't spoken to her in months, and it just made me realize how very much it was a friendship of convenience. We worked together in the same place, so we were friends. But now my best friends are literally my family as I marry into this huge group that's filled with women I respect, admire, and adore.

So they're all standing up with me today, just as all of Miller's brothers are standing up with him. Cassie is my matron of honor. Tanner is his best man, and he also has Lincoln, Grayson, Spencer, and Asher with him.

But all that matters is that today we will be vowing forever to each other.

I was so scared that getting involved with Miller was going to spell the end of such a long, important friendship. Instead, that friendship became the foundation on which we've built literally everything.

People always say they're marrying their best friend…and I am, too. Literally. I can't honestly remember being closer to someone else in my life than I am with him, and even more so now that we've added the side of intimacy.

We've gone through growing pains, and that only tells me that we're strong enough now to handle anything that comes our way. We both realize it's communication that's the key—especially when we're forced to spend time apart because of circumstances beyond our control.

The season has been incredible so far. Watching Miller play football was always exciting, but knowing he's stepping off the field and coming home to me takes it to another level entirely.

Jamie, the wedding planner, pops into the room where I've been hidden away getting ready the last few hours.

"Are you ready?" she asks.

"I'm definitely ready," I say confidently. I thought I'd be a nervous wreck when a wedding planner told me it was time to walk down the aisle, but that's not the case at all. I know I'm marrying my perfect match, and I know he will continue to show up for me in all the ways that matter.

"Miller wanted me to give you this," she says, and she hands me a small box.

I open it and find a gorgeous diamond bracelet inside with a little note from Miller.

"April's birthstone is the diamond, so this is for you in honor of our baby. Our future starts now, and I couldn't be more excited about it. I love you. See you at the other side of the aisle."

Tears heat behind my eyes as I pull the bracelet out and show it to the women in the room with me.

"He's just the sweetest," Jolene murmurs.

"His note says it's because April's birthstone is a diamond," I say, my voice breaking as Cassie helps secure it onto my wrist.

It's absolutely gorgeous, and I couldn't be more excited about the future we have before us as well.

The ladies line up, and they start their walk down the aisle. My dad joins me, and he nudges my shoulder with his.

"You look beautiful, Sophie."

"Thanks, Dad."

"I'm so proud of you. You chose well with that one, and we're thrilled to welcome him into our family."

I smile. I half expect him to say something like how just because his marriage ended in divorce doesn't mean mine will, but he doesn't mention it. We already talked about that, anyway.

The doors open, and it's my turn to walk.

I see Miller standing at the other end of the aisle, and my face breaks out into a smile as I watch him looking at me. He wipes his eyes as if the very sight of me brought tears to them, and I close my eyes and take a deep breath as I memorize this moment.

A pianist plays a slowed-down version of Ed Sheeran's "Photograph" as I start my walk toward Miller, and he starts to chuckle as he recognizes the song.

It's true that loving can heal, and it's true that love conquers all. My belief in that wavered for a minute, but then Miller Banks showed up for me the way he has the entire time I've known him, and that was the end of the wavering.

Nothing will ever make me waver from him again.

"We are gathered here today to witness the joining of Miller Matthew Banks and Sophie June Summers," our officiant begins, and the rest of the ceremony is a blur.

He says something about having loved me half his life. I say something about how the love of my life was right in front of me the whole time.

We both wrote down our vows, and we'll share them again later since this is all a blur at the moment. We'll read them. We'll frame them. We'll live by them for the rest of our lives.

All I know is that twenty minutes later, I'm wearing a ring Miller slid onto my finger, and he's bending me backward and kissing the hell out of me because I'm officially his *wife*.

Because it's Miller, of course he has a plan to give us a moment for just the two of us. We walk down the aisle with huge smiles on our faces as the photographer walks backward capturing every second, and instead of stopping to greet our guests, Miller grabs my hand and pulls me into the room where he got ready. We take a moment before we'll be rushed by our bridal party and our families.

He leans his forehead to mine. "I love you, Sophie Banks," he says, and a thrill darts along my spine as I hear my new name for the very first time.

"I love you, my husband," I murmur, and our lips crash together.

He pulls back and doesn't hide the fact that he's ogling me. "You're gorgeous. That dress…"

"I have big plans for you to get me out of it later."

"Later?" he whines.

I raise my brows. "We do have a party to get to. But maybe we can sneak out halfway through—once everyone's drunk and dancing. No one will notice."

He grins. "Deal."

He kisses me one more time before we head back to our wedding party, and we do make good on that deal a couple hours later.

I married my best friend today, and soon we'll have a baby together. We might've known each other for the better part of half our lives, but it feels like today is truly the start of our happily ever after.

The End

Want more Miller and Sophie?
Scan this QR code to download a bonus epilogue!

Scan this code to join Lisa on Facebook
at Team LS: Lisa Suzanne's Reader Group!

Acknowledgments

Big thanks first as always to my family. Thank you to Matt for the love and support and to our kids who all this is for.

Thank you to Valentine PR for your incredible work on the launch of this book.

Thank you to Valentine Grinstead, Diane Holtry, Christine Yates, Billie DeSchalit, Serena Cracchiolo, and Patricia Rohrs for beta and proofreading. I value your insight and comments so much.

Big thanks to my ride or die bestie, Julie Saman. We'll always push each other to hit those deadlines no matter how impossible they may seem!

Thank you to my ARC Team for loving this sports world that is so real to us. Thank you to the members of the Vegas Aces Spoiler Room and Team LS, and all the influencers and bloggers for reading, reviewing, posting, and sharing.

Thank you to my ARC Team for loving this sports world that is so real to us. Thank you to the members of the <u>Vegas Aces and Vegas Heat Recovery Room</u> and <u>Team LS</u>, and all the influencers and bloggers for reading, reviewing, posting, and sharing.

And finally, thank YOU for reading. I can't wait to bring you more sports romances where swoony superstar heroes ride emotional roller coasters to their happily ever afters.

Cheers until next season!

xoxo,
Lisa Suzanne

About the Author

Lisa Suzanne is an Amazon Top Ten Bestselling author of swoon-worthy superstar heroes, emotional roller coasters, and all the angst. She resides in Arizona with her husband and two kids. When she's not chasing her kids, she can be found working on her latest romance book or watching reruns of *Friends*.